"NOW, WHAT I'D LIKE YE TO DO IS TOUCH ME. . . ."

"Touch ye?" she exclaimed, becoming alarmed.

"Just glide yer hand across my chest," he coaxed, his voice a soft caress. "Or wherever else ye wish."

She stared into his intense, gray gaze. She wanted to touch him, to feel his muscles rippling beneath her hand.

Reaching out, Rob traced her fingertips across his naked chest to his shoulder and then down to the powerful muscles in his upper arm. Becoming bolder, she glided the palm of her hand up to his neck and then slid it down his chest, reveling in the feel of the mat of brown hair covering it.

Gordon nearly groaned at the exquisite sweetness of her touch. He held the back of her neck and, leaning close, covered her mouth with his lips.

And she responded, returning his kiss in kind.

"Now I want to touch ye the way yer touchin' me," he said in a husky whisper. "May I touch ye, angel?"

"Yes," she answered. . . .

Patricia Grasso

Courting An Angel

A DELL BOOK

Published by
Dell Publishing
a division of
Bantam Doubleday Dell Publishing Group, Inc.
1540 Broadway
New York, New York 10036

ISBN: 0-440-22085-8

Printed in the United States of America

Published simultaneously in Canada

December 1995

10 9 8 7 6 5 4 3 2 1

For Linda Grasso-Kaplan, my dearest sister:

Roses are red and violets are blue.
I'm younger, cuter, and Mom's favorite too . . .

Gotcha last!

Prologue

Dunridge Castle, Scotland, 1576

She was going to give him grief.

Fifteen-year-old Gordon Campbell marched across the torchlit great hall and stared at his eight-year-old bride. Nervous apprehension made his heart sink to his stomach and his clenched hands felt clammy with sweat, yet his unconcerned expression never altered. As the Marquess of Inverary and the Duke of Argyll's heir, Gordon had a reputation to safeguard, and he would never allow any eight-year-old to gain the upper hand with him. If the watching MacArthurs and Campbells guessed how uncertain he felt at that moment, Gordon knew he'd be the laughingstock of the Highlands until the day he died. God's balls, imagine the scandal of the Duke of Argyll's heir trembling before his future duchess—an eight-year-old bairn.

Not in this lifetime, Gordon vowed, fixing his gray-eyed gaze on her.

The lass was trouble all right. Gordon knew that as surely as he knew his own name.

Dressed in virginal white and wearing a wreath of orange blossoms in her ebony hair, the girl looked as innocent as an angel, but gleaming trouble leaped at him from the depths of her emerald green eyes. The tilt of her upturned nose and the stubborn chiseling of her chin gave proof to her less than passive temperament. The lass even had the audacity to stare right back at him. *Without blushing.*

She gave him an ambiguous smile. Standing with her arms behind her back, the girl seemed as demure as a shy angel. In contrast, the thick mane of ebony that cascaded to her waist and those disarming emerald eyes with their thick fringe of sooty lashes lent her a seductive appearance beyond her years.

Feeling a hundred interested gazes on his back, Gordon decided to use his superior sophistication to win the girl's affection. He gave her his most charming smile, the same one that worked so successfully with Inverary Castle's maids.

In answer, the girl raised her perfectly shaped ebony brows at him. *Did the wee witch know what he was thinking?*

"Yer as cute as a kitten," Gordon remarked, crouching down to be eye level with her.

"I'm a girl," she said flatly.

Gordon forced himself to smile. "A verra bonny girl," he complimented her, thinking flattery would soften her attitude. "I'm Gordon Campbell, the Marquess of Inverary."

"I know who ye are," she said, apparently unimpressed by his title.

"What's yer name?"

"Rob B. MacArthur."

"Ye've a boy's name."

"I'm a girl."

"What's the B signify?" Gordon asked.

"Brat," shouted the girl's three older brothers.

Rob turned her head and cast each of them a reproving look. She flicked a smile filled with love at her father, the earl, and then returned her attention to Gordon, saying, "The B stands for Bruce. My father named me in honor of his special hero, Robert the Bruce. Have ye ever heard of him?"

God's balls, Gordon thought in disgusted dismay. How could he hope to live down the fact that he'd married a girl named Rob Bruce? What kind of daft parents did the lass have?

"And I dinna give a tinker's damn if my name pleases ye or no," she added.

"Rob is a lovely name," Gordon said, wondering how she'd known what he was thinking. "As a matter of fact, Robert the Bruce is my own special hero."

That made her smile. The sweetness of it tugged at his heartstrings. She really was as cute as a kitten and held the promise of growing into a great beauty.

"Did ye know I'm goin' to marry ye today?" Gordon asked.

Rob nodded, but asked in a loud whisper, "Dinna ye think yer a bit elderly to be my husband?"

Pockets of smothered laughter erupted in the hall. Embarrassed, Gordon cast his father a meaningful look.

"Dinna look to me for help," Magnus Campbell called to him, apparently amused by his son's discomfort. "Each man makes his own way in the world."

"Speak to yer daughter, Brie," Iain MacArthur ordered his wife. "She's givin' the lad a hard time."

Lady Brigette started forward.

"Brie, stay where ye are." Magnus countermanded the order. "Gordon will be dealin' with her for his whole life. The lad may as well make a beginnin' of it now."

" 'Tis my father, the Duke of Argyll," Gordon told Rob. "If ye marry me, I'll make ye a duchess someday."

"I dinna want to be a duchess," she replied.

"The devil take ye," he exclaimed, but his piercing gray eyes flickered with interest. "What do ye—?"

"This is *my* hall," Rob interrupted him. "I'll thank ye to keep a civil tongue in yer head when yer speakin' to me."

"I do apologize," Gordon said with laughter lurking in his voice. For a child of eight, the lass already issued orders like a seasoned duchess. "If ye dinna mind me askin', what would ye like to be?"

"An English lady like my mother."

Holy horseshit, Gordon thought, his charming smile never wavering. "If ye marry me, I'll be yer knight," he coaxed. "That means I'll slay yer dragons."

Now *her* eyes flickered with interest. "What aboot the monster that lives under my bed?" she asked.

"Ye've a monster livin' beneath yer bed?" Gordon echoed, feigning shocked dismay.

Rob nodded gravely.

Drawing Gordon's attention, thirteen-year-old Ross MacArthur called, "The only monster in her room is the one who sleeps *in* the bed."

"Show the marquess yer devil's hand," ten-year-old Jamie MacArthur added, then quickly sidestepped out of his father's reach.

"Both of ye shut yer mouths, or ye'll answer to me," fifteen-year-old Dubh MacArthur threatened.

Gordon cast the three MacArthur brothers a long, measuring look and wondered at their words. When he turned back to the girl, his heart nearly broke at the startling transformation in her demeanor. One moment she'd been a proud Highland lass and the next moment a pathetic angel complete with quivering bottom lip as if she waged a fierce inner battle to prevent the flood of tears that threatened to spill. What would he do if she started to weep?

"Why dinna ye ask yer da to kill the monster?" Gordon asked.

"Old people canna see him," she answered, making everyone but her father smile.

"What does he look like?"

"Da or the monster?"

Gordon swallowed the chuckle he felt bubbling up. The lass was more entertaining than a band of traveling players. "I meant the monster," he said.

"I never saw him but—" Rob broke off, lowered her gaze, and worried her bottom lip with her teeth.

"Share it with me, lass," Gordon said in a soothing tone of voice.

"The monster touched me once," she whispered, holding her left hand out for his inspection. "See what he did."

A dark, flower-shaped birthmark stained the back of her left hand. The six-petaled flower of Aphrodite signified sin, or so the church authorities taught their faithful. Most people regarded the mark as a sure sign of the devil.

Gordon slowly raised his gray-eyed gaze to hers and noted the unshed tears glistening in her disarming eyes. Without forethought, he lifted the offending hand to his lips and kissed the birthmark.

"I'll kill that monster for darin' to touch ye," Gordon promised, smiling at her surprised expression. "As soon as ye place yer mark on the marriage contract."

Rob shook her head and said, "Ye must kill the monster first."

"Dinna ye trust me to keep my word?"

"Everyone in the Highlands knows that *Campbell* means 'crooked mouth.'"

Gordon flushed when he heard the smothered chuckles emanating from the MacArthur section of their audience. "So ye'll wed me if I slay him first?" he asked.

Rob nodded.

"Dinna do it," Ross MacArthur called.

"Yer a gonner for sure if ye do," Jamie MacArthur warned.

Dubh MacArthur reached out and slapped first one brother and then the other. "Open yer mouths again," he threatened them, "and Ma will be wearin' mournin' black in yer memory."

Ignoring his future brothers-in-law, Gordon stood and offered the girl his hand. He glanced at his father who cast him a look that said "well done." Together, the fifteen-year-old marquess and his eight-year-old bride left the hall.

"Ye'll wait here where 'tis safe," Gordon ordered, halting at the bottom of the stairs. "Which chamber is yers?"

"The last door on the left."

Gordon started up the stairs but stopped when he heard her speak.

"Ye'll be careful?" she called, sounding worried.

Gordon paused and turned around. He smiled at her and nodded, then continued up the stairs. Gordon walked into her chamber, leaned against the door, and waited. He judged ten minutes would be the appropriate amount of time for monster slaying. Anything less would be suspect, anything more would bring the girl in search of him.

Glancing at the spartanly furnished chamber, Gordon assumed it was the usual little girl's room but didn't know for sure. As an only child, he'd never stepped inside a young girl's chamber.

Gordon reached up and ran a hand through his chestnut brown hair at the same moment his gaze touched the bed. For some unknown reason, Gordon pushed away from the door and sauntered across the chamber toward the bed. He dropped to his knees, lifted the coverlet, and peered beneath the bed. *No monster.*

Ten minutes later, Gordon emerged from the chamber and retraced his steps down the corridor to the stairs. He smiled when he caught sight of his bride-to-be.

Rob stood at the base of the stairs. With her eyes closed and a frightened expression fixed on her face, she moved her lips in a silent prayer.

Gordon flicked a glance toward the great hall. Lady Brigette stood outside the hall's entrance. When he looked in her direction, she mouthed the words *thank you* and then disappeared inside.

" 'Tis done," Gordon announced. "That nasty monster willna be botherin' ye again."

Rob opened her eyes and gave him a relieved smile. "What did ye do with his body?" she asked.

"The thin' disappeared when he died."

"Yer certain sure he isna hidin'?"

Gordon nodded and sat down on the bottom stair. He reached into his pocket and said, "I've a gift for ye."

"I love receivin' gifts," Rob cried, her emerald eyes sparkling with delight.

"I was certain ye did," Gordon said dryly. He lifted her left hand and slipped a scrolled band of gold onto her third finger. "The ring has a secret message inside. *Vous et Nul Autre* means 'Ye and No Other.' Yer my lady-wife, and I'll always be true to ye."

Rob looked at the ring on her finger and then gazed at him, saying, "My mother told me ye'd bring me somethin' pretty, and ye did." She batted her ebony lashes at him and smiled winsomely, adding, "I was hopin' for a new doll."

Gordon burst out laughing. "I believe ye'll make me a

grand duchess, and I promise to send ye a dolly as soon as I return to Inverary. Will that do?"

Rob nodded.

Several minutes later the Duke of Argyll's only son married the Earl of Dunridge's only daughter. With all of her heart and soul, Rob MacArthur loved her gallant husband for a long, long time. Gordon Campbell left Dunridge Castle and, in true fifteen-year-old fashion, dismissed his child bride from his mind as if she'd never existed.

He never sent her the promised doll.

Chapter 1

Devereux House, London, 1586

 Autumn wore its most serene expression that final day of October. Clear blue skies kissed the distant horizon, and gentle breezes caressed the land.

The changing season painted vivid colors within the perfect setting of the Earl of Basildon's garden. In addition to nature's orange, gold, and red-leafed trees, an army of gardeners had landscaped the grounds in a rainbow of autumnal shades. Chrysanthemums in a variety of hues adorned the manicured lawns along with flowering cabbage, marigold, and sweet alyssum.

A shining white birch tree, an evergreen yew, and a majestic oak stood together like old friends in the rear of the earl's garden. The earl's five daughters, ranging in age from three to ten, and his countess circled the yew tree and stared up at the ebony-haired woman perched comfortably on its thickest branch.

"Are you listening?" called the eight-month-pregnant Countess of Basildon.

Rob MacArthur inhaled deeply of the mingling scents

of the garden's flowers and then looked down at her audience. "I hear ye, Aunt Keely."

The countess turned to her daughters and asked, "Are *you* listening?"

Rob smiled at the sight of the five young girls nodding their heads with exaggerated vigor, their ebony braids bobbing up and down with the movement. Having passed the previous year in England with Uncle Richard and his family, Rob loved her younger cousins and considered them the sisters she'd never had.

"All the participants around the bonfire tonight will receive a sprig of yew," Lady Keely instructed. "Samhuinn—known in England as Halloween—is the festival of our ancestors, and the yew tree symbolizes death and rebirth. These sprigs of yew represent our ability to commune with those loved ones who have gone before us into the Great Adventure. Do you understand?"

"Yes," the five little girls chorused.

The countess looked up at her niece and asked, "Do you understand?"

"I ken what yer sayin', Aunt Keely." Rob dropped a handful of yew sprigs, and her cousins scrambled to pick them up. She glanced toward the mansion and saw her uncle headed in their direction.

"Here comes yer father," she announced.

In the distance behind the earl, Henry Talbot walked onto the Devereux estate. Spying the family gathering in the rear of the garden, the twenty-five-year-old Marquess of Ludlow sauntered in their direction.

Rob sighed when she saw him. "Isna he the handsomest man ye've ever seen?"

" 'Tis one of the many reasons why I married him," the countess replied.

"I dinna mean Uncle Richard." Rob giggled at the

absurd notion that her uncle was the handsomest man. "I meant yer brother Henry."

"Rob loves Henry," eight-year-old Bliss Devereux chanted in a singsong voice. "Rob loves Henry."

"Quiet, Lady Blister," Rob hushed her. "He'll hear ye."

"I'm no blister," Bliss replied.

"You're a terrible pain in the arse," ten-year-old Blythe Devereux told her sister.

" 'Tis unkind of you to say that," Lady Keely chided her eldest.

"Cousin Blythe, lyin' is sometimes kinder than the truth," Rob called, then smiled at her aunt's reproving frown.

"How are the Halloween preparations progressing?" asked the earl, reaching the yew tree.

"Fine." The countess smiled and patted her swollen belly. "As ordered, I refrained from climbing the tree this year."

"Daddy?"

Richard Devereux looked down at six-year-old Aurora, usually as silent as the hushed moments for which she'd been named. When the child offered him a sprig of yew, the earl smiled and crouched down to be eye level with her.

"Thank you, sweetling," he said, accepting the sprig.

"Daddy," two voices chimed together.

Richard glanced first to the left and then to the right. On either side of him stood his three-year-old twins, Summer and Autumn.

"What do you call an Englishman who eats ants?" Summer asked.

"Uncle," Autumn shouted.

Everyone but the earl laughed. "Who told you that?" Richard demanded.

"Uncle Henry," Blythe, Bliss, and Aurora answered at the same time.

The earl stood and faced his wife, saying, "Tell your brother to refrain from spreading his wickedness to our daughters."

"Great Bruce's ghost," Rob cried indignantly from her perch in the tree. "Henry isna wicked."

"Thank you for defending me, my lady," said a husky voice behind the earl.

Rob smiled at Henry Talbot, and all of the tender affection she felt for him shone in her expression. Noting the grim set to her uncle's jaw, Rob prevented his intended tirade by calling, "Henry, will you help me down?"

"With pleasure." Henry stood beneath the yew tree, and when she leaped off the branch, his arms were there to steady her. They stood so close their bodies touched.

The masculine feel and the clean scent of him made Rob's senses reel. Staring up into his sky-blue eyes, Rob became mesmerized by the tender emotion mirrored in them.

Silently refusing to relinquish her, Henry dipped his head toward her. His face inched closer, and his lips sought to claim hers.

Rob turned her head at the very last moment. Her heart pounded frantically within her breast at the near contact of their lips. How she wished she were free to succumb to his kiss.

Henry chuckled and planted a kiss on her cheek. "I almost had you that time," he teased.

"Almost doesna count," Rob replied. She glanced at her frowning uncle and blushed with embarrassment. "Daddy?"

Richard Devereux turned away from his niece and his

brother-in-law who were still clinging to each other like a couple of vines. He looked down at Aurora.

"Yesterday I seen Uncle Henry trying to kiss Cousin Rob," the little girl told him. "She wouldn't let him."

"Daughters, let your cousin's behavior be an example to you," Richard said, beginning his favorite lecture on the inherent evil in men. "All men—like Uncle Henry— have wicked intentions. Never let them near you."

"Daddy?"

"Yes, Blythe?"

"You're a man," the ten-year-old observed. "Do you have wicked intentions too?"

Henry and Rob burst out laughing while the countess covered her smile with one hand. The earl cast them a quelling look, which only served to make Rob giggle even more.

"Daughters, if a man tries to kiss you," Richard asked, "what are you going to say to him?"

"Yuch-yuch-yuch," the five little girls chorused.

The earl cast the three watching adults a look of triumph and then asked his daughters, "If a man *does* kiss you, what are you going to do?"

"Slap his face," they shouted.

"Daddy, Uncle Odo told us—" Blythe began.

"—to kick the gent's balls," Bliss finished.

"What balls?" Aurora asked.

"Never mind," the earl answered.

"Daughters, if you plan to celebrate tonight," Lady Keely spoke up, "you must nap this afternoon. Mrs. Ashemole is waiting inside for you."

The earl knelt in front of his three-year-old twins and put an arm around each. "Give Daddy a kiss good-bye," he said.

"Yuch-yuch-yuch," Summer and Autumn shouted.

Lady Keely, Rob, and Henry burst out laughing. Even the earl smiled.

Henry turned to Rob and asked, "Would you care to ride with me this afternoon?"

"There's nothin' I'd love more," she answered, "but Isabelle will be here soon. Ye know she's comin' for an extended visit."

"Then I'll wait with you at the quay," Henry said.

Hand in hand, the two walked in the direction of the quay. The earl and the countess stared after them for a moment.

Richard and Keely exchanged concerned glances. The earl raised his brows at his wife in a silent question. She shrugged in answer and smiled.

"Henry fancies himself in love with her," Lady Keely said. "Rob will have him if her parents can manage to win her an annulment."

"Does your brother know about her previous marriage?" Richard asked.

Keely shook her head. " 'Tisn't my place to tell him, and I doubt Rob has shared it. She's hoping for good news from Scotland."

Both the earl and his lady watched the retreating couple. Appearing very much in love, Henry and Rob strolled across the lawns to the quay. At one point, the marquess tried to kiss her, but she managed to elude his lips and giggled at her victory.

"Send Henry to court for a few weeks," Keely suggested, looping her arm through her husband's. "By the time he returns, we shall have heard if an annulment is possible."

"You're very wise, dearest," Richard said, escorting her to the house.

"You once told me I had no common sense," she reminded him.

Richard smiled. "True, but you proved me wrong when you married me."

Meanwhile, Rob sat beside Henry on a stone bench near the quay. Her right hand clasped his, and her left hand hid inside her pocket. When she peeked at the handsome marquess and found him watching her, Rob blushed and smiled.

"I saved ye from one of my uncle's tongue-lashin's," she teased him. "Why do ye persist in tellin' his daughters vulgar jokes? They canna even understand them."

" 'Tis precisely the reason," Henry told her. "For the past ten years, Richard has been obsessed with guarding his daughters' maidenheads. I love sending him into a high dudgeon."

" 'Tis cruel of ye to do so," Rob said.

Henry chuckled. "Before he married my sister, your uncle was the wildest and most successful rake at the Tudor court."

"Uncle Richard?" Rob couldn't credit that. "He seems so proper."

"My sister tamed him."

"How did she manage that?"

"By kissing him whenever he wished," Henry lied. "You should strive to emulate her behavior. Besides, you wound me whenever you turn your lips away from mine."

"Disappointment is a part of life, my lord," Rob said, flicking a sidelong glance at him. "Ye'll survive."

"Won't you feel guilty if I expire before your eyes?" he asked with a wicked grin.

"Yer incorrigible," she replied, laughing. "I willna kiss ye until my previous betrothal is annulled. Remember, my lord, those who wait long at the ferry are bound to get across sometime."

Henry slipped his arm around her shoulder and drew

her close, so close his well-muscled thigh teased her skirt. When she looked up at him, he gazed deeply and longingly into the fathomless pools of her emerald eyes and whispered in a seductively husky voice, "Darling, you do remind me of a thunderstorm at a picnic."

Rob giggled. "You resemble a *waistie wanis.*"

Henry cocked an ebony brow at her. "What's that?"

"A spoiled child."

"Sorry, darling. Let's kiss and make up."

"Yer forgiven and may kiss my hand." Rob offered him her right hand to kiss in a courtly manner.

"Uncle Henry!"

Both Rob and Henry looked over their shoulders. Blythe hurried across the lawns toward them.

"Uncle Henry," Blythe called. "Daddy wants to see you. *Now.*"

Henry waved at his niece and then turned back to Rob. "Darling, I fear you only delayed your uncle's tonguelashing. Will you accompany me to the house?"

Rob glanced toward the Thames River and shook her head. In the distance, a barge had just rounded the bend. "Isabelle is almost here."

"I'll return in a few minutes," Henry said, rising from the bench. "Be warned, my bonny lassie. I plan to steal one of your kisses at the Samhuinn celebration tonight."

"Ye can always try," she countered with a flirtatious smile.

Rob watched Henry and Blythe walk back to Devereux House. With his ebony hair and sky-blue eyes, the Marquess of Ludlow was every maiden's dream man. Rob sighed. She loved him, but why couldn't he understand that she wasn't going to allow him liberties with her person until her annulment was finalized?

Because he doesn't know I'm already married, Rob answered her own question. Guilty remorse coiled itself around her heart. Though she wasn't deceitful by nature, Rob couldn't chance losing Henry's tender regard by telling him the truth of the matter.

Gordon Campbell will welcome the opportunity to dissolve our marriage, Rob told herself. *If he even remembers he has a wife.* The Marquess of Inverary had never sent her any trinket or letter. When he left Dunridge Castle after their wedding, the man seemed to have fallen off the edge of the world.

Banishing the painful memory, Rob smiled inwardly. She had achieved her goal in life. Like her mother before her, she was a real English lady. Having found happiness in England, she vowed never to return to the Highlands.

Rob pulled her left hand out of her pocket and stared at the birthmark shaped like the devil's flower. She ran a finger across it. The mark felt no different from the skin on her right hand, yet it had brought her a lifetime of trouble. Amazing, how an innocuous-looking stain could create so much heartache.

"Rob?"

Rob focused on the voice, then leaped off the bench and cried, "Isabelle!"

The boatman helped the blonde disembark, and the two petite women flew into each other's arms. Materializing from nowhere, the earl's footmen carried the young woman's bags to the house.

"I missed you," Rob exclaimed.

"I missed you more," Isabelle Debrett said with a smile.

" 'Tis warm today. Let's sit in the garden and chat," Rob suggested, slipping her left hand into her pocket. "Or would ye prefer to rest awhile?"

"I'm too excited to rest," Isabelle admitted. Then ordered, "Get that hand out of your pocket."

"But—"

"Do as I say."

When Rob reluctantly did as she was told, Isabelle took her blemished hand in hers. Together, they walked to one of the stone benches.

Uncomfortable with the other girl touching her marked hand, Rob sat stiffly beside her on the bench. She itched to yank her hand back and hide it in her pocket, but would never chance offending the other girl.

Without warning, Isabelle reached out with one finger and traced the six-petaled flower stain. "Delicately distinctive," she murmured, then looked up and smiled.

Horrified by the gesture and surprised by the words, Rob turned a stricken expression upon the other girl. Didn't she recognize the mark of the devil? What would she do if Isabelle suddenly made the sign of the cross to ward the evil eye off? How could she bear losing her only friend?

"I'm so glad we're friends," Isabelle said.

Tears welled up in Rob's eyes. "I—I never had a friend before I met ye," she confessed.

"That makes us even," the other girl admitted. "You're the only real friend I ever had."

"Ye've two sisters."

"Stepsisters," Isabelle qualified. "They never considered me their real sister."

"'Tis pure jealousy," Rob replied, indignant for her friend's sake. "Yer so bonny, and whenever Lobelia and Rue go out and aboot, their ugly faces scare wee bairns."

"'Tis unkind of you to say that," Isabelle said with a mischievous grin. "Lobelia and Rue are merely a tad plain."

"Belle, how can ye sit there and defend them?" Rob asked. "They force ye to attend them as if yer their personal servant. Unpaid servant, I might add. Yer stepmother's no better."

Isabelle shrugged. "Delphinia, Lobelia, and Rue are the only family I have now that Papa is gone."

"What aboot yer cousin Roger?"

"I meant immediate family. Besides, accumulating a mountain of gold keeps Roger too busy to bother with me." Isabelle spied the handsome man advancing on them and whispered, "Here comes the Marquess of Ludlow."

Rob yanked her hand out of her friend's and slipped it into her pocket. Masking her abrupt gesture, she said, "I feel a bit chilled. Do ye?"

Isabelle shook her head and cast her friend a curious look. She flicked a glance at the marquess and then the pocket where her friend's blemished hand was hidden.

"Lady Isabelle, welcome to Devereux House." Henry greeted the blonde with an easy smile. Before she could reply, he dismissed her presence just as easily. Turning to Rob, Henry said, "Your uncle needs me to go to court. I won't be here for tonight's celebration. How about an early Samhuinn kiss, sweetheart?"

Rob blushed, embarrassed that he would speak so boldly in front of her guest. "I'll consider givin' ye a welcome-home kiss when ye return," she said, refusing him.

Henry lifted her right hand to his lips, gazed deeply into her eyes, and said, "Darling, you're making me daft."

Isabelle burst out laughing.

Rob giggled and then parried, "My lord, ye already were daft when I met ye."

As she watched the marquess walk toward the quay, a vague sense of relief surged through Rob. She loved him with all of her heart, but needed a bit of breathing space. Rob wanted to savor each moment with the only friend she'd ever had, and Henry's departure would give her that opportunity.

"Ludlow seems smitten," Isabelle remarked.

"So he says," Rob replied, her gaze still fixed on the retreating marquess. "I willna kiss him until I'm free."

"Do you think Campbell will agree to that?" Isabelle asked.

"I dinna know." Rob slipped her left hand out of her pocket, removed the scrolled band of gold that she now wore on her smallest finger, and stared at it.

Lifting the wedding ring from her hand, Isabelle admired it and then said, "There's something written inside."

" 'Ye and No Other,' " Rob supplied.

"How romantic," Isabelle gushed, momentarily forgetting her friend's preference for Henry Talbot. "The Marquess of Inverary must love you. What did he say when he gave you the ring?"

"Somethin' aboot bein' his lady and how he'd always remain true to me," Rob answered, hoping her friend proved wrong about the marquess's feelings. "What a crock of dung that was."

"Campbell adores you," the other girl disagreed. "No man would say such things to a lady unless he meant them."

Rob gave her an affectionate smile. "Isabelle, ye always see the good in people. Campbell never even wrote me a letter during all those years."

"Perhaps he's been busy."

"For ten years?" Rob countered, cocking an ebony brow at her.

" 'Tis possible," Isabelle said with a nod, then sighed dreamily. " 'Ye and No Other.' Aye, the Marquess of Inverary loves you madly. I warrant 'tis the very reason he's kept himself away. Campbell refused to tempt himself while you were growing into womanhood. Imagine, Rob. All those long, long years Gordon Campbell remained faithful to you . . ."

Holyroodhouse Palace, Edinburgh

"Come back to bed and warm me," the Countess of Galbraith purred throatily.

Twenty-five–year–old Gordon Campbell ignored the blatantly sensual invitation. Dressed only in black breeches and boots, he stared out the bedchamber window that overlooked Holyrood Park.

That first morning of November had dawned depressingly gray and frosted. October's crowning glory of gold, orange, and red leaves lay scattered across the brown lawns. Bare branches etched stark silhouettes against a bleak sky.

Gordon studied the fallen leaves and the barren branches. "No wind" registered in his mind. The overcast day appeared ideal for his golf game with King James. Losing to the king without seeming to do so was much easier on a windless day.

"Gordy, did ye hear me?" twenty-two-year-old Lavinia Kerr asked in a whining voice. "I'm freezin'."

Gordon turned around and smiled lazily at the voluptuous redhead snuggled beneath the coverlet on the four-poster, curtained bed. His latest mistress possessed all the qualities he liked best in a woman—stupid, shallow, and married to someone else.

No commitments was rule number one in Gordon's personal philosophy. He needed no tender attachments impeding his soaring ambitions and was glad he'd followed his father's advice by marrying MacArthur's daughter when he turned fifteen. His marriage to her had saved him from myriad pretty vultures like Lavinia. When doing so suited him, Gordon intended to end his affair with the fiery-haired beauty in his usual way. He'd gift her with an outrageously expensive trinket, give her adorable derriere a final pat, and send her on her way. To her next lover, no doubt.

"At what are ye starin'?" she asked, a flirtatious smile curving her full lips.

"I'm admirin' the most beautiful woman in Edinburgh," Gordon answered, sauntering across the chamber to sit on the edge of the bed.

Lavinia sat up and let the coverlet drop to her waist, exposing her breasts. "Ye have a remarkable way with words," she murmured, gliding the palm of her hand across his bare chest. "Take yer boots and breeches off. I have urgent need of ye."

"When ye slipped into my bed this mornin'," Gordon reminded her, "I told ye I couldna linger. I'm golfin' with James."

"The king willna golf in the rain," she argued.

" 'Tisna rainin'," he told her. "Why dinna ye join us?"

"I hate golfin'."

"How unfortunate." Gordon cast her a long look and added in feigned dismay, "Ye possess the perfect stance for an excellent golf game."

"I do?"

"Aye, widespread legs."

"Yer crude," Lavinia said, lifting her nose into the air. Then, "When are ye goin' to marry me?"

Gordon leaned close and nuzzled the side of her neck. With laughter lurking in his voice, he reminded her, "Did ye forget, hinny? Ye've already got yerself a husband."

"Galbraith is an old man and canna last verra much

longer," Lavinia countered. "Challenge him to a duel and be done with it."

"I expected better of ye," Gordon replied, giving her a reproving look. "Where's the honor in challengin' a man too old to defend himself? Dinna forget, lovey, I have a wife."

"The MacArthur chit?" Lavinia laughed derisively. "Annul her."

Gordon opened his mouth to reply but heard a knock on the door. He flicked a measuring look at Lavinia and hoped this wasn't one of her tricks intended for Galbraith to find them together in a compromising position. Murdering a man old enough to be his grandfather wasn't something he'd enjoy. Perhaps he'd better shop for that farewell trinket after his round of golf.

"Gordy? Are ye in there?" The voice belonged to his friend, Mungo MacKinnon.

"Here's yer cousin. Cover yerself," Gordon said to Lavinia. Then called, "Come in, Mungo."

The door swung open, and twenty-six–year-old Mungo MacKinnon walked into the chamber. Standing well under six feet, Mungo was slenderly built and a good six inches shorter than Gordon. He sported a crown of pale blond hair and deep-set blue eyes. Mungo leaned his bag of golf clubs against the wall and then grinned at Lavinia.

"Cousin, ye look delightfully disheveled," he teased her. "How's yer husband?"

"Verra funny."

"Are ye almost ready?" Mungo asked Gordon. "We dare na keep Himself waitin'."

Rising from his perch on the edge of the bed, Gordon pulled his white shirt on over his head and then reached for his black leather jerkin. "I was tryin' to persuade Lavinia to join us," he said, his gray eyes sparkling with mischief.

Lavinia tossed the pillow at him, but in the movement, the coverlet dropped to reveal her breasts. She blushed prettily and yanked it up.

The two men hooted at her embarrassment, but an insistent knocking on the door cut their laughter short. While Mungo hastily pulled the bed draperies shut to hide his cousin, Gordon crossed the chamber and opened the door a crack. A man, dressed in the black and green Campbell plaid, stood there.

Recognizing the Marquess of Inverary, the Campbell courier offered him a sealed parchment, saying, "From His Grace."

"I'll be returnin' to Campbell Mansion this afternoon," Gordon said, accepting the parchment. "I'll see ye there later if this requires an answer."

The courier nodded and left.

Gordon closed the door and leaned back against it. He started to break the wax seal on the missive.

"What's the news from Argyll?" Lavinia called. With the coverlet wrapped around herself, she emerged from the curtained bed.

Suppressing a smile, Gordon glanced at his friend. Mungo rolled his eyes at his cousin's curiosity.

Gordon opened the missive, and keeping its contents hidden from view, began to read. He'd been expecting this particular order, but actually seeing it in writing startled his senses. Ten years seemed to have passed in the blink of an eye.

Closing his eyes, Gordon tried to conjure the image of his bride as she would now appear, a full-grown woman. All he saw was an eight-year-old angel who feared the monster living under her bed. What did Rob MacArthur look like now? he wondered. Had the promise of beauty been fulfilled?

"Ye dinna look especially pleased," Lavinia remarked.

Gordon stared at her for a long moment and hoped she wouldn't succumb to one of her tantrums. "My MacArthur bride is ripe," he said. "Argyll orders me to fetch her."

"Ye canna leave me," Lavinia cried. Then, "Cousin, speak to him."

"Livy, the man must do his father's biddin'," Mungo replied with a shrug.

"If ye dinna consummate yer vows," Lavinia advised, "ye can annul the marriage."

"I willna do that," Gordon told her. " 'Twould cause a breach between our families."

"Why, ye never loved me at all," Lavinia said in an accusing voice.

She has the right of that, Gordon thought. He didn't love her. Love was for women and fools.

Gordon reached out and pulled her close, saying, "Livy, love has naught to do with marriage. Ye know that as well as anyone."

"Ye promised ye'd escort me to the king's masque tomorrow evenin'," she whined.

"Do ye see me leapin' on my horse and ridin' off to the Highlands?" Gordon asked. "The MacArthur brat has kept for ten years. Another couple of days willna matter."

Lavinia smiled and entwined her arms around his neck. She pressed herself against his hard, muscular frame and asked, "So, ye'll leave me heartbroken in a couple of days?"

Her delicately seductive scent assailed his senses. Steeling himself against her wiles, Gordon set her back a pace.

"God's balls, Livy. Dinna wrap yerself around me," he scolded. "Ye know I detest bein' smothered."

Mungo burst out laughing. Gordon Campbell was the only man he knew who possessed the willpower to resist his beautiful cousin.

Glorious in her anger, Lavinia rounded on her Mac-Kinnon cousin. "Yer laughin' at my heartache?"

The absurd thought of Lavinia being heartbroken over any man made Gordon chuckle. Lavinia whirled around and raised her hand to slap him.

Gordon was faster. He grabbed her wrist and yanked her against his unyielding body. His lips captured hers in a kiss that left her breathless and yearning for more.

"Dinna be daft," Gordon whispered against her lips. "I'm plannin' to deposit the chit at Inverary Castle and then return to Edinburgh posthaste."

Lavinia's expression cleared, and she smiled with satisfaction.

"Sneak back to yer own chamber after I leave," Gordon ordered. "Be dressed for shoppin' by the time I return."

"Shoppin'?" Lavinia echoed, her interest primed.

Gordon smiled. "Aye, lovey. I'll buy ye somethin' wildly extravagant." At that, he lifted his bag of golf clubs and gestured to the other man.

"I'll ride with ye to Argyll," Mungo said as the two of them walked out the door.

"I thought ye disliked the MacArthurs," Gordon replied.

"My Edinburgh creditors are breathin' down my neck," Mungo told him. "At the moment the MacArthurs seem the lesser of two evils."

Gordon's chuckle ended abruptly when something heavy hit the door as it closed behind them. The two men stopped short and turned around to stare at it.

"Lavinia is ventin' her anger," Mungo said. "The MacArthur lass is gettin' the title to which she aspired."

Gordon glanced at him. "She'll survive. To the best of my knowledge, disappointment never killed anyone."

The two men lifted their golf bags to their shoulders and started down the corridor again.

"I'll be leavin' for Argyll in the mornin'," Gordon informed his friend. "Be ready to ride at dawn if ye've a mind to accompany me."

Mungo looked at him in surprise. "Ye told Lavinia—"

"Livy willna know until after I've gone." Gordon winked at the other man and added, "The gift I buy her today will smooth her ruffled feathers . . . Ah, a double dose of trouble walks this way."

Mungo glanced down the long length of the corridor. From the opposite direction, Lady Armstrong and Lady Elliott advanced on them and smiled when they spied the two men.

"Good mornin', ladies," Gordon greeted his two former mistresses. He flashed them one of his most charming smiles.

"Will ye be attendin' the king's masque tomorrow evenin'?" Lady Elliott asked, giving Mungo her attention.

"We'll be leavin' Edinburgh in the mornin'," Gordon spoke up.

"Poor Lavinia will be so disappointed," Lady Armstrong remarked, her insincerity apparent in her voice.

"To hell with Lavinia Kerr," Lady Elliott quipped, her inviting gaze still fixed on Mungo. "*I'm* disappointed."

"We've an appointment with His Majesty and dinna want to keep him waitin'," Gordon said, drawing his friend away. "Excuse us, ladies."

"Why d'ye do that?" Mungo asked as they continued down the corridor. "Lady Elliott seemed interested in me."

"Lady Elliott is married," Gordon reminded him.

"Well, *ye* had her," Mungo replied. "Her bein' married never bothered ye."

"Married mistresses are a wealthy man's luxury," Gordon informed him. "Beddin' other men's wives is a waste of yer time. Ye need to woo an heiress."

"And how am I to do that when I've got no prospects?" Mungo asked.

"For one thing, always tell the ladies what they want to hear," Gordon advised. "Tell a beautiful woman she's smart, and a smart woman she's beautiful."

"What if the lady in question is both beautiful and smart?"

"Run in the other direction, my friend," Gordon warned. "The point is give the ladies what they desire in their secret hearts, and they'll trip over their pretty feet to do yer biddin'. 'Tis a lot like dealin' with the king."

Mungo cast his friend a sidelong glance and said, "I guess what they say is true."

"What's that?"

"There are more reivers amongst the Campbells than honest men in other clans."

Gordon grinned. "Thank ye for the high praise." He reached out and put his arm around his friend's shoulder in easy camaraderie, saying, "Did ye hear the story aboot the Reverend John Knox playin' golf on the Sabbath?"

Mungo shook his head.

"One glorious Sabbath morn, that righteous reformer sneaked away for an illicit solo round," Gordon told him. "God saw what the hypocrite was doin', so He punished the man by givin' him a hole in one."

"That's no punishment," Mungo remarked.

"Strange ye should say that," Gordon replied, giving him a sidelong glance. "Saint Peter uttered those verra same words. God cocked one holy eyebrow at Saint Pete and replied, 'Oh, no? And whom can he be tellin'?'"

Mungo chuckled. "Serves the bastard right. My uncle told me Sunday was the best day of the week before John Knoxious had his way with it."

Gordon burst out laughing. "My own father said the verra same thing . . . Let's hurry, or Himself will be waitin' for us. Ye know what that means."

"Aye, partin' with more money than I can afford to lose."

In their haste to reach the king, Gordon and Mungo quickened their pace. Turning down another passageway, the two men nearly crashed into someone rounding the corner from the opposite direction. In the dimly lit corridor, the man appeared as dark and sinister as Lucifer himself.

"The devil's bairns have the devil's own luck," the stranger said, flashing the marquess a smile. "I've found ye without any trouble."

Gordon noted the man's green and black, yellow-pinstriped plaid. *A MacArthur clansman,* he concluded, *come to tell me my bride is ripe.* Lifting his gaze to the stranger's dark eyes, Gordon realized he was looking at one of his brothers-in-law.

Six feet tall and muscularly built, Dubh MacArthur had hair and eyes as black as a moonless midnight and a devilish smile that could charm the chastity out of a nun. At twenty-five, this MacArthur son was the image of his father as a young man.

"Greetin's, Cousin Dubh," Gordon said, returning the other man's smile. "What brings ye to Holyroodhouse?"

"Ye do."

Gordon raised his eyebrows at him. He turned to introduce his companion, but faltered at the cold hatred gleaming at the other man from his friend's blue eyes. Why did MacKinnon harbor such a strong dislike for the

MacArthurs? This aversion didn't bode well for their continued friendship. After all, his bride was the MacArthur laird's only daughter.

Recovering himself, Gordon pasted a gracious smile on his face and said, "Meet Mungo MacKinnon, one of my closest friends."

"Are ye, perchance, related to my cousin Glenda?" Dubh asked the slight, blond man.

"Her mother Antonia was one of my late father's sisters," Mungo answered.

Dubh offered the man his hand in friendship, saying, "Then I'm certainly pleased to make yer acquaintance."

Mungo hesitated and dropped his gaze from MacArthur's dark eyes to his offered hand. Finally, he accepted the outstretched hand, but his smile did not reach his pale blue eyes.

"We're late for a round of golf with the king," Gordon told Dubh. "Come with us, and I'll introduce ye to him. We can talk as we walk."

As the three of them started down the corridor, Gordon cast his MacArthur kinsman a sidelong glance. When Dubh grinned broadly at him, Gordon suffered the sudden and uncomfortable feeling that he was the butt of a hilarious jest to which only his brother-in-law was privy.

" 'Tis strange ye should arrive in Edinburgh today," Gordon remarked. "Mungo and I are leaving for Dunridge Castle in the mornin'. 'Tis past time I fetched my wife to Inverary."

"Dinna bother, brother-in-law." Dubh gave him a long look. "Yer wife isna there."

Gordon halted abruptly and turned to him. "What do ye mean?" he asked, confused. "Is she dead?"

"Rob is in England," Dubh told him. "She's been visitin' Uncle Richard for the past year."

"Ye mean the Earl of Basildon?" Gordon asked.

"The English queen's Midas?" Mungo echoed, obviously impressed.

"Aye," Dubh answered.

"When is the lass due home?" Gordon asked, relieved for the reprieve from the drudgery of beginning his married life.

Dubh hesitated. He flicked a glance at the blond man and then said to his cousin, "Send Mungo ahead, and we'll speak privately aboot this."

"Ye can say whatever ye want in front of my friend," Gordon told him. "Make it fast, though. We've kept the king waitin' long enough."

Ignoring his kinsman's rudeness, Dubh inclined his head and smiled. "Rob says she's stayin' in England and wants yer marriage annulled."

Mungo reacted first. He hooted with derisive laughter, but one quelling look from the surprised marquess ended it abruptly.

"*She* wants to annul *me*?" Gordon echoed, unable to credit what he'd heard. No woman had ever refused him. That the MacArthur twit even considered annulling him was shockingly humiliating.

Dubh grinned and nodded. "Ye've the gist of it, cousin."

"I willna allow it," Gordon said, masking his embarrassment with sternness. "Tell yer father to order her home."

"With all due respect, my lord marquess, Rob is yer wife," Dubh countered. "If ye want her, fetch her yerself."

"The earl approves of her rebellion?" Gordon asked.

"I didna say that," Dubh replied. "We MacArthurs havena heard a peep out of ye in ten years. How could we guess yer intentions? 'Tis the reason I'm here."

Gordon had the good grace to flush but then defended himself, saying, "I've been makin' my way at court for the good of the clan." He turned to his friend and asked, "Are ye up for ridin' to England?"

Mungo nodded. "Perhaps the king will have messages for his ambassadors."

"I'll ride with ye," Dubh said. "I've always been able to reason with my baby sister."

Gordon grinned. " 'Twill be the last adventure of my bachelor days. The three of us will go trystin' with the Sassenach devils."

"My sweet mother is English," Dubh reminded him. "The English are na devils, Gordy, merely men."

"Only a devil would seduce an innocent bride into turning her tender regard away from her noble husband," Gordon replied.

"Perhaps the husband lost the bride's tender regard without anyone else's help," Dubh countered with an easy smile.

Mungo MacKinnon chuckled, earning a censorious look from the irritated marquess.

"Whatever the cause of my bride's waywardness," Gordon told his kinsman, "I'm determined to take her in hand and set her straight."

Chapter 2

 "Whatever the outcome, I'm determined to take Henry aside and tell him the truth of the matter," Rob announced. Noting her friend's dubious expression, she added, "I swear I'll do it the moment he returns from court."

"Do you think 'tis wise?" Isabelle asked. "The fact that you've kept your marriage a secret for over a year will probably anger him."

"I'll take my chances," Rob said with a dainty shrug. "If he truly loves me, Henry will see my annulment through to its end."

"I'll be here to help you through the worst of it," Isabelle promised, taking Rob's right hand in her own.

"I'm so lucky yer cousin Roger brought ye along with him to visit us last summer," Rob said, smiling at the only friend she'd ever had. "However would I cope with this whole situation if ye werena aboot to hold my hand?"

"I'm the lucky one," Isabelle insisted, returning her smile. "When do you think Henry will return?"

"I dinna know," Rob answered. "I was hopin' he'd come home in time for tonight's celebration."

The two friends strolled around the Earl of Basildon's garden and enjoyed the early winter's afternoon. Opposites yet complementary, the two young women were like magnificent jewels—beautiful if solitary yet startlingly exquisite when placed in the perfect setting of the other's company. Both were petite, but Rob's ebony hair and emerald eyes contrasted strikingly with Isabelle's golden tresses and sky-blue eyes.

A powdery light blanket of snow, the first of the season, muffled the sounds of their footsteps on that December afternoon. Several starlings gathered in the hackberry elms and dined on its few remaining berries while wrens, so secretive during the summer nesting season, flaunted themselves boldly on the barren branches of a birch tree. Woodsmoke scented the Strand's crisp, crystalline air.

"Aunt Keely says 'tis a Welsh custom to kiss beneath the Yule mistletoe," Rob told her friend. "I've decided to allow Henry one kiss."

"Your aunt is a bit of a pagan, isn't she?" Isabelle said with a fond smile. "By the way, your uncle seems in especially good spirits for a man who's just fathered his sixth daughter."

"Aunt Keely assures Uncle Richard that the next one will be a boy," Rob replied. " 'Tis why they've named the new babe Hope."

"How can she possibly know what her next child will be?"

Rob shrugged. "She hasn't been wrong yet . . . *Ouch!*"

"Owww," Isabelle cried.

Something struck their backs, and the two women whirled around as a second barrage of snowballs sailed through the air toward them. The telltale giggling of little girls reached their ears.

"We got you good," ten-year-old Blythe called, materializing from behind a hedgerow.

Eight-year-old Bliss, trailed by her three younger sisters, stepped from behind the hedgerow and asked, "Will you play with us?"

"Please?" three-year-old Summer and Autumn chimed together.

"Pretty please with sugar on it," added six-year-old Aurora.

"I thought I felt pryin' eyes watchin' my back," Rob said. "Come along then."

Beside her, Isabelle chuckled as the five Devereux girls dashed toward them. "I too felt someone watching us," she said.

"I still do." Rob glanced around but could detect no one watching them. Yet, the uncomfortable feeling persisted.

"Grandmama Talbot's birthday party is tonight," Aurora announced when she reached them.

"Mama said we may attend," Blythe added. "If we nap today."

"We can eat all the pudding we want," Bliss told them.

"Apples and nuts," Summer and Autumn shouted with childish glee, making all of them laugh.

"Do ye think anyone will invite me to dance?" Blythe asked, hope and fear warring upon her pretty face.

Rob noted her cousin's anxious expression. "Do ye wish to dance?"

Blythe nodded and blushed, admitting, "With Roger Debrett."

"He's an old man," Bliss said.

"Is not," Blythe countered, rounding on her sister.

"He is—"

"—Not!"

"At twenty-two years, Roger Debrett scarcely qualifies as aged," Rob informed Bliss. She smiled at Blythe, adding, "I'm certain sure he'll be invitin' you to dance."

"Shall we try to make a snowman?" Isabelle asked, hiding a smile.

"There isn't enough snow," Bliss complained.

"Watch this," Rob ordered her cousins, starting toward the rear of the garden where the snow was virgin, untouched by their footprints.

Rob removed her left hand from her pocket, tightened her cloak around herself, and then lay on her back in the snow. She brushed her arms upward in the snow toward her head and down again. Finally, Rob stood and stepped away from the spot, then beckoned the five little girls to her side.

"What is it?" Aurora asked, inspecting the impression in the snow.

Rob opened her mouth to reply but then frowned as an uncanny feeling of being watched overwhelmed her senses.

"Are you going to tell us or no?" Bliss demanded, drawing her attention.

"What d'ye think it is?" Rob asked, suppressing the overpowering urge to look over her shoulder and catch whoever was watching them.

" 'Tis an angel," Blythe answered.

Rob grinned. "Correct."

"Me make angel," Summer demanded.

"Me too," Autumn said.

"Isabelle and I will show ye how 'tis done," Rob agreed. "Come here where the snow is still unblemished and wrap yer cloaks tightly around yerselves . . ."

* * *

False Solomon's-seal with its blackberry clusters and an arum plant bearing bright red fruit nodded just above the snow-dusted lawns next to the stone wall of Devereux House. A pair of piercing gray eyes peered out of the high-styled windows of the Earl of Basildon's study and watched the two young women surrounded by five little girls in the garden.

Gordon Campbell fixed his gaze on the petite, ebony-haired woman—*his wife.* At this distance, he was unable to see her features clearly but distinctly recalled a pair of disarming emerald-green eyes that had stared up at him from the pretty face of an angelic eight-year-old. Had the promise of her beauty been fulfilled?

From somewhere behind him, Gordon heard Mungo say to the Earl of Basildon, "I'm verra honored to make yer acquaintance, my lord. Yer fame has even reached the Highlands of Scotland."

Gordon smiled inwardly. Mungo always failed to look beyond a man's possessions to see the true worth that lay beneath. A poor man's flaw, but utter folly.

Sensing someone beside him, Gordon glanced to his left and saw Dubh MacArthur silently offering him a glass of whiskey. Accepting it, Gordon took a healthy swig and then coughed as the potent liquid burned a path to his stomach.

"Fine spirits," Gordon managed to say finally.

"A gift from Dubh's father," Earl Richard said with an easy smile. "You know, I never understood how Iain enjoyed this particular poison until I met my illogical wife."

The three younger men smiled. Apparently, English-women could be as troublesome as their northern counterparts.

Dubh gestured toward the window, asking, "Who's the blonde?"

"Isabelle Debrett, a cousin of one of my business associates," Earl Richard answered. He stood on Gordon's right side and gazed out the window. "Rob and Isabelle have become fast friends."

"Strange," Dubh murmured.

Gordon turned his head to look at his brother-in-law and asked, "What's strange?"

"I canna remember Rob havin' a friend," Dubh answered absently, his interested gaze riveted on the blond beauty walking beside his sister. "Whenever I picture her in my mind, I see her strollin' aboot the garden with our mother."

"Everyone has friends," Gordon scoffed, gazing out the window again.

"I dinna recall any."

"Who are those little girls?" Gordon asked.

"My daughters," the earl answered.

Gordon turned a horrified expression on him and echoed, "Ye've *five* daughters?"

"Six." Earl Richard grinned. "Baby Hope is barely ten days old and much too young for romping in the garden with her sisters."

"If ye want a son, do it with yer boots on," Gordon advised, casting the earl a pitying look.

Dubh and Mungo nodded in agreement. Earl Richard smiled and would have replied, but the door opened, drawing his attention.

"My lord, the barge is ready for travel," Jennings, the earl's majordomo, informed him.

"My barge will carry you upriver to Hampton Court," Earl Richard told Mungo. " 'Tis the fastest route. Of course, my bargemen will remain there at your pleasure."

"Thank ye, my lord." Mungo turned to Dubh, asking, "Are ye accompanyin' me upriver?"

Dubh flicked a glance out the window at his sister's friend and then shook his head, answering, "The English rose in the garden interests me. I believe I'll be stayin' here a few days."

"Why take a chance with one pretty flower?" Mungo argued. "There'll be dozens of beauties at court to pluck."

Gordon snapped his head around and cast his friend a puzzled look. Along the road to England, he would have bet the Campbell fortune that Mungo disliked Dubh. Now it appeared that Mungo could hardly bear to part with the man.

"I'll take my chances," Dubh said with a smile. "If I'm disappointed, I'll meet ye at court in a few days."

"As ye wish." Mungo followed Jennings out of the study.

"Shall I send for Rob?" Earl Richard asked Gordon.

"Their playin' in the snow makes such a fetchin' picture," he said, refusing, his gaze returning to his wife. " 'Tis certain she'll balk when I order her to pack her belongin's."

"Ye've plenty of time for arguin'," Dubh said. He looked at his uncle, adding, "We'll be stayin' next door at the Dowager House."

"The countess and I are hosting a party tonight to honor my mother-in-law's birthday," Earl Richard told them. "Of course, both of you are welcome. Gordon can begin wooing Rob tonight."

"Court my own wife?" His suggestion surprised Gordon. "Ye must be jokin'?"

"Rob wishes to remain in England. She and my young brother-in-law—" Earl Richard broke off, leaving unspoken whatever he'd intended to say. Instead, the earl smiled and added, "Heed my advice. Your married life will enjoy peace if you seduce my niece to your will."

Gordon said nothing. He stared out the window at his wife and considered the earl's advice. He never intended to hurry back to Scotland, as traveling at this time of year could be treacherous, especially in the Highlands. Where was the harm in seducing his bride to do his bidding? Getting her home to Argyll would be easier if she developed a fondness for him. After all, arguing with a reluctant bride across the long length of England and Scotland was a less than appealing notion.

Beside him, Dubh MacArthur asked, "Will the Debrett lass be attendin' yer party?"

"Isabelle is Rob's guest until after the first of the year," the earl answered.

"Will ye do me a favor?" Gordon asked the earl. "Dinna tell Rob of my arrival. I'd much prefer meetin' her again before she's aware of who I am."

"As you wish."

"What are they doin' now?" Gordon asked, a puzzled smile on his lips.

Earl Richard's gaze followed the young marquess's, and then he smiled too. "Making angels in the snow."

"Great Bruce's ghost," Rob muttered in frustration, inspecting herself in the pier glass. She wore an exquisite garnet and gold brocaded gown with a squared neckline and long, tight-fitting sleeves that ended in a point at her wrists. Though she'd never looked more beautiful, Rob only saw the despised devil's flower staining the back of her left hand.

Why me? Rob wondered. Couldn't the Lord have bestowed this particular disfigurement upon some other woman? Or even one of her own brothers?

Rob sighed with instant remorse. Wishing her shame on another was a terrible sin. She didn't mind being flawed and could have managed to live happily with an overly long nose or a rotund body. After all, nobody shunned a fat lady. *Or made a protective sign of the cross when a fat woman passed by.* Why couldn't this particular flaw have been located elsewhere on her body, a place that wasn't so visible?

Watching her movements in the pier glass, Rob practiced hiding her left hand within the folds of her gown. Too bad, the damned skirt had no pockets. Well, dancing was definitely out of the question. Unless Henry stood beside her, she couldn't chance flaunting her shame beneath the noses of London's elite.

Rob whirled around when the door swung open. Music from the great hall drifted into her chamber, the sound wafting through the air like the delicate song of the nightingale.

"Isabelle said she'll meet you in the hall," Blythe announced, walking into the chamber with Bliss.

Rob smiled at the pretty picture they presented in identical gowns of pink velvet. "Ye do remind me of rosebuds aboot to bloom," she said.

"You look pretty too," Blythe returned the compliment.

"Too bad Uncle Henry isn't here to admire the sight," Bliss added. "You'll probably never look that good again. I mean—"

"We know what you mean," Blythe interrupted.

"I look like a changelin'-witch," Rob said miserably, frustrated tears welling up in her eyes. "This gown doesna hide Old Clootie's touch."

"Who's Old Clootie?" Bliss asked.

"Satan himself," Rob answered in a hushed tone of voice as if speaking his name could summon him into their presence. She held her left hand out for their inspection. "Most in the Highlands believe 'tis Old Clootie's mark upon me."

"What stupid people," Bliss blurted out. "No offense to your kinsmen, Cousin Rob."

"None taken."

"Satan does not exist," Blythe informed her. "Mama said so, and she knows absolutely everything."

" 'Tis so," Bliss agreed, bobbing her head.

"Whether Old Clootie actually exists or not doesna matter," Rob told them. "He lives if people believe he does, and I'm a changelin'-witch if they think so."

Blythe shook her head. " 'Tis true only if *you* think it."

Rob stared in surprise at her younger cousin and wondered at the wisdom in the ten-year-old's words. Finally, she smiled and said, "How verra perceptive of ye, Blythe."

"At the moment of your creation, the great mother goddess touched you with her blessed hand," Blythe told her. "I wish I wore her flower."

"Me too," Bliss added.

"Sweet cousins, I do love ye," Rob said, her flagging spirits rising with their comforting words. "Dinna speak such blasphemy aloud in the presence of those who wouldna understand."

"We won't," they chimed together.

"Rob?" Blythe hesitated and worried her bottom lip with her teeth before continuing, "Do you really think Roger Debrett will invite me to dance?"

"She wants to marry him," Bliss announced, rolling her eyes.

"I'm positive Lord Roger will find ye irresistibly enchantin'," Rob assured the ten-year-old. "Shall we go below and see if he's arrived?"

On either side of Rob, the two girls placed their hands in hers. Together, they left the bedchamber and started down the corridor.

"I wish Uncle Rhys and Aunt Morgana could have come from Wales," Bliss remarked as they descended the stairs to the foyer. "I do love listening to them argue."

Rob and Blythe looked at each other and giggled, and Bliss grinned. Reaching the hall, the two sisters dashed inside to greet the guests, but Rob paused in the entrance and hid her left hand within the folds of her gown.

Situated at each of the short ends of the rectangular chamber, two gigantic hearths blazed and crackled and warmed the hall's occupants. The flames from dozens of torches cast eerily dancing shadows against the walls.

Rob gazed through the crowd toward the high table, directly opposite the hall's entrance. Lady Dawn, whose birthday they were celebrating, sat with Duke Robert in the place of honor. With the duke and the duchess were Uncle Richard and Aunt Keely. A group of guests gathered in front of the high table and chatted with them.

To the left of the high table, a band of London's finest musicians played the spritely, five-step galliard for the throng of nobles dancing in the center of the chamber. Long trestle tables had been erected around the inner perimeter of the hall and held every kind of seasonal fare imaginable from a variety of roasted meats and fowl to mince pies, cheeses, apples, nuts, and a generous supply of red wine.

Summoning her courage, Rob verified her left hand was hidden and then plunged into that noble mob. Ten steps inside the hall, she stopped short as an uncomfortable feeling of being watched assailed her senses. Nonchalantly, she looked around but detected no one paying her any particular attention.

Giving the casual observer the impression of demure femininity, Rob hid her left hand behind her right hand and walked around the dance floor toward the high table. She saw Roger Debrett dancing with Lady Darnel and slid her gaze to Blythe. The ten-year-old wore a mask of disappointment upon her pretty face, and Rob decided to speak with Lord Roger as soon as the music ended.

As she neared the high table, Rob recognized the familiar profile of the man who was speaking with her uncle. A smile of pure joy lit her face.

"Dubh" she cried. Forgetting to hide her birthmarked hand, Rob threw herself into her older brother's arms and hugged him.

"Ye've grown more bonny," Dubh said, smiling down at her upturned face.

"Do ye carry news of my annulment?" Rob asked, ignoring his compliment.

"What must be said will be said in the mornin'," he told her.

"Is the news good or bad?" she persisted, tugging on his sleeve. "At least, tell me that."

" 'Tis interestin'," Dubh teased her, an amused smile lighting his dark eyes. "Yer bein' rude, baby sister."

Rob turned to the others seated at the high table and smiled apologetically. "I beg yer pardons. Best wishes on yer birthday, Yer Grace."

"Thank you, darling," the Duchess of Ludlow replied.

Rob would have spoken with the others, but again suffered the uncomfortable feeling of being watched. She hid her left hand within the folds of her gown and glanced around at the dancers, but was unable to detect anyone staring at her. She did, however, catch Roger Debrett's attention and gave him an arch look that traveled from him to her cousin.

Roger nodded almost imperceptibly, and when the music ended a moment later, excused himself from Lady Darnel. The dashing young lord approached the group gathered in front of the high table and stopped before Blythe.

"My lady, how lovely you look tonight," Roger remarked, bowing low over her hand.

" 'Tis kind of you to notice my unassuming presence," Blythe replied, a high blush rising on her cheeks.

Lord Roger gifted the ten-year-old with his most charming smile and inclined his head toward the dance floor, asking, "Would you do me the honor of partnering me for the pavane?"

Blythe's answering smile could have lit the whole mansion. "I'd be delighted," she said, accepting his hand.

Pleased with herself, Rob watched Roger escort Blythe onto the dance floor. From beside her, she heard Bliss say in a loud voice, "What a relief. I wasn't relishing the thought of—" Rob snaked her right hand out and covered the eight-year-old's mouth, making everyone laugh.

Rob turned to her brother and asked, "Are Ross and Jamie with ye?"

"No."

"Ye rode alone to London?"

Dubh shook his head. "While in Edinburgh, I chanced to meet a couple of friends who were bound for England. One's gone along to Hampton Court, but the other is stayin' with me at Grandmother's and will be here shortly."

Rob nodded. Outwardly, she appeared the picture of serenity, but every fiber of her being tingled in a riot of suppressed excitement. Her brother's sole purpose in traveling to Edinburgh would have been to gain an annulment for her. Rob knew her life was about to change as surely as she knew her own name.

"I saw ye walkin' in the garden this afternoon," Dubh remarked. "I'd like to meet yer friend. Where is she?"

Rob never heard her brother's question. Once again, the uncanny feeling of being watched overwhelmed her senses. Without thinking, Rob hid her left hand in the folds of her gown and scanned the hall.

And then she saw him.

With his arms folded across his chest, he leaned non-chalantly against the wall opposite the high table. Easily the most incredibly handsome man she'd ever seen, the black-clad stranger stared at her with an intensity that made Rob feel weak legged as if she'd been struck with the blunt end of a claymore.

Unexpectedly, the corners of his lips turned up into a lazy smile. He inclined his head in her direction by way of a long-distance greeting.

Rob read the supreme arrogance in his stance and his gesture. Even his irresistible smile was much too confident and strangely proprietary. Rob suffered the illogical urge to slap it off his handsome face.

"Did ye hear me?"

By sheer force of will, Rob yanked her gaze from the stranger's and looked at her brother. "I beg yer pardon?"

Dubh grinned. "I'd like to meet yer friend. Isabelle, is it?"

Rob nodded distractedly. Like a flower beneath the noonday sun, she felt the stranger's heated gaze. Its intensity flustered her and made logical thinking difficult.

"Would ye care to dance with yer brother?"

"I beg yer—?" Dubh's question registered in her mind. She shook her head and said, "Later, perhaps."

Rob ran one finger across the detested stain. Living in England this past year had been almost like heaven, but flaunting her deformity beneath the noses of London's elite could abruptly end the plans she'd begun to make for herself. She flicked a glance across the hall. The black-clad stranger still watched her.

"Rob?"

"Isabelle, this is my brother Dubh," she said, focusing on the voice beside her. "He's just arrived from Scotland."

"I'm pleased to meet you," the blonde said with a smile.

"I'm *more* than pleased to meet ye," Dubh replied, returning her smile.

"Isabelle is the Earl of Eden's niece and a countess in her own right," Rob interjected, but neither her brother nor her friend spared a glance for her.

"What a coincidence," Dubh remarked, raising his brows at the blonde. "I'm the Earl of Dunridge's heir . . . May I call ye Belle?"

"Please do," she answered.

Dubh gestured to the dancers and asked in a husky voice, "Would ye care to partner me, Belle?"

Without saying a word, Isabelle placed her hand in his.

Surprised, Rob watched her oldest brother and her only friend join the dancing couples. She turned to speak with the others at the high table, but they seemed engrossed in their own conversations. Even her cousin Blythe still danced with Roger Debrett.

Standing alone in the midst of that noble crowd, Rob felt as conspicuously out of place as she had in the Highlands. Was she forever destined to play the outcast? Old Clootie's flower made her different, set her apart from others.

And then Rob thought of Henry. If only he had returned from Hampton Court in time for the party. Rob knew she could brave anything with Henry by her side.

What she needed was a breath of winter's fresh air to clear the old worries from her mind. Wending her way slowly around the perimeter of the dance floor, Rob reached the hall's entrance and stepped into the deserted foyer.

As she reached for her cloak, a hand covered hers, and a voice behind her said, "Dinna leave, bright angel."

"Great Bruce's ghost," Rob cried, startled.

She whirled around and found herself staring into piercing gray eyes. And they belonged to the black-clad stranger.

Like a proper English lady, Rob steeled herself against his smoldering look and tried to withdraw her hand, but the stranger refused to release her. When he spoke, his sensuously husky voice conspired with his disarming gray-eyed gaze to hold her in thrall.

"If my unworthy hand profanes yer angelic shrine," the stranger said, "consider my lips as pilgrims to smooth the roughness of my touch." At that, he pressed his warm lips to her hand and then gifted her with a devastating smile.

Enchanted by his chivalrous speech and gesture, Rob ignored the fluttering riot in the pit of her stomach and returned his smile in kind. She felt safe enough; some part of her mind heard the northern accent that announced his identity as her brother's Edinburgh acquaintance. Out of habit, she hid her left hand within the folds of her gown.

"Ye do wrong yer hand, gentle Scotsman," Rob told him. "With true devotion do pilgrims' hands touch statues of angels and saints. 'Tis the way they kiss."

"Dinna pilgrims and angels and saints have lips?" the stranger asked, inching closer.

"For prayer."

"Why dinna we let lips do what hands do?" he suggested in a seductive whisper. His face came dangerously close, and he lightly brushed his lips across hers.

Shocked and excited, Rob kept her eyes open. The oh-so-gentle touch of his lips on hers sent a heated shiver coursing down her body to the tips of her toes. The delicious sensation ended in an instant.

What possessed her? She had an unwanted husband in the Highlands and a would-be betrothed at court. How did she dare stand in her uncle's foyer and allow this stranger a liberty she'd denied both husband and suitor?

"Yer holy lips have absolved mine of sin," the stranger teased, drawing her attention from troubling thoughts.

"Do my lips now possess yer sin?" Rob asked with a smile.

"God forbid," he said. "Give me back my sin again."

He moved to capture her mouth with his own, but Rob held him off with the palm of her right hand pressed against his chest. "My lord, I do protest—"

"—but not overly much."

The stranger reached down, and capturing her hands in his own, brought them to his lips. He kissed the back of her right hand. After gazing for a long moment at the delicate devil's flower staining her left hand, he pressed his lips on it.

His tender action nagged at an elusive memory. "Though rudeness to my brother's friend troubles me," Rob said, yanking her hand out of his, "I must inform ye that ye are maulin' a married lady."

"Madam, I'm better acquainted with yer marital state than any man," he replied.

Rob heard the rueful tone in his voice and narrowed her gaze on him. "Who are ye?" she demanded, arching one perfectly shaped ebony brow at him. "Identify yerself."

He leaned closer, and as a smile slashed across his handsome features, said, "Call me . . . *husband*."

"Great Bruce's ghost," Rob cried.

The foyer spun dizzyingly, and the floor rushed up to meet her. For a few moments, Rob found refuge from shocked disappointment in a faint. All too soon, she began to swim up from the depths of unconsciousness, and a strange floating sensation permeated her senses. Then

Rob heard the voices reaching out to her from a great distance, recalling her to cruel reality.

"Why won't she awaken?" a man asked.

"She's had a bad shock," a woman answered.

"Why dinna we pitch cold water on her face?" suggested a second man.

"*No.*" Both Earl Richard and Lady Keely rejected the Marquess of Inverary's idea.

Almost reluctantly, Rob opened her eyes and focused on her uncle's and her aunt's concerned expressions. In the background behind them rose a wall of books, and Rob realized she reclined in a chair within her uncle's study. And then she saw the piercing gray-eyed gaze fixed on her.

"Oh, God," Rob moaned. "Yer real."

Gordon refused to smile at her insulting impertinence, though his lips twitched with the urge to laugh. Silently, he offered her a dram of whiskey.

Rob shook her head and looked away.

" 'Twill revive ye," he said.

She flicked him a sidelong glance and said, "I dinna want to revive."

The absurdity of her remark made Gordon smile. "Drink it," he ordered in a pleasant voice, "or I'll force it down yer throat."

Of all the arrogant, insufferable—Rob looked at her uncle and then her aunt. No help there.

Lifting the dram of whiskey from the Marquess of Inverary's hand without actually touching him, Rob pinched her nostrils together with her left hand and gulped the whiskey down in one suicidal swig. Her reaction to the dark amber liquid was swift. First, her emerald eyes widened in pained surprise; and then she coughed and wheezed as the potent whiskey blazed a path to her stomach. When she finally recovered herself, Rob passed the empty glass to her aunt.

Gordon grinned, seemingly amused by her gesture. "My wee kitten has grown into a sleek, temperamental she cat," he drawled.

"I'm not yer anythin'," Rob insisted, then turned a pleading gaze upon her uncle.

"Let us sit in front of the hearth and discuss this gently," Earl Richard suggested, succumbing to her silent plea for help.

"Verra well," Gordon agreed, moving to assist his bride out of the chair and escort her across the chamber.

"I've revived," Rob said, yanking her arm out of his grasp.

Gordon and Rob sat in the two chairs placed in front of the hearth. Peeking at him from beneath the thick fringe of her ebony lashes, Rob saw him staring at her hands. As casually as she could, Rob moved her right hand to cover the devil's flower on her left hand. When his piercing gaze traveled from her hands to her face, Rob quickly fixed her own gaze on the flames in the hearth. Though she refused to gift him with a glance, Rob felt the marquess's overpowering presence with every fiber of her being.

Standing beside her husband, Lady Keely wore an ambiguous smile while Earl Richard stood directly in front of them and folded his arms across his chest. He cleared his throat and said, "We seem to have a problem here."

"I dinna perceive any problem," Gordon replied, stretching his long legs out as though he hadn't a worry in the world. "I've come to collect my wife."

"Dinna call me that," Rob said, her voice tinged with barely suppressed panic.

"Yer the Marchioness of Inverary, angel, whether ye like it or no," Gordon said with an easy smile.

Rob felt like screaming but forced a sweet patience into her voice when she replied, "My lord, I do desire an annulment."

" 'Tis impossible, angel."

"We never consum—" Rob broke off, her complexion reddening with hot embarrassment. She dropped her gaze to her lap and informed her white-knuckled hands, " 'Tis possible, I say."

Gordon chuckled huskily, the sensual sound of it flustering her even more. "I ken yer meanin', hinny, but 'tis Highland tradition for the Marquess of Inverary to wed the MacArthur laird's daughter whenever possible."

"Yer own father married a Gordon," Rob said, forcing herself to look at him though it disturbed her to do so. She felt as though his piercing gaze could see into her soul.

"Aye, but the MacArthur laird—namely, yer grandfather—had no daughters," Gordon replied. "Our parents desired this union. Failin' to honor our vows can only cause a breach between the two families and dissension within the entire clan."

"Ye needn't concern yerself with my parents," Rob assured him. She forced herself to smile, but her lips trembled with the effort. "They wish for my happiness, which I can never have if married to ye."

God's balls, Gordon thought, bristling beneath her innocently spoken insult. The lass could test the patience of a saint, which he damned well wasn't.

"Ye dinna know that, angel," Gordon replied in a deceptively quiet voice.

"I do," Rob insisted. "I'm an English lady and no longer belong in the Highlands."

That a Highlander would forsake her native land appalled Gordon. Unable to control himself, he snorted with angry contempt and said, "I see that a white ram may sire a black lamb."

"What d'ye mean by that?" Rob asked. There was no mistaking the challenge in her voice.

Gordon opened his mouth to answer, but Lady Keely stuck a fortifying dram of whiskey in front of his face. Accepting the glass without a word, Gordon downed its contents in one healthy swig, but his anger numbed him to its burning sensation. He handed the countess the empty glass and then rounded on his bride.

"I slew yer damned monster," Gordon reminded her.

"To what are ye referrin', my lord?" Rob asked, surprised by his words.

"The monster that was livin' beneath yer bed on the day we married." Gordon cocked a dark brow at her. "Dinna ye recall him?"

Rob flushed with angry embarrassment. She flicked a humiliated glance at her uncle and her aunt who appeared to be enjoying themselves.

"Shame on such a fierce Highland warrior as yerself for takin' unfair advantage of an eight-year-old bairn," Rob said, her voice filled with scorn.

"I do believe a compromise is in order." Earl Richard intervened before the marquess could respond to his niece's insulting accusation.

"I agree," Lady Keely said, then turned to Gordon. "My lord, you cannot expect my niece to ride to Scotland in the company of a man she hardly knows, albeit her lawful husband."

Rob smiled with relief. "Thank ye, Aunt Keely."

"And you cannot expect the marquess to forsake his marriage vows so easily," Earl Richard said to her. " 'Tis obvious your parents desired this union."

"Ye married for love," Rob argued.

"And so will we find a fondness together," Gordon said, drawing her attention.

"Ye dinna ken," Rob tried to explain, her voice an aching whisper. "I canna love ye. I love—"

"Lord Campbell will winter in England," Earl Richard interrupted. He looked pointedly at the marquess and added, "He will allow people to believe that you were *betrothed* as children, and he will not seduce you into his bed, which would void any chance for annulment."

"Nor force me either," Rob added.

"Yer safe with me," Gordon snapped, losing patience, thinking his bride was a viper masquerading as a desirable woman. This whole scene was humiliating. Unexpectedly, he gave her a lazy smile and added, "Ye may not believe this, but women have always dropped most willin'ly into my arms."

For some unknown reason, that bit of unsolicited information irritated Rob. She narrowed her gaze on him, and her usually sweet expression became a mask of disgust.

"You will spend as much time with Lord Campbell as he desires and become acquainted with him." Lady Keely spoke up before her niece could level another insult at the marquess.

"On or before the first day of spring, Rob will decide whether to return to Scotland or to remain in England," Earl Richard told the marquess. "Do we have an acceptable understanding?"

"She'll behave without any trace of sullenness?" Gordon asked, purposefully perverse.

"I guarantee it," the earl replied without bothering to glance at her.

Gordon stared for a long moment at his beautiful, reluctant bride but perceived no real contest in this battle of their wills. The chit would be sighing in his arms and begging for his kisses before Hogmanay, which wasn't such a terrible way to greet the new year.

"I agree," Gordon said finally.

Rob sagged with relief in her chair. The longer she remained in England, the less chance there was she'd be forced to return to Scotland. Soon, Henry would return from Hampton Court and set the arrogant Marquess of Inverary in his place. In fact, she could hardly wait to witness the womanizer's comeuppance. That satisfying thought brought the hint of a smile to her lips, and without thinking, she traced a finger across the devil's flower staining her left hand.

"Verra well," Rob agreed, looking up at her uncle's expectant expression. Abruptly, she rose from the chair and announced, "I have the headache and wish to retire for the evenin'."

"We'll begin our courtship in the mornin'," Gordon announced, standing when she did. "Be ready to go ridin' at ten o'clock."

"As ye wish." Rob turned and, feeling that piercing gaze on her back, crossed the chamber to the door. A distant memory surfaced, and she paused. "My lord?"

"Yes, my lady?"

"Ye never sent the doll," she said in a soft, accusing voice.

Gordon raised his brows. "What doll?"

Without bothering to answer him, Rob lifted her up-turned nose into the air in a gesture of dismissal and walked out the door. Dubh and Isabelle stood outside in the corridor, but Rob ignored their presence and headed for the stairs. Tears welled up in her eyes as soon as she reached the privacy of her bedchamber, but she held them in check through sheer force of will.

Dinna cry, Rob told herself. Weepin' willna gain ye an annulment.

Rob stared out the window at the night sky. A crescent moon hung overhead, and thousands of glittering stars winked at her from their bed of black velvet. Mysterious night shrouded all manner of flaws, and Rob loved it.

'Tis imperative I remain in England, she thought, desperation rising within her breast.

Changelin'-witch. Loch Awe Monster.

The crushing taunts of the MacArthur clansmen's children came rushing back to her in a flood of memory. For over a year those painful memories had lain dormant within the deepest recesses of her mind, but Gordon Campbell's unexpected appearance had awakened them.

Rob sighed raggedly. The devil's flower had rendered her unacceptable to the Highlanders. How could she return to that land of lonely misery? Was she forever doomed to play the feared and distrusted outcast?

The Marquess of Ludlow loved her, and the English accepted her as one of their own. Not once had she noticed anyone make a protective sign of the cross when she passed by. She just had to marry Henry and remain in England. Living in Scotland would destroy her.

An elopement was out of the question. She already had a husband.

Adultery leaped into her mind, but Rob banished that sinful thought without any consideration. In good conscience, she could never compromise her virtue and integrity in order to save herself from heartache. What she needed was an honorable solution to her problem. An annulment was the only thing possible, but she needed his permission to get it.

As she stared out the window and pondered the bleakness of her future, Rob spied the dark figure of a man walking across the snow-covered lawns toward the Dowager House. Mist, sheer as a bride's veil, crept up the banks of the Thames and swirled around the Marquess of Inverary's legs.

Gordon Campbell's piercing gray gaze and chestnut brown hair conspired with his rugged features to make him an unusually attractive man, the kind about whom maidens dream. Too bad he hadn't been born English. Rob knew she wouldn't have minded being his wife. On the other hand, the marquess admitted being a womanizer and did seem overly proud.

That was it! No self-respecting Highlander would keep a woman who loved another. In the morning, she would explain—ever so gently and tactfully, of course—that Henry and she shared true love. Campbell would bow out with his pride intact and, hopefully, return to Scotland posthaste to annul their marriage. If he wished, he was welcome to use Old Clootie's mark as the reason.

That dim hope buoyed Rob's sagging spirits, but it was a long, long time before sleep seduced her into sweet oblivion.

Chapter 3

 "Good morning."

Rob awakened to the cheerful greeting but refused to open her eyes. In a futile attempt to shut the intruder out, she yanked the coverlet over her head.

" 'Tis time to awaken," the insistent voice told her. "I've brought you a breakfast tray."

Reluctantly, Rob pulled the coverlet off her face. Lady Keely sat on the edge of the bed. Brilliant, blinding sunshine streamed into the chamber through the window behind her aunt.

Rob moaned as if in pain and snapped her eyes shut. Great Bruce's ghost, she despised mornings and much preferred the night's dark beauty.

"The morning ages," Lady Keely said. "Your handsome marquess will soon arrive."

"Tell Henry to come back later," Rob replied without bothering to open her eyes.

"I'm referring to the Marquess of Inverary," the countess said.

The memory of the previous evening seeped into Rob's sleep-befuddled mind and made her gasp. She bolted up in the bed and would have thrown the coverlet off, but then thought better of it and leaned back against the headboard.

"Campbell kept me waitin' for ten long years," Rob said, noting her aunt's puzzled expression. "I dinna think expectin' an hour or two of waitin' on his part is unreasonable. Do ye?"

"Gobbling one's food is certainly unhealthy," Lady Keely agreed with a conspiratorial smile. She set the breakfast tray across her niece's lap. " 'Tis wise to eat slowly."

Rob looked over the usual morning fare of bread, ham, hard-cooked eggs, and apple cider. A sudden, unexpected wave of homesickness washed over her, and she suffered an acute craving for a Highland breakfast. Barley bannocks, oatmeal porridge, and Old Man's milk would certainly fortify her for the inevitable confrontation with the Marquess of Inverary.

"Do ye ever miss the mountains of Wales?" Rob asked, her gaze rising to meet her aunt's.

"Every day of my life," Lady Keely admitted. " 'Tis the reason we summer there each year instead of accompanying Queen Elizabeth on her annual progress."

"I'd give my eyetooth for a mug of Moireach's Old Man's milk," Rob said, her voice wistful.

"Who's Moireach?" the countess asked. "And what is Old Man's milk?"

"Moireach is the undisputed queen of Dunridge Castle's kitchen," Rob answered. "Old Man's milk consists of egg and milk beaten together, sweetened with sugar, and zested with whiskey."

"I'll tell Jennings to give Cook instructions," the countess said.

Rob shook her head, saying, "Thank ye, Aunt Keely, but 'twouldna be the same." Shrugging her mantle of homesickness off, she asked, "Is Belle aboot yet?"

"Isabelle is still abed," Lady Keely answered. "Your brother and she danced until dawn."

That bit of information lifted Rob's mood considerably. "Wouldna it be grand if Dubh married Belle? Then my verra best friend would be my sister-by-marriage. No, that wouldna do because I'm stayin' in England and would never see her again."

"Give the Marquess of Inverary a chance," the countess advised.

"I know ye possess magical talents," Rob said, reaching out to touch her aunt's hand. "Can ye tell me who my husband will be?"

"You already have a husband," Lady Keely answered, giving her an ambiguous smile.

"I mean, will I spend my life with Henry or Gordon?"

"You will live with the man destined to be your mate."

"Which one is that?" Rob cried in frustration. "Dinna ye know?"

"Being druid means knowing." Before her niece could plead with her to share that special knowledge, the countess added, "I've brought you a gift."

Lady Keely reached into her pocket and withdrew a necklace. Each of its wirelike, golden cages contained a different gemstone. One of the cages, larger than the others, held a star ruby, that rare stone with a six-pointed star inside.

" 'Tis a necklace fit for royalty," Rob gasped.

The countess smiled, pleased with her niece's response. She held the necklace up and instructed her, "A necklace is a large circle, the symbol of eternity, and a magical guardian that wards negativity off. This particular piece is my own version of lucky beggar beads which, legend says, will grant your wishes. The purple amethyst calms fears and raises hopes, the rose quartz opens the heart to attract love and happiness in relationships, the lucky green aventurine soothes troubled emotions, the brandy carnelian bolsters courage, and the white agate brings pure truth to your lips."

Slipping the necklace over Rob's head, Lady Keely added, "This star ruby, resting against your breast, offers potent protection because a guardian spirit dwells within it. If danger approaches its owner, the ruby will grow darker than pigeon's blood."

"Yer concern for me makes the necklace priceless," Rob said, touching the ruby. "I thank ye and will cherish it always."

Rob stared into space for a long moment as if mulling an idea over in her mind. Out of habit, she traced a finger across the devil's flower on the back of her left hand. Finally, she asked, "Ye did say that whatever I wished would be granted?"

Lady Keely nodded.

Rob closed her eyes, touched the ruby, and whispered, "By the power of the spirit dwellin' within this stone, I wish that Henry and I—"

"No," Lady Keely cried, touching her niece's hand, breaking the spell.

Startled, Rob opened her eyes and stared in surprise at her aunt.

"Interfering with another's destiny is forbidden," Lady Keely explained. "We cannot alter what is to be, merely accept it. Do you understand?"

Rob shook her head. She had absolutely no idea what her aunt was talking about.

"You may wish for love and happiness," the countess told her, "but the goddess will decide which man is meant for you."

"I ken what yer sayin'." Rob closed her eyes again and touched the ruby. "By the power dwellin' within this special stone, I wish for true love and happiness with whomever the goddess deems suitable for me."

"Well said." Lady Keely rose from her perch on the edge of the bed and crossed the chamber to the door, saying, " 'Tis nearly ten o'clock. I wouldn't keep the marquess waiting overly long, as patience doesn't appear to be one of his virtues."

Alone again, Rob fingered the beggar bead necklace. If danger approached, the ruby would darken redder than pigeon's blood. She intended to keep a watchful eye on it whenever Gordon Campbell crossed her path.

Unbidden, the marquess's image arose in her mind's eye, and the hint of a smile touched her lips. Campbell was an exceedingly attractive rogue, to be sure. His ruggedly handsome features and his sensuously chiseled lips conspired to make her heartbeat quicken. Those piercing gray eyes of his disturbed her, though. Their intensity seemed to see past all of her pretense to the frightened insecurity that dwelled in the depths of her soul.

And then Rob remembered Henry Talbot. Try as she did, conjuring the pleasing image of the Marquess of Ludlow proved impossible. Guilt and shame coiled around her heart. Why couldn't she picture his smiling face? She loved him, didn't she?

Rob banished those disturbing questions from her thoughts and rose from the bed. She dressed as plainly as possible in a black woolen skirt, a white linen blouse, and her oldest pair of scuffed leather boots in a poor attempt to discourage the Marquess of Inverary. The severe clothing only served to enhance the youthful beauty of her face. Around her neck hung the gold and gemstone necklace, its star ruby resting above the blouse's scooped neckline. After plaiting her ebony hair into one thick braid, she slung a black woolen cloak over her arm and grabbed her black riding gloves.

At exactly eleven o'clock, Rob left her bedchamber and strolled leisurely down the corridor. Though her strategy in handling the marquess satisfied her, she dared not keep him waiting above an hour. Nearing the bottom of the stairs, Rob spied her uncle's majordomo opening the door to admit a guest.

Dressed completely in black like Old Clootie himself, Gordon Campbell strode into the foyer. Why, he hadn't been waiting for her at all.

"Yer late," Rob called.

With a smile of greeting slashed across his face, the marquess looked at her, and Rob felt a melting sensation in the pit of her stomach. His smile could light the whole mansion.

"I believe I'm right on time," Gordon said, sauntering across the foyer.

"Ye said ten o'clock," Rob reminded him, her voice mildly accusing. "Yer an hour late."

"I meant, ten o'clock plus the hour ye intended to keep me waitin'."

The truth in his words surprised Rob. She tilted her head back to stare up at him. How could he have known what she'd intended?

"I've been ready and waitin' for an hour," Rob lied, trying to put him on the defensive. "I saw yer approach from my window."

"In that case, I do apologize for my tardiness," Gordon replied, lifting her hand to his lips. He grinned and added, "Didna yer mother ever teach ye to play coy? A lady should never admit to waitin' anxiously for her man."

With embarrassment flushing her cheeks, Rob opened her mouth to tell him exactly how *unanxious* she was to see him. Unfortunately, Gordon had more practice at verbal sparring, and so his tongue and his wit were faster.

"Close yer mouth," he teased with laughter lurking in his voice. "Unless yer invitin' my tongue inside?"

It was the wrong thing to say to an unsophisticated virgin. Gordon realized that as soon as the words slipped from his lips.

"Go to hell with Old Clootie," Rob snapped, turning away, intending to retrace her steps upstairs.

Gently but firmly, Gordon grasped her upper arm and prevented her flight. "I'm verra sorry," he apologized.

That he spoke sincerely was apparent to Rob. She stared at his chest but refused to budge one way or the other. Without another word, Gordon lifted the cloak from her arm and wrapped it around her shoulders.

"I'll do it myself," Rob said, pushing his hands away when he started to fasten it.

Gordon watched her for a moment and then reached out to cup her chin gently in one of his hands. He waited patiently until she raised her disarming, emerald gaze to his. "Give me a chance, angel," he said. *"Please?"*

That one word *please* was Rob's undoing. She relaxed, and her expression softened. A smile kissed her lips when she said, "I suppose I owe ye that much for killin' the monster beneath my bed."

"Rescuin' a beautiful damsel in distress is its own reward," Gordon replied with an answering, thoroughly devastating, smile.

Rob felt herself blush heatedly at his compliment. When he offered her his hand, she hesitated for the briefest moment and then accepted it.

"One chance, my lord, doesna mean victory is yers," she warned, though her smile lingered upon her lips.

"A verra puir choice of words, my lady," Gordon

chided as he escorted her outside to the courtyard. "Victory implies battle, and I have gentler pursuits in mind."

Rob inclined her head. "I stand corrected, my lord."

"I applaud ye for that," Gordon said. "Admittin' yer wrong is a rare ability that I've always admired."

"Which ye dinna possess yerself?"

"I'm afraid not," Gordon said. His honest admission made Rob laugh, a sweet melodious sound that reminded him of the angelic eight-year-old he'd married ten years earlier.

"I'm ridin' astride instead of sidesaddle?" Rob exclaimed, spying the horse he'd had saddled for her. "Why, I havena properly felt a mount between my legs in more than a year."

God's balls, Gordon thought as his privates swelled with need. Didn't the lass realize how arousing her words sounded? Could an eighteen-year-old actually be that naive, or had jades like Lavinia colored his outlook on women? More important, how the hell was he to face the world with his groin bulging like a boulder?

Hearing his muffled groan, Rob rounded on him and noted his choked expression. "Is aught wrong?" she asked, touching his forearm. "Ye dinna look well. Are ye ill?"

"I'm fine." His brusqueness masked his embarrassed discomfort.

Gordon grasped her waist and lifted her onto the saddle. One of his hands accidentally brushed against the side of her left leg and detected a foreign object there. It seemed the lass had a bulge of her own.

Without permission, Gordon lifted the bottom edge of her skirt and saw the infamous *sgian dubh,* the Highlander's weapon of last resort. Attached to the garter strapped on her leg was a small, black leather sheath decorated with a thistle and an acorn motif. The blade it carried appeared to be about four inches long.

" 'Tis my last resort," Rob said without anger or embarrassment.

"I'm wearin' one of my own inside the top of my boot," Gordon replied.

He looked up and caught her gaze. The intense, smoldering expression in his piercing gray eyes made her feel as if a thousand airy butterflies had suddenly taken flight inside the pit of her stomach.

"Yer lips say English lady," Gordon teased, "but yer habits scream Highlander."

"Old habits die hard," Rob told him. "Nevertheless, I will get my annulment."

"Dinna bet the family fortune on it," Gordon replied, mounting his own horse.

"What does that mean?"

He flashed her a winning smile. "I mean, I've got the next three months to change that adorable mind of yers."

Early winter wore its most placid expression. The morning appeared as if Easter, instead of the Yule, lay around the bend in the road of time. The sky was a heavenly blanket of blue, and radiant sunshine melted the coating of powdery snow that had fallen two days earlier. The springlike warmth of the day, like one of the fabled siren's of yore, lulled the world of men into a false sense of security; bleak winter seemed as far away as the New World across the seas.

Turning their horses northeast, Gordon and Rob rode at a leisurely pace down the Strand. Londontown, their destination, lay to the east.

"Does my presence in England trouble ye?" Gordon asked. "Ye look like ye didna' sleep a wink last night."

"I slept like the dead," Rob lied, flicking him a sidelong glance. Letting the marquess know that his presence made her edgy was a satisfaction she wasn't about to give him.

"That good, huh? Why do ye have dark smudges of fatigue beneath yer eyes?"

"Decoration."

"I see . . . Ye know, there's many a fine shop in London," Gordon remarked. "Perhaps I'll buy ye that doll after all."

Rob snapped her head around to fix a frigid look upon him. "Yer ten years too late."

"Better late than never," he said, his voice coaxing, his smile as sunny as the day.

"Forget it, my lord." Rob gave her attention to the road ahead as if it were the most interesting sight in the world.

"I'll make amends somehow."

" 'Tisna necessary."

" 'Tis, I say."

Without bothering to look at him, Rob inclined her head in deference to his wishes. Seeming to acquiesce was easier than arguing with a stone wall.

Suddenly, Rob remembered her ruby. After giving him a surreptitious glance to verify he wasn't watching, she peeked inside her cloak. Much to her surprise, the ruby appeared as placid as when she'd donned it. There had to be some mistake. She was riding to London with a man bent on ruining her life. She peeked at the ruby again, just to be sure.

"What are ye doin'?" Gordon asked, startling her. "Checkin' yer titties?"

Rob refused to rise to his outrageous bait. Every instinct she possessed demanded she fling back whatever he threw at her.

"Everyone in the Highlands knows the Campbells are born reivers," Rob said, arching one ebony brow at him.

"I wanted to be certain ye hadna lifted them off my chest."

Gordon cast her a wry smile and countered, "I dinna need to steal what I already own, angel."

"Ye dinna own me," she snapped.

"A man is his wife's lord and master," Gordon told her. "The sooner ye learn that fact, the happier our married life will be."

"We are na' havin' a married life together," Rob informed him. "Remember, ye swore ye'd admit only to bein' my childhood betrothed."

"And ye promised to refrain from sullenness," he shot back.

"I wasna' sullen."

"What do ye call yer attitude, then?"

The marquess was correct, Rob thought. And she couldn't expect him to honor his promise if she failed to honor hers.

Rob quirked her lips into a sheepish smile. "Childishly insultin'?" she suggested.

Gordon grinned at the unexpected change for the better in her attitude. "I stand corrected, my lady. Childishly insultin' isna anythin' like bein' sullen."

"Great Bruce's ghost, do my ears deceive me?" she teased. "I thought I heard ye admit to bein' wrong."

"Ye bring out the verra best in me, angel." Gordon winked at her. "I believe I'll keep ye around forever."

Rob ignored his loaded comment, and as they rode down the length of the Strand, she pointed to its more interesting landmarks. On the left stood Leicester House, separated from Arundel House by the Milford Stairs. On their right sat Durham House where Edward VI had once lived. Up ahead rose Westminster Abbey where Henry Tudor and his beloved Jane Seymour lay together for all of eternity.

" 'Tis Lennox House," Rob said, pointing at one of the mansions they passed.

"Jamie's late grandfather's house?"

"Humph! I'm verra surprised Darnley even managed to sire one heir."

"What ever can ye mean by that, lass?" Gordon asked.

"I'm no innocent," Rob informed the marquess, making him smile. "I've heard the tales aboot Darnley's preference for boys."

"King James is partial to his father's memory," Gordon told her. "Ye willna be repeatin' those tales if ye accompany me to court."

"Jamie's an unnatural brat," she muttered.

"That royal brat is two years older than ye," he reminded her, his voice stern.

Rob halted her mount unexpectedly. When the marquess reined in beside her, she lowered her voice and said, as if revealing a secret, "I met her last summer, ye know."

"Who?"

"The queen."

"Elizabeth?"

Rob shook her head and inched her horse closer to his, so close her leg teased the side of his thigh. She glanced around to verify that no passerby could hear and then whispered, "Mary Stuart."

Gordon raised his brows and silently gestured for her to embellish her story.

"They were keepin' her at Chartley House then," Rob explained. "I was in Shropshire with Uncle Richard and persuaded him to stop there. My uncle is a verra important man in England and enjoys vast privileges that—"

"What did ye think of her?" the marquess interrupted.

" 'Twas heartbreakin'," Rob cried. "The puir lady seemed so alone in the world. He betrayed her, ye know."

"Who betrayed her, lass?"

"That ungrateful whelp who sits upon the throne of Scotland."

"Ye dare call the King of Scotland a whelp?"

Rob nodded. "Aye, and I'd call him worse if I wasna a lady."

Gordon's first instinct, which he successfully squelched, was to reprimand her for slandering their king. Cognizant of the fact that the Earl of Basildon was forcing him to court his own bride, Gordon decided to be reasonable. Though, he doubted logic would be effective with the beauty beside him.

"What makes ye think Jamie betrayed Mary?" he asked.

"I overheard a conversation between Uncle Richard and Duke Robert," she told him. "Believin' themselves alone in my uncle's study, they mentioned Elizabeth's offer to return Mary to Scotland. King James refused the offer."

Gordon stared at her for a long moment while he digested this less-than-surprising information. He was the king's man, but felt there *was* something unnatural about a son rejecting his own mother, especially since the woman—a queen anointed by God—would remain imprisoned in a foreign country.

"Ye canna expect the man to harbor tender feelin's for a woman he's never met," Gordon said finally. He wanted no trouble from the chit when they returned to Edinburgh. Voicing such treasonous opinions would cause Clan Campbell infinite problems.

"Never met?" Rob countered. "The woman carried him within her body and gave him life."

Without another word, Rob nudged her horse forward, and they continued down the Strand toward Charing Cross where they veered to the right and rode into

London proper. Here the crowds of Londoners grew increasingly larger and forced them to pick their way carefully down the city's narrow, twisting lanes.

"Are ye hungry, lass?" Gordon asked.

"Famished," she answered. "I skipped breakfast."

" 'Cuz ye didna wish to keep me waitin'?"

"No, I am tired of the bland English fare. At the moment, I'd kill for a mug of Old Man's milk."

Gordon chuckled. Rob looked at him from beneath her fringe of sooty lashes and smiled.

Like a breath of fresh mountain air, speaking with someone who understood her habits and preferences felt good. The marquess wasn't so bad after all. Too bad living in the Highlands was no option for her. She'd rather brave an eternity of bland breakfasts than see one more person make the sign of the cross as she walked by.

"Do ye know of a decent tavern where we can eat?" Gordon asked, interrupting her thoughts.

"Aye, and Uncle Richard told me an interestin' tale that goes along with it."

Rob led Gordon through Cheapside Market and past St. Paul's Cathedral. Finally, they turned their horses up Friday Street and dismounted in front of the Royal Rooster Tavern.

The Rooster's common room was surprisingly spacious, large enough for a hearth and a bar. On the left side of the chamber, near the narrow stairway that led to the second floor, stood the hearth. The bar sat in the corner on the opposite side of the room. Tables and chairs were positioned around the chamber.

Gordon escorted Rob to a secluded table in the corner near the hearth. Ever the courtier, he assisted her into her chair and then sat down.

"What's the tale that goes along with the tavern?" Gordon asked, leaning close.

Beneath his amused gaze, Rob inched away from the danger his disturbing nearness presented. His clean masculine scent reminded her of mountain heather and made her senses reel. She flicked him a skittish, sidelong glance.

"What'll it be, folks?" a voice beside the table asked loudly.

Both Gordon and Rob looked up at the proprietor's wife, a handsome middle-aged woman. Shrewd intelligence shone from her hazel eyes. And then recognition.

"Robbie, 'tis a pleasure seein' ya again," the woman greeted her. "How's yer ma? Nothin's happened, has it?"

Rob shook her head. "My parents enjoy the best of health, Mistress Jacques."

"I told ya before to call me Randi," the woman chided her. "All my friends do, and I won't take *no* for an answer."

"Verra well, Randi." Rob smiled. "I'd like ye to meet Gordon Campbell, a friend from Scotland."

"A pleasure to meet ye," Gordon said, inclining his head toward the older woman.

She stared hard at him for a long moment. "Gawd, ya look familiar."

Rob giggled. "Gordon is Magnus Campbell's son. Do ye remember Lord Magnus?"

"Do I ever!" Randi burst out laughing. "Gawd, I ain't washed me right hand in the twenty-five years since that rascal kissed it . . . I'll fetch ya some vittles right away," she added when she heard her husband calling her.

"What was that aboot?" Gordon asked, a puzzled smile flirting with his lips.

"A verra long time ago, my mother ran away from my father," Rob told him. "Along the road to England, she met your father who escorted her to London where she found employment as a servin' wench at this verra tavern. Your father's mission was to invite the Earl of Lennox and his son, Lord Darnley, to the Scots court. Queen Mary was in search of a husband."

"I never knew aboot that," Gordon said. "How excitin' the times must've been with two bonny, rival queens rulin' over virtually the same island kingdom." He winked at her and dropped his voice to a husky whisper, adding, "See the heritage we share? I'd love to share ever so much more with ye."

Rob felt the hot blush rising upon her cheeks. His oh-so-sensual voice made her tingle all over—in secret places she'd never imagined *could* tingle.

"Gawd, he's as handsome as his father," Mistress Jacques said, materializing with their stew and ale. "Grab him if ya can, Robbie-girl; I warrant ya'll never shiver with the cold on those long, winter nights."

Embarrassed almost beyond bearing, Rob suffered the powerful urge to slip beneath the table to hide. Her stricken expression and her telltale blush told them exactly how she felt because both Gordon and Randi chuckled at her apparent discomfort.

"Have ya taken him to see the queen's menagerie?" Randi asked.

Rob shook her head, too embarrassed to look either of them directly in the eye.

" 'Tis a startlin' sight," Randi said, winking at Gordon. "Them growlin' lions always put me in the mood for a parcel of protection—if ya know what I mean."

As soon as the woman left them to continue her duties, Rob lifted her spoon and began to eat. She reached for a hunk of brown bread; but without any warning, the marquess snaked his hand out and grasped her left hand. Rob froze and wished she'd kept her gloves on. She despised anyone looking at her evil deformity.

"Yer still wearin' my weddin' ring," Gordon said, inspecting the scrolled band she now wore on her smallest finger. He planted a kiss on the stain and murmured, "Ye and No Other."

Rob felt her stomach lurch at his words. The marquess remembered the ring's inscription. That boded ill for her future with Henry Talbot.

"There's a matter of importance we must discuss," Rob said, giving him a nervous smile as she extracted her hand and hid it on her lap.

"Discuss away, angel."

Rob hesitated. She knew the heartache of rejection better than most and felt reluctant to cause the marquess any unnecessary pain. On the other hand, she could never live happily with him in the Highlands. The choice was a smidgen of heartache for him now or a ton of heartache for herself later.

"Henry Talbot—the Marquess of Ludlow—and I love each other," Rob blurted out. "We wish to marry."

"The English marquess isna the man for ye," Gordon said, his voice and his expression colder than a Highland blizzard. "Ye've already got yerself a husband."

"Why are ye bein' difficult?" Rob cried, determined in spite of his forbidding expression. "There must be dozens of women in Scotland who'd love to call ye husband."

"Naturally. However, yer my wife and I want ye," Gordon said. "Tell me, does Talbot usually run aboot courtin' other men's wives?"

Rob stared at the hands she was wringing in her lap and refused to meet his gaze. She peeked at her ruby and saw that its color remained surprisingly placid.

"And which popinjay was Talbot last night?" Gordon asked.

"Henry is away at Hampton Court," Rob answered, summoning the courage to meet his gaze. "Can ye not be reasonable aboot this?"

"If I wasna a reasonable man, angel, I'd dispatch the dirty Sassenach." His lips turned up into a ghost of a smile. "And ye too."

Rob swallowed nervously and dropped her gaze. Though her demeanor appeared pathetically meek, her thoughts veered toward mutiny.

How dare the arrogant lout ride into England and threaten her! How dare he . . .

Gordon rose from his chair so abruptly its legs scraped the wooden floor. He tossed a few coins on the table and said, "I've had enough tourin' for one day. Let's go."

In miserable silence, they retraced their path through London's crowded streets toward the Strand. The marquess's profile seemed chiseled in stone, frightening Rob too much to speak. She refused to give him the satisfaction of hearing her voice quaver like a coward's.

Rob realized she needed to make the marquess understand that her rejection was nothing personal. How could she do that without revealing that her own MacArthur kinsmen had made her an outcast in her native land? Her happiness hinged on remaining in England, but she would never share that supreme humiliation with the marquess. She wanted no man's pity.

Afternoon aged into long shadows as the sun drifted westward on its eternal journey. At Charing Cross, Gordon and Rob veered to the left and rode down the Strand, London's most elite section, where the English nobility lived in their stately mansions.

Reaching the circular lane that led to Devereux House, Rob flicked the marquess a sidelong glance filled with regret. Bitter rejection had dogged her life for eighteen years because of the fear and the mistrust Old Clootie's flower evoked in others. Now Rob understood that hurting another caused the perpetrator pain. She longed to recall her hasty outburst and to begin again, this time to speak more gently.

Two Devereux grooms rushed forward to take their horses when they reached her uncle's courtyard. Gordon dismounted and tossed his reins to one of the men. Then he turned and, without a word, lifted her out of the saddle.

"I'm sincerely sorry for hurtin' yer feelin's," Rob apologized, determined to make amends for her unpardonable behavior.

Gordon gave her a measuring look, an unrecognizable emotion flickering in his gray-eyed gaze. "Only a man who loved ye would be hurt by what ye revealed," he told her. "True love—if there be such a thin'—takes time. I scarcely know ye, lass."

"Why are ye angry?" Rob asked, strangely disgruntled that he cared not a whit for her.

"Yer my wife," Gordon answered. "No man takes what's mine."

"I belong to myself."

"Ye spoke yer vows before God and man, lass. And, ye shouldna have played the English marquess for a fool. 'Twas ill done of ye."

Rob opened her mouth to reply, but he pressed one finger across her lips in a gesture for silence. She stared up at him, mesmerized by the gleaming intensity in his eyes, oblivious to the effect her own disarming gaze was having on him at the moment.

"I'm sorry for frightenin' ye," Gordon apologized in a voice no louder than a husky whisper.

Rob straightened her back proudly, unable to cast her fierce heritage off completely. " 'Twasna fear ye saw on my face, merely a smidgen of uneasiness," she lied. "I knew 'twas yer anger talkin' and didna believe ye'd do anythin' rash."

"Is that so?" Gordon raised his brows at her and warned, "I always mean what I say, and make no mistake aboot it."

"An admirable trait that few men possess," Rob said with a conciliatory smile, purposefully deflecting what could have become another argument.

"Thank ye, *I think*."

"Would ye care to step inside and share a goblet of wine?" she invited him.

"Aye, lass." Gordon flashed her one of his devastating smiles. "I love bein' in yer company."

Carelessly spoken words uttered by a sophisticated man of the world, Rob told herself as a warm, melting sensation heated the pit of her stomach and then spread through her body, making her limbs weak. Great Bruce's ghost, his effect on her verged on sickening.

Rob dropped her gaze to the hand he offered her in truce and then peered up at him from beneath the fringe of her sooty lashes. With a shy smile, she placed her hand in his.

At that hour of the afternoon, the great hall was nearly deserted. In fact, only the earl and his countess sat in chairs drawn up in front of the hearth. Earl Richard rose when they entered the hall and offered Rob his seat. As if on cue, Jennings arrived and nodded once at his lord's unspoken command to bring refreshment.

"I assumed the girls would be aboot," Rob remarked, feeling horribly awkward. She loved her aunt's brother, yet here she sat in the company of her Scots husband and her aunt.

"Last night wearied them," Lady Keely told her. "They willingly went down for a nap. Even Blythe and Bliss."

Rob smiled. "Where's Isabelle?"

"She's gone," the countess answered.

"Lady Delphinia recalled her to court," Earl Richard explained. "The message arrived shortly after you'd ridden out."

"I didna get the chance to bid her farewell," Rob cried.

As she always did when upset, Rob traced a finger back and forth across her birthmark. She turned an angry glare on the marquess whom she blamed for taking her away from Devereux House. She should have been here with her friend.

The marquess missed her accusing glare. His interested gaze rested on the movement of her hands as she furiously ran a finger back and forth across the devil's flower.

Rob despised anyone but family seeing the mark, and she quickly moved her right hand to cover the stain. When the marquess raised his gaze to hers, Rob flushed with embarrassment and looked away.

"Dubh escorted Isabelle to Hampton Court," Earl Richard said, noting the byplay between them.

"Dubh too?" Rob echoed, her spirits sinking. Who would help her entertain the marquess? At least, her brother could have kept the man busy. If only Henry would come home from court . . .

Jennings chose that moment to return to the great hall. Instead of refreshments, the earl's majordomo carried a sealed parchment and bouquet of flowers—a single, perfect orchid in the midst of six red roses.

"A courier just delivered these from Hampton Court," Jennings announced, handing both to her.

"How lovely." Rob opened the missive and read it. Without looking up at the others, she said in a voice filled with disappointment, "Elizabeth has chosen Henry to be this year's Lord of Misrule. Plannin' the Yule's activities prevents him from returnin' home for a visit."

Uneasy about what she would see, Rob peeked at

Gordon. His expression of satisfaction reminded her of a sleek predator with its quarry trapped. She quickly dropped her gaze.

"Roses signify love," Earl Richard said to his wife in an unnecessarily loud voice. "What do orchids represent?"

"In the language of flowers," Gordon answered before the countess could speak, "a man who gifts a woman with a single orchid means to seduce her."

Staring at her hands in her lap, Rob refused to look at the marquess though she did feel his gaze upon her. She already knew what emotion would be written across his face. Henry's sensuous message would certainly irritate him, and knowing that made her uneasy.

"Since Dubh has deserted you, stay with us at Devereux House," Earl Richard invited the marquess.

Rob snapped her head up and stared in surprised dismay at her uncle. How could her own flesh and blood betray her? That the marquess slept next door disturbed her enough, but how could she survive with him in the same house? Just thinking about it was enough to give her the hives.

"Yes, do." This encouragement came from Lady Keely.

Gordon smiled. " 'Tis kind of ye . . . I'll go next door and fetch my belongin's." Without even a glance in her direction, the marquess left the hall.

"How could ye do this to me?" Rob exclaimed. "I willna be able to get away from him."

Earl Richard snapped his brows together at his niece's impertinence and then, in a deceptively calm voice, reminded her, "You did promise to become acquainted with him."

"A world of difference lies between becomin' acquainted and livin' beneath the same roof," Rob protested. "I willna enjoy any privacy."

"The Marquess of Inverary is a stranger in England," the earl said. " 'Twould be shameful to expect him to stay alone at the Dowager House. Where are your manners and your Highlander's code of hospitality?"

"Gordon isna an ordinary traveler," Rob argued. "He is—"

"—your husband," the countess interrupted.

"I dinna want him," Rob cried, frustrated with their logic. "Whether ye approve or no, I intend to remain in England and marry the man I love."

"Do you want to remain in England because you love Henry?" Lady Keely asked in a quiet voice. "Or do you love Henry because you want to remain in England?"

That loaded question shocked the anger out of Rob. Before she could profess her love for Henry, Jennings returned to the hall.

"The Marquess of Inverary asked me to give you this," the majordomo announced, handing her a bunch of sweet alyssum. The man turned to his mistress and whispered, "I think he stole them from your garden."

Lady Keely bit her bottom lip to keep from laughing. With a flick of her hand and a nod, she dismissed the majordomo.

"Look at the common flowers he sends me," Rob complained, as if that were reason enough to banish him to the Dowager House.

Lady Keely smiled knowingly and then informed her, "In the language of flowers, sweet alyssum signify 'worth beyond beauty.' "

The marquess's sentiment surprised Rob. He didn't seem like a man concerned with a woman's worth. She gazed at the flowers in her hands and steeled herself against him. His sweet thoughtfulness was a ploy to get her to ride north where she would live unhappily ever after. Not only did she need to discourage Gordon

Campbell but also to guard her heart against the arrogant Highlander. Danger to her peace of mind lurked in his gray-eyed gaze and his devastating smile.

Rob sighed. Too bad Gordon Campbell hadn't been born English . . . Too bad she'd been cursed with Old Clootie's flower . . . Too bad her aunt's probing question was beginning to give her a headache.

Did she want to remain in England because she loved Henry? Or did she love Henry because she wanted to remain in England?

Chapter 4

Drinking Old Man's milk . . . Riding her horse astride . . . Wearing a last resort strapped to her leg.

His MacArthur bride was a Highlander all right. Gordon knew that as surely as he knew he was standing in the English Earl of Basildon's study and looking out the window at the River Thames.

Gordon lifted his gaze from the mist-shrouded river to the blazing sun dying in the western sky and wondered what motivated his bride's behavior. Did the not-so-timid angel he'd married want to be an English lady because she truly loved the English marquess? Or was it something else that incited her to speak so disparagingly of her homeland? Sooner or later, he'd learn the answer to that. Time favored him. His bride had nowhere to run. Except into his arms.

Abruptly, Gordon turned away from the window. The bottom edge of his plaid whirled slightly with the sudden movement. He sat in the chair in front of the hearth and stretched his long legs out.

What would his reluctant bride do when she saw him dressed in the northern mode? That thought brought a hint of a smile to his lips. He could hardly wait for their next encounter, which would happen very soon now since he'd instructed the earl's majordomo to direct Rob to the study where he'd be waiting. And just what was taking her so long to answer his summons? Was she perhaps preening in front of a pier glass to verify she appeared attractive enough to interest him?

Thoroughly relaxed by the warmth of the fire, Gordon yawned and stretched. He might as well steal a ten-minute catnap. Gordon closed his eyes and drifted off into a light slumber, but he'd only dozed five minutes when the sound of voices penetrated his mind.

"That's him," a voice said.

"Holy stones, he's wearing a skirt."

" 'Tis his kilt," came the explanation.

Gordon awakened, but kept his eyes closed in feigned sleep. The voices belonged to young girls, and he thought to learn new information regarding his bride. After all, children were notoriously honest. At times, brutally so.

"His knees are naked."

"Yes, I see."

Unable to resist the urge, Gordon opened his eyes a crack. From beneath his dark lashes, he spied two girls standing in front of him.

"He's got dimples on them," the younger of the two remarked, leaning closer to inspect his knees. "Do you think Uncle Iain also wears a skirt?"

"I suppose so," the older girl replied. " 'Tis their manner of dress in the Highlands."

"Does Daddy have knees too?" a third child asked from where she stood beside his chair.

Like a multitude of cherubs, the angelic sound of giggling girls echoed within the study. Unable to feign sleep another moment, Gordon opened his eyes and sat up straight. He glanced around and saw that *five* ebony-haired, violet-eyed angels surrounded him.

"I'm Blythe," said the oldest who appeared to be about ten years.

"And I'm Bliss," the eight-year-old added.

"Summer and Autumn stand on your right," Blythe said. "On your left is Aurora."

"Summer and Autumn are twins," Bliss told him.

"The man can see they're twins," Blythe informed her sister.

Six-year-old Aurora leaned close, and wearing a childishly flirtatious smile, asked, "What do you call a Highlander who eats ants?"

"Uncle!" shouted Summer and Autumn.

Gordon burst out laughing. "And I suppose yer the earl's daughters?"

All five of them bobbed their heads in unison.

"Do you love Cousin Rob?" Blythe asked baldly.

Before he could reply, Bliss said, "Uncle Henry loves her too."

"Uncle Henry tried to kiss Rob," Aurora told him, "but she wouldn't let him."

"Hush, sister." This came from Blythe.

"If Henry marries Rob, she'll be our aunt," Bliss said.

Aurora giggled. "How can a cousin be an aunt?"

Enchanted, Gordon looked from one little girl to the next. With their barrage of questions and comments, he couldn't edge a single word into their conversation. How did the earl survive the chatter of five such adorable angels?

"If Rob marries Henry, I'll marry you," Aurora promised, making her two older sisters laugh.

"Thank ye, poppet," Gordon said with a smile. "Tell me, why would ye marry a man ye dinna know?"

"Because, silly, your eyes are the color of mist," the six-year-old answered.

"Mist?" he echoed, puzzled.

"We love mist," the three oldest girls chorused.

Gordon grinned. "I always believed wee lasses loved blue skies, gentle breezes, warm sunshine, and sweet flowers."

"Heavy mist lets us see beyond the horizon," Blythe told him.

" 'Tis a game?" Gordon asked.

The ten-year-old cast him an ambiguous smile and answered, "In a manner of speaking."

"Tell me, poppets," Gordon said. "Whilst I'm courtin' yer cousin, will ye be givin' us any private time to be alone?"

"How much is it worth to you?" Bliss asked.

"I dinna ken why yer parents named ye Bliss," Gordon said dryly, taken aback by the eight-year-old's precociousness.

" 'Tis short for Blister," Blythe told him.

Bliss cast her older sister an unamused look and then rounded on him. With her hands on her hips in a challenging stance, she asked again, "Well, my lord. How much are you willing to pay for private time?"

Gordon cocked a dark eyebrow at her. "Name yer price, lass."

"Two gold pieces a day for each of us."

"One gold piece."

"My lord, you have yourself a deal," Bliss said with the sweetest of smiles. "And 'tis payable at the end of each day. No gold coins, no privacy the next day. We never extend credit, so don't bother to ask."

Gordon stared at the eight-year-old for a long moment

and then nodded. He gave a silent prayer of thanks that Bliss wasn't his intended and felt almost sorry for whomever fate doomed to wed her.

"What will ye do with the gold ye earn?" he asked, glancing around at the five of them.

"Invest it with Daddy," the girls chorused.

Gordon threw back his head and shouted with laughter. The women of his acquaintance would squander their coins on trinkets and gewgaws, but the English queen's Midas had managed to sire females interested in business ventures. How delightful.

"What time is supper served?" Gordon asked.

"Six o'clock," Blythe answered.

"I'll give each of ye an extra shillin' if ye go tell Rob I've been waitin' for her in the study."

" 'Tis passing strange," Bliss remarked. "Rob sent us here to tell you that she won't be down for supper. She'll see you in the morning."

"The hell she will." Gordon rose from his chair and marched across the study. Pausing at the door as if just remembering something, he turned around and asked, "Which chamber is Rob's?"

Bliss smiled as winsomely as she could. "That information will cost you extra, my lord."

"How much?"

"An extra gold piece." When he nodded at her, Bliss added, "For each of us."

" 'Tis a pleasure doin' business with ye, my lady," Gordon said dryly, agreeing to her terms.

"The pleasure is ours, my lord," Bliss replied. "Rob's chamber is upstairs, second door on the left."

Gordon hesitated for only an instant when he reached the second door on the left upstairs. A boyishly wicked smile flirted with his lips, and without bothering to knock, he opened the door and stepped inside his bride's bedchamber. In spite of the room's dim light, he spied her immediately, and his smile grew into a delighted grin.

Rob was leaning against the windowsill directly opposite the door and staring outside at the early winter's twilight. Her silken bed robe accentuated every alluring curve she possessed, especially her gently rounded derriere.

God's balls, but his bride had herself a nice arse, Gordon thought as he stood two feet inside the chamber. His appreciative gaze perused the enchanting sight of her silk-clad buttocks thrust high into the air.

"Well, Blythe?" Rob asked without turning around. "What did the marquess say when you told him I'd see him in the mornin'?"

"He said, 'the hell she will.' "

Rob whirled around at the sound of his voice, shocked that he dared to enter her bedroom uninvited. She clutched the silken bed robe tightly against her bosom, which only served to enhance the pleasing roundness of her breasts.

"What d'ye do here?" Rob demanded in an angry whisper.

"Avoidin' me willna be easy, angel," Gordon told her. "I've come to escort ye to supper."

"Leave this chamber before someone sees ye."

"What do I care aboot that?"

"*I* care," Rob said. " 'Tis improper for a gentleman to visit a lady's bedchamber."

Gordon gifted her with a lopsided grin, folded his arms across his chest, and silently refused to budge. "Is it also improper for a husband to visit his wife's chamber?"

"Ye swore to Uncle Richard—"

"And ye also promised several thin's yerself," he reminded her. "Ye are na makin' this easy, lass."

"I never promised to make thin's easy," Rob shot

back. She dropped her gaze and groaned in dismay as his choice of clothing registered in her mind.

The Marquess of Inverary had donned traditional Highland garb, the black and the green Campbell plaid. The great kilt's folds fastened around his waist with a black leather belt; the long length of material hanging from the belt had been gathered and secured at his shoulder with an enormous gold broach encrusted with emeralds. Beneath the kilt he wore a white silk shirt.

"Yer wearin' a—"

"Skirt?" Gordon supplied, sauntering toward her with arrogant grace. " 'Tis what yer wee cousins said."

Instinctively, Rob clutched her bed robe tighter and wished she hadn't undressed down to her chemise. Her flimsy silk robe seemed no protection at all against his masculine presence and made her feel vulnerable.

"Yer wearin' that to embarrass me," she said in an accusing voice. "Or was yer purpose a not-so-subtle reminder of our shared heritage?"

"Dinna get yer back up, kitten. Yer married to me, not my clothes."

"Dinna condescend to me," Rob warned him, standing her ground in spite of his disturbing nearness. "Or this kitten's fur will surely be flyin'."

"I'm tryin' real hard to be agreeable, lass," Gordon said, holding his hands up in a conciliatory gesture. "Yer company for the evenin' is what I desire. I've come to escort ye to supper and willna be leavin' this chamber without ye."

"Verra well," she acquiesced. "Wait outside while I dress."

"I dinna relish seein' ye in rags again," Gordon said, already crossing the chamber to her dressing room. "I'll choose yer gown."

Though his outrageous arrogance irritated her, Rob

remained silent and seized the opportunity to inspect her star ruby. The stone appeared as placid as ever. Didn't the marquess present a danger to her? The damned ruby wasn't doing what it should. Could Aunt Keely have been mistaken?

"Are ye checkin' yer titties again?"

Rob snapped her head up. Her cheeks flamed with embarrassment, but her emerald eyes glinted with barely suppressed anger.

"Wear this," the marquess ordered, offering her a green silk gown.

"So I'll match the green in yer plaid?"

"No, angel. The emerald accentuates yer beautiful eyes."

His words flustered her, and the fight left her as quickly as it had come. "I'll be down in a few minutes," Rob said, lowering her gaze.

"I'll wait."

Rob lifted her gaze to his. "Then step outside while I change."

Gordon raised his brows at her and teased, "What's a little bared flesh between husband and wife? Besides, if I stepped into the corridor, ye'd lock me out and hide in here for the evenin'."

"Ye dinna trust me?" Rob asked.

"Yer behavior hardly inspires that feelin' in me," Gordon answered. "I promise I willna peek at ye."

"*Yer* behavior doesna inspire that much trust in me," she countered.

"*Touché*, angel." Still, he made no move to leave.

Rob whirled away, and mumbling to herself about his Highland pigheadedness, marched across the chamber to her privacy screen. She'd spoken truthfully to the marquess; she didn't trust him not to peek. Rob slipped the bed robe off and let it drop to the floor where she stood, then slipped into the emerald gown and pulled it up. She fastened the two top buttons first and then the two just above her waist. At that point the battle with her gown began in earnest. Though the top and the bottom buttons were deceptively easy to fasten, the ones running down the middle of her back were unreachable.

Rob contorted this way and that but only managed to become flushed and damp from her exertions. Oh, why was a grown woman incapable of dressing herself?

"Great Bruce's ghost," she grumbled, frustrated with her uncooperative gown.

"Did ye say somethin'?" the marquess called.

With a high blush coloring her cheeks, Rob stepped from behind the screen. "I said, would ye—?"

A wolfish gleam of understanding lit his eyes. Gordon sauntered across the chamber toward her and said, "Turn around then."

Rob suffered the worst embarrassment of their renewed acquaintance. Asking for his assistance with such an intimate task humiliated her. Without a word, she showed him her back.

Exhibiting the practiced skill of a man who has fastened hundreds of women's gowns, Gordon completed his task within seconds. He leaned close and pressed his lips against her ear, whispering, " 'Tis done, angel."

A delicious shiver slid down the length of her spine. Steeling herself against his disturbing nearness, Rob turned around and said to his chest, "Thank ye for yer assistance, my lord."

"I assure ye 'twas my pleasure."

Only when he offered her his arm did Rob lift her gaze to his. They stared at each other in silence for a long moment. Gordon raised his brows, and reluctantly Rob accepted his arm. Together, they left the bedchamber and walked down the corridor to the stairs.

Supper was a huge success.

Almost.

Rob breathed a sigh of relief when she managed to sit on Gordon's left side at the high table, which meant Old Clootie's mark upon her left hand would be easier to hide from his piercing gaze. Beyond Gordon sat Uncle Richard, Aunt Keely, Summer, Autumn, and Blythe. Aurora and Bliss were seated on Rob's left.

Earl Richard and Gordon spoke almost nonstop about business, politics, and their respective monarchs throughout the meal. Being neglected didn't bother Rob. The marquess's inattention gave her the opportunity to study him without being observed.

When he reached for his goblet of wine, Rob noticed his hands. With their long fingers, his hands looked strong enough to handle a claymore with deadly ease and expertise. Yet his touch on the delicate goblet stem appeared gentle, as feathery light as his hand upon her had been when he'd fastened the buttons on her gown.

Rob slid her gaze upward slowly. His posture was arrogantly erect yet relaxed, his profile pleasingly chiseled, his chestnut brown hair a mite too long on his neck.

Great Bruce's ghost! The man even possessed attractive ears.

Rob quickly glanced away when she sensed him beginning to turn in her direction. Had he felt her interested gaze upon him? His hand reached for hers in her lap, and he leaned close to whisper in her ear.

"Would ye care to walk aboot the garden before ye retire for the night?" Gordon asked.

"Aye," Rob answered, raising her gaze to his. She loved the night's dark beauty because it shrouded all manner of flaws. She felt safe enough; her five young cousins would surely accompany them.

Rob looked down the length of the high table toward Blythe and asked, "Would ye care to join us?"

Blythe, Summer, and Autumn smiled at her but shook their heads. That surprised Rob. Usually, she was unable to enjoy a moment's privacy without one of them clinging to her side.

Rob mentally shrugged their refusal off and turned to the left, intending to invite Bliss to walk in the garden with them. She caught the eight-year-old giving the marquess an exaggerated wink. Puzzled, Rob glanced over at the marquess who seemed oblivious to the eight-year-old's behavior.

Turning back to her cousin, Rob began, "Would ye care—?"

Bliss yawned loudly and stretched. "I'm *sooo* tired," she said.

Rob dropped her gaze to Aurora, but then heard Bliss say, "Poor Aurora, her exhaustion may force us to carry her all the way to bed."

Gordon chuckled huskily and said, "I never realized how entertainin' wee lasses could be. I hope we produce enough to fill Inverary Castle with them." He stood then and touched her shoulder, adding, "For now, let's walk aboot the garden."

With a resigned sigh, Rob nodded and rose from her chair. She couldn't very well change her mind once she'd agreed to accompany him. As she crossed the great hall with the marquess, Rob spared a glance over her shoulder. Her five cousins sat at the high table and smiled at her as if they were privy to a secret joke at her expense. When she paused in the hall's entrance and cast them a long measuring look, all five of them yawned loudly and stretched with exaggerated weariness.

Rob wasn't fooled for a moment and intended to visit their bedchamber as soon as she returned from her walk.

She needed their help in keeping the marquess at bay. If need be, she'd pay her cousins to follow the marquess and her about.

Stepping into the garden, Rob sighed deeply as she gazed at the night's dark beauty. Accompanied by hundreds of glittering stars, a crescent moon hung overhead in the perfect setting of a black velvet sky. Evening mist covered the Thames River like a lover and swirled up its earthen banks onto the shore. Wood smoke from the Strand's great houses scented the crisp air and mingled with the fragrances in the earl's winter-landscaped garden.

Gordon and Rob strolled across the lawns toward the river. Because the night shrouded her shame, Rob didn't bother to hide her birthmarked hand in her pocket.

"What has brought that smile to yer lips?" Gordon asked.

Rob glanced sidelong at him. "The English call this weather winter," she answered.

"Aye, 'tis yet warm for us sturdy Highlanders," Gordon replied. "Look up, lass. Do ye see how lovely the moon and the stars appear in the sky? They are na as pretty as ye are."

"How strange that an admitted womanizer would compare me with the *fickle* moon," Rob said, gazing up at the sky.

"'Tis a marvelous time of the year," Gordon remarked, ignoring her jibe. "The season signifies youth in old age and old age in youth."

"Life in death and death in life," Rob added in a soft voice.

"Aye, lass, the endin' and the beginnin' of the year's cycle," Gordon said. "Soon the 'secret of the unhewn stone' will be upon us."

"What's that?"

"The Great Blank Day in the ancient calendar. The twenty-third day of December when anythin' can happen and usually does. Ye can always expect the unexpected on that special day."

"Are ye a pagan too?" she asked.

"I'm a reader," he answered. "And what d'ye mean by *too*?"

"I meant, in addition to bein' a Highland barbarian," Rob lied. She knew her aunt believed in the Old Ways but had no idea if others did. Was the marquess hiding a dangerous secret?

Gordon gifted her with his devastatingly boyish grin. "Ye've a quick wit, lass."

"And ye like that in a woman?"

"No, 'tis an irritatin' trait for a female to possess," he teased, "but all of us have a cross to bear in this life. I'll accustom myself to yer insultin' tongue."

"Verra funny, my lord," Rob said, lifting her upturned nose into the air. She wished she could think of something insulting to hurl at him; but her quick wit failed her, and her mind remained embarrassingly blank.

As they walked closer to the Thames, the delicately fine veil of mist grew into a thick shroud. The ground fog swirled around their ankles and crept up their legs.

"I canna see my feet," Rob said. "If we go much farther, we'll disappear in this."

Without warning, Gordon reached out and pulled her close against the side of his body. "I canna think of anyone with whom I'd rather disappear," he said in a husky voice.

"Thank ye, my lord," Rob teased him, "but I'd wager the family fortune that ye say those verra same words to all the ladies."

Gordon ignored that loaded comment. Instead he asked, "So what've ye been doin' with yerself?"

"For ten years?" she quipped. "Well, I grew up and moved to England."

"Ye *visited* England," he corrected her. "Tell me aboot the doll, angel."

"Why would ye care to hear that story?"

"I'd like to know what crime I'm accused of."

"Ye are na accused, my lord. Yer guilty," Rob told him, the teasing playfulness gone from her voice. "That day ye visited Dunridge Castle—"

"Ye mean the day we married?" Gordon interrupted.

Rob didn't like the way he described that day, but she refused to argue about his choice of words. "Ye promised to send me a new dolly once ye'd returned to Inverary Castle, but ye never did."

"I was fifteen at the time and couldna see beyond my immediate desires." Gordon paused before continuing and gently forced her to face him. "Will ye forgive me, lass?"

"I forgave ye long ago." Rob pulled out of his grasp and again started walking toward the river.

"Then why are ye angry with me?" Gordon asked, falling in beside her.

"I never said I was angry," she answered, looking straight ahead. "The fact is that I love Henry Talbot and wish to remain in England."

Her professed love for another man irritated Gordon. "We'll become acquainted without speakin' aboot others," he said in a stern voice.

"Yer welcome to speak of any woman ye like," Rob replied, casting him a sidelong glance. " 'Twill never bother me."

"Are ye *tryin'* to aggravate me?" Gordon asked, his disbelief apparent in his voice.

Rob cast him a winsome smile and feigned innocence

when she said, "I dinna care enough aboot ye to—
Dinna get too close to the water."

Gordon kept walking but halted at the embankment.
He couldn't see the Thames because of the fog, but he
sensed its nearness and heard the water lapping against
the land.

"Did ye hear me?" Rob cried in a panic. "Back away
from that water!"

Gordon turned around and closed the distance between them. Even in the darkness, he saw that apprehension had etched itself across her features.

"What's the problem, angel?"

"I—I dinna like the water."

"Ye canna be afraid of it. Did ye never learn to swim?"
Gordon asked. "I'd find that a difficult notion to believe,
since Loch Awe touches the backside of Dunridge Castle."

Rob refused to meet his gaze. His mention of Loch
Awe brought a flood of unwanted memories rushing
back to her. In her mind's eye Rob saw the ghastly white
face of the crofter's daughter. She saw her own father
frantically pounding the swallowed water from the girl's
body. And then she heard those familiar taunts again.
Loch Awe monster . . . Changelin'-witch.

"What's wrong, angel?" Gordon asked, his strong
hands on her upper arms yanking her back to the present.

"I—I was thinkin' of a friend who almost drowned
once," Rob answered. "Since that day, an uneasiness
comes upon me whenever I get too close to the water.
'Twas the fog shroudin' the river's edge that made me
nervous."

"Then we shall sit on that bench beneath those trees
and let the mist tickle our ankles," Gordon suggested.

Rob forced herself to smile and nodded agreement.
"So, my lord, tell me aboot yerself," she said as they

crossed the lawns to the stone bench. "What've ye been doin' for the past ten years?"

"On the advice of my father, I've been makin' my way at court for the good of the clan," Gordon answered, casually placing his arm around her shoulder when they sat down.

Nervous with his masculine nearness, Rob sat rigidly. She dropped her gaze to the hand resting so nonchalantly on her shoulder and then glanced sidelong at him. The marquess seemed perfectly relaxed as if he was unaware that his hand was touching her. His apparent innocence put her at ease, and she sighed.

"I've become great friends with the king who especially enjoys huntin' and golfin' with me," Gordon was saying. "The court holds other pleasures as well, such as dancin' and gamin'. Do ye golf, angel?"

"I never tried my hand at that," Rob answered, turning her head to look at him.

"I'll teach ye then," Gordon said, and the hand resting on her shoulder began a slow caress.

"Dinna go to any trouble for me," Rob replied, so neatly caught by the intensity in his gray gaze that she never noticed his hand caressing her shoulder.

"Why, angel, 'tis no trouble at all," Gordon assured her in a husky whisper as his lips slowly descended to hers.

Mesmerized by the seductively intense expression on his face, Rob was unable to resist as his mouth came closer and closer to claim hers. She'd never kissed a man before. What was expected of her? Surely, a man of the world like the marquess would laugh at her inexperience.

That humiliating thought spurred Rob into action. At the very last moment before their lips touched, she turned her head away.

"'Twas ill done of ye, angel," Gordon chided her

softly, his face so close the warmth of his breath tickled her flushed cheek.

"I've only really known ye since yesterday," Rob said in an aching whisper, turning a pleading expression on him. "Please give me time."

"I willna force ye, lass." Gordon cupped her chin in one hand and gazed into her eyes. "Whenever yer ready, so will I be."

"Thank ye," Rob said with a relieved smile. "Ye are na such a barbarian after all."

"Thank ye, *I think*." He stood then and offered her his arm. "Shall we return to the house, angel? Ye need yer beauty sleep, and I've business to discuss with yer uncle."

"What business?" Rob asked with a mildly curious smile.

"Ye wouldna understand," Gordon answered as they walked into the foyer.

Rob lost her smile. She looked him straight in the eye and said, "Try me."

"I plan to do just that some other night," Gordon said, teasing her, one long finger playfully touching the tip of her upturned nose. At that, he turned on his heel and crossed the foyer toward her uncle's study.

Irritated at being so rudely dismissed, Rob glared at his retreating back for a long moment and then whirled away. She'd set the arrogant marquess straight in the morning. Right now she intended to enlist her cousins' aid in keeping him at bay.

As Rob reached the chamber that Blythe and Bliss shared, the door swung open unexpectedly, and Mrs. Ashemole brushed past her. The obviously disgruntled nanny was mumbling beneath her breath about paganish manners and discarded nightcaps.

Rob stared after the woman and wondered what her problem was, then walked into the bedchamber. Closing the door behind her, she heard Bliss saying, "Ashemole is an arsehole."

"Tsk. Tsk. Such unkind vulgarity from an earl's daughter," Rob scolded. She sat on the edge of the bed and noted the two nightcaps lying on the floor, apparently the reason for the nanny's aggravation.

"I need yer help," Rob told her cousins. "I want ye to pester the marquess and me every possible moment."

"I'm sorry," Blythe apologized, flicking a glance at her younger sister. "We cannot do that."

"I'll pay ye."

"How much?" Bliss asked.

"A shillin' every day for both of ye."

Blythe and Bliss looked at each other and burst out laughing. Then Bliss gave her the surprising news, "The marquess is paying us more to stay away."

"That sneaky Highland bastard," Rob swore.

"Tsk. Tsk. Such unkind vulgarity from an earl's daughter," Bliss said with the sweetest of smiles.

"Aye, sister," Blythe agreed. " 'Tis shameful the way she speaks in front of innocent children."

Rob narrowed her gaze on them. "How much is he payin' ye?" she asked.

"A gold piece each for the five of us," Blythe answered.

Great Bruce's ghost, Rob thought. There was no way she could match that price, never mind beat it. Her budget didn't allow for bribery.

"Might I appeal to yer sense of family loyalty?" Rob asked, pasting a persuasive smile onto her face.

"Appeal all you want," Bliss told her, "but we shan't change our minds. Business is business, you know."

"We're sorry, Cousin Rob," Blythe tried to soften their refusal. "You aren't angry with us?"

Rob looked from one expectant expression to the

other and then shook her head. "I could never be upset with my favorite cousins. I'll see ye in the mornin'."

After leaving the girls' bedchamber, Rob retired to her own in order to ponder her dilemma. She couldn't very well blame her cousins for taking advantage of this opportunity. After all, they were their father's daughters. No, indeed, Rob reserved all of her anger for that reiver from Argyll, Gordon Campbell. How dare a sophisticated man of the world use innocent children for his own advantage. How deplorably immoral. First thing in the morning, she intended to set him straight about his lack of integrity. If she didn't lose her nerve.

She lost her nerve.

In an effort to avoid the marquess, Rob had lingered within the safety of her chamber all morning long. Now the sun shone high in a heavenly blue sky. Appearing more like a harbinger of spring than winter, the day called out, enticing her to venture outside.

I willna allow him to keep me prisoner in my own uncle's house, Rob decided as she watched her five cousins romping in the garden below her bedchamber window.

Rob grabbed her cloak, hurried to the door, and then hesitated. The marquess would certainly be lurking about somewhere and waiting for her to make an appearance. Perhaps avoiding him would be easier if she located his whereabouts first.

What would she do if he tried to kiss her again? She'd never actually kissed a man except for her father and brothers, and that certainly didn't count. Oh, why had Dubh deserted her and gone to court? If only Henry would return.

Opening the door a crack, Rob peered outside. No one was about. She stepped into the corridor and walked slowly, almost stealthily toward the stairs. Reaching the deserted foyer below, she scurried on tiptoes to the great hall's entrance and peeked inside.

"He's gone," said a voice behind her.

"Great Bruce's ghost," Rob cried, startled, whirling around.

Her aunt smiled. "Lord Campbell left this morning—"

"He returned to Scotland?" Rob interrupted. For some unknown reason, that possibility failed to give her any emotional relief. Strangely enough, she felt letdown.

"No, dearest. Lord Campbell rode into London to attend to a few errands."

"What errands?"

"I don't know," Lady Keely answered with a shrug, "but he did say he would return after dinner."

"Well, why didna ye tell me?" Rob asked. "I've wasted a whole mornin' of freedom hidin' inside my chamber."

"I had no idea you were avoiding the marquess," her aunt replied. "I thought you were sleeping late."

Rob reached out and touched her aunt's arm. "What should I do if he tries to kiss me?" she asked, embarrassed but determined to prepare herself.

The corners of the countess's lips twitched as if she suffered the urge to laugh. "Say 'yuch-yuch-yuch'?"

"I'm verra serious aboot this, Aunt Keely."

"Do you *wish* to kiss Lord Campbell?" Lady Keely asked.

"Of course not," Rob answered. "But even if I did, I dinna know how."

"Press your lips against his," the countess told her. "The rest comes naturally."

"But what aboot my hands?"

"People use their lips to kiss, dearest, not their hands."

"I know that much," Rob replied, becoming frustrated. "I meant, where do I put them?"

Lady Keely cast her an ambiguous smile. "Trust me, dearest. All of your body parts will know what to do when the marquess kisses you."

Still, Rob remained unconvinced. "One more thin', Aunt Keely, and then I'll let ye go," she said, fingering the beggar bead necklace. "Are ye certain sure this ruby will warn me of approachin' danger? It hasna darkened to the color of pigeon's blood."

"Then you haven't been in any danger," the countess replied.

"But I've repeatedly checked it whenever the marquess is aboot," Rob told her. "The stone remains placid."

"Have you considered the possibility that the marquess presents no danger to you?" Lady Keely suggested.

"He wants to ruin my life."

"No, dearest. He wants to change it."

"Livin' with him in the Highlands will ruin my life," Rob insisted.

"We can live happily anywhere as long as we are happy with ourselves," Lady Keely told her. "Now, run along. The girls have been waiting for you."

"Thank ye, Aunt Keely." Taking the long route in order to digest her aunt's advice, Rob went out the door into the front courtyard and then strolled around the mansion in the direction of the garden where her cousins were playing. She inhaled deeply of the clean, mild air. Unseasonably warm and sunny, the day only hinted at impending winter because of the stark, leaf-barren trees.

How different this day would be in the mountains of Argyll, Rob thought. Even this early in the season, heavy snows blanket the land. Most December days dawned depressingly overcast and cold. Like an unwelcome guest, winter always arrived early and stayed late in those northern climes.

Rob heard the unmistakable sound of arguing angels as

she rounded the corner of the mansion and stepped into the garden. Only a budding brat named Bliss could cause dissension amongst angels.

"You're cheating," Blythe accused her sister.

"I am not," Bliss defended herself.

"You've chosen Aurora," Blythe said, "leaving me Summer and Autumn."

"Both Summer and Autumn are three years old, which totals six, and that is exactly Aurora's age," Bliss argued. "You are the one with the advantage. All other things being equal, you're two years older than I am."

"What are ye playin'?" Rob called, crossing the lawns toward them.

"Bliss is cheating at dodge the ball," Blythe told her.

"I am not cheating," Bliss insisted.

"Two three-year-olds hardly equal one six-year-old," Rob said, arching an ebony brow at her cousin. "Perhaps *I* should join Blythe's team."

"That would be grossly unfair," Bliss complained.

" 'Tis precisely the point, my connivin' cousin," Rob said with a smile. "Now ye know how—"

"Never mind," Bliss interrupted, her gaze fixed on something behind Rob. "You're very welcome to join Blythe's team. I'll even the sides by taking the marquess."

Rob whirled around and saw him strolling across the lawns toward them. Quickly, she hid her left hand within the folds of her cloak and then watched his approach.

Gordon Campbell looked like a magnificent god sprung to life. While Englishmen huddled within their cloaks, the Marquess of Inverary kept chill at bay with only a black leather jerkin over his shirt and breeches. Dressed completely in black, Gordon Campbell was as darkly handsome as Old Clootie was rumored to be, and more attractive than original sin.

With arrogant grace, Gordon sauntered toward them.

He carried an enormous satchel of golf clubs slung over his right shoulder.

Rob heard a noise behind her and glanced over her shoulder. With great exaggeration, the five Devereux girls yawned and stretched as if the hour were midnight.

"Stay where ye are," Rob ordered them, hiding a smile at their performance. Then she rounded on the marquess and said, "My lord, we've somethin' important to discuss."

"What's that?" Gordon asked, leaning his bag against the oak tree beside her.

"Yer lack of integrity."

Gordon stared at her in apparent confusion. "Whatever d'ye mean?" he asked.

"Bribery, my lord." Rob gestured at her cousins. "Yer usin' these innocent bairns for yer own advantage."

At that, Gordon fixed his gaze on the eight-year-old.

"Cousin Rob made us an offer we had to refuse," Bliss blurted out. "She tried to bribe us too, but the price was too low."

Rob felt the heated blush rising on her cheeks when Gordon raised his eyebrows at her and said, "As I told ye yesterday, yer habits scream 'Highlander.'"

He looked at the girls again and said, "I've brought ye gifts from Londontown and left them for ye in the great hall."

With squeals of excitement, the five Devereux girls dashed across the lawns toward the mansion. As they vanished from sight, Gordon cast Rob his devastatingly boyish smile.

" 'Twas well done of ye, my lord," Rob remarked, ignoring the melting sensation in the pit of her stomach. "Is there a second act?"

Gordon took a step toward her.

"I wasna bein' sullen," she said hastily, stepping back a pace.

"Aye, but sarcasm doesna become ye either," he said, reaching for his bag of golf clubs.

Gordon produced a black leather glove with no fingers and pulled it onto his left hand. Next came several leather-covered balls, a wooden tee, and an ash driving club.

Turning his back on her, Gordon walked several paces away, stuck the tee into the lawn, and set the ball on top of it. He winked at her over his shoulder and then gave his full attention to the ball.

As soon as he showed her his back, Rob dropped her gaze to his magnificently masculine physique. With his broad shoulders, tapered waist, and well-muscled legs, Gordon Campbell was the perfect specimen of manhood.

Too bad he'd been born a Highlander, Rob thought.

Gordon hit the ball with so much power that it sailed high into the air and flew toward the Duke of Ludlow's estate. Then it disappeared. Glancing over his shoulder at her, he asked, "Would ye care to try?"

"I dinna know how," Rob refused.

"I'll teach ye," he replied, offering her the black leather glove.

Eager as a young girl, Rob doffed her cloak and stepped forward. She pulled the glove on and looked at her left hand. The glove hid Old Clootie's mark. Too bad she couldn't wear it whenever people were about.

"What do I do now?" she asked.

Gordon set another ball on top of the tee. Handing her the golf club, he said, "Face the ball, angel."

Rob showed him her back. She sensed him close behind her. *Too close for comfort.* Unexpectedly, his arms encircled her body.

"What are ye doin'?" The prospect of being held within his embrace sent her into a minor panic.

"Dinna fret, lass. I'm helpin' ye through it."

His words did nothing to calm her. Standing so close their bodies touched, Rob felt his strength and his heat through her gown. His breath tickled the side of her neck, and his clean masculine scent reminded her of mountain heather, making her senses reel pleasurably.

"Spread yer legs for me," he whispered into her ear.

Blissfully innocent, Rob did as he told her and then asked, "How's that? Wide enough for ye?"

"Simply perfect, angel. Yer an apt pupil," he said, laughter lurking in his voice. "Gently but firmly, grip my shaft. Without takin' yer eyes off the ball, ye'll swing in an arc and then follow through until the club is over yer left shoulder."

Rob felt the long length of his body pressed against her backside. His hands, covering hers on the golf club, moved with her as she began to swing.

Wham! The ball sailed through the air. With a loud plop, it landed in the Thames River.

"Ye owe me five shillin's for the loss of the ball, angel."

Rob whirled around and told his chest, "If ye can afford five gold pieces a day to purchase my cousins' loyalty, ye can certainly afford to lose a few shillin's for a golf ball."

"Look up, angel," he said in a husky whisper.

Rob wet her lips with her tongue and, ever so slowly, raised her gaze to his face. His piercing gray eyes seemed to soften on her with an emotion she failed to recognize.

"I've also brought ye a gift from Londontown." Gordon reached into his pocket and produced a heavy gold band set with an enormous emerald. Lifting her left hand, he slipped the ring onto her third finger and said,

"The stone reminded me of yer beautiful eyes. I've had the inside engraved with *our* words, 'Ye and No Other.' "

Surprised by his gesture, Rob stared in silence at the ring. No man except her father and her brothers had ever given her a gift. When she finally raised her gaze to his again, Rob saw only his handsome face as he inched closer to capture her lips with his own.

Yuch-yuch-yuch, Rob thought. But she made no move to pull away.

Rob closed her eyes at the very last moment. Their lips met. His mouth felt warm and gently insistent on hers.

"Yer so sweet," he murmured, his breath mingling with hers.

The intoxicating feel of his lips on hers and the husky sound of his voice conspired against Rob. Surrendering to his kiss, she sagged against his hard unyielding body. His strong arms encircled her and kept her imprisoned within his embrace.

With nerves tingling in a wild riot, Rob reveled in these new and exciting feelings. And then it was over as unexpectedly as it had begun.

"Thank ye for the gift of yer kiss, angel."

Rob opened her eyes when he spoke and stared at him in a dreamy daze. And then relief that she'd finally experienced her first real kiss surged through her.

"Aunt Keely was correct," Rob blurted out. "Kissin' does come naturally."

Gordon smiled. Putting his arm around her shoulder, he drew her against the side of his body, and they started across the lawns toward the mansion.

"What did ye buy the girls?" Rob asked, trying to mask the pounding of her heart with the sound of her voice.

"Marchpane and dolls," Gordon answered, casting her a sidelong glance. "Are ye back to checkin' yer titties?"

"If ye must know, I'm checkin' my ruby," Rob told

him. "Aunt Keely says this special ruby will darken redder than pigeon's blood if danger approaches me." She gave him an unconsciously flirtatious smile. "And I'm positive that yer a danger to my peace of mind."

"Thank ye for the high praise," Gordon replied as they walked into the foyer.

Rob paused at the great hall's entrance and asked when he looked at her, "When we kissed, my lord, do ye remember what I did with my hands?"

"No, why d'ye ask?"

"Never mind," she said, her complexion scarlet. "I'll pay better attention next time."

Gordon gave her a wolfish, thoroughly satisfied grin.

"If there is a next time," Rob amended, wiping the smile off his face.

When she started to brush past him, he reached out and gently grasped her forearm. "I've also brought ye a doll from London."

"I told ye yesterday—" she began.

Gordon placed one finger across her mouth and ordered, "Say 'thank ye,' angel, and then shut yer temptin' lips."

Rob smiled in spite of herself. "Thank ye, my lord." She made a gesture as though she were buttoning her lips together.

"Yer so sweet," Gordon said, leaning close to plant a chaste kiss on her lips. "I believe I'll keep ye around forever."

Chapter 5

December the twenty-third . . . the Great Blank Day with the secret of the unhewn stone . . . expect the unexpected.

Rob shivered as she recalled Gordon's words. Anything could happen today, and she knew for a fact that she didn't possess enough inner strength to survive more of the unexpected.

Since that day three weeks earlier when the Marquess of Inverary had barged into her life, Rob had felt her emotional fortitude slipping away slowly but surely. She'd passed the better part of each day with him and, thus far, had managed to keep him and his oh-so-inviting lips at bay; but she lacked the necessary strength to guard her heart from him indefinitely.

In spite of his arrogance, Gordon Campbell attracted her like no other man ever had. Rob knew that as surely as she knew that she had to marry Henry Talbot and remain in England forever.

And yet, the past three weeks had been pleasantly exciting. No court would ever find the Marquess of Inverary guilty of inciting boredom. Rob never felt so wonderfully alive than when she was in his presence.

Gordon and she rode in the morning and golfed in the garden during the afternoon. Each evening they sat in front of the hearth in the great hall and played a spirited game of chess while her five cousins watched.

Immediately following their chess game, which he always won, Gordon would disappear into her uncle's study to discuss business ventures. He insisted their clan's interests needed diversifying.

Rob felt certain her uncle was trying to maneuver her into the untenable position of being unable to refuse the marquess when the first day of spring arrived. His forming alliances with the man she planned to reject was risky business.

On the other hand, perhaps Uncle Richard believed that James Stuart was destined to succeed Queen Elizabeth. If the Scots king sat on the throne of England, then those Englishmen who enjoyed high-ranking Scots friends would secure their positions at the new court. How like Uncle Richard to solve problems before they arose.

Rob shivered in spite of the fire that blazed in the hearth, grabbed her black cashmere shawl, and wrapped it around her shoulders. Then she crossed the chamber to gaze out the window.

The weather, springlike until a few days ago, had taken a turn for the worse. A raw, bone-chilling rain fell steadily; and the angry, east wind beat against the windows, making them rattle. Its lonely howl reminded her of the Highlands and made her homesick. Though she never wanted to live there again, Rob missed her parents and her brothers.

And how would she entertain Gordon Campbell on such a miserable day? Rob wondered, giving herself a mental shake. She'd probably pass the next ten hours fending off his kisses. How could she survive a whole day of that tender torture?

She wasn't immune to his charm, and her firm resolve was weakening. Shielding her heart against his amorous advances was becoming more difficult with each passing day, even more draining than ignoring the taunts of the MacArthur clan's children.

The Great Blank Day . . . expect the unexpected.

Rob sighed, squared her shoulders, and started for the door. She might as well venture downstairs and meet whatever was destined to happen that day.

When she heard the knocking, Rob stopped short and stared at the door as if it had suddenly become a living entity. Apparently, the "unexpected" had wearied of waiting and had decided to come looking for her.

"My lady?" The voice on the other side of the door belonged to Jennings, the earl's majordomo. "My lady, are you there?"

Rob opened the door. "Yes, Mr. Jennin's?"

"A guest awaits you in the great hall," he announced.

That surprised Rob. "Is Lord Campbell aboot?"

Jennings shook his head. "The marquess rode out this morning and hasn't returned yet."

"He went ridin' in this weather?"

"Yes, my lady."

"Thank ye, Mr. Jennin's." Rob walked past him and hurried down the corridor to the stairs.

Reaching the foyer, Rob hid her stained left hand in the pocket of her gown. A smile of pure joy lit her face when she stepped inside the great hall.

"Henry!" she cried.

In her excitement, Rob pulled her hand from her pocket and rushed across the hall. She leaped into Henry Talbot's open arms and hugged him as if she'd never let him go. Her gallant knight had returned to rescue her from a life in the hostile Highlands.

Rob looked up in time to see his handsome face descending to hers. She quickly turned her face away, and his kiss landed on her cheek.

"Am I to assume your annulment hasn't been granted?" Henry asked, his voice tinged with amused irritation.

" 'Tis been delayed," Rob lied, stepping back a pace and taking his hand in hers. "Ye must be terribly chilled, my lord. Come and warm yerself in front of the hearth. How long can ye stay?"

Ignoring her question, Henry let himself be led to one of the chairs in front of the hearth. He grasped her wrist as he sat down and pulled her onto his lap.

Rob giggled. "Henry, please. 'Tis unseemly."

"I've been gone for six weeks and still you refuse to kiss me," he complained. "The least you can do is perch upon my lap."

Rob hastily moved her right hand to cover her left hand. She was almost as concerned with hiding the ring Gordon had given her as she was with masking her devil's flower.

For a long moment, Rob gazed at Henry's handsome face. He was the same man she'd known and loved for more than a year but, somehow, not quite as irresistibly appealing as he'd been two months earlier. She knew without a doubt that he wanted her, but her aunt's probing questions slammed into her consciousness.

Did she want to remain in England because she loved Henry? Or did she love Henry because she wanted to remain in England?

"Darling, tell me how much you missed me," Henry said, drawing her attention from troubling thoughts.

"Ye know I amna free to tell ye any such thin'," Rob chided him gently, a flirtatious smile touching her lips.

"God's balls, lass," drawled a familiar voice behind them. "Surely ye can tell the man how *little* ye missed him?"

"Great Bruce's ghost," Rob exclaimed, leaping off Henry's lap. She whirled around and saw a grim-faced Gordon Campbell advancing on them.

Wearing a puzzled expression, Henry rose from the chair and turned around. "Who is this?" he asked.

"Gordon Campbell, the Marquess of Inverary," Rob said in a voice barely louder than a whisper. "Gordon, this is Henry Talbot, the Marquess of Ludlow."

The two rivals stared at each other in hostile silence. Watching them, Rob furiously ran a finger back and forth across the devil's flower staining her hand.

"Has Campbell ridden the long distance from Scotland to deliver the betrothal annulment in person?" Henry asked, flicking a glance at her.

"Well, no," she hedged, mentally squirming. "But all I need to do is behave agreeably until the first day of spring. Then he'll give me the annulment if I wish."

Gordon caught Henry's attention and then insolently perused Rob from the top of her head to the tips of her dainty feet, his heated gaze lingering on her more interesting curves. "Rob's been ever so agreeable," he said, his tone of voice implying more than companionship. "Why, ye canna imagine how verra agreeable she's been."

"Fuck you and the horse you rode in on," Henry said in a clipped voice.

Gordon merely smiled at him.

"Annul your betrothal," Henry threatened, "or we'll see you in court."

In a flash of movement, Gordon pulled his last resort

from his boot. "Courts are for cowards," he said. "Draw yer dagger, and we'll settle this here and now."

"No!" Rob screamed as Henry pulled his own dagger from his belt.

"Sheath your weapons," ordered the voice of authority.

Rob whirled toward the hall's entrance. Much to her relief, Uncle Richard and Aunt Keely hurried across the chamber toward them.

"Campbell is trying to steal my intended," Henry complained, sheathing his dagger.

"She belonged to me long before ye ever met her," Gordon shot back, returning his blade to its hiding place. "The lass played ye for a fool, man. Ye'd be wise to forget aboot her."

Ready to argue, Rob began, "Now just one minute—"

"Silence," Earl Richard ordered.

"Arguing is so futile an activity," the countess added, casting both marquesses a reproving look.

Lady Keely took Rob's hand and led her to the chairs in front of the hearth. The three men followed and stood nearby. Earl Richard began to question Henry about what was happening at court.

Feeling horribly awkward, Rob refused to meet either suitor's gaze. She stared at her lap and rubbed a finger back and forth across her devil's flower. The conversation about court life swirled around her; but, so immersed in her own misery, Rob was unable to focus on it.

What if Gordon Campbell broke his promise? What if he told Henry that they were already married? Her dream to remain in England would be destroyed. She'd lied to Henry, and never again would he trust her once he realized how unworthy she was.

Rob stole a peek at Gordon. His attention was fixed on

the movement of her hands. She instantly dropped her gaze and hid her deformity behind her right hand.

Unexpectedly, a hand offered her a linen-wrapped package. Rob snapped her gaze up.

"I've brought you a gift," Henry said with a smile.

"Thank ye, my lord." Accepting it, Rob flicked a nervous glance at Gordon and then slowly unwrapped the linen. Relief surged through her when she saw the wonderfully innocuous book. She flipped through the first few pages and realized the words were written in a foreign language.

Was she now required to admit to being ignorant in addition to being deformed? Rob thought as humiliation stained her cheeks pink. How could Henry gift her with this? Didn't he realize that her education could never equal that of a sophisticated lady of the Tudor court? Well, she would pretend to read it.

"French love poems," Henry was saying for the benefit of the others.

"Apparently, my sweet *betrothed* is unschooled in French," Gordon remarked with obvious satisfaction. He offered her his gift, saying, "I rode into Londontown this mornin' to fetch these for ye, angel."

Crimson with angry embarrassment, Rob wondered how he'd known she was unable to read French. She squelched the almost overpowering urge to toss Gordon's gift into his face; instead, she managed an insincere smile and reluctantly opened the box. Inside lay at least a dozen pairs of lacy gloves—fashioned without any fingers like his golf gloves—in colors that matched the gowns in her wardrobe.

"How lovely," Lady Keely said.

"The merchants cheated you, Campbell," Henry said, his voice tinged with sarcasm. "You've purchased gloves without any fingers."

Gordon said nothing.

Ignoring their byplay, Rob stared in misery at the fingerless gloves. *Old Clootie's mark disturbed Gordon.* He would never admit it, but his actions did speak louder than his words. Her husband had purchased these gloves so that neither he nor anyone else would be forced to see the devil's flower staining the back of her left hand. How embarrassing it would be if others discovered how flawed his bride was.

"Did you hear me, sweetheart?"

Rob raised her gaze to Henry. "I beg yer pardon?"

"We've business to discuss in the study," he said. "I'll see you again before I return to Hampton Court."

"Yer leavin' today?"

Henry gave her an apologetic smile. "The Lord of Misrule presides over all the holiday entertainments. You wouldn't want me to shirk my duties to the queen, would you?"

"I understand," Rob said. Glancing back over her shoulder, she watched him follow Uncle Richard and Gordon out of the hall.

Bleak melancholy and aching regret mingled within her breast. Rob sensed that her relationship with Henry would never be quite the same after that day. Even if she did manage to rid herself of her arrogant Highland marquess, happiness would elude her, and misery would follow every step she took in life.

Absently, Rob fingered the beggar bead necklace and stared into the hearth's hypnotic flames. Glistening tears welled up in her eyes and then slid slowly down her cheeks.

Great Bruce's ghost, what a coil! Was she falling in love with the man she refused to marry? Would she never find heart's ease?

Rob looked at the two gifts that sat in her lap, a book

of love poems she was unable to read and a dozen pairs of fingerless gloves to hide her shame. *Ignorant and deformed, a vile freak to be cast out.* That's what she was.

"Do you wish to talk about it?" Lady Keely asked, her voice soothingly gentle.

"The jest is on me," Rob said, brushing her tears away with her hand. "I am fortune's greatest fool."

"Life jostles everyone, dearest. Your problem isn't that bad."

Rob looked at her aunt. " 'Tis worse than words can express."

"What is so tragic about two wealthy, attractive noblemen vying for your affection?" the countess asked.

"Henry's too busy dancin' to the queen's tune to rescue me from Gordon who's determined to drag me north," Rob answered. "Livin' in the Highlands will destroy me."

" 'Tis untrue, dearest."

" 'Tis, I say." Rob held her left hand out toward her aunt. "This cursed devil's flower made me an outcast within my own clan."

"The stain you wear is no curse," Lady Keely disagreed, mirroring her daughter's words. "At the moment of your conception, the great mother goddess blessed you with her touch."

"If I'm so damned blessed, why did my own clansmen avoid me like the black plague and make a protective sign of the cross whenever I chanced to pass by?" Rob asked, a lifetime of anguish making her voice crack with raw emotion. "Why did their children refuse to play with me? Why did they taunt me with names like 'changelin'-witch' and 'Lock Awe monster'?"

"Ignorance governed their actions and their words," Lady Keely answered.

"The Highlands abound with ignorant people," Rob

said. "I canna return to Scotland now that I have experienced acceptance in England."

"Did you know that I lived my first eighteen years as an outcast at my stepfather's holding in Wales because I am the Duke of Ludlow's bastard?" Lady Keely asked, reaching out to touch Rob's hand. "I can see that surprises you, but I swear 'tis truth. When I married Richard, I felt conspicuously out of place and was positive Elizabeth's courtiers considered me a backwoods Welsh bastard, a nobody who'd somehow managed to entrap England's premier earl into marriage. How wrong I was. When I accepted myself, they accepted me. And the same will hold for you."

" 'Tis different with me," Rob replied, shaking her head sadly. "Ye carried yer stigma hidden within yer heart where none were privy to it, but I carry mine on the back of my hand for the whole world to see."

"Adversity builds character," Lady Keely said. "The bigger the adversity, the nobler one's character grows. Indeed, you are truly blessed."

Rob smiled without humor. "If I had any more character, the pope would surely canonize me a saint," she replied, her voice tinged with bitterness. "I know ye possess unworldly talents, Aunt Keely. Can ye help me?"

"Well, what is it you really want?" the countess asked.

"Acceptance," Rob answered without hesitation, though her heart felt heavy with regret. "Ye must help me send 'Old Clootie' Campbell back to the Highland hell from whence he came."

"Success cannot be guaranteed," the countess warned. "The force you send out to control Campbell may return to control you instead."

Rob perked up at her aunt's words. "I accept full responsibility for whatever happens," she replied, nervously rubbing a finger back and forth across her devil's flower.

"Gordon willna be injured in any way, will he? I wouldna want to hurt him."

Lady Keely cast her a knowing smile as if she were privy to a secret that eluded Rob. "Cockle bread and white heather wine are our only hope to remedy this delicate situation without angering the goddess."

"I never heard of such thin's."

"White heather, a sacred herb, cools the ardor of unwanted suitors," Lady Keely explained. "I'll grind a bunch into fine powder, and you'll serve it in wine to Gordon. 'Tis perfectly safe."

"And the other?" Rob asked.

"Cockle bread is an aphrodisiac cake," the countess answered. "You'll knead a small piece of dough and then press it to your vulva—"

"I dinna have any vulva," Rob moaned in dismay.

Lady Keely burst out laughing. "Dearest, your vulva lies between your legs. Mold the dough to your privates, bake it, and then serve it to Henry. Do you still wish to do this?"

Shocked embarrassment colored Rob's cheeks a vivid scarlet. "Yes," she agreed in a choked voice.

"We'll serve them in Richard's study whilst their attention is fixed on business," the countess said, rising from the chair.

"And where are we goin' to perform this magic?" Rob asked, standing when her aunt did.

"The pantry, of course."

An hour later the two women stood outside the earl's study. Rob held the tray steady while her aunt positioned the three crystal goblets of mulled wine, the small loaf of cockle bread, and the two round tartlets topped with sweet-curd cottage cheese called maids of honor cakes. The wine laced with white heather, destined for Gordon, sported a cinnamon stick and perched on the opposite side of the tray from Henry's cockle bread.

"Richard will be sitting behind his desk," Lady Keely said, arranging the food and the beverage, "so I'll place one wine goblet and a tart here. The white heather wine and the other tart should go here. If 'tis necessary, we'll turn the tray around after I serve Richard."

"That seems logical," Rob replied.

"And may the great mother goddess smile with approval upon our venture," Lady Keely said, reaching out to knock on the door.

"Amen."

Pasting a smile onto her face, Lady Keely opened the door and stepped inside the study. Rob, carrying the tray, followed behind her.

"Don't bother to stand for us," Lady Keely called as they crossed the chamber. "We've brought refreshment."

Relief surged through Rob when she caught her first glimpse of the seating arrangement. Earl Richard sat behind his desk just as her aunt had predicted. Henry and Gordon, perfectly positioned in relation to the tray's contents, sat in the two chairs pulled up in front of the desk. Arousing their suspicion by rearranging the refreshments would be unnecessary.

"And how is your business discussion progressing?" Lady Keely asked as Rob set the tray on the desk.

"Peaceful, at the moment," the earl answered, giving his wife a meaningful look. "We've been discussing commodities. Lord Campbell is also interested in my Levant Trading Company."

"May the one who hears all bless us with prosperity." Lady Keely smiled and asked, "Do you mind if I browse for a book?"

"Me too," Rob said, noting her uncle's surprised expression.

Without waiting for her husband's permission to stay, Lady Keely grabbed Rob's hand and led her across the chamber to stand in front of one of the walls of books in her uncle's extensive collection. Nonchalantly, Rob peeked over her shoulder and decided she didn't trust the expression on her uncle's face. He appeared to sense something was amiss.

Rob didn't doubt that he felt suspicious. In the year since she'd arrived in England, neither her aunt nor she had read even one book.

"Dearest, why don't you read *Lives of the Saints?*" the earl suggested, an amused smile flirting with the corners of his lips. "I gave it to you eleven years ago."

"I'm in the mood for romance," the countess replied.

"Then I'd do well to finish my business," the earl remarked in a low voice, making the two younger men smile.

"My sweet betrothed has a book of French love poems, if that appeals to ye," Gordon suggested, his voice tinged with sarcasm.

Rob shifted her gaze to Henry. He appeared ready to pounce on Gordon.

"Shall we conduct ourselves like gentlemen?" the earl asked, obviously trying to prevent trouble.

Henry smirked and said, "Expecting a Highland barbarian to behave like a gentleman is like expecting a pig to sing like a skylark."

Before Gordon could defend himself, Rob whirled around and marched across the study. "I'm a Highlander," she said in a challenging voice. "Apologize at once."

Gordon relaxed in his chair. He caught the other man's attention and grinned at him.

"I'd never refer to you as a barbarian," Henry told Rob.

"My father and my brothers are Highlanders," she countered. "Are ye callin' them barbaric pigs?"

"No, but you always refer to Highlanders as barbarians," he answered.

"I've the right to say whatever I wish," Rob told him. "I was born there."

"I do apologize," Henry said, taking her right hand in his and planting a kiss on it. "I'd never hurt you in any way."

"I'm sorry too," Rob relented, hoping her reprimand hadn't offended him. She wouldn't want him to return to court while he harbored angry feelings toward her. "Drink yer wine, my lord."

Henry released her hand. Instead of choosing the wine closest to him, he reached for the one with the cinnamon stick.

" 'Tis for Gordon," Rob told him, staying his hand.

"But I like mulled wine with cinnamon sticks," Henry said.

Great Bruce's ghost, Rob thought in a near panic. If she'd known that, she would have left the white heather wine plain. Had her aunt known that Henry liked cinnamon sticks with his wine? No, that couldn't be. She trusted that her aunt desired what was best for her.

"The cinnamon willna taste good with the bread I baked," Rob told him.

"I don't want bread," Henry replied. "I'll take the pastry."

"I'll taste yer bread," Gordon said.

"No!" Rob cried, whirling around in time to see him reach for it. Without thinking, she raised her hand to slap his hand away, but her aunt was faster.

"Let them choose whatever they wish," Lady Keely said, grasping her wrist and giving her a reproachful look.

Rob knew what her aunt was telling her. The goddess would decide who ate what. Though she could try to influence her fate, the final decision lay with the greater power.

Rob nodded, accepting the inevitable. She let her aunt lead her back across the study.

Staring at the books without actually seeing them, Rob kept her senses alert to the men as they resumed their conversation. Nervously, she ran her thumb back and forth across her devil's flower and focused on their mundane words about sheep and cattle production and turning milk into cheese for sale.

Time slowed to a crawl. Each passing moment felt like twenty years.

Finally, unable to endure the suspense another agonizing moment, Rob peered over her shoulder. She fixed her gaze on the tray. Both the white heather wine and the cockle bread had vanished.

Rob closed her eyes, almost afraid to look at either of her suitors. Summoning her courage, she peeked at Gordon who wasn't eating or drinking. Then she slid her gaze to Henry who sat there and chewed on a cinnamon stick.

Rob dashed across the study and asked Henry, "Have ye drunk the wine and eaten the bread too?"

"I ate the bread," Gordon said. " 'Twas verra well done of ye, angel."

"The wine with the cinnamon was meant for ye," Rob blurted out, rounding on him. "Ye werena supposed to eat the bread."

"Keely, explain what this is all about," Earl Richard ordered his wife.

Ignoring him, Lady Keely touched Rob's arm and spoke in a gentle voice, "Child, the goddess has chosen."

"I dinna give a tinker's damn aboot yer goddess," Rob cried as tears of frustration welled up in her eyes. "I refuse to live in the Highlands." At that, she ran out of the study.

The two marquesses rose from their chairs at the same time, intending to go after her, but the countess gestured for them to sit and said, "Let her go."

Lady Keely looked at her husband and shrugged, saying, "Rob made cockle bread for Henry and white heather wine for Gordon, but 'twould appear the goddess has her own opinion about the way things must be."

Earl Richard threw back his head and shouted with laughter, and his countess giggled. A smile of unmistakable satisfaction appeared on Henry Talbot's face.

Gordon looked at the three of them in confusion. God's balls, what the hell was so funny?

"Shall I share our knowledge with Lord Campbell?" Lady Keely asked her husband.

"Oh, please do," Henry Talbot spoke up.

Gordon looked at his rival. The other man's expression told him that he wouldn't care for the explanation.

"You see, my lord, the wrong marquess consumed the wrong food," Lady Keely said when her husband nodded his permission. "The cockle bread, meant for Henry, primes a suitor's interest while the white heather wine, meant for you, cools a suitor's ardor."

Though irritated, Gordon kept his face expressionless. He flicked an unconcerned glance at the Marquess of Ludlow and said, " 'Twould take more than cockle bread and white heather wine to convince me to annul my ma—"

"Brother, perhaps you ought to return to Hampton

Court now," the countess interrupted. "You did wish to arrive there by nightfall?"

"Tell Rob I'll try to visit on New Year's though I cannot promise until I know the queen's schedule," Henry said, rising from his chair. Before turning away, he paused and offered Gordon his hand, saying with a sincere smile, "Inverary, I'm pleased to have made your acquaintance. And may the best man win."

"I have no doubt 'twill be me," Gordon said, standing to shake his rival's offered hand.

Henry inclined his head. "Or me . . ."

As her two suitors were shaking hands, Rob stood alone in her chamber and gazed out the window at the rain. The bleakness of the day matched the bleakness within her soul.

I willna weep, she told herself, holding back the flood of tears that threatened to spill. Henry would never forsake her because he'd drunk the white heather wine.

And then she saw him. The Marquess of Ludlow dashed across the lawns toward the quay and the barge that would carry him away from her to Hampton Court.

Her dismal future had arrived. The man she wanted to marry had drunk the magical white heather wine. Now he was leaving without even bidding her farewell.

What did the future hold for her? Gordon Campbell, a womanizer who wanted to hide her deformity with gloves. And yet, more than once, the Marquess of Inverary had pressed his lips to her devil's flower. Was that a self-serving act meant to lull her into believing that he cared for her?

Rob felt the panic rising in her breast. Gordon had eaten the magical cockle bread. Did that mean he would be beating down the door for love of her?

Rob whirled around at the sound of someone knocking on her chamber door. Had her outrageous thoughts somehow conjured the man?

"Who is it?"

"Gordon."

"Go away."

The door swung open slowly, and Gordon walked into her chamber.

"I said, go away."

"Oh, I'm sorry," he apologized, casting her his devastating smile. "I thought ye said 'come in.' "

"What d'ye want?" Rob asked, unamused at the obvious lie.

Gordon held the box of gloves up. "Ye left these in the hall."

Rob flicked a glance at the hateful box. Then she raised her gaze to his and said, "I dinna want them."

Or you was left unspoken.

Almost imperceptibly, Gordon flinched as if he'd been struck. All pleasantness vanished from his expression, and his gray-eyed gaze darkened like a storm cloud. Without a word, he set the box down on a nearby table and turned to leave.

"I told ye I dinna want them," Rob said, steeling herself against the aching regret beginning to swell within her.

Gordon turned to face her and said in a surprisingly quiet voice, "I rode all the way to Londontown in that peltin' rain to get them for ye when what ye deserve is a tremendous whack on yer arse."

Ever so slowly, he perused her body from the ebony crown of her head to the tips of her slippered feet. "Ye look like a desirable woman, but ye behave like a willful brat. When ye grow up, angel, yer welcome to come courtin' me."

Rob showed him her back and waited for him to slam the door in anger as he left the chamber.

He didn't. Almost noiselessly, the door clicked shut behind him.

The quietness of that click echoed within her soul, tugging painfully at her already raw emotions. Had she been wrong about him? Had he purchased those gloves to mask her flaw or because she'd so admired his golf gloves?

Rob held her hand up and stared at her devil's flower. Winking at her from its golden bed was the exquisite emerald he'd said matched her eyes.

Rob sighed raggedly. He'd been kind to her, but she'd been cruel to him.

Was she stubbornly childish to want to marry Henry and to remain in England? Didn't everyone have hopes and dreams? Aye, they did. Courtiers wished for noble commissions, lawyers longed for high fees, and soldiers dreamed of the glory in battle. Maidens desired handsome husbands while young matrons yearned for healthy babes . . .

And then her aunt's probing questions slammed into her consciousness. *Did she want to remain in England because she loved Henry? Or did she love Henry because she wanted to remain in England?*

Each passing moment made that answer clearer within her heart, her mind, her soul. No matter, though.

Rob *craved* acceptance.

Chapter 6

 God's balls, but wooing the MacArthur chit was proving damned near impossible.

With his golf bag slung over his right shoulder, Gordon grumbled to himself as he marched across the lawns. At dawn, after passing a restless night, he decided to take his frustrations out on his golf balls.

The skies had cleared under cover of darkness, and the early morning promised a near perfect day. The rolling mist had already receded from the earl's grounds but still shrouded the river. By mid morning the fog would evaporate as if it had never existed. The comforting scent of wood smoke wafted through the crisp air as myriad servants along the Strand stoked the morning fires in preparation for a new day.

Gordon leaned his golf bag against an oak tree, withdrew his ash driving club, and walked several paces away. After sticking the tee in the winter-brown lawn, he pulled a golf ball from his pocket and set it down on top of the tee, then readied his stance and swung the club with all of his pent-up strength.

Wham! The ball sailed through the air and disappeared into the Duke of Ludlow's estate.

What the bloody hell was he doing wrong with the MacArthur lass? Gordon wondered, staring—without seeing—in the direction his golf ball had vanished. Apparently, the saucy angel he'd married preferred a book of unreadable love poems to his own thoughtful gift.

That Rob MacArthur might truly love the Marquess of Ludlow never entered his mind. Henry Talbot was a dish-cloth when compared to himself. Gordon was certain that he was the handsomer of the two, possessed greater wealth, and enjoyed considerably more status. While Ludlow played the Lord of Misrule for an ageing queen whose time was nearly past, he had the young king's ear. When Gordon inherited his father's dukedom, Rob Mac-Arthur would become the undisputed "Queen of Argyll." What was so objectionable about that?

Muttering to himself about the folly of women, Gordon took another ball from his pocket and set it down on top of the tee. Keeping his gaze riveted on the ball, he swung hard. This time the ball flew over the treetops and landed in the Thames River.

"Are you hitting balls or killing them?" called a voice from behind him.

Gordon whirled around. The garden was deserted. Had he become so distracted by the MacArthur chit's rejection that he now heard imaginary voices?

"Good morning, my lord." Laughter lurked in that female voice.

"Where are ye?" Gordon called, turning in a circle. "Show yerself."

"I'm perched in the oak tree."

Gordon turned toward the tree and looked up. His

mouth dropped open at the astounding sight that greeted him. The Countess of Basildon, the wife of England's premier earl, sat on a thick branch.

"What are ye doin' up there?" Gordon asked, sauntering toward the tree.

"Collecting sprigs of mistletoe." Lady Keely inhaled deeply of the morning's fresh scent and surveyed the kingdom of her garden from her perch in the tree. "I love the dawn. 'Tis the reason I named my daughter Aurora."

Gordon smiled. "Can I help ye down?" he asked.

"My twenty-nine-year-old bones aren't brittle yet," the countess refused. She leaped gracefully from the branch and landed like a cat on her feet, then remarked, "You've risen unusually early."

"I doubt I closed my eyes for more than an hour or two," Gordon admitted.

"And what has stolen your peaceful sleep?" Lady Keely asked, reaching out to touch his arm in concern.

"I believe ye already know," Gordon answered. He flicked a glance at the mansion's second-floor bedchamber windows and added, "Perhaps abductin' her would be for the best."

" 'Twould destroy any chance you have of winning her heart," Lady Keely warned him. "You've made such good progress with her. Why ruin that now?"

Gordon stared at the countess in surprise. If anything, the opposite was true. Even before he'd reached full manhood, women had thrown themselves at him. A few wanted his money and his title. Most contented themselves with his body. Now that he'd met a woman singularly unimpressed with him, Gordon had no idea how to go about changing her mind. It was an eventuality for which he'd never prepared.

"I dinna ken what goes on inside that pretty head of

hers," he admitted with a rueful smile. "She isna like any woman I've ever met."

"Trust me, my lord. Rob and you are destined for each other," the countess told him. "I knew that the very first moment I saw you."

Gordon glanced sidelong toward the mansion again and said, " 'Tis a pity she doesna know it."

"Today marks the start of the birch tree month, which signifies new beginnings," Lady Keely said with an encouraging smile. "Besides, a tiny spark can kindle a flame."

"What d'ye mean?"

"Rob worried that the white heather wine might harm you," the countess said. Then she asked, "Why did you give her those gloves?"

"To hide the birthmark she carries on the back of her left hand."

His honest answer seemed to anger her. "But why?" she asked.

"Rob's always been uncomfortable aboot that stain, though I dinna ken why," Gordon answered. "On the day we wed ten years ago, she hid it behind her back and told me that the monster livin' beneath her bed had touched her hand. I thought the gloves would give her freedom of movement. Too bad she doesna want them."

"So, you don't find the mark repulsive." Lady Keely visibly relaxed and then said, "My lord, courtship is emotional seduction. Absence has been known to make a reluctant heart grow fonder. It did for me when the earl determined to force me to the altar. You see, I'd rejected his advances, but with my stepmother's assistance, Richard engineered me into a compromising position which forced me to accept his marriage proposal. No sooner had we signed the betrothal contract than the earl left for court."

Gordon chuckled. "And what did ye do aboot that, my lady?"

"As I recall, those two weeks were the longest of my entire life," the countess admitted. "I worried that one of the acclaimed beauties at court would catch his eye and win his heart. I've always wondered if Richard purposefully abandoned me because he knew I'd realize how much I wanted him."

"Ye never asked the earl?"

"Part of life's pleasure lies in its mysteries."

"What are ye suggestin' I do, my lady?" Gordon asked, a smile flirting with his lips. That she had something in mind was all too obvious.

"My husband has documents that must be delivered posthaste to Queen Elizabeth," Lady Keely said. "Unfortunately, he forgot to give them to Henry. Why don't you offer to deliver them? You could pass several days at Hampton Court and enjoy a few of the Yule's festivities. When you return, Rob may have reexamined her feelings."

Gordon narrowed his gaze on her. "Is this a trick to get rid of me?"

The countess cast him a suitably offended look. Then she turned her back and started to walk away.

"I'm verra sorry," Gordon said, reaching out with one hand to prevent her flight. "I meant, do ye really believe 'twould help? I'm unused to reluctant females."

"Modest, aren't you?" she quipped.

Gordon gave her a sheepish smile and shrugged.

"Making a woman desire something is easy when you lead her to believe she cannot have it," Lady Keely told him. "Besides, your gray eyes do resemble mountain mist, and only a blind woman could be immune to their mysterious depths."

In courtly manner, Gordon bowed low over her hand

and said, "May the wisdom from yer lips travel directly to God's ears."

"You mean *goddess*, my lord. The Supreme Being is female."

Gordon grinned at that absurd notion but said, "My lady, ye may be correct."

"Gather your golfing paraphernalia and breakfast with me," Lady Keely ordered. "Together we'll plan your strategy for stealing your wife's sensitive heart."

Your wife. Gordon felt strangely comforted by those two words. Could he be developing a fondness for the angel he'd married?

"Ludlow is yer brother," Gordon remarked as he reached for his bag of golf clubs. "Why are ye willin' to help me?"

"I desire happiness for all involved," the countess explained. "My brother could never truly be happy if he married a woman meant for another man."

"Do ye think Rob loves me, then?"

"The answer to that question hides within the shadows of her heart."

"How does a woman gain such wisdom in only twenty-nine years?" Gordon asked, escorting her across the lawns toward the mansion.

"The same way a man does."

"Which is?"

Lady Keely cast him an ambiguous smile. "Either you are born with wisdom, my lord, or you make do without it . . ."

"*. . . a desirable woman, but . . . a willful brat . . .*" Rob stared out her bedchamber window and recalled the words Gordon had spoken the previous evening.

Her downcast mood contrasted sharply with the scene

outside, a near-perfect day with the sun riding high in a heavenly blue sky and the angelic sound of her five Devereux cousins playing a rousing game of blind-man's buff. She watched her cousins without actually seeing them, her thoughts fixed on her would-be husband.

Rob knew from personal experience that anger sometimes hid an injured heart. Her rejection of his gloves had hurt Gordon's feelings; his insulting her had probably never been his intent.

Had living like an outcast for eighteen years made her overly sensitive and jaded her thinking concerning his true motive for that gift? And wasn't that proof that she could never be happy living with him in the Highlands? No one could erase the lifetime of harsh lessons learned at the hands of ignorant, superstitious people.

She should apologize to him for her churlish behavior and then ask him what motivated his giving her those gloves. That would be the adult thing to do.

As Rob turned away from the window, another thought occurred to her. Whenever her mother felt the need to apologize to her father, she wore her prettiest, most daringly low-cut gown.

If she was seeking Gordon's forgiveness, then she had better look damned good. To that end, Rob dressed in a rose silk gown with scooped neckline and matching shoes. She slipped her beggar bead necklace over her head. If the ruby darkened redder than pigeon's blood, she'd make a run for her chamber. Checking her reflection in the pier glass, she pinched her cheeks for color and then left the room.

Anxious thoughts slowed Rob's steps as she descended the stairs to the foyer below. If Gordon had failed to send a servant to awaken her for their morning ride, then he must still be very angry. Had he missed her company on his morning jaunt? She certainly hoped so. That would make obtaining his forgiveness easier. The one thing she dreaded was staring into his piercing gray eyes that seemed to see to the dark depths of her soul.

Reaching the great hall, Rob found it nearly deserted. A few servants prepared the high table for dinner while her aunt sat in a chair in front of the hearth.

"What are ye doin?" Rob asked.

"I'm reading," the countess answered, holding a book up.

That surprised Rob. "Shall I come back later?"

"Actually, I'm relieved you've interrupted me," Lady Keely admitted, setting the book aside. " 'Tis *Lives of the Saints*. So much needless sacrifice gives me the shivery creeps."

"I ken what yer sayin'." Then Rob asked casually, "Do ye know where Gordon is?"

"Lord Campbell is completing an errand for your uncle."

"Oh." Rob failed to mask the disappointment in her voice. She'd mustered her courage for nothing; he wasn't even home.

"You look especially lovely," Lady Keely complimented her.

"Thank ye, Aunt Keely." Rob blushed with embarrassment like a child caught stealing marchpane. "I thought dressin' up would lift my spirits after yesterday's fiasco. If ye see Gordon, would ye tell him I'd like to speak with him?"

Lady Keely nodded. "Of course, dearest."

Rob passed the afternoon watching her cousins romping in the garden and waiting for Gordon to appear, but he never showed for his usual golf session. When he also failed to appear for supper, she couldn't bear the anticipation another moment.

"Where is Gordon?" Rob asked, turning to her aunt as the family supped together at the high table.

"Doing an errand for your uncle," Lady Keely answered. "I told you that this afternoon."

"Great Bruce's ghost, 'twas hours ago. He should have returned by now," Rob said, becoming alarmed. "He could have suffered an accident or—"

"Campbell is delivering several financial reports due the queen at Hampton Court," Uncle Richard interjected.

"Do ye mean he went to court and never told me?" Rob asked, surprised.

"Did the marquess need your permission to leave?" her uncle countered.

"No, but ye could've had Henry deliver those reports."

The earl cocked a copper brow at her, the same warning gesture her own mother used for conveying irritation. "And do *I* need to explain my actions to you?" he asked in a quiet voice.

Rob lowered her gaze. "I'm verra sorry, Uncle Richard, and meant no disrespect."

"Your uncle forgot to give the reports to Henry," Lady Keely spoke up. "Old people tend toward forgetfulness, you know."

"Thank you, dearest," the earl said dryly.

Lady Keely turned to her husband and teased him, "Well, you are a lot older than you were eleven years ago."

"So are you."

"True, but you'll *always* be older than I am."

Earl Richard's gaze warmed on his wife. "I'm not too old to—"

"No, you're not," Lady Keely interrupted, casting him

a blatantly seductive smile. "You'll never be too old for that."

Rob saw the heated look that passed between them. After eleven years of marriage and six daughters, the earl and his countess still loved each other.

Would she ever possess such a lasting love in her own life? Rob wondered. No, she didn't think so. Wonderful things only happened to nice people. Her devil's flower damned her to a lifetime of misery.

Taking control of her emotions, Rob gave herself a mental shake. She should be enjoying this evening of freedom, the first she'd had in weeks. Tomorrow was Christmas. The marquess would certainly return then.

Christmas came and went without Gordon making an appearance. Rob pasted a smile onto her face and refrained from asking questions about him, but at odd moments, irritation and heartache mingled within her breast. She had a would-be husband and a would-be betrothed. Both had abandoned her on Christmas.

The next four days passed excruciatingly slowly. Rob awakened late each morning and spent the afternoon with her cousins in the garden. Each evening she sat in front of the hearth in the great hall and wondered what Gordon was doing and with whom.

Then Henry Talbot's image would form in her mind's eye. Guilt over neglecting his memory made her squirm mentally.

Rob awakened late on the fifth morning. Gazing out the window at the day, she spied her uncle's barge docked at the quay. The sight of that barge lifted the heaviness from her heart like the midday sun evaporating the morning mists from the Thames. Unexpectedly, she became fully aware of how glad she was that Gordon had returned home.

'Tis nothin', Rob told herself. Of course, she was happy

that he'd finally returned. Hadn't he kept her entertained while Henry was busy at court? Soon Henry would complete his duties to the queen, and Gordon would leave for Scotland. Only then would she be able to secure permanent happiness here in England.

Though she told herself repeatedly that she cared nothing for Gordon, Rob took special pains with her toilet that morning. She dressed in one of her favorite outfits, an emerald silk gown and matching satin slippers. Should she don one of the pairs of gloves he'd given her? No, that would be too obvious, and he might begin to believe that she cared for him.

Rob hurried downstairs and, expecting to see Gordon, slowed to a casual stroll when she walked into the hall. Lady Keely, surrounded by her five oldest daughters, sat in a chair in front of the hearth. No one else was in attendance except for Mrs. Ashemole who lifted a sleeping baby Hope from her mother's arms and carried her out of the hall.

"Good morning," the countess called, watching her cross the hall. "Or should I say 'good afternoon'?"

"Good day to all of ye," Rob returned the greeting.

"Good afternoon, Cousin Rob," the five little girls chorused.

"I saw a barge docked at the quay," Rob remarked, trying—*but failing*—to hide the excitement in her voice. "Do we have company?"

"Lord Campbell returned from Hampton Court this morning," Lady Keely told her. "He went directly to bed. The poor man said he hadn't slept for more than five hours in as many days."

"I see." A surging wave of jealousy crashed through Rob, and in its wake the heaviness returned to weigh her heart down. Her husband had been carousing at the Tudor court with beauties who bore no evil deformity.

"Want to play with us in the garden?" Bliss asked her. Rob shook her head. "Later perhaps."

"No shouting," Lady Keely warned as her daughters started to leave. "We don't want to awaken the marquess."

Rob sat in the chair beside her aunt's, folded her hands in her lap, and waited for Gordon to awaken. He never appeared, and that afternoon stretched out longer than the preceding four days put together.

When suppertime arrived, Rob kept her gaze riveted on the hall's entrance. Four days and one exceedingly long afternoon of waiting had taken its toll on her nerves. With her hands hidden on her lap, she furiously ran her thumb back and forth across her devil's flower. Surely, Gordon would join them for supper. The man required food, didn't he?

When the earl's majordomo appeared, Lady Keely instructed him, "Please serve the marquess a supper tray upstairs."

"Dinna bother, Jennin's. I'll take it," Rob said, leaping out of her chair. Hurrying across the hall, she never saw the smiles that passed between her uncle and her aunt.

With tray in hand, Rob stood outside Gordon's bedchamber door. She balanced the tray on her left forearm and reached out with her right hand, but then hesitated.

Should I knock? she asked herself.

No answered an inner voice.

Summoning every ounce of courage she possessed, Rob opened the door and stepped inside the chamber. She closed the door behind her lest she flee.

Melancholy dusk cast the chamber in semidarkness. Only one night candle burned on a nearby table.

Rob focused her gaze on the bed. Its brocaded curtains had been left open, and though unable to see his features, she discerned the form of a sleeping man and started forward slowly. She set the tray on the bedside table, turned to stare at her husband, and nearly swooned at the seductive picture he presented.

Bare chested, Gordon lay on his back with the coverlet pulled up to his waist. In sleep his face appeared boyishly vulnerable, yet he exuded an aura of power.

Unhurriedly, Rob studied his handsome features. His jaw was strongly chiseled and his lips sensuously formed, inviting sweet surrender to his kiss. She slid her gaze lower, saw the strength in his well-muscled chest with its mat of brown hair, and struggled against the sudden urge to touch him and feel his muscles rippling beneath her fingertips.

When her interested gaze reached the boundary line of body and coverlet, Rob wondered if he wore anything at all. Could that flimsy coverlet be the only barrier between his nakedness and her? That tantalizing thought frightened and excited her.

As if he sensed another's presence, Gordon opened his eyes and asked in a sleep-husky voice, "What are ye doin' there, Livy?"

"Who's Livy?" Rob demanded. Her voice sounded overly loud in the chamber's hushed atmosphere.

Gordon focused on her and yawned. "Ah, angel. Good mornin' to ye."

"'Tis evenin'," Rob snapped. She folded her arms across her chest and cocked an ebony brow at him to indicate her irritation. "Did ye travel to England to attend court or to court me?"

"I see that ye missed me," he remarked.

"Missed ye?" she echoed, incredulous. "Dinna flatter yerself, my lord. Yer the wart on my existence."

"I'm growin' on ye, then?" Gordon asked with a wry smile.

"Yer verra funny, my lord."

"Sit beside me," he invited her, patting the bed. "I promise I'll give ye the attention ye deserve."

Rob bristled at his conceited arrogance. "No, thank ye," she replied, lifting her chin a notch. "There's a tray here for ye if ye've the energy to eat after carousin' at court for long days and even longer nights." She marched back across the chamber to the door but leveled one final parting shot at him, "And I hope ye didna catch anythin' fatal from galavantin' aboot."

Rob slammed the door behind her and started down the corridor to her own chamber, but the sound of Gordon's laughter dogged her every step. She passed a sleepless night wondering about the woman named Livy.

Rob awakened later than usual the next day. The heaviness in her heart kept her weighted to the bed until early afternoon.

The last day of December was Hogmanay Eve in the Highlands. Homesickness for her parents and her brothers coiled itself around her heart. At Dunridge Castle, her ancestral home, that festive night would be celebrated with guising as animals, burning smoking sticks to ward off evil sprites, and eating special cakes. The doors would be thrown open at midnight, and everyone would rattle utensils to scare off the last vestiges of the old year, paving the way for all that was new.

Rob emerged from her chamber just before supper. Entering the great hall, she hesitated for a fraction of a moment. Gordon stood with her uncle and her aunt near the hearth and smiled warmly at her when he caught her gaze. Out of habit, Rob hid her stained hand within the folds of her gown and joined them.

"Good evening, my dear," Lady Keely greeted her.

Rob smiled at her aunt and then her uncle. Finally, unable to delay the moment, she turned her gaze on the marquess.

"What's the news from Hampton Court?" Rob asked, assuming a casual attitude, determined to show her husband that the woman named Livy meant nothing to her.

"The usual court doin's," Gordon said with a shrug. He gifted her with his devastating smile as if he knew what game she was playing.

"How fares Dubh?" she asked. "And Isabelle?"

"I do believe yer brother and yer friend share a fondness for each other," he answered. "They pass all of their spare hours together . . . By the way, Mungo will be ready to leave for Scotland by the first day of spring."

"Mungo?" Rob echoed. "Is he yer other travelin' companion?"

Instead of answering her question, Gordon smiled and said, "Look up, angel."

Rob looked up. Her aunt was waving a sprig of mistletoe over her head.

Before she could utter a word of protest, Gordon captured her within the circle of his embrace and claimed her lips. Caught off guard and reeling from his appealing scent of mountain heather, Rob succumbed to the enticingly sensuous feeling of his mouth on hers and returned his kiss in kind.

As if from a great distance, Rob heard her cousins' disgusted exclamations, "Yuch-yuch-yuch." And then Gordon ended the kiss as quickly and as unexpectedly as he'd begun it.

"Rob loves Gordon," six-year-old Aurora chanted in a sing-song voice. "Rob loves Gordon."

"Hush," Rob said, rounding on her cousins. She could feel the heated blush staining her cheeks.

"Well, you must love him," Blythe began.

"Because you never even tried to kick his balls," Bliss finished baldly.

Gordon threw back his head and shouted with laughter. Earl Richard nodded with proud approval of his daughters, and Lady Keely smiled at her husband's gesture.

Only Rob remained unamused. Was it true? she wondered. Was she beginning to care for Gordon Campbell? If that was true, she would be doomed to eternal misery. Never could she live with him in the Highlands. But if she loved him, how could she live in England without him?

I care naught for the Marquess of Inverary, Rob told herself. Gordon Campbell was simply a not-so-pleasant diversion until Henry returned from court.

When supper ended, Gordon turned to her and asked, "Would ye care to pass the hours until midnight with a game of chess?"

"Why dinna ye play with *Livy?*" Rob replied, lifting her upturned nose into the air in a gesture of dismissal.

"Och, angel," Gordon whispered, leaning close to her ear. "Livy doesna care much for games."

Rob turned her whole body away from him.

"Livy happens to be the housekeeper at Campbell Mansion in Edinburgh," he lied. "She changed my nappies when I was a bairn."

Rob closed her eyes against the burning humiliation she felt. Her imagination had run wild, and now she must pay for it.

"I'm verra sorry for my behavior," she apologized with a sheepish smile. "I *would* like to play chess with ye."

For long hours the two of them sat across the chessboard like adversaries on a battlefield. When the three youngest Devereux girls succumbed to sleep, Blythe and Bliss joined them for several games of the ladies against the gent. The ladies surprised Gordon by winning every game until the last one when he caught them cheating.

A moment before midnight, everyone grabbed their designated utensils and ran to the front door. Laughing and shouting, they banged their pots and pans together to scare off the old year and welcome the new.

"Are you going to give her the gift now?" Blythe asked Gordon as they returned to the hall.

"Aye, lass. I am."

"I'll fetch it," Bliss offered.

"*I'll* fetch it," Earl Richard informed his daughter.

"Ye must sit down," Gordon said, escorting Rob to one of the chairs in front of the hearth. "Get those hands off yer lap, and close yer eyes."

Rob did as she was told. All was silent in the hall. Then she heard her uncle's footsteps as he returned. At Gordon's command, Rob opened her eyes and cried in pleased surprise, "Great Bruce's ghost, 'tis what I've always wanted."

Against his chest, Gordon cuddled a tiny ball of squirming fur. With a smile, he set the pup in her lap.

The English toy spaniel had a well-rounded head, a turned-up nose, and an aristocratic expression. Its fur was pearly white with well distributed chestnut-red patches.

"Oh, she's so sweet," Rob cooed, gathering the pup against her breast like a baby.

" 'Tis a boy," Blythe told her.

Rob lifted her gaze to Gordon and caught the tender emotion mirrored in his. "Thank ye, my lord," she said. " 'Tis the best Hogmanay gift I've ever received."

The pup chose that moment to lick her neck, and Rob giggled at the tickling sensation.

"He likes you," Bliss said. "He's giving you smooches."

" 'Tis what I'll call him then." Rob gazed into the pup's dark eyes and told him, "Yer name is Smooches. Ye ken what I'm sayin'?"

Smooches barked the shrill yelp of a puppy. Everyone laughed.

Gordon leaned close and planted a chaste kiss on her cheek, whispering, "Happy New Year, angel."

"I'm sorry I've no gift for ye," Rob said, a sudden frown marring her expression.

Gordon traced one long finger down the side of her cheek. "Yer smile will be gift enough," he told her.

Rob gifted him with an angelic smile, and a look of unguarded emotion passed between them.

Cradling the pup in her arms like a baby, Rob took Smooches to bed with her that night. She gently stroked the top of his rounded head and gazed into his dark doleful eyes.

Patting Smooches relaxed her. His silky fur reminded her of the satin blanket she'd carried around as a child; his miniature size conspired with the woebegone expression in his dark eyes and brought her maternal instincts to the surface.

"What a wonderful gift ye are," she cooed to the pup.

Rob's thoughts traveled the short distance down the corridor to the man who'd given her Smooches. Contrary to her first impression of him, the Marquess of Inverary had a kind streak in him. Handsome and wealthy and powerful and kind, Gordon Campbell would make an excellent husband for any woman. *Except her.* Too bad he hadn't been born English. They could have lived as man and wife in England, but not in Scotland. *Never in the Highlands.*

Rob tried to picture his smiling face as he'd appeared that evening in the great hall. All she managed to conjure in her mind was the image of him lying all but naked in his bed as she'd seen him the previous evening. Rob tried but failed to banish that seductive scene from her thoughts and finally, with a sigh of surrender, savored the remembered sight.

Slurp! Slurp! Slurp!

A tiny tongue licking her face awakened Rob the next morning. Opening her eyes a crack, she peered into the pup's dark eyes. Rob reached up with one hand to caress him as a drowsy smile touched her lips.

"Good mornin', Smooches," she said in a sleep-husky voice.

The sound of giggling girls awakened Rob fully. Blythe and Bliss sat on the edge of the bed, and beside them stood her aunt.

Rob yawned and stretched, then sat up and leaned back against the headboard. "Happy New Year, Aunt Keely," she said. "Happy New Year, cousins."

"Happy New Year, Cousin Rob," chimed Blythe and Bliss.

"Happy New Year, dearest. We've brought you a breakfast tray," Lady Keely said. "You know, I do believe Smooches is small enough to be trained for a box of sand. I'll have one brought up later."

"I never considered *that*," Rob said. "I hope he hasna messed the floor."

Blythe and Bliss giggled.

"Smooches accompanied me when I greeted the dawn this morning," Lady Keely told her. "Afterwards, Jennings served him breakfast."

"Thank ye, Aunt Keely. I'm supposin' I'll need to awaken earlier from now on."

" 'Twill be unnecessary if you train him to a box."

"We'll help you train Smooches," Blythe offered.

"Can we take him out to play with us?" Bliss asked.

"Of course," Rob answered. "I'll meet ye outside later."

Blythe lifted Smooches into her arms. Followed by Bliss, she headed for the door.

"You have a visitor waiting in the study," Lady Keely said, drawing Rob's attention.

" 'Tis Uncle Henry," Blythe called over her shoulder.

"And he's brought you a gift," Bliss added, then disappeared out of the door after her sister.

Rob looked at her aunt and opened her mouth to speak, but the countess was faster.

"Lord Campbell had already left for his morning ride," Lady Keely told her.

"But how could ye have known what I was thinkin'?" Rob asked, surprised.

The countess cast her an ambiguous smile. "Being druid means knowing." At that, she quit the chamber.

Ignoring the breakfast tray, Rob leaped from the bed and dashed across the chamber. She would have taken special pains with her morning toilet, but the threat of Gordon returning while Henry and she were together spurred her into action.

Rob splashed water on her face to clear the sleep from her expression and dressed hurriedly in the emerald-green gown she'd worn the previous evening. Then she grabbed her brush and swept her ebony hair away from her face, letting the dark mane cascade down her back to her waist. When she emerged from her chamber in record time, Rob appeared delightfully disheveled as if she'd just come from a lover's tryst instead of her virgin's bed.

Wearing that endearingly easy smile of his, Henry Talbot stepped forward when she walked into the study. Rob hid Old Clootie's mark within the folds of her gown and started toward him. They met in the center of the chamber.

"Happy New Year, darling," Henry greeted her, bowing low over her right hand.

"Happy New Year, my lord." Rob gave him one of her warmest smiles. "I've missed ye."

"I missed you more," he said.

"With all of those acclaimed beauties at court?" she countered. "I canna credit that."

"I swear 'tis truth," Henry vowed. "Those alleged beauties wither when compared to your lovely face and sweet disposition."

"Thank ye for the pretty compliment," Rob said, casting him an unconsciously flirtatious smile. "Have ye chanced to meet my brother Dubh at court?"

"Aye, and he's a man I'd be proud to call my brother-in-law."

"How fares Belle?"

"Isabelle is well but concerned for you," Henry told her. "Your brother and she spend a good deal of time together. That is, when she's not serving her stepmother or stepsisters."

" 'Tis shameful the way they order Belle aboot," Rob exclaimed, angry for her friend's sake.

"Darling, I haven't traveled all the way from Hampton Court to discuss Isabelle Debrett's personal problems," Henry said. "Though I do commend your loyalty, my time here is short." He produced a small, midnight blue velvet box from inside his doublet and offered it to her. "I've brought you a New Year's gift."

Rob smiled and accepted the gift, saying, "Thank ye, my lord. Shall I open it now?"

Henry chuckled. "Would you wait if I asked?"

"I love receivin' gifts," she said, shaking her head like a young girl.

Rob opened the box and gasped at what lay inside, a magnificent broach in the shape of nesting lovebirds. The charming gold lovebirds perched on either side of a golden nest that contained four pearl eggs. The birds' eyes were gleaming rubies, as were the leaves on the diamond and gold branches in which their nest sat.

" 'Tis fit for royalty," Rob cried softly.

"Allow me, darling," Henry said, lifting the broach from her hand. As he reached to pin the broach on her bodice, his fingertips lightly brushed against her breasts.

Rob sucked in her breath at the accidental contact, and her heartbeat quickened. Flustered by his intimate touch, she stammered, "I—I d-dinna know how to thank ye."

"A kiss will do."

Rob blushed and shyly dropped her gaze to the carpet.

"I've waited forever for this," Henry said, with one hand tilting her chin up. Gently, he pressed his lips to hers.

Rob enjoyed the pleasant feeling of his mouth covering hers, but an inner voice told her that the spark needed to ignite warm fondness into blazing love was missing. Gordon Campbell's drugging kiss had spoiled her for anyone else's.

"Get yer hands off my *wife*," ordered an angry voice.

Rob leaped away from Henry and whirled around to face the door. Heart-stopping fright made her complexion pale to a sickly white.

Gordon Campbell marched across the study toward them. There was no mistaking the fury etched across his features.

"If ye ever touch my wife again," Gordon warned, "I'll kill ye."

"This will decide that," Henry shot back, fingering the hilt of his dagger. "Rob isn't your wife yet. Her heart belongs to me, and her body will follow as soon as your betrothal is annulled."

Gordon fixed his frigid gaze on Rob and said, " 'Tis time for the truth of the matter, angel. Tell him."

Rob felt the earth move dizzyingly beneath her feet as

her world crumbled around her. Her bottom lip trembled, and when she spoke, her words came out in an aching whisper. "Ye odious rogue, how could ye—"

"Tell Talbot the truth," Gordon snapped.

"I'm verra sorry," Rob said, turning to Henry. "My father married me to Gordon when we were children." Unable to bear the shocked disappointment in his expressive blue eyes, she rounded on her husband and said in an accusing voice, "Ye promised ye'd keep this a secret until the first day of spring when I was supposed to decide between ye. Ye broke yer solemn word."

"I was humorin' ye," Gordon told her, his voice colder than the bitter north wind in winter. "I never intended to annul ye."

"Would you live with a woman who loved another man?" Henry asked.

"The lass doesna ken what real love is," Gordon replied. "However unintentional, she played ye for a fool." He turned to Rob, ordering, "Pack yer bags, *wife*. We leave for Scotland within the hour."

"No," she cried.

"I'll see her a widow before I let her leave with you," Henry threatened, drawing his dagger.

"Yer a dead man, Talbot." From inside the top of his boot, Gordon pulled his weapon of last resort.

"Sheath your daggers!"

The three of them turned toward the voice. Earl Richard and Lady Keely stood just inside the study.

"Gentlemen, please do as my husband says," the countess ordered. "We allow no violent dramatics in our home."

Reluctantly, both men sheathed their daggers as the earl and his countess advanced on them. At his wife's nod of unspoken agreement, Earl Richard turned to his young brother-in-law. "Return to court until the first day of spring," he ordered. "Leave now."

Henry gave Gordon a murderous glare and started to leave.

"Henry," Rob called, stopping him. Removing the broach from her bodice, she crossed the chamber and offered it to him, saying, "I canna accept this now."

Henry smiled and, ever so gently, closed her fingers around it. " 'Tis yours, darling," he said. "Think of me when you wear it." And then he disappeared out the door.

Rob struggled against the tears welling up in her eyes. Rising anger helped her win the battle to control her aching emotion, and she rounded on her husband. At that moment, she'd suffer no qualms about making herself a widow.

"My lord, I appeal to your common sense," Lady Keely was saying to Gordon. She looped her arm through the furious Scotsman's and led him past Rob toward the door. "Traveling in winter is exceedingly dangerous. I assure you that your wife has been properly chaperoned, and nothing illicit has happened between my brother and her."

The door clicked shut behind them. Sudden silence reigned inside the study.

Rob lifted her gaze to her uncle, who stared back at her. There was no mistaking the irritation in his expression.

"Shame on you for creating such harsh feelings between those two men," Earl Richard reprimanded her. "You promised to be amenable to Inverary."

"But uncle, I—" Rob tried to defend herself.

"Remember this, niece," the earl interrupted. "Legally, I can do nothing if Campbell decides to haul your arse north." He shook his head in disgust and added,

"You're more trouble than your mother ever was." At that, the earl quit the chamber too.

Finally alone, Rob succumbed to her tears. She couldn't face anyone at the moment, most especially Gordon Campbell.

Rob headed for her favorite hiding place, the overly large chair set in front of one of the windows on the opposite side of the chamber from her uncle's desk. Anyone entering the study would believe the room empty.

She plopped down in the chair and curled her legs up under herself. Gordon never intended to grant her an annulment. There appeared to be no way out of this dilemma for her.

Studying Old Clootie's mark on her hand, Rob wondered how she would survive the remainder of her years. Living in the Highlands would certainly destroy her; those superstitious Highlanders would never accept her.

Would Gordon be more understanding if she told him the reason why she'd refused him? No, she could never reveal her shame by admitting that her own MacArthur clansmen shunned her.

All she possessed in this world were her virginity and her pride. Oh, Gordon Campbell would eventually take her virginity, but never would she willingly hand him her pride.

Rob sighed in defeat and closed her eyes. The thought of the stinging lecture that Gordon would certainly deliver at first opportunity kept her glued to that chair until she fell asleep.

Chapter 7

He ignored her for a week.

Gordon resumed the daily routine he'd followed since his arrival at Devereux House. He rode in the morning, practiced his golf game during the afternoon, and closeted himself within her uncle's study each evening. However, he did not seek out her company.

Alert to her husband's every movement, Rob felt him watching her from across the distance he'd placed between them; yet whenever she summoned the courage to steal a peek in his direction, his attention lay elsewhere. Still, shaking the uncanny feeling of being watched proved impossible.

Each morning when she dressed, Rob donned her beggar bead necklace to warn her of impending danger and her last resort in order to resist Gordon if he decided to haul her north. Her star ruby never darkened, and her last resort remained in its sheath strapped to her leg. However, her frazzled nerves had stretched to the breaking point by the end of that one week of silence.

In the end, Smooches brought them together again.

The eighth day of their cold war of silence dawned depressingly rainy and raw. Rob lingered in her chamber all morning but decided to venture downstairs during the afternoon. On impulse, she wore a pair of the fingerless gloves that Gordon had given her and hoped that would elicit a reaction from him. She was beginning to think that arguing was better than watching and being watched in return.

Sitting in one of the chairs in front of the hearth, Rob reached inside her tapestry bag for her knitting needles and the sweater she'd begun two days earlier. From behind her in the center of the hall came the sounds of Gordon practicing his golf putting. One of her aunt's crystal goblets turned on its side played the role of the hole on the green. Rob's lips twitched with the urge to laugh as she listened to her six-year-old cousin tormenting the marquess.

"You missed it," Aurora was saying.

"I know, lass."

"The ball looked like it would go in, but then swerved away," the little girl said.

" 'Tis exactly what I'm tryin' to do," Gordon told her.

"You're practicing to lose?" There was no mistaking the surprise in her cousin's voice.

"Aye, but without seemin' to do so."

"Why?"

"Because, lass, losin' to the king is good politics," Gordon explained.

"Why?"

"Because the king favors good golfers who lose to him."

"Why?"

There was no mistaking the frustration that crept into

he marquess's voice when he answered, "Because the
ing likes to win."

"Don't *you* like to win?" Aurora asked.

"Aye, but I prefer pleasin' the king."

"Why?"

"Because—"

"Aurora, stop pestering Lord Campbell," Rob heard
er aunt calling from the high table.

"Am I pestering you?" Aurora asked.

"No, lass," he answered. "But 'tis time we took a
break from all of this practicin'."

Resuming her knitting, Rob wondered what the silence
behind her meant, and then she saw the pair of black
boots planted on the floor in front of her. Slowly, she
lifted her gaze and stared into her husband's piercing
gray eyes.

"Yer wearin' the gloves I gave ye," Gordon said, as if
their week of silence had never occurred.

His casual remark caught Rob by surprise. Of all the
things she'd imagined him saying, his innocuous observa-
tion was not one of them. She glanced at her hands, as if
to verify the truth of his words, and then looked up at
him again.

"Yes, I am," she said simply.

"What are ye knittin'?" he asked.

"A sweater for Smooches," she answered.

Gordon smiled at that. Rob relaxed and returned his
smile.

In the next instant, their serenity shattered. Barking his
shrill puppy yelp, Smooches dashed full speed into the
great hall; and chasing him, Blythe and Bliss ran into the
room and shouted for someone to catch him. All three
were soaking wet and mud splattered.

"Great Bruce's ghost," Rob cried, leaping from her
chair to see what the commotion was about.

Gordon reached down as Smooches tried to scoot ▮ him and scooped the dirty pup into his arms. Witho regard for his wife's gown, he dumped the mud-cover▮ pup into her arms and said, "He's yer dog."

"We took Smooches outside," Blythe explained, "b▮ he rolled in the mud."

"Then he made us chase him all around the garden Bliss added.

"All three of them will need a bath," Lady Keely sai▮ crossing the hall toward them. Over her shoulder, s▮ called, "Jennings, have a bath set in the girls' chamb▮ and a smaller one here for Smooches. Come alon▮ daughters."

When a large stewing pot had been placed in front ▮ the hearth and filled with warmed water, Gordon rolle his sleeves up and held his hands out for the pup. "I▮ take care of this," he said. "Or ye'll both end up in th▮ pot."

Gordon placed a struggling Smooches into the pot an▮ held him steady by the scruff of his neck. Then he washe▮ the mud from the pup. When Smooches had been rinse▮ Gordon passed him to his wife.

Rob toweled Smooches briskly and folded him like a▮ infant within a dry linen. When the pup sneezed, sh▮ turned a worried gaze on her husband and asked, "D'y▮ think he's warm enough? I dinna want him to catch chill."

"Then come with me," Gordon said, and started f▮ the hall's entrance.

With Smooches cradled in her arms, Rob followe▮ Gordon out of the hall and up the stairs. She hesitated fo a moment when he opened his chamber door and walke inside.

"I've somethin' here that will chase the chill out ▮ Smooches," Gordon called.

Rob glanced at her beggar bead necklace; the star ruby remained placid. She stepped five paces inside the room and saw her husband rummaging through his belongings. A smile of relief lit her whole expression when he turned around and showed her the black and green woolen Campbell plaid.

Gordon held the plaid open, and when Rob passed him Smooches, wrapped the pup in it. "Good boy," he said, stroking the underside of the pup's chin.

Rob reached for Smooches, but in the movement, their hands touched. She looked up at him quickly. The intensity in his gray gaze mesmerized her, held her captive.

Inching closer, so close only their garments and the pup separated them, Gordon lowered his head and pressed his lips to hers in a lingering kiss. And Rob responded. She closed her eyes and returned his kiss in kind, savoring the incredible sensation of his warm mouth on hers.

In the end, Smooches forced them to part. Crushed between their bodies, the pup struggled wildly in her arms.

Rob stepped back a pace. Much to her embarrassment, she could feel the heated blush rising on her cheeks.

With tender emotion gleaming at her from his disarming gaze, Gordon pressed the palm of his right hand against her flaming cheek. Then he showed her his hand and teased, "Is it burnt?"

Mortified, Rob reddened to a vibrant scarlet.

"I'm verra sorry for losin' control of my temper that day in the study," Gordon apologized, surprising her. " 'Twas wrong of me to break my solemn word. Can ye forgive me, angel?"

"I forgive ye," Rob said, a smile flirting with her lips. "Do ye realize ye just admitted to bein' wrong aboot somethin'?"

Gordon grinned. "Ye bring out the verra best in me, lass."

"I was wrong too," Rob told him. "My parents instilled honor in me, and I'd never let another man kiss me whilst I was forsworn to ye. Henry never kissed me before that day in the study."

Gordon gave her a wry smile. "I knew that already."

His reply puzzled her. "But how could ye have known?" she asked.

"A man can always tell when he's given his lady her verra first kiss," Gordon told her.

Rob moaned inwardly. She must be an incompetent kisser, and kissing wasn't a thing that a virtuous maiden could practice.

"But how can the man tell?" she forced herself to ask.

"Well, now, every circumstance is different," he answered. "Ye asked me what ye'd done with yer hands. Remember?"

Rob smiled with relief. Perhaps she wasn't such an incompetent kisser after all.

"Shall we go downstairs and sit with Smooches in front of the hearth?" Gordon suggested. When she nodded, he added, "Perhaps ye'd care to kill a few hours' with a game of chess."

"Aye, my lord. I'd like that verra much . . ."

Gordon and Rob resumed the daily routine they'd followed the previous month. She accompanied him on his morning rides, practiced the skill of golfing during the afternoon, and played chess with him each evening. Neither mentioned Henry Talbot nor the fact that on the first day of spring Gordon expected her to ride north with him to Scotland.

The winter cooled as Gordon and Rob warmed to each other. With frosted trees and sparkling icicles, January turned bitterly cold. Angry flocks of starlings gathered in the trees within the earl's garden and complained loudly about the dearth of berries. Ever so gradually, those melancholy days lengthened and warmed into February with its receding blanket of snow. Candlemas came and went, as did the full storm moon.

The tenth day of February dawned surprisingly springlike and teased the world of men. At mid morning, Gordon and Rob left Devereux House. The earl's ostler had their horses waiting for them in the courtyard.

Rob flicked a sidelong glance at her husband as they walked toward their mounts. Dressed completely in black, Gordon appeared as Old Clootie would *wish* to look in order to seduce more souls than he already did. If the devil possessed her husband's devastatingly good looks, parades of women would surely follow him through the gates of hell.

" 'Tis a fair enough day, and I've a mind to see the queen's menagerie before goin' home," Gordon said as he lifted her into her saddle. "Let's ride to London."

Rob nodded in agreement, but as they started down the private lane that led to the thoroughfare, disturbing thoughts leaped into her mind. Another six weeks would bring the first day of spring, and then she'd be forced to ride north and to begin living unhappily ever after.

"Is somethin' troublin' ye?" Gordon asked, drawing her attention.

Rob pasted a bright smile onto her face. "No, my lord. I'm merely pensive today."

"Pensive, are ye?" he teased her. " 'Tis comfortin' to know I've married a woman with thoughts of her own."

"Are ye ridiculin' me?" she asked.

"Och, lass. Yer accusation wounds me."

"I'm askin', not accusin'."

Gordon grinned at her. "In that case, angel, my answer is no."

Rob nodded but remained unconvinced. She didn't believe for a moment that her husband appreciated women who thought for themselves.

They passed Leicester and Durham houses and then veered to the right at Charing Cross. When they entered London proper, the crowds grew increasingly larger and forced them to pick their way carefully down the narrow, twisting streets.

Reaching St. Paul's Cathedral, Gordon and Rob turned right onto the Old Change, and at the end of that street, they went left onto Thames Street. The palace of White Tower loomed before them at the end of Thames Street.

They rode through the Middle Tower, the castle's main entrance, and halted their horses. When two scarlet-clad yeomen rushed forward to attend their mounts, Gordon tossed each man a coin for his trouble.

Suddenly, an unearthly growl rent the air behind them, and Rob reacted instinctively. She threw herself into her husband's arms and cried, " 'Tis frightenin'."

"I'll protect ye, hinny," Gordon said, his arms encircling her. " 'Tis perfectly safe. The lions live inside a pit."

Setting her back a pace, Gordon took her by the hand and led her toward the Lion Tower where the menagerie was kept. "Yer uncle told me the menagerie began when the King of France gifted Henry III with an elephant," he said conversationally.

"What's that?" Rob asked.

Gordon had never actually seen an elephant, but he wasn't about to admit his ignorance to his young wife. "Why, an elephant is the largest of God's creatures and has a long nose called a trunk."

The semicircular bastion just outside the Middle Tower was known as the Lion Tower. Cages, pits, and trapdoors filled the area.

Here the crowd of spectators swelled to a crush of humanity. Apprehensive about stepping into that throng of strangers, Rob clutched her husband's hand and mouthed a silent prayer of thanks that she'd worn her gloves that day.

For his part, Gordon smiled down at her and mentally rubbed his hands together. As that tavern wench at the Royal Rooster had predicted, his wife would be ripe for a parcel of protection after this. Perhaps, crossing the border into Scotland before making her his wife in the truest sense would be unnecessary.

"Dinna be scared," he whispered in her ear as they wended their way through the milling crowds.

Rob gaped in astonishment at the elephant and then the Norwegian bear, but the lions' roars attracted her attention the most. Reaching the lions' pit, Gordon paved a way for them through the crowd of commoners who parted for the nobleman and his lady, and then closed in behind them again.

"Great Bruce's ghost," Rob exclaimed softly, catching her first glimpse of the iron bars across the top of the pit and hearing the loud roars from its shadowy depth.

Closer and closer, Rob inched forward in an effort to see the ferocious beasts below. Suddenly, unexpectedly, she felt two hands on her back giving her a tremendous shove. At the same moment, a foot kicked her legs out from under her. Caught off balance, Rob slid legs-first toward the pit. One of her legs dangled through the pit's iron bars.

"Help!" she cried, desperately reaching for her husband.

Gordon yanked her to safety just as one of the lions leaped for her dangling leg. Both landed on the ground as the shocked spectators surrounded them.

"Are ye injured?" Gordon asked.

Too frightened to speak, Rob shook her head and trembled like a woman afflicted with palsy. She pressed one hand to her breast in an effort to calm her pounding heart and bent her head to catch her breath.

And that was when she saw it. The star ruby had darkened redder than pigeon's blood.

"I think we've seen enough," Gordon said, standing. He helped her rise, put his arm around her shoulder, and drew her close against his body. "God's balls, lass. What happened back there?" he asked, leading her toward the Middle Tower. "Did yer foot slip?"

"Someone pushed me," Rob answered in a quavering voice.

Gordon stopped short and looked at her. "I canna credit that, hinny."

"I tell you, I felt two hands pushing me," she insisted, her voice rising in direct proportion to her extreme agitation. His disbelief was adding insult to near-fatal injury.

"Ye must be mistaken," Gordon said. "The crowd merely jostled ye."

"I know what I felt," Rob cried, becoming irritated. She'd nearly been devoured by a lion, and her husband was brushing her explanations aside as nonsense. "Someone tried to kill me. Yer my husband; find out who it is."

"Men dinna kill without motivation." Gordon tried to reason with her as they mounted their horses. "Who in God's great universe would gain by yer untimely death?"

"If ye are na up to the task of protectin' me, then ye are na up to bein' my husband," Rob said tartly. "Henry would find and punish the culprit."

"Henry—Henry—Henry!" Gordon roared as ferociously as the lions. "I am sick unto death of Henry. I'm surprised Ludlow canna walk across water."

"Well, he'd be more apt to do that than ye," Rob shot back.

Gordon snapped his head around and stared coldly at her. "Keep yer lips buttoned," he warned, "or I'll take ye across my knee and give ye the spankin' ye deserve."

Instinctively, Rob reacted as her own mother did whenever her father behaved outrageously pigheadedly. She gave him a frosty glare and then lifted her upturned nose into the air in a defiant gesture of dismissal.

Gordon ignored her silent tantrum.

During the long ride through London to the Strand, Rob seethed in silence. She knew what she'd felt; someone had purposefully pushed her toward the lions' pit. But, who could possibly want her dead? Did the culprit harbor a grudge against her family? Rob couldn't credit that; no one in England knew them. That left her uncle's enemies. But, why would this assassin choose to murder her? She was merely the earl's niece.

Rob flicked a glance at her lucky beggar beads. The farther they rode from the White Tower, the lighter the star ruby faded into its original color. At one point Rob peeked at Gordon, who was watching her. "And I amna checkin' my titties," she told him.

Gordon's expression was a mask of irritation. He turned his attention to the road again and said, "If ye truly think someone tried to kill ye, then I believe ye. We'll be leavin' for Argyll this afternoon."

"I willna be accompanyin' ye anywhere, my lord," Rob told him. "I willna debate this further."

"Aye, ye'll be safe with my father at Inverary Castle," Gordon went on, as if she hadn't spoken.

Rob ignored him, but fumed in aggravated silence. The Marquess of Inverary was an insufferable, pigheaded lout, and those were his *good* qualities. If he thought to force her to ride north before the first day of spring, then he'd better reconsider his position.

"Pack yer bags, angel," Gordon ordered as they rode

down the private lane that led to Devereux House's front courtyard. "We're leavin' for Scotland within the hour."

"Are ye deaf? I just told ye—" Rob broke off when she spied the two men exiting Devereux House. Spurring her horse forward, she shouted, "Dubh!"

Rob reined her horse to an abrupt halt when she reached her brother and his companion. Before anyone could help her dismount, she leaped from her saddle and threw herself into her brother's arms. "Oh, Dubh. I'm so happy to see ye," she cried, hugging him as if she'd never let him go.

"How are ye, sister?" Dubh asked.

"Fine, now that yer here to protect me," Rob answered, gazing into his dark eyes. She'd always felt safer with her oldest brother around because he resembled their father.

"Protect ye from what?" Dubh asked with an amused smile. "Yer husband?"

"Yer sister swears that someone tried to push her into the lions' pit at the White Tower," Gordon told him. "Did ye ever hear of anythin' so ridiculous?"

"There's nothin' ridiculous aboot bein' a lion's dinner," Rob replied, turning within the circle of her brother's arms to look at him. She flicked a glance at the slight, blond man and asked, "Who's yer friend, Dubh? Ye havena introduced us."

"Meet Mungo MacKinnon, the Earl of Skye's grandson," her brother said. "Mungo is yer husband's friend and also related to Cousin Glenda."

"Mungo, meet Rob MacArthur," Gordon finished the introduction. "My wife, the Marchioness of Inverary."

"I'm verra pleased to make yer acquaintance," Mungo said with a smile, bowing low over her hand.

Out of politeness, Rob returned the blond man's smile, but decided in that very instant that she didn't like him.

She recognized only too well the poorly masked hatred gleaming at her from his pale blue eyes. Neither her brother nor her husband seemed aware of the man's sinister attitude toward her, but Rob had seen enough hatred cast in her direction to recognize it when she saw it.

Why did this stranger whom she'd never met harbor a hatred for her? Rob wondered. Her riding gloves covered Old Clootie's mark, so that could not be his reason.

"Well, now, we're all together," Mungo said, turning to her brother. "Perhaps we can make plans for returnin' to Scotland."

Watching his eyes, Rob sucked in her breath at the intense hatred leaping at her brother from the blond man. That Dubh failed to recognize it was understandable. As the earl's heir and mirror image, her brother had always been the clan's beloved prince. No man in clan MacArthur had ever looked at him with evil intent.

"I wouldna want to be caught ridin' north if this weather changes," Dubh was saying. "Waiting another week or two would give me peace of mind, especially since my sister will be travelin' with us. What do ye think, Gordy?"

Rob watched Mungo turn to Gordon and saw the intense hatred fade from the blond man's gaze. Why did MacKinnon harbor such a dislike for the MacArthurs whom he had never met? she wondered. Why, they even shared a cousin with him.

"I carry missives for the king and shouldna delay deliverin' them," Mungo told Rob's husband.

"Safety lies across the border," Gordon said, flicking a glance at her. "Since my wife fears for her life, we'll be ridin' north this afternoon."

"I amna steppin' a foot outside Devereux House until the first day of spring," Rob insisted, then turned her back and started walking toward the house.

"Get back here," Gordon called.

Rob quickened her pace and then broke into a run when she heard her brother's deep rumble of laughter and her husband's muttered curse. Slamming the door shut behind her, she leaned back against it and sighed in defeat. Rob knew she had no way to escape the inevitable if her husband insisted they leave England.

And then an idea came to her, bringing the hint of a smile to her lips. She'd sit in her favorite hiding place inside her uncle's study until the day aged into evening. No sane person began such a long journey at night. She'd be safe until the morning, at least.

Praying her uncle's study was empty, Rob hurried across the foyer and closed its door behind her. She crossed the study to her chair, but paused to peek out the window first. Gordon, Dubh, and Mungo were walking toward the Dowager House. Could her husband have changed his mind?

Unwilling to risk being forced north, Rob plopped down in the chair and curled her legs up under herself. If her husband came searching for her now, he would believe the study was deserted.

Rob leaned her head back against the chair and pondered her untenable predicament. Tears welled up in her eyes as she realized she was beginning to care for her arrogant husband.

Her feelings defied logic. She could never live happily with him in the Highlands. Old Clootie's mark prevented that. If she rode north with him, she'd be doomed forever to play the outcast.

And then her aunt's probing questions slammed into her consciousness. *Did she want to remain in England because she loved Henry? Or did she love Henry because she wanted to remain in England?*

Now Rob knew the answer. She loved Gordon Campbell but could never be his wife.

An imperfect world required that she compromise her dreams of love and acceptance. She would take the acceptance and learn to love Henry Talbot.

A sudden swell of painful guilt surged through her. Henry Talbot deserved more than a wife who would learn to love him. Although, there were worse things in life than beginning a marriage without earth-moving love. Her own parents' marriage had been arranged, but that didn't count since her father and her mother had fallen madly in love at first sight of each other. Or so her mother said.

Thinking wearied Rob and gave her a dull headache. With a sigh, she closed her eyes and tried to wipe the emotional clutter from her mind.

That task proved difficult. A long hour passed before she drifted into a restless doze.

The low sounds of men's voices brought Rob slowly back to the reality of her uncle's study, but lethargy kept her from moving. She opened her eyes and stared in a drowsy daze outside the window at the rapidly advancing dusk. When she heard her uncle's voice, Rob realized she hadn't been dreaming. The talking men were inside the study with her.

"Welcome to Devereux House, Lord Burghley," Earl Richard greeted his visitors. "And welcome to you, Walsingham."

Those particular names jerked Rob into full alertness. Two of Queen Elizabeth's most important counselors were conferring with her uncle. Lord Burghley was the queen's most trusted minister, and Walsingham her secretary of state specializing in foreign affairs.

Rob felt like a fool to be caught napping in her hiding chair. Should she stand up now and make her presence known or sit there until they left and pretend she'd never heard their conversation?

"Henry, I told you to remain at court until the first day of spring," her uncle was saying.

Rob cursed her bad luck when she heard that remark. Her husband already suffered a mood foul enough to force her to ride north. If he spied Henry, Gordon wouldn't even give her the chance to pack her belongings. Indecision about what to do kept Rob rooted to the chair.

"As my father's representative, I've been traveling with Lords Burghley and Walsingham," Henry told her uncle.

"Traveling at this season of the year can be difficult," Earl Richard remarked. "So, I assume 'tis a matter of importance."

"We are en route from Fotheringhay Castle to Richmond Palace," Burghley replied.

"We decided to stop here on our way because you'd voiced such a negative opinion concerning possible actions against Mary Stuart," Walsingham added.

At that comment, Rob froze in her seat. Every nerve in her body tingled in a riot of expectation about what she was going to overhear. All thoughts of making her presence known vanished from her mind.

"And what have you decided?" her uncle asked.

Rob heard one of the men clear his throat as though in preparation for revealing a matter of utmost importance.

"A panel of judges found Mary Stuart guilty of treason against the Crown," Lord Burghley announced.

Rob covered her mouth with both of her hands in order to keep from crying out. The punishment for treason was death. The English queen and her minions could not possibly be considering executing a queen, a woman whom God had anointed. That would be regicide.

"*Bloody Christ!* Was this an impartial panel of judges?"

Earl Richard exploded, his outrage apparent. "How convenient for you, Walsingham. Did you falsify evidence against her as you've falsified other various reports to Elizabeth in order to get your own way?"

"Now, Richard—" Lord Burghley began.

"Do *not* 'now Richard' me, Cecil," her uncle snapped at his illustrious mentor. "Walsingham has been angling to catch Mary Stuart in a trap for years. Tell me, how can you possibly punish a queen found guilty of treason? Why, that pathetic woman has already been imprisoned for twenty years."

"What will be done has been done," Walsingham announced, his voice harsh.

Rob held her breath in anticipation. When he spoke, Lord Burghley nearly felled her with his shocking words.

"Mary Stuart was beheaded at Fotheringhay Castle two days ago," Burghley informed her uncle. "We three witnessed the execution."

"*You idiots!* Nothing now stands between England and Spain," Uncle Richard exploded. "Mark my words, gentlemen. The Spanish Don will be threatening our shores before six months have passed."

"We'll cross that bridge when we come to it," Walsingham said. "Right now, 'tis imperative we keep Mary's death a secret until Elizabeth sends official condolences to James."

Rob heard a loud defeated sigh, presumably her uncle's, and then he asked, "How did it go at Fotheringhay?"

"Mary Stuart redeemed herself in death by humiliating us with her dignity," Burghley answered, his tone of voice quietly respectful. "Regicide is bad business, though."

Rob was unable to contain her raging fury another

moment. She shot to her feet and rounded on the men, surprising them with her presence.

"Ye wretched Sassenach swine! How dare ye murder my queen," Rob cried. "We Highlanders will burn this England into a wasteland. Great Bruce's ghost, we'll—"

"Shut up," Uncle Richard snapped.

Accustomed to obeying orders, Rob abruptly clamped her lips together. The fires of unreasoning fury leaped at the men from her gaze.

"Who is this eavesdropper?" Walsingham demanded.

"His niece from Scotland," Henry told him.

The queen's secretary of state turned to Rob's uncle and said, "Tell her to pack her bags. We'll keep her in the Tower until Elizabeth deems the time is ripe for announcing Mary's death to the world."

"I beg your pardon?" the earl said, his disbelief apparent in his voice.

"Francis, 'tis unnecessary," Lord Burghley said, after flicking a measuring glance at his former protégé. "If Richard can guarantee . . ."

"You cannot lock Rob in the Tower," Henry added his own opinion. " 'Twould be unnecessarily cruel."

Ignoring their protests, Walsingham started across the study toward her, saying, "I promise you won't be harmed in any way."

In a flash of movement, Rob reached down and pulled her last resort from its sheath strapped to her leg. She pointed the deadly little dagger in the general vicinity of the secretary of state's throat.

Walsingham stopped short.

"I'm skilled with this blade and unafraid to use it on a Sassenach swine like yerself," Rob threatened him. "In fact, I eagerly await yer takin' another step forward."

"Rob, what do you think you're doing?" Henry exclaimed. "No one draws a dagger on the queen's man."

"I'm verra sorry, Henry," she said, her voice deceptively calm and pleasant, the dagger fortifying her with courage. " 'Twould seem I'm a Highlander first and a lady second." She flicked a glance at her uncle. Though he did appear ready to explode, she recognized the grudging respect gleaming at her from his eyes.

"Basildon, control your niece or our plans will go awry," Walsingham ordered her uncle.

"Richard, her visiting the Tower for a few weeks would give me infinite peace of mind," Burghley said. "I can guarantee her safety."

Rob stared at her uncle who, in turn, was staring at her. He gave her an encouraging smile when their gazes met. What did that mean? she wondered. Was he about to hand her over to the queen's men?

"If you want to send my sister's daughter to the Tower," Richard announced, "you'll need to procure an arrest warrant."

"Very well, but the queen will hear of this," Walsingham replied. "I trust you can keep the chit quiet until the morning."

"Of course."

Without another word, the secretary of state marched toward the door. "I'll await you in the courtyard," he said to the prime minister, and then disappeared out the door.

" 'Tis ill done of you," Burghley chided her uncle.

The earl shrugged. "My sister entrusted her daughter into my care."

"I understand," Burghley replied. "I only hope that Elizabeth will understand too. Are you coming, Talbot?"

"No, I'm spending the night at Talbot House," Henry answered. "I'll return to Richmond in the morning."

"As you wish." At that, Burghley followed the secretary of state out.

With her blade still drawn, Rob stood motionless. She felt uncertain of what to do or say.

The earl walked to one of the windows behind his desk and watched the queen's men cross the lawns to the quay. Finally, after long uncomfortable silent moments, he turned around and said, "Sheath your dagger, niece. Come over here and sit down."

"You never told me you wore a dagger strapped—" Henry began to scold her.

"Henry, run next door to the Dowager House," Richard interrupted him. "Fetch my nephew and the marquess, but tell them their companion is to be told nothing."

Henry nodded and left the study.

A few minutes later, the two Scotsmen marched into the study with Henry. Behind them walked Lady Keely.

"What's this aboot?" Dubh asked, crossing the chamber toward his sister.

"And what's Talbot doin' here before the first day of spring?" Gordon asked, one step behind Dubh.

"Thank God, yer here," Rob cried, leaping out of her chair and running across the study toward them. Ignoring her brother, she flew into her husband's arms.

Surprised, Gordon gathered her into the protective circle of his embrace. He felt her trembling and planted a kiss on the top of her head, then looked expectantly at the earl for an explanation.

"What I am about to tell you must remain a secret," the earl began. "Not even your traveling companion can be told. If word of this leaks out, I will be arrested and thrown into the Tower. Can I depend upon your silence?"

"I swear to it," Gordon vowed.

"Me too," Dubh said.

Richard nodded. "Lords Burghley and Walsingham just informed me of Mary Stuart's execution, but—"

"They've murdered our queen?" Dubh exclaimed. "How dare—"

"Let yer uncle speak," Gordon interrupted him.

"As I was about to say," Richard continued, "Rob was eavesdropping and—"

"I *wasna* eaves—"

Nonchalantly, Gordon reached up and covered her mouth with his hand. Then he grinned at the earl and gestured at him to continue.

"Thank you, Inverary," Richard said dryly, the ghost of a smile flirting with his lips. "Rob failed to make her presence known to us. Walsingham is determined to send her to the Tower until Elizabeth sends official condolences to James."

Gordon nodded in understanding. "We'll take to the heather within the hour."

"Take to the heather?" Lady Keely echoed, apparently unfamiliar with the phrase.

Dubh smiled at her. "Escape to freedom."

"I'd rather brave the Tower than return to Scotland," Rob announced, lifting her chin a notch.

"No one asked ye what ye preferred, angel," Gordon said.

"Rob, nothin' will bring our queen back from the dead," Dubh reasoned with her. "Placin' yerself in danger can only complicate matters."

"Verra well, I'll keep the silence," she agreed. "I wouldna want to be the cause of Uncle Richard bein' locked away."

"Ye willna be thrown into the Tower when the queen's men discover Rob missin'?" Dubh asked his uncle.

"I'll tell them she escaped with you in the night," the earl answered. "Burghley will not doubt me, and Walsingham doesn't have the courage to challenge Elizabeth's most trusted advisor."

Gordon turned to the countess and asked, "My lady, will ye help Rob pack a few necessities? Whatever she leaves behind can be sent to Scotland later."

Lady Keely nodded. "I think 'tis best Rob dress as a boy until you're safely away from London." She turned to her brother, asking, "Do you still have any older clothing at Talbot House? I mean, from when you were a boy."

"I'll scrounge something up," Henry answered, and headed for the door.

An hour later, Rob arrived at the stables with her uncle and her aunt. Dressed completely in black, she looked like a scrawny stableboy in raggedy garb much too big for her. Matching her breeches, shirt, jerkin, and cloak, a black woolen cap hid her ebony mane. A leather satchel served as a carrier for Smooches and had been strapped to her chest beneath the cloak. Her uncle carried a second satchel with two changes of boy's clothing as well as a few other necessities.

Gordon, Dubh, Mungo, and Henry stood silently in the stableyard. Four horses had already been saddled and only awaited her appearance.

Gordon looked up at the dark, moonless night and said, " 'Tis a Highlander's night, created for raidin' and takin' to the heather. Are ye ready to ride, angel?"

Rob nodded at him, but his apparent eagerness irritated her. How like a Highlander to enjoy dangerous escapades and mad flights to freedom. She turned to her uncle and her aunt and said, "Thank ye for the best year of my life. I hope the girls willna be hurt or angry that I didna say farewell to them."

"I'll make certain they understand," Lady Keely answered her.

The earl flicked a meaningful glance at Gordon and then said to her, "Devereux House is always open to you."

Rob hugged and kissed them, and then turned to Henry. "My lord, I'm verra sorry—"

"You've done nothing for which you should apologize," Henry interrupted her, pressing a finger across her lips. He planted a chaste kiss on her cheek and said, "Be happy, darling."

Rob felt like weeping. In an aching whisper she said, "Thank ye for yer understandin', my lord."

Rob turned to her husband to tell him she was ready, but stepped back when she caught the foul smell emanating from her brother and him. Gordon reached out and placed an object in each of her two pockets, but she couldn't see what it was.

" 'Tis nasty like swill," Rob cried, as Smooches began sneezing. "What is it?"

"Horseshit."

"Are ye cursin' me already?" she asked, making the others chuckle. "We didna even leave yet."

"I wasna cursin' ye," Gordon answered, wearing a mischievous grin. "Horseshit in our pockets will discourage the curious we pass."

" 'Tis revoltin', and I dinna want my pockets fouled," Rob said. " 'Twill make Smooches and me sick."

"Sorry, angel." Gordon led her toward her horse and helped her into the saddle. "I promise we'll clean ourselves once we're well away from London."

Dubh and Mungo mounted their horses. As Gordon reached for his reins, Henry Talbot stopped him.

"Inverary, I want five words with you."

Gordon turned around and nodded. He walked over to the other man. "Well?"

"Take good care of her," Henry said, his voice low.

Gordon looked the English marquess straight in the eye and told him, "Rob willna be returnin' to England."

"I know."

Gordon offered the other man his hand in friendship and assured him, "I swear I'll be guardin' her with my life."

"See that you do," Henry replied, shaking his hand. "Or you'll answer to me."

Gordon turned away and then mounted his own horse. The four young Highlanders rode out of the stableyard and started down the lane that led to the Strand.

Rob glanced over her shoulder once to catch a last glimpse of Devereux House and said a silent farewell to her dream of acceptance. She knew she'd never return to England; her husband would never permit it.

Summoning every ounce of her Highlander's fierceness of spirit, Rob decided to meet her destiny bravely and challenge it at every opportunity. She fixed her gaze on the road ahead and schooled her features into a grim look of determination.

Never would she surrender to the inevitable and meekly accept a life of lonely misery.

Never would she permit cruel destiny to defeat her and destroy her spirit.

Chapter 8

Never had he been more miserable in his life. Damn, but his wife was a terrible pain in the arse, Gordon thought. How would he keep his sanity during the next two weeks on their journey across the long length of England and Scotland from London to Argyll? For that matter, how would he survive the next forty years married to her?

Murder leaped into his mind, but Gordon dismissed that outrageous idea out of hand. Gone were the good old days when a nobleman could dispatch a nagging wife and never answer for the deed in a court of law.

Reaching the end of the Strand, they'd veered to the left at Charing Cross and started down Oxford Street. The more distance they put between Devereux House and themselves, the safer his wife apparently felt. Her complaints grew in direct proportion to the miles they placed between her and the queen's men.

She was cold. She was tired. She was hungry—in spite of the nausea that the smell of the horse droppings elicited in her.

Did she think that he actually *enjoyed* smelling like shit?

Gordon flicked a sidelong glance at her, the hint of a smile flirting with the corners of his lips. Rob appeared pink cheeked, sultry eyed, and expectant rather than cold, tired, and hungry. Hardship became her.

Aye, her nagging was a royal pain in the arse, but he was unable to envision Lavinia Kerr enduring what Rob was. Perhaps the difference between the two women lay in the fact that Rob was a Highlander and Lavinia a Lowlander. Whatever the reason, his wife was stouthearted enough to be his marchioness and, eventually, the Duchess of Argyll.

"Smooches and I need to stop," Rob announced suddenly, her voice sounding overly loud in the night.

"No," Gordon and Dubh said simultaneously.

" 'Tis an emergency."

"No."

The four of them rode on seemingly endlessly, trying to put as much distance as they could between Devereux House and themselves by daybreak. They passed through the villages of Harrow, Cookham, Marlow, and Henley.

"Tell me, angel," Gordon said, making conversation in order to keep his wife's thoughts off her physical discomfort. "How did Basildon keep Walsingham and Burghley from takin' ye away?"

"Uncle Richard insisted Walsingham needed an arrest warrant, and Lord Burghley reluctantly sided with him," Rob answered. "Besides, I—" She broke off, embarrassed to reveal her own unladylike behavior.

"Besides what?"

Rob felt the blush rising on her cheeks. "I kept Walsingham at bay with my last resort," she admitted.

Both Gordon and Dubh burst out laughing.

"Ye drew yer dagger on Queen Elizabeth's secretary of

state?" Mungo exclaimed, his voice mirroring his appalled surprise.

"I said it before, bright angel, and I'll say it again," Gordon spoke up before she could reply to his friend. "Yer lips say English lady, but yer habits positively scream Highlander."

"But why did ye pull yer dagger on him?" Mungo asked.

Rob cleared her throat and tried to think of a plausible reason other than the truth. She'd promised her uncle she'd keep the secret of Mary Stuart's execution and intended to honor her solemn word.

"I didna care for the way the man looked at me," Rob lied unconvincingly. " 'Twas highly insultin'."

She peered at her husband's friend. The grim set to his jaw told her that he didn't believe a word she'd spoken. Even more, he appeared irritated at being left out of what the three of them obviously knew.

"We'll stop for a couple of hours' rest once we reach Oxford," Gordon said, changing the subject. "What d'ye think, Dubh?"

"Aye, the horses need feedin' and waterin'," her brother replied. "Thirty miles from Devereux House is safe enough to grab a couple of hours' sleep."

Orange light streaked the eastern horizon as they rode through the Chiltern Hills and into the heavily wooded county of Oxfordshire. Rob's mood brightened at her first sight of Oxford, a market town that offered plenty of accommodations for weary pilgrims. In the distance beyond the town rose the forbidding walls of Oxford Castle, but the town itself was invitingly picturesque with its partly stone, partly timber-framed houses.

"Let's stop at that inn over there," Rob suggested.

"Och, lass. We havena the time to spare," Gordon

replied, leading them across a stone bridge over the Thames River.

Rob grimaced and sighed, but said nothing. She'd already realized that her complaints fell on deaf ears.

On the opposite side of the Thames River stood the royal forest of Wynchwood, better known as Shotover Wood. Here they sought refuge from the possibility of prying eyes, and finally halted their horses in a small clearing beside a gentle stream.

"I'll feed the horses," Dubh said as they dismounted.

"I'll help ye," Mungo offered.

Gordon lifted Rob out of the saddle and set her on her feet. Her legs wobbled from the long hours of riding.

"We'll find a place for Smooches and ye to take care of yer private needs," he said, removing the pieces of dung from her pockets and tossing them away.

"Dinna worry aboot Smooches," Rob informed him, an impish smile lighting her weary expression. "He satisfied his needs about ten miles back."

"The pup soiled the satchel?"

"No." Rob lifted Smooches out of his nest and removed his woolen wrapper, a Campbell plaid. Beneath that, the pup wore the sweater she'd knitted for him and a baby's nappy. Divested of his confining garments, Smooches scampered around wildly like a man released from the darkest dungeon.

Gordon's smile told Rob that he appreciated her ingenuity. "I'll put another nappy on him before we leave," she said as her husband took her arm and led her away from the clearing. " 'Tisna necessary to accompany me."

"A woman alone is always in danger," he replied.

"Well, if ye promise not to peek."

Gordon flashed her a boyishly wicked smile and asked, "What's a bit of bared arse between husband and wife?"

Rob refused to blush at his vulgarity. No, that would

only encourage him. Instead, she gave him a sweet smile and countered, "Have I told ye yet today how ex-ceedin'ly crass ye are?"

"No, angel, but thank ye for noticin' my finer points of character," Gordon said dryly. Then added, "Dinna ye realize that men have 'needs' too?"

Rob did blush then. She hadn't thought of that.

"Take that oak tree over there," Gordon ordered. "I'll use this one over here. Scream if ye need me."

Rob emerged from behind the oak a few minutes later. She blushed when she saw Gordon waiting for her.

"Feelin' better?" he asked.

"Much."

When they returned to the clearing, Rob knelt beside the stream and rinsed her face and hands in its frigid water. "I wish I had a hot bath," she murmured wistfully.

"I promise ye'll sleep in a bed tonight," Gordon said, standing beside her. "Let's eat now and then catch a nap."

Rob sat on the ground between her husband and her brother, opposite Mungo MacKinnon. The four of them shared a cold meal of cheese, bread, and ham slices that Lady Keely had prepared for them. They passed one flask of wine between them.

"Tell us what happened at the royal menagerie," Dubh said to her.

"Someone purposefully pushed me toward the lions' pit," Rob told him. "I know Gordon doesna believe me, but *he* never felt the hands on his back. My footin' was secure, I didna slip."

"What a coincidence that both of us should experience a near-fatal accident within hours of each other," her brother remarked. "Just the other day at Richmond, an arrow almost felled me. Though Mungo and I searched high and low for the culprit, we couldna find him."

"Two accidents dinna seem a coincidence to me. Perhaps someone harbors a grudge against yer family," Mungo speculated. "Since he failed to dispatch ye, the villain aimed for yer sister."

"Do ye really think so?" Rob asked, inching closer to her husband.

"I dinna believe the two events are connected," Gordon said. "What d'ye think, Dubh?"

"I agree with ye," her brother replied. "Who would want to harm Rob? She's so sweet."

Rob smiled at her favorite brother, who'd always championed her causes. She reached for Smooches in order to feed him a slice of ham, but in the movement, her cloak opened. Her star ruby had darkened redder than pigeon's blood.

Rob looked at her husband and asked in alarm, "Do ye think we're in danger?"

Gordon snapped his brows together. "Why do ye ask such a question?"

"My ruby—"

" 'Tis merely a stone," he interrupted. "Besides, yer perfectly safe with me around to protect ye."

"Pass the wine, lass," Mungo said.

With her husband on one side and her brother on the other, Rob felt so comfortably safe that she forgot about her devil's flower and its effect on strangers. She offered Mungo the wine flask but then froze when she saw his gaze riveted on Old Clootie's mark.

Great Bruce's ghost, she should have switched Smooches to her left arm and then passed the flask with her right hand. She wasn't usually this careless. Perhaps exhaustion had impaired her reflexes.

Mungo MacKinnon apparently possessed the presence of mind to keep from shrinking back while her husband sat beside her. He lifted the flask from her hand without actually touching her and then made a protective sign of the cross.

And so it begins, Rob thought with a sinking feeling in the pit of her stomach.

They'd only traveled thirty miles, and already this man had crossed himself. The closer they got to Scotland, the greater the number of people who'd be crossing themselves at the sight of her deformity.

Rob longed to hide her hand inside her cloak, but Smooches prevented her from doing that. Instead, she dropped her gaze to her lap and prayed that the expression of horrified surprise would fade from the blond man's eyes.

"Why did ye do that?" she heard her husband ask his friend.

"Do what?"

"Ye just blessed yerself," Gordon told him.

Rob cast a sidelong glance at her brother who appeared ready to pounce on the blond man. Her wonderful brother had always championed her cause and defended her against the ignorance of others. She only hoped there wouldn't be trouble while the queen's men were chasing them.

"I—I blessed myself for luck," Mungo told them. "We're only thirty miles from London, and the English queen possesses many fast horses. I wouldna want to be caught unaware."

"We'd better catch a few winks," Dubh said, wrapping himself in his plaid.

Relieved that the trouble had passed, Rob peered at Gordon, who held his plaid open in an unspoken invitation. With Smooches cradled beneath her cloak, she lay down and cuddled against her husband's warm body. Too tired to fret about improprieties, Rob closed her eyes and dropped into a deep dreamless sleep . . .

"Wake up, angel."

Rob felt a hand nudging her shoulder. She opened her eyes, focused on her husband's face, and groaned as if in pain. Two hours felt suspiciously like two minutes.

"If ye get up, ye'll sleep in a bed tonight," he coaxed her.

Rob yawned and stretched, then said, "I want to sleep in a bed *now*."

"There are na any beds in these woods," Gordon told her, forcing her to stand.

"Where's my dog?" she asked.

"Smooches is ready and anxious to ride."

Rob spotted the pup and smiled drowsily. Her husband had fastened a clean nappy on him and dressed him in his sweater. After strapping the leather satchel to her chest, Rob wrapped the dog in the Campbell plaid and set him inside.

Riding northwest, they passed through the Cotswold Hills with their wooded glens and serene streams and, as dusk descended upon them, entered the market town of Stratford upon the Avon River. Crossing the Clopton Bridge, Rob peered down at the Avon's swirling waters. Two swans, one black and one white, swam gracefully below the bridge.

They halted their horses in front of the first inn they saw, appropriately named the Black Swan Inn. Sitting between her husband and her brother inside the inn's crowded common room, Rob carefully hid her disfigured hand on her lap while she ate. She gave a silent prayer of thanks that Smooches had ensconced himself in her husband's arms.

With supper ended and a hot bath waiting in each of the two rooms they'd rented for the night, the four Highlanders went upstairs. Dubh and Mungo shared a chamber while Gordon and she took the other. Rob would have preferred sharing the room with her brother, but she knew without asking that her husband would object.

"I think 'twould be wise if we left the nappy on Smooches," Gordon said, sitting down on the only seat in the room, the edge of the bed. "There's yer bath, angel."

In the act of pulling her night shift out of her satchel, Rob snapped her head up in surprise. "My lord, 'twould be improper for me to bathe with ye in the room."

Gordon flashed her a devastatingly boyish smile and said, "I willna peek at ye."

After riding for almost twenty-four hours straight, Rob was unable to muster the energy to argue. She gave him a long, measuring look and then shifted her gaze to the steam that rose oh-so-invitingly from the tub. Rob positively yearned to submerge her aching muscles in that water.

Gordon set a towel down on the bottom edge of the bed and turned his back, making an exaggerated show of ignoring her. "I dinna hear splashin' water," he said after a long silent moment had passed. "If ye dinna get into that tub right now, I'll go first."

Rob stripped hurriedly. She stepped into the tub, only slightly larger than a hip bath, and plopped down in the water. The thought of her husband squeezing his warrior's body into the tub made her smile.

Too nervous with him in the room to soak for long, Rob quickly lathered and scrubbed and rinsed each part of her aching body. Gradually, she began to feel almost human again.

Dripping water, Rob stood and turned around to reach for the towel on the edge of the bed, but froze in surprised embarrassment at what she saw. With his arms folded across his chest, her husband relaxed on the bed and watched her.

Their gazes met. The unmasked desire in his intense stare made her vulnerable.

Rob yanked the towel up to cover her nakedness and reminded him in an accusing voice, "Ye said ye wouldna peek."

"I lied," Gordon admitted, his smile charmingly unrepentant. "But I crossed my fingers so it doesna count as a real fib."

Rob tried to think of something suitably insulting to hurl at him, but her mind remained humiliatingly blank. She stepped out of the tub, and being careful to keep herself covered, struggled to pull her nightgown over her head.

"Do ye need a hand with that?" Gordon asked.

Rob cast him an unamused look. With her virgin's frilly, high-necked nightgown in place, she tossed the towel at him and said, "Yer turn, my lord."

Turning her back on him, Rob sat down on the edge of the bed and lifted Smooches onto her lap. She heard her husband disrobing and then the sound of him stepping into the tub.

"God's balls, 'tis only fit for dwarfs," she heard him mutter.

Rob swallowed the bubble of laughter she felt rising in her throat. She glanced over her shoulder to steal a peek at her husband; he sat uncomfortably with his legs bent and his knees high.

That didn't seem to bother him, though. He sat in that tiny tub and hummed a spritely tune while he lathered and rinsed himself.

Rob let her gaze wander across the broad expanse of his shoulders and well-muscled back. Great Bruce's ghost, but the man was the image of every maiden's dream.

And he belonged to her. That realization brought a smile to her lips and incited her to impure thoughts. Would his buttocks and his thighs be as pleasing as the rest of him? What if he stood up suddenly and turned around? What would she do if she saw *that* part of him?

"No peekin'," Gordon called over his shoulder.

Rob snapped her head around, mortified that he knew she was watching him. She heard the sound of his chuckle, the water sloshing, and then the whip of the towel as he dried himself.

"Are ye goin' to sit there and blush all night, or were ye plannin' on sleepin'?" Gordon asked.

Rob rounded on him, intending to give him a piece of her mind, and nearly swooned at what she saw. With only the towel covering his privates from his waist to mid thigh, her husband stood there and smiled at her. His chest was as magnificently formed as his back.

"What are ye doin'?" Rob cried when he pulled the bed's coverlet back.

"I'm goin' to sleep."

"Like that?"

"Well, I forgot my nighty," he said dryly. "Do ye have an extra I could borrow?"

Rob glared at him. "I dinna find yer humor amusin', my lord. And, if ye think I'm sleepin' with ye in this bed, then ye'd better think again."

"Listen, angel. I'm too tired to scale the bulwarks," Gordon told her.

"What bulwarks?"

"The walls of yer virginal defenses. Are ye sleepin' or no?"

Rob nodded, her exhaustion overruling her modesty.

She clutched the pup tightly in her arms and lay back on the bed.

"The dog's sleepin' with us?"

"Between us," she corrected him.

Rob knew by the wholly exasperated look on her husband's face that he intended to put an end to that as soon as they reached Inverary Castle. She snapped her eyes shut when he moved to drop the towel and lay down on the bed. Smooches struggled out of her arms and cuddled into his chest.

"Betrayin' cur," Rob muttered, and turned her back on both of them.

Long silent moments passed.

"Angel, have I told ye how cute ye are when yer angry?" Gordon asked, a smile lurking in his voice.

No response.

Gordon shifted the pup in his arms, leaned close, and peered down at her. Fatigue had already claimed his wife in sleep.

He planted a chaste kiss on the side of her cheek and whispered, "Good night, angel. Sweet dreams."

Her life became an endless nightmare.

At dawn the following morning, Rob began the most exhausting week of her entire eighteen years. They turned their horses northeast and rode through Coventry, a cathedral city with defensive walls, and Leicestershire with its rolling landscapes, ancient gnarled trees, and stone villages. Physical exhaustion blinded Rob to Leicestershire's stark beauty.

After riding from dawn to dusk, the four young Highlanders camped in the surrounding woodlands beneath the stars. Rob slept snuggled against her husband, the safest place in the world at that moment. In spite of the fact that his smiling arrogance infuriated her, Rob never doubted that Gordon would protect her with his life.

They rode through Derby and then crossed the windswept moors and heaths of Yorkshire while skirting the towns of Leeds, Sheffield, Wakefield, and Ripon. Completely exhausted by then, Rob did whatever she was told without argument or even thinking. She did, however, keep a guarded eye on her star ruby. That magical stone remained darker than pigeon's blood despite the distance between the queen's men and herself.

Inspecting the star ruby on the eighth morning of their northward trek, Rob realized that she was hopelessly caught in an untenable position. Danger followed her from England and awaited her in Scotland. Trapped as she was between two evil forces, how could she survive?

"Look," Dubh called, drawing her attention.

Rob snapped her head up and stared in the direction her brother pointed.

The Cheviot Hills rose in the distance. Making the hills appear spectacularly tall, a fine mist enveloped the low-lying areas around them.

Gordon and Dubh halted their horses at the sight of Scotland, forcing Rob and Mungo to stop with them. Dubh sighed with exaggeration and breathed deeply as if the northern air was somehow purer than England's.

"What a beautiful sight," he exclaimed.

" 'Tis Scotland," Mungo said flatly, apparently unimpressed by the sight of their homeland.

"Ye see Scotland but I see paradise," Gordon remarked.

Staring straight ahead at the beckoning hills, Rob felt the panic beginning to swell within her breast. She had no idea what terrified her most, facing the queen's men or a multitude of Highlanders making the sign of the cross as she passed by.

" 'Tis paradise for some," Rob said, her voice tinged with bitterness, "but hell-on-earth for others." Feeling her husband's gaze, she asked, "Well, are ye plannin' on passin' the day admirin' the sight, or are we goin' home?"

An eternally disputed tract of land between Scotland and England, the Cheviot's main road was the pass connecting Redesdale in Northumberland and the valley of Jed. Smoothly rounded and dissected by deep glens, the hills were deserted except for an occasional shepherd's cottage.

Unexpectedly, two men on horseback appeared in the distance. The riders halted their horses abruptly as if surprised to see them there and then started forward in their direction.

"Be ready for trouble in the event they prove unfriendly," Gordon warned, gesturing for them to halt.

Galloping at full speed, the riders came closer and closer. And then the color of their plaids became visible. The two gigantic men wore the Earl of Bothwell's red and green plaid. They reined their horses to an abrupt halt five feet away and studied the four of them in silence for a long, tense moment.

"And what do we have here?" the first man asked, his smile flippantly wary.

"Pilgrims, do ye think?" the second man suggested.

" 'Tis the Campbell plaid the man's wearin'," the first man replied. "All of Scotland knows there are na any Campbells holy enough to go pilgrimin'."

"Yer correct aboot that," Gordon said with a smile. "Could ye possibly belong to Bothwell's borderers?"

"Who's askin'?" the first man demanded.

"Gordon Campbell, the Marquess of Inverary, Argyll's heir."

"Dubh MacArthur, Dunridge's heir."

"Mungo MacKinnon, the Earl of Skye's heir."

"Who's the lad?" the second man asked. "An English hostage?"

Gordon reached over and yanked the cap off Rob's head, letting her ebony mane cascade down her back to her waist. "My wife, the Marchioness of Inverary."

"Who happens to be my sister," Dubh added for good measure. Borderer or no, these men wouldn't wish for the MacArthur-Campbell clan to hunt them down.

"Well, what can we do for ye?" the first man asked.

"If Bothwell's in residence at Hermitage, we'd like to enjoy his hospitality for tonight," Gordon answered. "Sleepin' with a roof over her head would do my wife a world of good."

"Aye, we've been runnin' through the heather for over a week," Mungo added.

"Who's chasin' ye?" the second borderer asked.

"Sassenach swine," Mungo spat, ignoring Gordon's gesture for silence. With a flick of his hand, he gestured toward Rob and said, "The twit had the temerity to draw her dagger on the English queen's secretary of state."

The two borderers shouted with laughter, and then turned warm smiles on her. There was no mistaking the admiration gleaming at her from their eyes.

"Hermitage is aboot ten miles from here," one said.

"Follow us," the other added, turning his horse around. "We'll escort ye there."

The largest and strongest border fortress, the H-shaped Hermitage Castle stood on the Hermitage Water between two streams and possessed an unusual double tower with central courtyard. Built in the thirteenth century by Walter Comyn, the ownership of Hermitage Castle had passed through several families until it became the property of Francis Hepburn-Stuart, an illegitimate grandson of James V and cousin to King James VI.

Their party of six reached Hermitage Castle as dusk

was descending and a light mist giving way to steady rain. They rode through the portcullis entrance and into the deserted courtyard.

As they dismounted, several stable boys materialized from nowhere and led their horses away. With one burly borderer in the lead and the other behind them, they entered the castle's main building and walked up the stairs to the great hall.

In sharp contrast to the deserted courtyard, the great hall buzzed in a beehive of activity. Bothwell's borderers and castle servants filled the hall to overflowing.

The tantalizing aroma of roasting meats and simmering stew wafted across the air and called out to Rob when she stepped inside the chamber. Her stomach answered with an unladylike growl, and Rob hoped that no one heard her hunger's roar.

"Ye'll eat soon," Gordon whispered, leaning close.

Rob blushed and stared straight ahead, refusing to look at him. Why couldn't she keep any secrets from her husband? This northward trek had been one of the most humiliating experiences of her life. This was her punishment for losing her temper and making her presence known to her uncle's associates.

A tall, well-built man started across the hall toward them; a puzzled but welcoming smile lit his entire expression. Francis Hepburn-Stuart, the Earl of Bothwell, was a handsome man with auburn hair, short beard, and heavenly blue eyes. As he advanced on them, their two escorts disappeared into the crowd of borderers.

"Welcome to my home," the Earl of Bothwell greeted them.

"I'm Gordon Campbell, and these are family and friend," Gordon made the introductions. "Dubh MacArthur, Mungo MacKinnon, and my wife, Rob MacArthur Campbell."

The earl shook the men's hands and then turned his charm on Rob. "I can see that yer journey's been long and tirin'," he said, bowing over her gloved hand. "Would ye care to eat and then retire to a chamber with a hot bath?"

"Aye, my lord," Rob answered, giving him a grateful smile. "Thank ye."

"And what's this creature yer carryin'?" Bothwell asked.

"Smooches, my puppy."

The earl held his hand out to the pup for him to catch his scent. In answer, Smooches licked the offered hand.

Bothwell smiled and escorted them across the hall to the high table. At a gesture from their lord, two serving women brought whiskey for the men and mulled wine for Rob.

"Yer verra far from Argyll," Bothwell remarked.

"Aye, we've been visitin' in England," Gordon answered. "Dubh and Rob's uncle is the Earl of Basildon."

"The English queen's Midas?" Bothwell asked.

"Aye, and the lass is Elizabeth's nemesis," Mungo piped up.

"What d'ye mean?"

"He means my sister had the audacity to draw her dagger on Walsingham," Dubh told him. " 'Tis the reason we took to the heather."

The Earl of Bothwell burst out laughing and nodded with approval at her. "Ah, here's supper," he said.

Several servants set loaves of bread, creamy butter, and bowls of hearty mutton stew on the table in front of them. Next came goblets of ale for the men and a refill of the mulled wine for the lady.

Shifting Smooches in her lap, Rob forced herself to remove her leather riding gloves. Wearing them at the

supper table would be rude though that was precisely
what she wished to do.

Rob fed the pup a few chunks of mutton from her bowl
and then lifted the spoon to eat. "My compliments to
Cook," she said after tasting it. " 'Tis delicious."

Gordon leaned close and whispered against her ear,
"Campbell soup tastes even better, angel."

Rob rolled her eyes heavenward. "If I listened to ye,
my lord, everythin' Campbell would be considered divine."

"And that would be the gospel truth."

"The gospel accordin' to Argyll?"

"Is there any other?"

Rob shifted Smooches to her right arm and reached
out with her left hand to pick the last few mutton chunks
out of the bowl for his supper. As one of the serving girls
refilled the men's goblets and started to turn away, Rob
lifted her gaze from the pup and caught the girl making a
protective sign of the cross.

Surprised, Rob froze for a fraction of an instant and
then hid her left hand in her lap. Great Bruce's ghost,
how could she have forgotten to hide her deformity? Had
she become so comfortable with the man beside her that
she'd forgotten about the frightened reaction Old Clootie's mark elicited in people?

Glancing sidelong at her husband, Rob felt a wave of
relief surge through her body. Gordon hadn't noticed the
girl's action. She slid her gaze to the Earl of Bothwell. He
was watching her intently. Was that pity she saw mirrored
in his eyes?

"Would ye care for yer bath, my lady?" the earl asked
kindly. " 'Tis waitin' for ye in yer chamber."

"Thank ye, my lord. I'd like that," Rob answered, her
cheeks pinkening because he'd witnessed her shame.

The earl gestured at two women. When she saw them

approaching the table, Rob recognized the fear couched in their eyes. She'd seen *that* expression thousands of times in the Highlands.

"I'll take care of Smooches," Gordon said, lifting the pup out of her arms.

Rob flicked him a grateful smile and then stood. Without another word, she followed the two women out of the hall.

"A braw lassie," the Earl of Bothwell said when she'd disappeared from sight. "Too bad she's marked."

Confused by his words, Gordon turned a questioning look on him. As far as he was concerned, his wife was pure perfection. Well, perhaps a mite headstrong at times, but that was a problem Gordon could easily solve.

"Dinna misunderstand," the earl added. "I dinna hold with superstitions. As ye know, I'm called the Wizard Earl behind my back, and my royal cousin fears me. But, life can be harsh for a tarnished angel like yer wife."

"There's nothin' tarnished aboot my sister," Dubh insisted. "The flaw lies with the beholder, not the bearer of that mark."

"What are ye talkin' aboot?" Gordon demanded, rounding on his brother-in-law.

"That flower stain on the back of her left hand frightens the misinformed," Bothwell told him.

"Old Clootie touched her for sure," Mungo piped up. "She's the devil's handmaiden."

Both Gordon and Dubh reached for MacKinnon at the same moment. Gordon moved faster, though. He grabbed his friend by the throat and threatened, "I'll kill ye if ye dinna take that back."

"The man canna recant while yer chokin' him," the Earl of Bothwell said, and then placed a hand on Gordon's shoulder. "Peace, Campbell. He canna help bein' ignorant."

With a warning growl, Gordon released his friend.

"I—I amna ignorant," Mungo gasped, slowly regaining his breath.

"Superstition is ignorance." The Earl of Bothwell turned to Gordon and advised, "Dinna present yer wife at court, man. Jamie believes in demons and witches. Yer lass will get hurt."

" 'Tis merely a birthin' blemish," Gordon said, shaking his head at such foolishness. "And a pretty flower at that."

His wife's enemies were his enemies. He'd kill the man who tried to hurt her.

"Wake up, angel."

At the sound of the familiar husky voice whispering in her ear, Rob swam up slowly from the deep depths of sleep. Was she dreaming? Or had she actually heard her husband uttering the three words she'd begun to hate?

"I said, wake up."

That voice was no dream. Rob opened her eyes and saw her husband still dressed for riding.

"Are ye comin' to bed?" she asked.

" 'Tis mornin'," he told her.

"Where did ye sleep?"

"Beside ye."

"Why dinna we rest here for a day or two?" she suggested, her voice a drowsy plea.

"Here's food on this tray," Gordon said, scooping Smooches into his arms. "Meet me in the courtyard, and dinna keep us waitin'." At that, he left the chamber.

Rob wondered if her husband was beginning to enjoy tormenting her, but she did as she was told. After washing her face and dressing hurriedly, Rob grabbed a piece of brown bread and a chunk of cheese and then headed for the door. She had no doubt that if she lingered within the chamber, her husband would return to shove the food down her throat and to dress her himself.

Dawn's orange streaks were brightening the eastern horizon when Rob stepped into the courtyard. Her husband and her brother spoke together in hushed voices. Near them, three horses stood saddled and waiting.

"Is MacKinnon stayin' at Hermitage?" Rob asked.

"No, I'm stayin' behind," Dubh answered.

"But why?"

"Yer safe from the queen's men now, and I've a mind to go raidin' the borders with Bothwell," he told her. " 'Twill be my own private revenge for Mary's murder."

"I wish I could go raidin' with ye." Rob looked at him through eyes that mirrored her worry. "Ye'll be careful, won't ye?"

"Of course." Dubh gathered her into his arms and gave her a hearty squeeze. "I couldna allow Ross or Jamie to inherit Dunridge. Those good-for-nothin' brothers of ours would pauper the family within a year."

Rob forced herself to smile. She felt sad at the thought of leaving her favorite brother behind, but understood his motives. Part of her sadness was pure selfishness. Though she knew her husband would protect her with his life, Rob had felt along the journey from London that Dubh was protecting her from Gordon. Now, from the borders to the Highlands, she would be forced to rely solely on Gordon. How absurd that one moment of foolishness, making her presence known to Elizabeth's ministers, could have such far-reaching consequences on the rest of her life.

Drawing their attention, Mungo MacKinnon hurried into the courtyard at that moment. Instead of looking rested, the man sported horribly bloodshot eyes and a pale-greenish complexion.

"Are ye hurtin', Mungo?" Gordon asked in an overly loud voice.

The blond man grimaced. "I'll never drink and dice with another borderer as long as I live."

Gordon grinned and slapped his back so hard the force of it nearly toppled the other man over. He turned to Rob and asked, "Are ye ready, angel?"

Rob threw herself into her brother's arms a final time and kissed his cheek. Then she stepped back a pace and nodded at her husband. Gordon set Smooches into her satchel and helped her mount.

"Dinna fear for her safety," Gordon told Dubh, reaching to shake his hand. "I'll be guardin' her with my life."

Gordon, Rob, and Mungo left Hermitage Castle and rode northwest. At Selkirk, Mungo took leave of them and headed northeast toward Edinburgh.

Feeling strangely relieved at his departure, Rob watched her husband's friend ride away. As she turned back to Gordon, she happened to glance down at her star ruby. Its color was fading into serenity. Puzzled, she looked at MacKinnon's retreating back and then her magical stone. Could there possibly be any connection between her husband's friend and the stone's color? Could the stone possibly be reflecting MacKinnon's negative feelings for her?

"Is aught wrong?" Gordon asked. "Or are ye back to checkin' yer titties again?"

Rob forced the fret from her expression. With a mischievous smile, she answered, "I want to be certain ye havena lifted them off my chest."

"Ah, lass. I told ye before and I'll tell ye again—" Gordon began.

"Ye dinna need to steal what ye already own," Rob finished for him.

Gordon grinned at her. "Yer a quick learner, angel. I believe I'll keep ye around."

"Unless I outwit ye by slippin' through yer fingers."

"Outwit me?" he echoed. " 'Twill never happen, lass."

"Dinna bet the family fortune, my lord." She flicked him an unconsciously flirtatious smile and teased, "Everyone knows that MacArthurs are smarter than Campbells."

Gordon burst out laughing. "Yer incorrigible. But, I guess we've got the next forty years to put that theory to the test."

Continuing northwest, Gordon and Rob passed through Lanark and Stirling, the jewel that clasped the Highlands with the rest of the world. Leaving Stirling behind, they rode into the Highlands of Scotland.

Like an unwelcome guest, winter lingered longer in those higher altitudes. A heavy blanket of snow muffled the sounds of the wilderness, its meadows remaining empty of animals. Only pawprints revealed the existence of life.

The howling voice of February's winds swirled around the brooding mountains, echoed through the hauntingly deserted glens, and rippled across once-serene lochs. Winter, the loneliest time of the year, was a season of solitude when people sought refuge from the elements within their humble dwellings and passed the hours weaving fantastic tales of yore.

The day had been a Highland rarity of blue skies and glistening snow. Wood smoke wafted across the crystalline air and grew stronger, urging them onward toward their final destination.

Reaching the crest of a modest incline, Gordon halted his horse and pointed toward the glen below. " 'Tis there," he said.

Rob reined her horse to a stop beside him and stared in

the direction he pointed. Pale yellow light of evening silhouetted the four-story high structure. From her vantage point, Rob saw that the castle stood on a promontory over Loch Fyne. The surrounding mountains and the loch combined to make Inverary Castle impregnable. Nearby, on the eastern and the western sides of the structure, lay two frozen streams apparently descended from the mountains.

"Welcome to Inverary Castle," Gordon said, smiling at her. "Welcome home, wife."

Rob flicked him a sidelong glance and then gazed at the castle below. "I willna say I'm glad to be here," she replied. "Inverary appears more like a castle of gloom than the Highland's wealthiest stronghold."

Gordon chuckled. " 'Tis forbiddin', I'll give ye that. The fact is we lovin'ly call it Castle Gloom. 'Twas built to be the ugliest castle in Scotland in order to discourage any foolhardy intruders."

"In that case, my lord, the Campbells have done an excellent job of it," Rob teased. "Inverary appears as if the devil himself cast his cloak over it."

"Thank ye for the high praise," Gordon replied.

"Where's Dunridge Castle from here?" she asked.

"Ye must go up into those mountains behind Inverary," Gordon told her. "Climb up the valley of Glen Aray, and then walk through the forest until ye arrive at the moors. When ye reach the crest of the moors, ye can see Loch Awe with its jewel, Dunridge Castle, and behind it rises Ben Cruachan."

Gordon nudged his horse forward toward home and called over his shoulder, "Are ye comin', angel?"

"Aye," Rob called, and reluctantly nudged her own horse forward to follow him down the incline. "Do ye think they'll be surprised to see us?"

"I doubt it," Gordon said without looking back at her.

"My father knows whenever anyone steps one foot into Argyll. No man catches a Campbell by surprise."

Perhaps, but I'm a woman, Rob thought. *The Campbells cannot see Old Clootie's mark from wherever they're standing. I'll bet my family's fortune that the sight of my devil's flower will catch every last Campbell off guard.*

Rob lifted her chin a notch, squared her shoulders proudly, and gazed at her new home. *Castle Gloom.* Today was the first day of the rest of her miserable life, and she'd better make the best of it. Perhaps she could wear those fingerless gloves and permanently keep her shame hidden . . . ?

Chapter 9

"Welcome to Inverary Castle." Magnus Campbell, the Duke of Argyll, smiled at Rob as he walked around the desk in his private study to greet her. "Come, lass, and warm yerself in front of the hearth. Let me take yer cloak and gloves."

With chestnut-brown hair, piercing gray eyes, and a charming smile that eased her apprehension, the fifty-year-old Duke of Argyll was still an exceedingly handsome man. The resemblance between his son and him was uncanny, and made her feel as if she were looking at a vision of her husband as an older man.

Still dressed in the boy's clothing borrowed from Henry Talbot, Rob felt positively ragged but let the duke divest her of cloak and gloves. She returned his smile shyly, followed him across the study to a chair in front of the hearth, and sat down. Lifting Smooches out of his satchel, she kept the pup imprisoned on her lap.

The duke handed his son a dram of whiskey and then offered her a goblet of mulled wine with a cinnamon stick. The unexpected sight of that cinnamon stick reminded Rob of the day in her uncle's study when she'd served her two suitors white heather wine and cockle bread.

Rob struggled against the bubble of laughter rising in her throat and managed to hold it down. She wondered what her husband was thinking at that moment, but refrained from looking in his direction lest the sight of him make her laugh. She didn't think he'd wish to tell his father about that particular day, and she couldn't very well laugh without explaining why. Her father-in-law would think she was a blinking idiot.

"Here's to yer safe arrival," Magnus said, lifting his glass of whiskey into the air in a toast. "May today be the first day of many happy years for my only son and his lovely wife."

"I'll drink to that," Gordon said, raising his own glass to his lips.

Though uncomfortable with his sentiment, Rob managed a smile for her father-in-law's gallantry. She did, however, refrain from joining in their toast.

"Lass, ye have the look of yer mother," the duke remarked. "Ye canna imagine how ecstatic I am that yer parents and I will share grandchildren."

In the act of sipping her wine, Rob choked on his words. A hard slap between her shoulder blades helped her catch her breath.

"Thank ye," Rob said, gazing through tear-blurred eyes at her husband. "The wine went down the wrong pipe." Fully composed again, she turned her attention on her father-in-law and said, "I'm verra sorry, Yer Grace, but my parents and ye may not be sharin' any grandchildren."

"*Rob.*" Her husband's voice held a warning note.

"Are ye barren?" Duke Magnus asked baldly.

Rob crimsoned with hot embarrassment. In spite of the pup sitting on her lap, she reached around his little body and began to rub her birthmark furiously.

"No, Yer Grace. I—I may be permanently returnin' to England this summer," she tried to explain.

Her statement confused him. The duke slid his gaze to his son and silently demanded an explanation.

"Dinna fret aboot this nonsense," Gordon told his father. He rounded on Rob who was about to argue with him, and added, "We'll discuss this later."

"Yer Grace, may I have a box of sand in my chamber?" Rob asked abruptly, switching to a more mundane subject than the possibility of her leaving Inverary Castle.

"Sand?" Duke Magnus echoed, thoroughly baffled by her request. He'd met myriad silly women in his time, including his own wife and Rob's mother, but the MacArthur chit seemed to outshine the lot of them.

"My young cousins trained Smooches to use a sandbox at night," Rob said, reading the confusion couched in his eyes.

The duke's expression cleared. "I'm certain we can find a box for yer pet." He flicked a glance at his son and added, "Duncan and Gavin will love playin' with Smooches."

"Duncan and Gavin?" Rob inquired, thinking the two must be the duke's own pets.

"A couple of Inverary's children to whom my father is partial," Gordon answered.

The duke coughed and cleared his throat, drawing her attention. Rob caught the pointed look his grace leveled on her husband but had no idea what it meant.

"Ye've suffered a long and tirin' journey," Duke Magnus said, turning his most solicitously charming smile on her. "I'm certain ye'd love a hot bath and a hearty meal to take the edge off yer hunger."

Without waiting for her to reply, the duke crossed the study to the door and called for service. Almost instantly, two women hurried into the room. One appeared to be about Rob's age and the other several years older than the duke.

Setting Smooches down on the floor, Rob stood to greet them. Out of habit, she discreetly covered her birthmark with her right hand.

"This is Biddy, Inverary's housekeeper," Duke Magnus said, introducing them.

In her late fifties, Biddy was plump and graying at the temples. Her expression was kind but brooked no nonsense.

"And this is Gabby, Biddy's granddaughter," the duke added. "Gabby will serve as yer tirin' woman."

Much taller than Rob's petite height of five feet, Gabby was strappingly well built and sported dark brown hair and eyes. Her expression seemed curious yet friendly.

When the two women smiled at her and moved to curtsey, Rob stopped them by saying, "Dinna curtsey to me. I'm nobody special."

"Why, yer the lady of Inverary Castle," Biddy said, obviously surprised by her words. "Yer the laird's daughter now."

"Only temporarily," Rob replied.

The housekeeper cast the duke a questioning look. Almost imperceptibly, he shook his head in a silent gesture to drop the subject.

"The long journey from London wearied Rob," Duke Magnus said. "Could we arrange a bath and supper for her upstairs?"

Biddy grinned. "Why, 'tis already waitin'."

"Oh, my new daughter-in-law will be borrowin' a few of Avril's gowns until her own belongin's arrive from England," Duke Magnus added.

"Avril?" Rob echoed, puzzled.

"Gordon's mother, my late wife," the duke told her.

"Thank ye, Yer Grace." Rob moved to curtsey, but she reached out and touched her arm to prevent her from doing so.

"Yer back in the Highlands," Duke Magnus said. "We'll have none of that bowin' and scrapin' takin' place within the family."

Rob nodded. She already liked her father-in-law immensely. He appeared to possess none of her husband's arrogant pigheadedness. Or had advanced age merely tempered those qualities?

"Leave Smooches with me, angel," Gordon said, scooping the pup into his arms. "I'll see he gets supper while yer bathin'."

"Thank ye, Gordy. Will I be seein' ye later?"

Gordon winked at her. "I've no doubt aboot that, wife."

No sooner had the door closed behind Rob than the Duke of Argyll rounded on his son. "Ye didna tell her?" he said, his disbelief apparent in his voice. "Lyin' to yer wife is bad business, no matter how worthy the cause."

"What does it matter when she learns aboot that?" Gordon countered. "A wife's duty is to accept her husband in spite of his flaws."

" 'Tis true only in theory, Gordy." The duke shook his head as if his son were a simpleton. "A wise man keeps the peace with his wife, especially here in the Highlands where winters are long and harsh. Do ye wish to live from November to April trapped inside this house with a wife who resents ye?"

Gordon knew his father's question was rhetorical. He filled his mug with whiskey, took a healthy swig of it, and sat in the chair vacated by his wife. Flicking a sidewise smile at his father, Gordon said finally, "My MacArthur bride isna the timid angel I'd expected. Since ridin' to England, I havena been able to accomplish quite a few thin's with her."

The Duke of Argyll stood with his arms folded across his chest. "Such as?" he asked, quirking an eyebrow at his son.

Gordon dropped his gaze and stared into the hearth's flames. "I havena breached her yet."

That unexpected announcement stunned the duke speechless for one long moment. Then he threw back his head and shouted with laughter.

"Are ye the man no woman could refuse?" Duke Magnus teased him. "Are ye the man whose near-legendary prowess I've been hearin' aboot for years?"

"Who's carryin' tales back to ye?" Gordon demanded.

The Duke of Argyll smiled. "I've got my spies, son."

"Why is it that whenever I speak with ye, I feel like a striplin' boy?" Gordon asked.

The Duke of Argyll's smile grew into a full-fledged grin. "Compared with my superior sophistication, ye *are* a striplin' boy."

"Verra funny, Father . . . When I arrived in London, my wife believed herself in love with the Marquess of Ludlow," Gordon told him. "I thought 'twas best to give her some breathin' space. Forcin' her into my bed could have ruined whatever chance we had for a happy marriage together. So I decided courtin' her for a time would be the best approach."

"Yer bride's here now. She must've changed her mind aboot ye," Duke Magnus replied. "My advice is to breach her first and then tell her aboot the other situation afterwards."

Gordon sipped his whiskey and decided to level with his father. "Rob isna here by choice," he admitted. "The queen's men chased us out of England."

"What did ye do?" the duke asked in a surprisingly calm tone of voice.

"*I* did nothin'." Gordon smiled at the memory. "My sweet-tempered wife drew her dagger on Elizabeth's secretary of state and threatened his life."

"Why did she do that?" Duke Magnus asked, obviously shocked by the revelation. He would never have guessed that the petite young woman could be capable of violence.

Gordon refused to meet his father's gaze when he answered, "Walsingham provoked her."

"Ye are na bein' honest with me, Gordy."

"I gave my solemn oath to Rob's uncle that I'd keep my silence," Gordon replied. "I can tell ye this much, ye'll hear all aboot it in the near future."

"Verra well, son." The duke placed his hand on the younger man's shoulder and said, "I'll trust yer judgment."

Covering his father's hand with his own, Gordon replied, "I knew ye would."

"Now, then. Ye know I canna wait forever to see the heir ye sire on yer wife," Duke Magnus said, changing their topic of conversation to one of his favorite subjects. "I need ye to get to work on makin' my heir. And 'twould appear that Cousin Iain's daughter is a braw lassie and will give the Campbells a dozen fine strong sons. Heed my advice, lad. Dinna lie needlessly to her. 'Twill only make a bad situation worse and could haunt yer whole life together."

Gordon cast his father a sidelong glance and asked in a rueful voice, "In that case, do ye know of an ugly, old woman named Livy whom we could hire as housekeeper for our Edinburgh home?"

"Ye neglected to warn her about Lavinia Kerr?" Duke Magnus replied, surprising his son.

"Ye know aboot her too?"

"The Duke of Argyll knows almost everythin' that happens in Scotland," he said with a smile. "What I dinna know, my MacArthur kinsman whispers in my ear; and what he doesna know, yer late mother's Gordon relatives tell me."

When she left the duke's study, Rob followed Gabby up the wheel stairs to the castle's third story and then down a long corridor to the east wing where the family's private apartments were located. She stepped into a spartanly furnished chamber and scanned it quickly. Against one wall stood a four-poster, curtained bed and a small table. Another wall had a door which, Rob assumed, led to the dressing room and closet.

Rob smiled with delight when her gaze turned in the direction of the hearth. Beckoning her, steam rose from the tub that had been set there.

Without regard to modesty, Rob began stripping as she walked toward the tub and left in her wake a trail of soiled, discarded clothing. She intended to submerge herself in that water for a fortnight.

"Ye'll probably redecorate this chamber," Gabby said, keeping up a steady stream of chatter as she washed her new mistress's hair. "Ye'll want it to look more like a lady's apartment. What d'ye think?"

Before Rob could reply, Gabby ungently dunked her head beneath the water to rinse her hair. Rob surfaced, coughing and gasping for air, and would have scolded her, but the other girl started talking again.

"Gordy will probably give ye the grand tour of Inverary in the mornin'," Gabby said. "Ye'll meet my Dewey then."

"Dewey?" Rob echoed.

"Gawd, what a hunk of man my Dewey is," Gabby

gushed. "He's my husband, ye know. Dewey is sooo verra handsome and burly and the fiercest of the laird's warriors." The girl paused for breath and then admitted, "He does have one tiny flaw, though."

"What's that?" Rob asked, thoroughly entertained by her chatter.

"Well, puir Dewey's candle is lit but usually there's nobody home, if ye ken my meanin'," Gabby told her. "When the good Lord was passin' out brains, my puir Dewey was outside pissin' in the wind."

Rob burst out laughing, but stifled it when the door swung open.

"Well, I'm glad to see yer becomin' acquainted with each other," Biddy called, marching into the chamber. She carried a tray with a bowl of stew and a chunk of brown bread, and slung across one arm were a clean night shift and a bed robe.

"Gabby, serve this to yer mistress while she soaks in the tub," Biddy ordered, passing her the tray. She set the night clothes across the chair that had been pushed aside to make room for the tub, and then turned to Rob.

"I'd stay and visit with ye too, but I ken yer tired and supper is waitin' to be served," Biddy said. "I canna tell ye how happy I am that Inverary has a lady again. Too many years have passed since I've heard the angelic sounds of a gurglin' baby."

The older woman smiled at her. Then she hurried across the chamber and disappeared out the door.

Rob swallowed uncomfortably. Though she did hope to become a mother some day, she wasn't about to sacrifice her own happiness so that the marquess could sleep easy at night because he'd produced an heir for Inverary.

In the act of reaching for the bowl of stew that Gabby offered, Rob froze with her hands in midair. The other girl was staring at her birthmarked hand.

Great Bruce's ghost, Rob thought. The girl's chatter had put her so much at ease that she'd forgotten to hide her shame.

"Ye needna act as my tirin'woman," Rob said in a voice that cracked with disappointment. "I—I release ye from my service."

Gabby snapped her gaze from the devil's flower to her mistress's face. "And why would ye do that?" she asked indignantly.

Her words surprised Rob. "Do ye *want* to serve me?"

"Would I be standin' here if I didna'?" Gabby countered with no regard for the gentle respect a tiring woman should accord her lady. " 'Twould seem my Dewey isna the only one hereaboots whose candle's lit with nobody home."

Rob cared not a whit that she'd just been insulted. She held her left hand out for the other girl's inspection and asked, "My birthmark doesna bother ye?"

"No." Gabby stared her straight in the eye and asked, "Does it bother ye?"

Rob knew the other girl was lyin' but loved her for it. She smiled at her, but when she answered only a deaf person would not have heard the bitterness in her voice. "Aye, Gabby. At times it gives me pain."

"Well, let me know when that happens," Gabby replied, deliberately misunderstanding. "I'll tell my Granny Biddy to mix ye a poultice."

"Thank ye."

"For what?"

"For bein' who ye are."

Gabby chuckled and shook her head, saying, "And who else could I be?"

Rob stood then and wrapped herself in a thick towel. She stepped out of the tub and let the other girl towel dry her hair. Then Rob donned the night shift that Biddy had brought her and sat on the edge of the bed.

"Fetch the comb from my satchel," Rob ordered. "Then take yerself downstairs to supper."

"Dinna ye want me to comb yer hair?" Gabby asked. " 'Tis one of my duties."

"True, but I'm goin' to sleep as soon as it's completely dry."

"Well, whatever blows yer gown up," the girl said, picking her mistress's discarded clothing off the floor as she headed for the door. "What should I do with these?"

"Burn them."

As soon as the door clicked shut behind Gabby, Rob rose from the edge of the bed and pulled a chair across the chamber to the window. She sat down, began combing the tangles out of her hair, and stared out the window at the Highland twilight.

Shadowy dusk, the night's herald, excited Rob more than any other time of the day. She loved the night's dark, mysterious beauty because it shrouded all manner of flaws.

A few minutes later the bedchamber door opened noiselessly, and Gordon stepped inside the room. He looked toward the empty bed first and then slid his gaze to the chair where his wife sat, oblivious to his presence. In spite of their differences, Gordon decided that his bride was an angel. No, she wasn't the timid girl he'd married ten years earlier, but somehow she was even more irresistibly wonderful than he'd expected or deserved.

Sauntering across the chamber, Gordon walked around her chair until he faced her. When he nonchalantly leaned against the windowsill, she looked up in surprise at him.

"I didna hear ye come in," she said.

"I've brought ye a cup of Biddy's Old Man's milk," he said with a smile, offering her the mug.

"Thank ye, my lord." Rob sipped the zested milk and then announced, "Why, 'tis every bit as delicious as Moireach's. By the way, where's Smooches?"

"The pup's enjoyin' supper with Biddy and friends," Gordon told her. "I'll fetch him later."

Without another word, Gordon pushed away from the windowsill and started across the chamber. Looking over her shoulder, Rob saw him sit on the edge of the bed and pull his boots off. Unceremoniously, he dropped them on the floor.

A swell of panic surged through her. Great Bruce's ghost, was he undressing here in her bedchamber?

When he tossed his shirt on the floor, Rob leaped to her feet and hurried across the chamber. "What are ye doin'?" she cried.

"I've a mind to wear clean clothes," Gordon said, then stood and reached for the top of his breeches.

Rob began running a finger furiously back and forth across her birthmark. "Why dinna ye do that in yer own chamber?"

Gordon snapped his head up in surprise and told her, "This *is* my chamber."

"Yer chamber?" she echoed. "Inverary's so big. Why do we need to share the chamber?"

"We're married. Remember?"

"Of course I remember," Rob cried, "but ye promised ye wouldna force me."

Gordon stared at her for a long moment, then said, "Sit down, angel. I need to explain a few thin's to ye." When she did as he asked, he continued, "I meant what I said aboot not forcin' ye, angel. However, we must keep that our secret. My father wouldna understand our sleepin' in separate beds, and soon enough the whole clan would be gossipin' aboot us. 'Twould mean a terrible loss of respect for me."

Rob looked past him and watched the flames in the hearth. Her husband had saved her life at the lions' pit and risked his own safety by rescuin' her from the queen's men. He'd also slain the monster living beneath her bed, which had given her hundreds of nights of peaceful sleep as a child. Humiliating him in front of his kin could hardly be considered the proper payment for all he'd done for her.

Rob sighed and lifted her gaze to meet his. "Verra well, my lord. We'll share the bed, and I willna let on that we never—" She broke off, too embarrassed to say the words.

"Thank ye, angel." Gordon leaned close and planted a chaste kiss on her forehead. Then he turned away and headed for the dressing room, tossing his clothing on the floor.

Rob stared straight ahead toward the window, too nervous to look over her shoulder and peek at him. Sharing his bed along the road to Scotland was far different from this. They'd been tired and dirty and chaperoned by Dubh and Mungo. There'd been no chance of any real intimacy between them.

How could she share this bedchamber with him and *not* see him naked? How many nights would pass before they turned to each other in the dark and—

"Rob?"

She glanced over her shoulder.

Gordon stood at the door. "Dinna wait up for me, hinny. I've hours and hours of reportin' to my father." And then he was gone.

Rob rose slowly from the edge of the bed and began picking his discarded garments off the floor. In spite of their soiled condition, she folded them neatly and set them across the chair, then paused to stare out the window at the night.

Gordon Campbell was oh-so-tempting. When the time came, would she leave Inverary Castle with her virginity intact? That was doubtful, no matter what he promised.

On the other hand, Gabby's lack of fright at the sight of her devil's flower encouraged hope to swell within her breast. Could the Campbells be considerably more stouthearted than the MacArthurs? If that was true, she'd have no reason to leave Inverary Castle because she'd find acceptance within its walls. The real test would come in the morning when her husband introduced her to his clansmen and retainers.

Rob held her left hand into the air and studied her devil's flower. She slid her gaze from the detested stain to her wedding ring with the emerald that her husband had said matched the color of her eyes.

"Ye and No Other."

If only those words were true.

Rob awakened late the following morning. Something cold and wet touched the tip of her nose, the tickling sensation making it twitch. She opened her eyes and saw Smooches. His face pressed against hers, and his dark eyes gazed at her dolefully.

"Good mornin', Smooches," Rob said, moving her arms to encircle the pup.

The sound of her voice brought an instant reaction from him. He wagged his tail and licked her face, which made her smile.

Setting the pup aside on the bed, Rob sat up and leaned back against the headboard. Where was her husband? She hadn't awakened when he returned to their chamber the previous night, but his side of the bed appeared rumpled so she knew he'd slept beside her.

Rob threw the coverlet back and swung her legs over the side of the bed. She yawned and then stretched like a sleek, half-grown she cat.

Should she dress and go below stairs? Rob wondered. Or should she wait for Gabby to attend her? Whatever happened today would color her relationship with her husband's clan for a long, long time.

Rob wished she could speak with her mother. Without an older woman's guidance, how was she to know what was expected of her? Insidious insecurity coiled itself around her heart; that familiar feeling of worthlessness surfaced like an old friend ready to renew their acquaintance.

The door swung open suddenly. With several garments slung across her arm, Gabby marched into the chamber like a smiling general.

"I'm glad yer awake," the girl said, advancing on the bed. " 'Tis verra late."

"Good mornin' to ye too," Rob greeted her.

"Sorry." Gabby placed a black woolen skirt and a white, scooped-neck linen blouse down on the bed. "Granny Biddy says ye'll wear this, and she'll help ye sort through the other gowns later. Should I help ye dress? 'Tis one of my duties, ye know."

"I believe I can manage on my own this mornin'," Rob said, refusing her offer. "Where's my breakfast tray?"

"Well, my lady—"

"Call me Rob."

"Lady Rob, yer husband said that breakin' the fast in yer bedchamber is a Sassenach custom," Gabby informed her. "He's waitin' for ye in the hall."

Rob smiled, pleased that Gordon was thinking of her. "Tell him I'll be down in a few minutes," she instructed the girl. It appeared that acquiring English habits had been easier than falling out of a tree. Hopefully, losing those habits would prove just as easy.

"Prepare yerself to meet the great clan Campbell," Gabby warned, and then disappeared out the door.

Rob washed the sleep from her face and then dressed in the skirt and the blouse that had once belonged to her husband's mother. She brushed her ebony mane and let it cascade loosely to her waist. Finished with her morning toilet, Rob donned her beggar bead necklace.

Though she was the MacArthur laird's daughter, Rob was a stranger at Inverary Castle. How could she know what forces might be set against her? Caution was never wasted; the MacArthur clan's children had taught her that important lesson.

" 'Tis yer turn," Rob told Smooches. She dressed him in the sweater she'd knitted and then scooped him up into the crook of her left arm.

The morning had aged into a feeble old man by the time Rob stood in the corridor outside the great hall. She paused before stepping toward the entrance and, with a badly shaking hand, smoothed an imaginary wrinkle from her skirt.

"Well, how do I look?" Rob asked the pup.

In answer, Smooches licked her hand.

"Thank ye, I think."

Rob took a deep, calming breath. She knew that first impressions were important and worried about not looking her best. She hoped that her husband's clan did not find her lacking in any way.

Summoning all of her courage, Rob forced herself to take that giant step forward. She stood in front of the hall's entrance and hesitated. Great Bruce's ghost, she'd never seen so many people in one place at the same time.

"She's here," a voice shouted over the noise.

Panic surged through Rob when she saw the sea of

strange faces turn toward her. Apparently, every Campbell in Argyll sat inside that chamber and waited to catch
a glimpse of Gordon's bride.

Out of habit, Rob moved to hide her stained left hand
within the folds of her skirt, but realized that was impossible with Smooches ensconced in the crook of her left
arm. Before she could shift the pup to the other side, her
husband stood in front of her.

Gordon took her right hand in his and raised it to his
lips. "I despaired of seein' ye this mornin'," he said with
a smile.

Rob calmed beneath the warmth of his smile and the
tender emotion in his disarming gray eyes. "Ye should
have awakened me earlier," she replied.

"Ye looked so peaceful," he told her. "I hadna the
heart to disturb ye."

The thought that he'd watched her sleeping made Rob
blush. She dropped her gaze in embarrassment, little
knowing the pleasing picture she presented to all of those
watching Campbells was demure femininity.

Without another word, Gordon gently forced her to
step forward with him; hand in hand, they walked
through that mass of Campbells toward the high table.
With her husband by her side, Rob wasn't nearly so
frightened as she would have been if she'd walked alone
through that crowd. Still, having all those unfamiliar
gazes fixed on her hardly inspired tranquility within her
breast. She much preferred blending into a crowd to being the center of attention.

"Is anyone guardin' the walls or tendin' the cattle?"
Rob whispered.

Gordon chuckled and gave her hand a gentle squeeze
which, she realized, was meant to bolster her courage.
Rob cast him an intimate, grateful smile.

"What's she carryin'?" a voice asked.

Gordon stopped walking and whispered to her, "Ye must meet this man personally."

With a polite smile fixed on her face, Rob stared at the dark-haired giant. He couldn't seem to decide whether to look at her or at Smooches.

"I'd like to present Dewey, one of our most valuable warriors," Gordon introduced them. "Dewey, say hello to Lady Rob."

"Hello." Dewey grinned, obviously flattered by his lord's description.

"I'm verra pleased to make yer acquaintance," Rob said to him. "Gabby has already told me good thin's aboot ye. I feel safe knowin' yer protectin' Inverary."

"Thank ye, Lady Rob." Dewey leaned closer to Gordon and in a worried whisper, said, "Gordy, she's got a boy's name."

"She's a girl," Gordon told him, winking at Rob. "Ye can take my word on it."

Another giant Campbell clansman stepped up beside Dewey. With him stood a voluptuous, dark-haired beauty holding a baby boy in her arms.

"Rob, I present my close friend Fergus," Gordon introduced them. His tone of voice altered when he added, "And this is his wife, Kendra."

The change in her husband's tone of voice alerted Rob to the abrupt change in his mood. She glanced sidelong at him. His profile appeared carved in stone as he stared at the dark-haired beauty. His cordial smile had vanished, and he appeared none too happy.

"I'm pleased to meet ye," Rob said, nodding politely at the man and the woman.

"What's that yer carryin'?" Fergus asked.

Rob smiled. " 'Tis Smooches, my dog."

"Dog?" Kendra said, her voice laced with barely disguised sarcasm. "It looks more like a cat."

Rob shifted her gaze to the woman and froze. With a fascinated expression on her face, the woman was staring at her exposed birthmark. Rob longed to hide her shame within the folds of her skirt, but the dog in her arms prevented movement. When the woman met her gaze, Rob recognized unmasked hatred gleaming at her.

What would she do if this woman made a protective sign of the cross? The crowd around them seemed to be hanging on their every word and watching with unusually rapt attention.

"The lad is as handsome as his mother is pretty," Rob forced herself to say conversationally.

"Thank ye, Lady Rob," Fergus spoke up. "Would ye care to hold him? 'Twould be practice for when Gordon and ye have yer own."

At that, Kendra shook her head and clutched her son as if the devil himself wanted to snatch him away. She shifted her gaze to Gordon and asked in a loud voice, "Have ye seen Duncan and Gavin yet?"

Rob heard several smothered gasps from clansmen standing nearby and flicked a puzzled glance at their audience. No one would meet her gaze. She looked up at Gordon, who had suddenly developed an angry twitch in his cheek.

"His Grace mentioned those boys yesterday," Rob said, cutting into the tense silence. "Are they yer sons?"

"Aye, Duncan and Gavin are mine," Kendra answered, a satisfied smile touching her lips. Her smile lacked warmth and did not reach her eyes.

"How fortunate ye are to have such a family," Rob remarked.

"The forge willna wait any longer," Fergus said, casting Gordon a meaningful glance. "Ye'll excuse us?" The man grasped his wife's upper arm with unnecessary force and escorted her from the hall.

Watching their retreat, Rob felt off balance. Something important had just transpired, but she didn't understand what it was nor could she question her husband. He appeared ready to pounce on anyone who even considered giving him a crooked look.

"Shall we?" Gordon asked, taking her hand in his again.

Duke Magnus stood when she finally reached the high table. He smiled and bowed in courtly manner over her right hand, which demonstrated to the watching Campbells that he approved of his son's bride.

"Good mornin', Yer Grace," Rob greeted him. "I see that I've kept the whole clan waitin'."

" 'Tis yer prerogative, my dear. How did ye sleep?" the duke asked.

"Like the dead," she answered. "I didna even rouse when Gordy joined me."

"Dinna sit down yet," Gordon said, lifting Smooches out of her arms. Then warned, "Brace yerself."

In a loud clear voice that carried to the far corners of the hall, Gordon announced, "I give ye Inverary's new lady, Rob MacArthur. When ye serve her faithfully, ye serve my father and me faithfully." He held Smooches up and said, "This is my wife's dog, *not a cat*."

Rumbles of chuckles echoed within the hall.

"Puir Smooches is exceedin'ly weak and, as ye can see, no bigger than a mite," Gordon told the crowd of kinsmen. " 'Tis because he's English."

Everyone laughed loudly. Rob cast her husband a sidewise smile.

"Lady Rob's a mite small herself," one warrior shouted.

"And she's got a boy's name," another man called.

"The MacArthur laird named his only daughter in honor of Robert the Bruce, and she's as fierce and fearless as he was," Gordon told them, his pride apparent in his voice. "Queen Elizabeth's men chased us out of England because my wee wife dared to draw her last resort on the English secretary of state."

The Campbell clansmen went wild. Their cheers and whistles erupted in the hall and shook the rafters overhead.

Unaccustomed to favorable attention, Rob nodded to acknowledge their approval and blushed from the top of her head to the tips of her toes. She only prayed they'd be just as amenable once they got a good look at her devil's flower.

"Say a few words, angel," Gordon whispered to her.

"I—I'm verra happy to be amongst my husband's clansmen," Rob said in a voice so soft the men in the hall strained to hear her. "I genuinely hope that ye'll soon consider me one of ye."

The men applauded her, and several banged the hilts of their daggers on the wooden trestle tables.

Gordon gestured for silence. "Ye've had yer peek at her. Now there's work to be done. Go on aboot yer business so my wee wife can eat in peace."

The hall cleared quickly. In a very few minutes only the three at the high table remained.

"Here we are," Biddy said, arriving with Rob's breakfast. The housekeeper set barley bannocks, oatmeal porridge, and a mug of Old Man's milk down on the table in front of her.

"Why, 'tis my favorite breakfast," Rob exclaimed with delight. She hadn't feasted on these delicacies in more than a year.

Biddy winked at her. "Gordy told me what ye liked."

"Thank ye for thinkin' of me, my lord," Rob said.

Gordon leaned close, so close she caught his fresh

scent of mountain heather. "Yer forever on my mind, angel."

Rob cast him a look that told him she didn't believe a word of that.

"Yer even lovelier than yer mother was at yer age," Duke Magnus remarked, smiling at the byplay between his son and his daughter-in-law. " 'Tis the Highland blood that spawns perfection."

"Thank ye, Yer Grace." Unused to all this flattery and approval, Rob wondered why she'd so desperately feared coming to Inverary. These Campbells weren't so bad as she had supposed, and this particular morning was fast becoming the happiest day of her entire life. Acceptance from her native Highlanders was a heady experience.

"Gordy and I ate at the Royal Rooster Tavern in London," Rob told him.

Duke Magnus stared at her blankly.

"Ye know, the tavern where my mother once worked as a servin' wench."

The duke's expression cleared, and he burst out laughing. "Dinna repeat this," he said, "but yer mother was the most incompetent servin' wench I've ever seen. I was half in love with her until I discovered she was actually Iain's runaway bride."

Duke Magnus glanced at his son and added, " 'Twas before I married yer mother, of course."

"What high times ye must have had," Gordon said. "How excitin' life must have been with two bonny young queens competin' with each other."

"I warrant the world had never seen anythin' like it," the duke agreed. "And never will again."

"I've a few thin's to do," Gordon said, turning to Rob. "Would ye care to take Smooches outside in the garden while I'm occupied?"

Rob nodded.

Gordon stood and grabbed a cloak from the chair beside his. After dropping the pup into her arms, he wrapped her cloak around her shoulders and fastened it, saying, " 'Twas my mother's cloak."

"I'm glad ye've finally come home to us," Duke Magnus said to her, rising when they did. "If anythin' troubles ye, come directly to me. I'm the law in Argyll."

When they left the great hall, Gordon and Rob walked down a long corridor and then descended the wheel stairs to the ground level. Rob saw two doors, one on her right and one on her left. She knew the one on her right led to the courtyard.

"I'm goin' out here," Gordon told her, pointing at the courtyard door. "That door leads to an enclosed, private garden that my father built for my mother. Smooches can run freely there without risk of bein' trampled."

Rob nodded and turned toward the garden door.

"Angel?" Her husband's voice stopped her.

"Yes?" Rob glanced over her shoulder at him.

Gordon said nothing more, but his expression appeared troubled as he stared at her. He opened his mouth to speak, but then apparently changed his mind and disappeared into the courtyard.

Banishing the disturbing thought that the morning was about to take a turn for the worse, Rob stepped outside into the walled garden and paused to breath deeply of the crisp mountain air. She could hardly believe she'd returned to the Highlands. The year she'd passed at her uncle's in England now seemed more like a pleasant dream than reality. But, she'd weathered her first meeting with her husband's people better than she would ever have thought possible. Dare she hope to find acceptance here at Inverary Castle?

The Campbells seemed to approve of her. Still, most hadn't caught a look at the back of her left hand, and there was no way to predict what their reaction would be once her devil's flower became common knowledge.

Rob sighed and surveyed her surroundings. Drooping clouds hung sadly overhead in a low overcast, but the air felt unusually warm for late February, more like rain than snow. Several nuthatches, finches, and sparrows chattered noisily on the barren branches of the garden's trees. Rob knew the hungry birds had several weeks of waiting before the plant life beneath the earth awakened. Yet, all of nature seemed poised, awaiting the coming of spring.

Rob set Smooches down. Invigorated by the crisp air, the pup scampered about wildly. Rob started to walk down the narrow stone path that led through the garden.

"Be ye friend or be ye enemy?" a voice demanded.

Rob stopped short and turned in a complete circle, but saw no one. She did, however, hear what sounded suspiciously like giggling children.

"Be ye friend or be ye enemy?" the voice called again, louder this time.

Rob swallowed the bubble of laughter she felt rising in her throat. "Show yerself," she ordered. "And then I'll tell ye."

"Speak first," the voice insisted.

"I'm yer MacArthur kinswoman from Loch Awe," Rob answered. "A damsel-eatin' dragon is chasin' me, and I've come in search of a hero to save me."

A dark-haired, dark-eyed boy about seven years old materialized from behind the evergreen hedgerow. Beside him appeared another boy, perhaps a year or two younger. With his chestnut brown hair and gray eyes, the younger of the two seemed vaguely familiar.

The older boy puffed his chest out and said, "Damsel, yer heroes are here."

Rob bit her bottom lip to keep from laughing. The lad

appeared so solemn that she knew her amusement would insult him.

"Be that the monster?" the younger boy asked, pointing a finger at Smooches.

Rob did chuckle then and shook her head. "No, 'tis my dog."

Smooches made a mad dash for the boys. Wagging his tail, he leaped at their legs and barked his shrill puppy yelp.

" 'Tis small for a dog," the older boy remarked.

"He's English."

"Ah." The boy nodded in understanding as if being an English dog explained the pup's miniature size.

Rob crossed the short distance between them and curtsied, saying, "I'm Rob MacArthur and have come with my husband to live at Inverary."

"Ye've a boy's name," the older boy said.

"I'm a girl," she replied. "My da named me in honor of his special hero, Robert the Bruce."

The boy nodded, but Rob surmised from his blank expression that he'd never heard of that great Scotsman. "And ye are?" she asked.

"I'm Duncan, which means warrior," the older boy told her. "This is my brother, Gavin. His name means hawk."

Rob wondered briefly what Kendra's sons were doing in the duke's private garden, but then recalled that her father-in-law was partial to them. "I'm verra pleased to meet ye," she said.

"How old are ye?" Duncan asked.

"Eighteen."

"Yer old!" Gavin exclaimed.

"Why, thank ye." Rob gestured to the pup. "This is Smooches, named because if ye lean verra close to him, he'll give ye plenty of kisses."

Instantly, both boys leaned close to the pup. True to his name, Smooches delighted in licking their faces and making them laugh with childish glee.

Duncan picked a twig up, threw it across the garden, and ordered, "Fetch, Smooches."

The pup wagged his tail and sat down.

"I'm afraid Smooches hasna learned to fetch yet," Rob explained.

"I'll teach him," Gavin offered.

"*We'll* teach him," Duncan corrected his brother.

"Perhaps 'twould be wise to begin with somethin' simple like 'sit' or 'give paw,' " Rob suggested.

"Sit," Gavin ordered the pup.

"He's already sittin'," Duncan told his brother.

"Stand," Gavin corrected himself.

Rob burst out laughing. The six-year-old cast her a flirtatious smile, obviously pleased that he'd entertained her.

"Do ye play here often?" Rob asked, sitting down on a nearby stone bench. She loved children and hoped she'd see them again.

Duncan nodded. "Every day at this hour."

"Weather permittin', I'll meet ye here tomorrow," Rob said. "Ye can train Smooches a little bit each day. Would ye like that?"

Surprisingly, the boys did not answer. They were looking at something behind her.

"Da!" Duncan shrieked and ran past her.

"Da!" Gavin echoed and followed his brother.

With a smile of greeting upon her face, Rob stood and turned to meet their father. The sight of him hit her with the impact of an avalanche, crushing whatever hopes for happiness she'd harbored in her heart. Shock weakened her legs as if she'd been struck with the broad end of a claymore, forcing her to plop down on the bench again.

Duke Magnus stood near the garden door. Beside him, Gordon crouched on one bended knee as he clutched his sons.

"How are my warrior and my hawk?" Gordon asked the boys.

"I missed ye," Duncan said.

"Me too," Gavin echoed.

"We've just saved that damsel from the dragon that was chasin' her," Duncan told his father.

Gordon shifted his gaze to Rob and told them, "I once slew the monster that was livin' beneath her bed."

"Ye did?" they chimed together.

Gordon smiled and nodded.

"She said we could train her dog and play together every day," Gavin told his father. The boy lowered his voice and whispered, "She's verra bonny."

"Aye, she's bonny," Gordon agreed, and smiled in her direction.

Meeting his gaze, Rob felt her blood heat to a boiling rage, and a tempest of anger swept through her. Duncan and Gavin were her husband's bastards, Kendra's sons sired after he'd married her. While she'd been dreaming of him rescuing her from the taunts of the MacArthur clan's children, Gordon had been nesting between Kendra's thighs.

Rob considered Duncan and Gavin innocent of their father's sins. She knew that many men sired children out of wedlock. Their existence didn't bother her. What hurt beyond forgiveness was his lack of regard for her as evidenced by his failure to tell her about his sons.

Everyone in the hall that morning knew that Kendra had borne Gordon his two sons.

Except his wife.

Chapter 10

 "God's balls, lass. Dinna just stand there lookin' like yer aboot to swoon," Gordon said, standing in front of her. "Say somethin', will ye?"

Having just suffered one of the worst shocks of her eighteen years, Rob knew she must be as pale as death itself. She looked up at her husband, and then gazed past him to the duke and the two young boys who stood near the door. All of them wore worried expressions, which meant she appeared as horrible as she felt.

Rob met her father-in-law's gaze and gave him a pointed stare. Oddly enough, Duke Magnus understood what she needed because he cast her an encouraging smile and inclined his head in her direction. Taking his grandsons in hand, he disappeared inside the building.

"Well, lass?"

Rob looked up at Gordon again. A surge of rage shot through her. Her husband was about to feel the sting of her anger, but not her pain. *Never her pain.* She'd always considered her pain a private matter to be kept locked away and never shared with anyone. Her MacArthur pride refused to allow anyone the sight of her vulnerable, aching heart.

Slowly and deliberately, Rob rose from her perch on the bench. She stepped closer to her husband and said in a deceptively quiet voice, "Tell me, my lord. How would *ye* feel if I'd been the one with children I'd neglected to mention?"

"Dinna be ridiculous," Gordon scoffed at the notion.

"How *dare* ye call me ridiculous," Rob said, her voice an angry whisper, her hands clenching into fists at her sides. "At least *I* possessed the integrity to tell ye aboot Henry. Ye should have told me aboot yer sons, Gordy." Her whisper grew into a shout, and her chest heaved with breathless rage as though she'd climbed a mountain. "I had the right to know aboot them before I stepped into that hall and faced the woman who bore them. Great Bruce's ghost, I'll *never* trust ye again."

Gordon snapped his eyebrows together. "Are ye finished?"

"Not quite," she replied in a clipped voice. "Yer an immoral, arrogant son of a bitch."

Without warning, Rob swung with her right arm and slapped his left cheek so hard the force of it snapped his face to the right. Scooping Smooches into her arms, she marched down the stone path and disappeared inside the house.

Rob went directly to her chamber. Shaking with fury, she set Smooches down on the bed and then sat in the chair in front of the hearth.

Tears welled up in her eyes, but she forced them back. How humiliating to meet her husband's mistress, the mother of his sons, and be unaware of it. Those watching Campbells in the hall that morning must have had a hearty laugh at her expense, and by now the tale would have spread to anyone unfortunate enough to have missed it.

And just how did Fergus figure into this? Didn't the man care that his wife had borne the laird's heir two children?

Rob sighed raggedly and struggled against the flood of tears threatening to spill, doggedly refusing to weep for Gordon. She'd lived through worse than this humiliation and never shed a tear. The proud MacArthurs never wept for trivialities like a miserable, friendless childhood or a husband's betrayal.

A startling thought suddenly slammed into her consciousness. She'd struck her husband. Never in her entire life had she done anyone violence. Why, in the holy name of God, had she started with him? Praise be to a merciful God, there'd been no witnesses. Gordon would be furious and bent on exacting some kind of retribution. What form would that take, and, more importantly, how would she deflect it?

Hours passed while she pondered her fateful near-future. Just before supper the door swung open. Startled, Rob glanced over her shoulder, certain that her husband had come to punish her for daring to raise her hand to him.

"Good evenin', Lady Rob," Gabby called.

"Is it evenin' already?" Rob asked, every nerve in her body relaxing at the welcome sight of her tiring woman.

"Have ye been sittin' there the whole day and never noticed the hours passin'?" Gabby asked, crossing the chamber to stand before her. "Ye dinna look well. Is yer hand painin' ye?"

Rob met the girl's worried gaze and answered, "No, 'tis my heart."

"Spill it, lady," Gabby ordered, heedless of the proper

protocol between a tiring woman and her mistress. "What's yer problem?"

Rob hesitated for a fraction of a moment, but then admitted, "My husband and I are in discord."

"Is that all?" Gabby chuckled, surprising her. "Would ye like me to help ye change yer gown before supper?" she asked. " 'Tis one of my duties, ye know."

Rob shook her head. "I'd rather ye tell me aboot Gordon and Kendra."

"What's to tell?"

"She bore him two sons."

"Oh, that." Gabby gestured with her hand as if the matter were of no consequence. " 'Twas an affair ended long ago. Besides, Gordy futtered dozens of Inverary's maids."

"Why, thank ye, Gabby," Rob said dryly. "Yer makin' me feel ever so much better."

"A man will always take what's offered," the girl told her. "Granny Biddy said so."

"What aboot Fergus?" Rob asked.

"Kendra married Fergus aboot three years ago when she realized havin' the laird's grandsons wasna gainin' her anythin'," Gabby said. "The laird ordered the boys moved into the main house last year so they could be educated and raised as befittin' a duke's grandsons. Tutors them himself, he does. Every week or two, Duncan and Gavin spend a day and a night with Fergus and Kendra. Ye are na harborin' a grudge against the lads, are ye?"

"No, but Gordon should have told me they existed," Rob replied.

"He never told ye?" Gabby shook her head in disbelief. " 'Tis just like a man to ignore the unpleasant truth until it leaps up and bites his arse. Granny Biddy says dinna ever let yer man get the upper hand with ye because—"

"I believe *I* got the upper hand with my husband," Rob interrupted, smiling in spite of her heartache.

"What d'ye mean?"

"I slapped him."

Gabby's lips formed a perfect O of surprise, and then she grinned. "Good for ye, my lady. I'm likin' ye better and better with each passin' moment."

Had she found a friend in Gabby? Rob wondered, returning the girl's smile. If so, it would be the second friend she'd ever had. Not bad, considering she'd never expected to have even one.

"Let me dress ye up pretty for supper," Gabby suggested.

"I canna go down there," Rob said, refusing. "Everyone except me knew aboot Duncan and Gavin bein' Gordy's sons. 'Twould be too embarrassin' to face them."

"The others dinna know that Gordy never told ye aboot the boys bein' his," Gabby reasoned with her. "In fact, I'm positive they assumed he told ye. I heard ye tell Kendra that the laird spoke aboot the boys to ye. What ye must do is *pretend* that ye knew all along."

"I dinna know," Rob replied uncertainly.

"Think of the fun ye'll have sittin' at the high table and givin' Gordy the cold shoulder," the girl coaxed. "Why, he'll be squirmin' in his chair like a man who's sufferin' from the crabs but doesna dare scratch his itch."

Rob smiled, though she had absolutely no idea to what the girl was referring. "Gabby, I'm likin' ye more and more," she said.

"Och, I never doubted ye would."

Rob dressed in one of her late mother-in-law's gowns created in dove gray velvet. The dress had long-flowing sleeves that ended in a point at her wrists, a tight-fitting bodice, and a moderately low-cut, squared neckline. Around her neck she set her beggar bead necklace, its star ruby resting provocatively just above the valley between her breasts. Rob would have worn a pair of the lacy fingerless gloves her husband had given her, but none quite matched the gown and would only have aroused curiosity about what she was hiding beneath it.

With Gabby trailing in her wake, Rob walked into the great hall. She kept her head held high and a serene expression on her face as she made her way through the crowd toward the high table. Most of the clansmen she passed bade her a good evening; Rob returned their greeting by nodding at them like a young queen acknowledging her subjects. Judging from her outward demeanor, no one would ever have imagined that she was a quivering mass of nerves on the inside.

Reaching the high table where Duke Magnus and Gordon stood with the two boys, Rob smiled and asked, "Who would care to sit beside me?"

"I do," all of them answered simultaneously.

Ignoring her husband, Rob cast her father-in-law a look of supreme regret and said, "I believe I'll sit between the two verra bravest Campbells. Gavin, ye sit here between yer grandfather and me. Smooches will sit on my lap; and, Duncan, ye sit over here between me and . . . *him*."

Rob heard Duke Magnus chuckle and then cough to cover it. Glancing over her shoulder, she cast him a look that said the entertainment was about to begin.

The duke's servants set supper on the table in front of them. There were sheep's haggis, Mashlan scones with butter, cheese, cider, and wine.

"Ye look especially lovely tonight," Gordon complimented her unexpectedly.

Rob inclined her head, acknowledging the compliment, and said, "Yes, I know." Then she turned away and scanned the hall's occupants.

"She isna here," the duke whispered over Gavin's head, drawing her attention.

"I dinna understand, Yer Grace," Rob said, giving him a puzzled look.

"Most couples, such as Fergus and Kendra, dinna sup in the hall," Duke Magnus told her. "Married couples usually enjoy the privacy of suppin' alone in their own quarters after a hard day's work."

Rob nodded. " 'Tis the same at Dunridge Castle."

"So, how was yer first full day at Inverary?" the duke asked.

"Enlightenin'."

"Any problems?"

"Only minor, certainly unworthy of yer attention," Rob replied, her voice loud enough for her husband to hear. She lifted her mug of cider to her lips and took a sip.

"I heard ye married our da," Gavin said, apparently unhappy with her inattention. "Should we call ye *Ma*?"

Rob choked on her cider. When she was able to speak again, she replied, "Well, yer own mother might feel puirly if ye gave me her title. What do ye call Fergus?"

"We call him Fergus," Duncan answered.

"Then call me Rob."

The boys nodded, their smiles telling her how relieved they felt to have that matter settled. "Well, Lady Rob," Duncan said. "Do ye suppose ye'll be givin' us brothers and sisters?"

Rob stared at him in surprise. And that was before she heard the little voice on her left speak up.

"Da, can we have a baby sister?" Gavin asked his father.

" 'Tis fine with me, son," Gordon answered, a wicked

smile lighting his expression. "Of course, ye'll have to clear it with my wife."

Rob sent her husband an unamused look.

"Would ye care for a game of chess after supper, hinny?" he asked.

"Ye canna get sisters from playin' chess," Duncan announced. "Even *I* know that."

Rob stifled a horrified giggle at the turn their conversation had taken. She cast her husband a long look and then said, "No, thank ye, my lord."

Before he could protest, Rob rose from her chair and, cradling the pup in her arms, said, "I'm still a bit weary from travelin'. I'll take Smooches outside for a few minutes and then retire." She turned to Gavin and asked, "Will I see ye in the mornin'?"

The little boy grinned and nodded.

"And ye too?" she asked his brother.

Duncan nodded. "We'll begin trainin' Smooches then."

Without glancing back at the high table, Rob slowly wended her way through the crowd of warriors and retainers, and then disappeared out the door. The four males at the high table, from the oldest to the youngest, watched her leave.

Duke Magnus chuckled as soon as she'd vanished from sight. "Well, she put ye in yer place," he told his son.

"Ye sound like yer enjoyin' this," Gordon replied, rounding on his father.

"Well, Inverary was becomin' a tad borin' until she arrived," the duke admitted. "Now I'm lookin' forward to bein' thoroughly entertained during my twilight years. At yer expense, of course."

"I dinna perceive any real contest of wills here," Gordon told his father.

"Remember this, son," Duke Magnus warned him. " 'Pride goeth before a fall.' "

"I canna credit what I'm hearin'," Gordon countered, rising from his chair. "Old Clootie himself is quotin' the Holy Scripture." At that, he followed his wife out of the hall.

The Duke of Argyll threw back his head and shouted with laughter. He glanced at his grandsons who were staring at him in confusion.

"At what are ye laughin'?" Duncan asked.

"Yer father," the duke answered.

"Why?" asked Gavin.

"Because yer father has the common sense of a donkey," Duke Magnus answered, still smiling. "And if ye repeat what I said, ye willna be receivin' ponies when yer birthdays come around again."

"I never heard nothin'," Duncan said.

"Me too," Gavin agreed.

When she left the great hall, Rob hurried down the long corridor and descended the wheel stairs to the ground level. Opening the door that led to the enclosed garden, she stepped outside and set Smooches down. "Go on," she ordered. "Do yer duty."

Rob paused before following the pup and looked up at the night sky. The west wind had blown the day's cloud cover away. Accompanied by thousands of glittering stars, a full moon hung overhead in the perfect setting of the black velvet sky.

Supper had been a success, Rob thought as she strolled down the stone path. So why did satisfaction elude her? Why did she have an empty feeling of loss deep within her heart?

As she walked along, the night's dark beauty and the serenity within the garden renewed her flagging spirits.

She could hardly wait for spring when this private sanctuary would certainly become nature's paradise.

"Rob?"

She turned around slowly at the sound of her husband's voice. "Yes, my lord?"

Gordon stood five feet away. Even in the darkness, her husband appeared a magnificent figure of a man, the kind about whom young maidens dream. No wonder he'd become a womanizer. How much inner strength could one man possess? Even Adam in his state of original grace hadn't been able to refuse that infamous apple.

"I apologize for not tellin' ye aboot Duncan and Gavin," Gordon said simply.

"I forgive ye and apologize for strikin' ye," Rob said. " 'Twas wrong of me."

Gordon stepped closer as a smile slashed across his handsome features. He reached out with one hand and touched her arm. "We could grant Gavin's request if we seal our forgiveness with a kiss," he suggested in a seductively husky voice.

"Request?"

"The lad wants a sister to cosset."

Rob stepped back two paces and scooped Smooches in her arms. Lifting her upturned nose into the air, she informed him, "All those verra willin' ladies have stunted yer emotional growth, my lord. Trust isna unlimited, and forgiveness doesna imply forgetfulness. This may be impossible for ye to ken, my lord, but *I* dinna desire ye."

At that, Rob marched down the path toward the door and disappeared inside. *Angel, ye know nothin' aboot desire,* Gordon thought, as he watched her retrace her steps, *but ye'll learn. Verra soon, my reluctant love.*

* * *

Rob opened her eyes and knew from the chamber's dim light that the hour was still early. She never awakened with the dawn. What had disturbed her sleep?

Turning toward her husband, Rob discovered his side of the bed empty. A noise from the other side of the chamber drew her attention, and she raised her head off the pillow to see what he was doing.

With his back turned to her, Gordon crouched in front of the hearth and stoked its embers to life. He was magnificently naked except for a loincloth, which he'd begun wearing to bed in deference to her easily offended modesty.

Watching him through heavy-lidded eyes, Rob admired the play of his sinewy, well-honed muscles across his shoulders and upper back as he worked. An unfamiliar, warm tingling heated the pit of her stomach as she stared at the ease of strength in her husband's muscles. A primitive feeling of being the only man and woman in the world surged through her, and she yearned for . . . what?

Breaking the spell his maleness had cast upon her, Rob snapped her eyes shut when he stood suddenly. She didn't want him to catch her peeking at him.

When the sound of splashing water reached her ears, Rob opened her eyes a crack. Her husband was standing across the chamber at the table where they kept the basin and rinsing the sleep from his face.

From this vantage point, Rob had an excellent view of the back of his thickly muscled thighs, a warrior's thighs developed from years of hard riding and, she supposed, more intimate activity. What would it feel like if those muscled thighs of his spread her legs apart and—

Gordon glanced toward the bed as if he could feel her interested gaze upon him.

Rob hastily closed her eyes again and then heard him

moving toward the chairs in front of the hearth. Her heart pounded rapidly as if watching her husband at his morning toilet was a terrible sin, but that possibility didn't stop her.

She opened first one eye and then the other. Apparently, he'd set his clothing across one of the chairs because he unexpectedly dropped his loincloth onto the floor and reached toward the chair. Rob nearly swooned from the incredible sight of his tight, rounded buttocks. The man even had an irresistible arse.

In the next instant Gordon ruined her pleasure by donning his long shirt, which covered his more interesting assets, and Rob nearly moaned with disappointment. Next came his wool stockings and black leather boots. Finally, Gordon wrapped his Campbell plaid around himself, secured it in place with a thick belt, and shrugged into his black leather jerkin.

Rob closed her eyes when he turned to leave the chamber. "Come, Smooches," she heard him call softly, and then felt the pup scrambling off the bed.

Silence reigned in the chamber for several, long moments. Rob opened her eyes and glanced toward the door through which her husband had disappeared.

" 'Tis early yet," Gordon said, a smile flirting with the corners of his lips as he watched her from the doorway. "Shall I rouse Gabby and send her to ye?"

"No," Rob squeaked, her face growing hot with embarrassment.

Gordon winked at her and said, "Well, I hope ye enjoyed the entertainment." Then he vanished with the pup out the door.

Great Bruce's ghost, he'd known all along that she'd been watching him strut naked about their chamber. How humiliating to be caught peeking at what he had to offer, especially since she'd insisted she didn't desire him.

Rob yanked the coverlet over her head. How she wished she could sink inside the mattress.

Later that morning Rob stepped into the enclosed garden and paused to inhale deeply of the pure mountain air, crisp yet surprisingly warmer than usual for that season of the year. Everywhere she looked, Rob saw the signs of winter's passing, and her spirit quickened with the promise of spring. The chaste full moon would begin waning that night, heralding days that waxed warmer as the sun's power increased.

Rob set Smooches on the ground and strolled down the stone path that led to the bench. She didn't have to wait long for Duncan and Gavin. Spying her from where they played at the opposite side of the garden, the two boys dashed toward her.

"Are ye ready to train Smooches?" Rob asked, making herself comfortable on the bench.

"Aye," both boys answered, standing in front of her.

Drawing their attention, the garden door opened unexpectedly, and Gordon appeared. He cast the three of them a smile as he advanced on them. Over his right shoulder, he'd slung his golf bag with one of Biddy's brooms sticking out of the end; in his left hand, he carried a bowl.

Watching him, Rob was unable to banish the naked image of him from her mind's eye, and felt the hot blush that stained her cheeks a becoming pink. Was he also remembering how she'd peeked at him that morning? she wondered when he winked at her.

"I've come to help the boys," Gordon said, leaning his golf bag against the bench beside her. "They canna train the pup unless they have treats to give him."

Rob, Duncan, and Gavin peered into the bowl. Tiny pieces of cold roast filled it.

"I'll handle this," Duncan said.

"No, I will," Gavin protested.

"Both of ye will get a turn," Gordon told them. He sat beside her on the bench, so close only the width of the golf bag separated them.

Rob looked down at his thigh teasing her skirt. In her mind's eye, she saw its muscled thickness and then his tight, rounded buttocks. The sensual memory of her naked husband heated her all over. She hoped he couldn't tell what she was thinking.

"What do ye think, angel?" Gordon was asking.

Rob lifted her gaze to his and blushed at being caught staring at his thigh. "Sounds reasonable to me," she answered in a soft voice. In truth, she couldn't recall what he'd been saying.

"Yer the oldest," Gordon said to Duncan. "Ye try first."

Smiling with seven-year-old bravado, Duncan took the bowl of meat and wafted it beneath the pup's nose, which twitched with eager anticipation. The boy shoved Smooches's backside down and ordered, "Sit." Then he reinforced his command by rewarding the pup with a morsel of meat.

Smooches learned this lesson quickly. Laughing at their success, Rob clapped her hands together for the boy and the dog.

"Well done," Gordon praised his oldest son. " 'Tis yer turn, Gavin."

The six-year-old took the bowl out of his brother's hands. Looking very much like his charming father, he gave Rob an exaggerated wink.

Unfortunately, *stay* was a little more difficult for the pup to learn. "Sit," Gavin ordered the pup. Then, "Stay."

Gavin walked three paces away and set a piece of meat on the ground. No sooner had he turned his back on

Smooches than the pup attacked the meat and gobbled it up.

"No, sit," Gavin scolded, pointing a finger at the pup. "Stay."

This time Gavin refused to turn his back on the dog. Walking backwards, he made a trail of meat leading away from the pup; but as soon as he placed a piece of meat on the ground, Smooches gobbled it up.

Gordon and Rob looked at each other and smiled. "Dinna laugh out loud," she whispered out the side of her mouth. "Ye'll hurt his feelin's."

"Stay," Gavin shouted, frustrated with his failure. Suddenly, the boy tripped over his own feet. The bowl flew out of his hands, and pieces of meat rained down around him. Faster than an eye could blink, Smooches gobbled all of it up.

"God's balls," Duncan exclaimed, sounding exactly like his father. "Now see what ye've done, brother."

" 'Twas an accident that could happen to anyone," Rob defended the six-year-old, struggling against a fit of the giggles.

"Bring more meat," Gavin ordered his father.

"Biddy will murder the lot of us if I steal another bowl of meat today," Gordon said, refusing, schooling the laughter out of his expression. "Besides, 'tis time for yer golf lesson. Ye do wish to play with the king some day?"

"Aye," Duncan and Gavin agreed.

Reaching into his golf bag, Gordon pulled the broom out first and proceeded to sweep the stone walk of any lingering winter debris. Next he withdrew a gold-plated goblet and set it down on its side. Taking his putter and a golf ball, he walked several yards away and gently hit the ball into the goblet.

"First, ye must learn to put it inside the goblet every single time," Gordon instructed his sons. "Then, ye must learn to make it a near miss whenever ye wish. 'Tis important to the clan that ye please the king's sons by losin' to them without seemin' to do so."

"Jamie doesna have any sons," Rob said. "He isna married."

"He'll have sons some day," Gordon replied. " 'Tis imperative that Duncan and Gavin be prepared."

"I want to go raidin' the other clans," Duncan told his father.

Gavin smiled at Rob. "I want to go dancin' with the ladies."

"I'll teach ye how 'tis done," Rob said, rising from her perch on the bench. "We'll begin with the pavane."

Rob curtsied to the six-year-old. In return, Gavin bowed from his waist.

"Press this part of yer arm against yer body," Rob instructed him, demonstrating as she spoke. "Hold yer open palms up toward me. Now sway yer right side toward my right side, and touch yer palm to mine." When he'd done that, she said, "Do the same thin' with yer left palm."

Rob and Gavin did each side two more times, and then, ending the dance, she curtsied to him. Taking his cue, the boy bowed from the waist again and then grinned at her.

Gavin had inherited his father's devastatingly charming smile, Rob thought. The lad would surely break dozens of female hearts.

"Let Rob try golfin'," Duncan told his father.

"I dinna think . . ." Rob began.

Gavin reached out and touched her hand, saying, "Do it for me."

Rob cast the six-year-old a rueful smile and nodded. "I dinna remember exactly how to hold the club," she told her husband.

"I'll help ye," Gordon said, his smile wolfish.

After setting a ball down on the walkway, Gordon passed her the club and stood behind her. Just like that day they'd practiced in the garden at Devereux House, he stood so close behind her only their garments separated them.

"Now then, angel," Gordon whispered against her ear.

His warm breath tickled the side of her face, and delightful chills of excitement danced down her spine. Unexpectedly, her husband caressed her neck with his lips.

" 'Tis exactly how we get baby sisters," Duncan announced.

Gordon chuckled huskily. Rob glanced over her shoulder and smiled shyly at him.

"Duncan! Gavin! Yer grandfather's lookin' for ye," Gabby called from the doorway. " 'Tis time for yer lessons."

"Comin'," Duncan answered and started toward the door.

"I'll see ye at supper," Gavin told Rob, and then followed his brother.

"I do believe that Gavin is fallin' in love with ye," Gordon said, returning his golfing paraphernalia to the bag.

"Ye've been blessed with two verra special boys, my lord," Rob replied.

Gordon lifted her hands to his lips and gazed deeply into her eyes. "Angel, I want to thank ye for not takin' my stupidity out on my sons."

"Likin' Gavin and Duncan is easy," she told him.

"As easy as likin' me?" Without waiting for her reply, Gordon scooped Smooches into his arms and then passed him to her. Together, they walked toward the door.

"Ye must admit I'm becomin' more sensitive to yer feelin's," Gordon said. "Why, we've been in this garden for more than an hour, and I never embarrassed ye by mentionin' that ye were peekin' at me this mornin'."

Rob flicked him an irritated, unamused look. Ruining the effect, a high blush stained her cheeks.

"Ooops, I guess I just mentioned it," Gordon said, wearing the most unrepentant grin she'd ever seen. "Well, if ye dinna get angry, I'll let ye peek at me tomorrow."

"Yer incorrigible," she told him.

"I know," he admitted. "And I thank ye for the high praise."

A week passed. And then another.

All around Inverary Castle the telltale signs of spring abounded. Courageous crocus broke through the still-frosty ground in the duke's garden. Migrating robins and finches appeared, returning to their northern haunts to prepare for their nesting season.

Anxious to see Duncan and Gavin, Rob stepped outside and scanned the deserted garden. The boys had passed the previous day and evening with Fergus and Kendra, and Rob had missed their company.

"Duncan and Gavin, I know yer here," she called, setting Smooches down to scamper wherever he would. "Are ye hidin' on me?"

Gavin appeared from behind an evergreen hedgerow. With a smile of greeting lighting his expression, the six-year-old started toward her.

"Stop!" Duncan shouted, materializing from behind the same hedgerow.

Gavin halted at his brother's command. He looked from Rob to Duncan and then at her again, seemingly torn between them.

"Come away, brother," Duncan said, grabbing his hand. "Or ye'll be hurt."

Rob stared at the seven-year-old in confusion. What

had happened to upset Duncan? Did the boys always behave strangely after spending time with their mother? Or was this merely a new game they were playing with her?

Rob decided a calm facade would be the best approach with them. She sat down on the stone bench and looked in their direction.

When Smooches tried to greet the boys, Duncan kicked the pup away. Then he flicked her a nervous, uneasy glance.

Rob recognized the frightened look in his eyes, but refused to believe what she saw. "Come, Gavin," she coaxed, casting the boy a winsome smile. "Sit beside me."

The six-year-old returned her smile and would have gone to her, but his brother held him back. "Mama said dinna get too near Old Clootie's witch," Duncan reminded him.

Hearing those words, Rob felt her promising new life crumble around her. " 'Tis untrue. I'm no monster," she pleaded in an aching whisper, holding her hand out in supplication to the boys. "Please, Gavin, sit with me."

"Begone, witch," Duncan shouted, and then made a protective sign of the cross.

"Begone, witch." Gavin imitated his brother.

Changelin'-witch. Loch Awe Monster. Those childhood taunts slammed into her mind and her heart with the impact of a crushing avalanche.

Rob covered her face with her hands and struggled against the familiar pain. The ache in her heart and the raw emotion swelling in her throat felt like old friends. Tears welled up in her eyes and streamed down her cheeks. Duncan and Gavin had accomplished what the MacArthur clan's children had been unable to do. Their rejection broke her heart.

I'm just like you, Rob wanted to shout at them. The stain on her hand didn't prove she was a witch. Evil lived within the heart, not on the back of a hand.

How many days would pass before everyone at Inverary made the sign of the cross when they saw her? The others didn't matter, though. Duncan and Gavin had already broken her heart.

Rob lifted her head and glanced in their direction. When both boys made the sign of the cross, she closed her burning eyes at the sight and took a ragged, painful breath.

Scooping Smooches into her arms, Rob flicked the boys one last look of regret. Slowly and wearily, as if the sins of the world rested upon her shoulders, Rob walked across the garden to the door. Their voices reached her just before she disappeared inside.

"Rob's weepin'," Gavin said. "We hurt her feelin's."

"Witches dinna have feelin's," Duncan told him.

"Then why's she weepin'?"

"I dinna know, so shut up."

Rob ran up the wheel stairs two at a time until she reached the third floor. Luckily, she made it to her chamber without being seen. After setting Smooches down on the floor, she plopped into the chair in front of the hearth and stared at the flames. In her mind's eye, Rob saw the boys crossing themselves at the sight of her, and a moan of aching regret slipped from her lips.

She should never have returned to Scotland. The Highlands abounded with ignorant and superstitious people. If only she hadn't behaved so impulsively that day in her uncle's study. And just what had enticed her into believing that life at Inverary Castle would be different from her previous life at Dunridge Castle?

A sudden, horrifying idea rooted in her mind, something she'd never considered before. Could she actually be Old Clootie's chosen? Had the real MacArthur daughter been abducted at birth? And was she the evil changelin' the fairies had left behind? These unanswerable questions and gnawing doubts gave Rob a headache.

Home. Like a siren's song the comforting arms of her family called to her. Yes, the MacArthur clansmen had rejected her, but Dunridge Castle housed a family who loved her. Inverary Castle offered none of that. Here she lived among strangers.

Ye ride into the mountains behind Inverary, through the valley of Glen Aray and then the forest. At the crest of the moors, ye'll see Loch Awe and its jewel, Dunridge Castle.

That was the path into her mother's comforting arms. Her wounds would heal within the shelter of her family. Come summer, she would return to England.

With her decision made, Rob knew there was no time to waste. She changed into the woolen skirt and linen blouse she'd worn her first day at Inverary. After strapping her leather satchel to her chest, she dressed Smooches in his sweater and set him inside, then grabbed her warmest cloak and wrapped herself in it.

Rob stepped into the courtyard and hurried in the direction of the smithy's and the stables. She saw Kendra standing with two women on the opposite side of the yard near the well. Spying her, the three women turned their backs and began talking with obvious excitement.

Rob cared not a whit. Acceptance by the Campbells was something she hadn't really expected. Only Gavin . . .

Rob forced herself to banish the six-year-old from her heart and her mind, as she'd exiled so many others who'd rejected her. She was going home. And then she reached the smithy's and stood uncertainly in his doorway.

"Lady Rob," Fergus greeted her with a broad smile. "Seein' ye here is a pleasant surprise."

"Good day to ye," Rob replied, forcing herself to return his smile. "I—I'm unsure of whom to ask, but I require a horse. Can ye help me?"

"Why do ye need a mount?" Fergus asked, puzzled.

"Do I need to explain myself to ye?" Rob countered defensively.

"Ye do," came his reply.

She inclined her head and said, "Verra well. I'm plannin' on visitin' my parents."

"Alone?" There was no mistaking the surprised disbelief in his voice.

"I have my husband's permission," Rob lied, determined to follow through with her plan to leave Inverary. She'd dared to draw her dagger on Queen Elizabeth's minister, so no Campbell smithy would thwart her plans. She just had to get away.

"I'm verra sorry, Lady Rob," Fergus said, refusing her request. "I'll need to hear Gordy tell me that ye have his permission."

"Are ye questionin' the veracity of my words?" she challenged him.

"No, yer honesty."

"Great Bruce's ghost, do ye realize to whom yer speakin'?" Rob asked, raising her voice with indignation. "*I* am Inverary's lady. How dare ye refuse me a horse."

"And do ye realize to whom yer speakin'?" Fergus asked, towering over her. "*I* am the laird's man in charge of the horses, and yer not gettin' one."

"My husband will hear aboot this," Rob threatened him.

"Yer damned right aboot that," Fergus met her threat with his own.

Rob gave up and walked away in a huff. Retracing her steps, she marched across the courtyard and then raced up the wheel stairs to the third story.

When she gained the privacy of her chamber, Rob dropped her cloak on the floor and freed Smooches from his confinement. Standing at the window, she gazed down at the enclosed garden. Duncan and Gavin sat in silence on the stone bench. They appeared as miserable as she felt. Unable to bear the depressing sight, Rob turned away from the window and began to pace the chamber.

What would she do now? Rob wondered. She refused to tell her husband that his sons had rejected her. Gordon would punish them, and she couldn't live with herself if he did that. The boys couldn't help believing she was a witch. How could she expect them to doubt their own mother?

The door crashed open. Rob whirled around and faced her husband. *Her angry husband.*

"Where did ye think ye were goin'?" Gordon demanded without preamble, marching across the chamber to confront her.

"Home," Rob answered honestly.

"Yer already home."

"Dunridge Castle is my home." Rob sighed and admitted, "I just wanted to see my mother."

"Is that why ye lied to Fergus?" Gordon asked, staring hard at her. "Do ye realize ye could have died out there if he hadna refused ye?"

"Argyll is safe," Rob replied.

"No place in the whole wide world is safe for a woman alone," Gordon said in a clipped voice. "I'll take ye home for a visit this summer."

"I want to go now."

Gordon narrowed his piercing gray gaze on her. "Ye never mentioned bein' homesick before. As a matter of fact, I nearly had to drag ye out of England. So, angel, what's the real reason ye've a mind to leave Inverary?"

"Kendra bore ye two sons," Rob cried, hating herself

for lying but determined to protect the little boys who'd stolen her heart and then broken it. "Ye dinna need me."

Gordon gave her a long, measuring look. Rob could tell from his skeptical expression that he knew she was lying.

"Duncan and Gavin are bastards," Gordon said baldly. "Neither can ever be the lord of Inverary Castle, but both will support the heir ye give me."

"Ye willna be gettin' an heir out of me," Rob announced.

"And why do ye say that?"

"Come summer, I'm returnin' to England."

Gordon stared at her as if she'd suddenly grown another head. "Ye willna be returnin' to England," he told her in a deceptively calm voice. "And, God willin', ye'll bear my sons and daughters. 'Tis past time to stop yer whinin' and grow up." He marched back across the chamber but paused at the door. "Dinna try for another horse. I've ordered the guards to stop ye if ye attempt to wander beyond Inverary's walls."

"Yer keepin' me prisoner?" Rob asked.

"Dinna be ridiculous. Yer Inverary's lady," Gordon said. "Try actin' like it." At that, he turned on his heels and left their chamber.

How would she survive among these enemies? Rob thought desperately. Being made outcast by the likes of Kendra didn't bother her overmuch, but the children would have nothing to do with her. The boys had insinuated themselves into her heart, and she'd miss playing with them in the garden. Especially Gavin, whose smile reminded her of her husband.

Chapter 11

 Damn, but his father sounded like the Inquisition.

The questions began as soon as Gordon stepped into the study and became increasingly more difficult to answer with each passing moment. His head ached with annoyance. But what could he do? The man was the Duke of Argyll, the laird of clan Campbell, and his own father.

"Well, did ye tell her?"

"No."

"She doesna know yer takin' her to the lodge?" Duke Magnus asked, passing him a dram of whiskey. "Where does she think she's goin'?"

Gordon gulped the whiskey in one long swig, fortifying himself for the eventual confrontation with his wife. Gazing out the window at the startlingly bright late-April day, he answered, "Rob believes I'm takin' her to Dunridge Castle for a visit with her mother."

"Ah, lad, will ye never learn?" Duke Magnus asked, an unmistakable smile lurking in his voice. "A wise man never lies to his wife. 'Twill eventually return to haunt ye."

"She would have refused me if I'd told her the truth," Gordon replied, facing his father. "I dinna ken what's made her so reclusive lately, but we canna continue like this. Why, she even avoids Duncan and Gavin."

"Have ye breached her yet?"

Gordon stared hard at his father. Their gray gazes, so much alike, met and clashed in a silent battle of wills.

"With all due respect, 'tis none of yer business," Gordon told his father.

Duke Magnus grinned at his son's defensive response and went in for the kill. "Since ye havena consummated yer vows, an annulment is still possible. Why dinna ye take her to Dunridge Castle and leave her there?"

"I didna say I havena breached her," Gordon hedged, embarrassed to be skirting around the truth and wondering why he was even bothering. His father always seemed to know when he was lying or evading. "As for the other, even if 'twas possible to annul her, 'twould cause dissension between our families."

"Dinna think twice aboot me," the duke said, waving his hand in a dismissive gesture. "I doubt Cousin Iain would be insulted either. After all, if the lass isna happy with ye and ye havena—"

"I said *no*," Gordon interrupted, his voice clipped with annoyance. God's balls, dealing with his wife was irritating enough. Was he now required to debate the merits of annulment with his father? Gordon had the feeling that the old fox was toying with him and enjoying himself immensely.

"Do ye love her?" Duke Magnus persisted.

"Drop it, Yer Grace," Gordon warned, his patience depleted.

"Well, ye must harbor a fondness for the lass," the

duke went on as if his son had never spoken. "Ye ordered puir Dewey to haul a real bed—mattress and all—up into those mountains. And what else did I hear? Ah, yes. A privacy screen, a chamber pot, scented soap, and the good Lord only knows what else."

"I dinna want her complainin' aboot bein' uncomfortable," Gordon said, by way of a plausible explanation. "Rob is a delicate woman, and 'twill be difficult enough without makin' her suffer. Consideration for my wife is a far cry from lovin' her."

"Yer underestimatin' her," Magnus told him. "Women and babies are always a lot stronger than we men believe."

Gordon snapped to alertness as the door swung open. With Smooches ensconced inside the satchel strapped to her chest, Rob hurried into the study. Her emerald eyes sparkled with excitement, and happiness at the prospect of going home had tinged her cheeks with a high blush; that worried look had vanished from her expression, and she appeared more vibrant than she had in more than a month. With her ebony hair woven into two braids, his wife seemed more like a young girl than the Marchioness of Inverary and the future Duchess of Argyll.

Admiring her youthful beauty and expectant smile, Gordon felt tight coils of guilt wrapping themselves around his chest. But what else could he do? Only by deceiving her into believing she was going home had he been able to get her to agree to leave their chamber. Why, she hardly even ventured into the garden anymore, and certainly never when his sons were about.

"Are ye ready, angel?" Gordon asked, unable to resist the boyish impulse of yanking her braids.

Rob giggled at his gesture and nodded.

"So, yer takin' the wee beastie with ye?" Duke Magnus asked.

"I wouldna leave Smooches behind," Rob answered. "My mother will adore him. I canna wait until she sees his sweet face."

The duke flicked a pointed glance at his son and added as they started for the door, "Dinna forget to give yer parents my regards."

Outside in the courtyard, two horses stood ready, awaiting their arrival. Beside them, a third horse had been laden with satchels and baskets.

"What's this?" Rob asked.

"Supplies," Gordon answered, lifting her into the saddle.

"For what?"

Gordon fastened the pack horse's reins to his own saddle and then flicked a sidelong glance at her. "I always prepare for the unexpected when I travel these mountains."

Leaving Inverary Castle behind, Gordon and Rob rode at a leisurely pace up into the mountains. The more distance they put between themselves and Inverary, the more carefree Rob grew.

The morning mists had evaporated, fulfilling the promise of a clear afternoon. The day was a Highland rarity of blue skies and brilliant sunshine.

Rob felt optimism swelling within her soul as they rode up toward the valley of Glen Aray. The recently born lambs were frolicking on the hillsides, and various kinds of birds flew hither and thither to their ancestral nests.

The whole of Argyll was a garden of wildflowers. God had landscaped the horizon with delicate white bloodroot blossoms and red trilliums. Rock columbine with crimson crowns nodded at her.

Rob smiled as she inhaled deeply of the mountain scents of heather mingling with pine. She could almost hear the fairies laughing and singing and dancing amidst the rocks and the wildflowers.

"At what are ye grinnin'?" Gordon asked.

"Can ye not hear the flower fairies singin'?" Rob asked.

Gordon halted his horse and cocked his head to one side as if straining to hear. "Ah, yes, I hear them now," he said, making her giggle. "I do believe they're a bit out of tune."

They rode into the silent grandeur of Glen Aray surrounded by rounded, massive peaks. The afternoon sun sparkled across the top of a serene pool of water formed by two mingling streams. All around them springtide flowers decorated the valley.

"What are those?" Rob asked, pointing at yellow flowers with red tendrils.

"Glenside sundew," Gordon answered. "The sweet-smelling tendrils attract and then ensnare insects. Then the plant eats them."

"I'm sorry I asked," Rob replied, surprised by the savagery in the innocuous-looking flower. "How can beauty be so deadly?"

"Everything dies, angel. The sundew would starve if it smelled like shit," Gordon teased her.

"Isna that unusual for those streams to form a pool?" Rob asked, pointing toward the water.

"Aye. Sorrow and Care—the Campbells' names for those streams—mingle in the pool as they do in life," Gordon told her. "Then they separate again on the journey down to Loch Fyne and Inverary."

Rob scanned the idyllic scenery. Tiny, beehive hovels of stone and turf dotted the sides of the hills around them. "What are those?" she asked.

"Why, angel, 'tis where the women and the children sleep during the summer shielin'," Gordon answered.

"The men sleep outside in their plaids. Everyone will be arrivin' tomorrow afternoon in time to celebrate Beltane Eve. Dinna the MacArthurs have a summer shielin'?"

"Yes, of course." Rob had never attended because nobody wanted her there. The MacArthurs feared she'd jinx the cattle.

At the far end of Glen Aray, Gordon and Rob rode into a magnificent virgin forest of pine, spruce, birch, and larch. Here beds of bracken grew out from the gnarled branches of beech.

Gordon halted his horse when they reached a clearing in the woodland. He looked at Rob, who was staring at the lodge and the stable.

"Does one of yer Campbells live here?" she asked.

"We live here," Gordon mumbled without looking at her.

Rob snapped her head around. "I dinna ken yer meanin'."

Gordon dismounted and then lifted her out of the saddle. He forced himself to smile pleasantly at her confused expression. "This is our destination, angel," he said. "We are na travelin' to Dunridge."

"Ye lied to me?" Rob's voice rose in anger.

Gordon took her by the hand, led her to a nearby tree stump, and gently forced her to sit down on it. Then he knelt on one bended knee in front of her.

"Ye havena been happy at Inverary, but I dinna ken why," Gordon said. "Ye and I havena had an ordinary marriage. Since last December, we havena enjoyed one moment alone in which we could become acquainted. What I'd like to do is pass the better part of the summer with ye up here. That is, if yer agreeable. Forgive me for lyin' to ye, sweetheart, but I couldna think of another way to get ye up here. If ye really dinna want to stay, I'll take ye along to Dunridge Castle to visit yer mother."

Rob dropped her gaze and stared at her hands folded in her lap. Her husband was correct; they were no more than intimate strangers. She refused to tell him why she'd become unhappy at Inverary, though. Her pain was a private matter, and her fear of rejection was a thing he could never understand. She was lonely. Only Gabby and Biddy had befriended her. And yet, Rob knew she cared for the handsome man kneeling in front of her. Perhaps if she passed the summer with him at the lodge, she could grab a few weeks of happiness for herself.

"What d'ye say, angel?" Gordon asked, his voice softly coaxing. "Will ye give us a chance?"

Rob lifted her gaze to his and smiled. One summer of happiness would bring her contentment for the remainder of her days.

"I'll stay," she said, "but ye'll need to do penance for yer lyin' ways. I'll expect sunshine and flowers and the gift of yer smile each and every day."

"For how many years?"

"I'll let ye know when I've decided."

Gordon flashed her his devastating grin. He kissed the back of her right hand and then pressed his lips to the devil's flower staining her left hand. His tender gesture brought back the memory of when she'd been his eight-year-old bride. Gallant and gentle and good, Gordon Campbell was the charming Prince of Argyll. Too bad he'd been forced to wed a tarnished princess.

Looking very much like Gavin, Gordon gestured toward the lodge and announced, "Damsel, yer castle awaits ye."

Rob accepted his offered hand. In courtly manner, they walked toward the lodge. Gordon opened the door, but before she could step inside, he surprised her by scooping her into his arms and carrying her across the threshold. Once inside, he planted a kiss on her cheek and gently set her down on her feet.

Rob quickly scanned her surroundings. The hunting lodge was one enormous room. A large unmade bed, the most commanding presence in the room, stood along the wall on her right. It seemed out of place, as though it had been brought here especially for their stay. Linens and a fur throw had been slung across its mattress. A privacy screen sat to the right of the bed in a corner that connected the bed wall to the wall facing her where the hearth was located. Pots and pans hung on the wall to the left of the hearth. A sturdy-looking oak table, two chairs, and two stools stood along the wall on the left side of the chamber. Shelves on the wall beside the table contained an ample supply of crockery.

" 'Tis more luxurious than my father's lodge," Rob remarked, her gaze fixed on the bed as she lifted Smooches out of his satchel and set him down on the floor.

"I didna want ye to suffer bein' out in the woods," Gordon told her.

Rob smiled at him. " 'Twas verra thoughtful of ye, Gordy."

"Give me a minute to bring the supplies inside," he said, turning away. "Then I'll help ye put the bed in order."

As soon as he stepped outside, Rob shook the linens out and started to make the bed. Did her husband think she was incapable of performing menial tasks? If so, he'd passed too many years with the pampered ladies at court and had a surprise coming his way. Yes, she was the Mac-Arthur laird's daughter, but a lonely young girl made friends with whomever she could, including a kindly housekeeper who'd taught her to do the minor tasks that keep a man's home running smoothly and comfortably.

The door opened. Laden like a pack horse, Gordon walked in and set the satchels and baskets down in the center of the chamber. Then he hurried across the room to help her make the bed.

Rob fluffed the second pillow in place, and Gordon spread the fur coverlet across the blanket. Standing on opposite sides of the bed, they touched each other with their gazes. Mesmerized by the tender expression in his eyes, Rob felt a melting sensation in the pit of her stomach and knew, without a doubt, that this was where her husband would make her his wife in fact as well as name.

"I'll light the fire," Gordon said in a husky voice, breaking the spell his piercing gray gaze had woven around her. "Biddy packed us a pot of stew. Could ye warm it while I feed the horses and bed them down for the night?"

"Fetch us a couple of buckets of water," she ordered.

Gordon grinned at her. "Damsel, yer merest wish is my command."

Rob watched her husband start the fire in the hearth and then return to their pile of supplies in the middle of the floor. When he pulled a covered pot from one of the baskets and retraced his steps toward the hearth, she stopped him.

"Gordy?"

He turned around. "Aye?"

Rob stepped up to him and lifted the pot out of his hands, saying, "I'll do that. Take care of the horses."

A doubtful expression appeared on his face. "Are ye certain?"

"I amna crippled," she assured him.

Gordon smiled. "The kitchen is yers, angel."

Rob set the pot of stew on the hook over the hearth and stirred it with a ladle. She headed across the room to the crockery shelves. Lifting two bowls, she used the bottom edge of her skirt to wipe the dust from them and then searched the food basket for the hunk of brown bread that Biddy always served with stew. She set that down on the table between their bowls.

Rob raced back to the hearth and stirred the stew again. She didn't want the first meal she'd ever cooked for her husband to stick to the bottom of the pot. When he returned, she was already hanging their clothing on the wooden pegs on either side of the door.

"It smells delicious," Gordon said, returning with a bucket of water in each of his hands. He set them down near the hearth and helped her unpack their belongings.

Deeming the stew sufficiently warmed, Rob filled their bowls and announced, "My lord, I give ye Campbell soup."

Surprising her, Gordon reached across the table and covered her hand with his own. "Have I told ye today how lovely ye are?" he asked.

Rob blushed and smiled at his compliment, but a low whining ruined the intimate moment. Both looked down and saw Smooches sitting beside the table.

"Stay where ye are," Gordon said when she started to rise. He filled a bowl with stew and set it on the floor beside the table for Smooches.

"Since we're here to become acquainted without pryin' eyes watchin' us," Gordon said, "tell me about yerself, angel."

"I've led a verra unexcitin' life," Rob replied, uncertain of what he wanted to know.

"How did ye come by yer name?" Gordon asked. "I ken yer father named ye in honor of Robert the Bruce, but 'tis puzzlin' why he didna name one of yer brothers after the man."

"Well, it happened like this," Rob said with a smile. "My parents decided they would take turns naming their children. When my oldest brother was born, my father named him John Andrew after my grandfather, but we call him Dubh because he's dark. My mother named their second son Ross, but when the third arrived, she insisted on calling him James after the king. My mother became pregnant again, and for nine months, my father reminded her that this time he'd name the babe. Unfortunately for my da, I was a girl, but he named me Rob Bruce anyway. I think 'twas revenge on my mother for takin' two turns in a row."

Gordon was chuckling by the time she finished her tale. "I dinna recall such goin's-on between my parents," he said. "My mother died when I was ten years. She was the youngest daughter of the Gordon chieftain, and 'tis the reason my parents called me Gordon. My oldest uncle, George Gordon, is now the Gordon chieftain. The 'Cock of the North,' as they say."

"Is that why the sayin' goes, 'the Gordons only talk to the Campbells, and the Campbells only talk to God'?" Rob teased him.

"We Campbells talk to the MacArthurs," Gordon said with a smile. "Tell me, lass. What did ye think of me that first day when we wed in yer father's hall?"

"Why would ye want to know that?"

Gordon shrugged. "Curiosity."

"As I recall, I thought ye were handsome and brave and gallant," Rob admitted. "I also thought ye were verra old. Elderly, in fact."

Gordon burst out laughing. "I thought ye were the sweetest angel I'd ever seen."

Rob blushed and dropped her gaze to her bowl of stew.

"The others will be arrivin' in the valley tomorrow," Gordon said, changing the subject. "As a boy, I always loved attendin' the summer shielin' . . . Dinna move. I'll be back in a minute."

Gordon left the lodge, and Rob wondered what he was doing. Ten minutes later, she heard him calling her name. With Smooches accompanying her, she stepped outside the lodge.

Smiling, Gordon stood there and offered her a wildflower bouquet of pale pink lady's smock, purple lady's slipper orchids, and white trilliums.

"Will ye accept starlight for tonight instead of the sunshine ye ordered?" he asked.

Rob looked up at the sky. Surrounded by thousands of glittering stars, a crescent moon hung overhead in a bed of black velvet.

"Aye, my lord," she answered, accepting his bouquet of wildflowers.

Standing beside her, Gordon drew her against his body. In silence, they watched Smooches scampering around, sniffing here and there.

"I'll stay here with the pup while ye take care of yer private needs," Gordon said, planting a kiss on the crown of her head.

Walking back inside the lodge, Rob washed her face and rinsed her teeth, and then changed into her nightgown. She dragged a chair close to the hearth, untied her braids, and then brushed her hair.

Gordon returned a short time later. He leaned close and kissed her cheek, saying, " 'Tis time for sleepin', angel."

While he smothered the fire in the hearth, Rob climbed into their bed and waited nervously. Was this the moment he'd make her his? She heard him moving around the room and then getting undressed. The bed creaked beneath his weight as he climbed in beside her.

"Good night, angel," Gordon whispered, and promptly fell asleep.

Rob lay there in surprise. Why had he bothered to bring her all the way up into the mountains if he wasn't going to make love to her? She didn't wonder about that long, though. Their journey and the day's unexpected events had wearied her, and she soon joined her husband in sleep.

"Wake up, angel."

Rob heard the voice but kept her eyes closed in the hope that if she feigned sleep, those three words she'd come to despise would go away. Ah, but the invitingly husky sound of her husband's voice warmed her all over, and the faintest of smiles touched her lips.

"See what I've brought ye," Gordon coaxed, sitting on the edge of the bed.

Rob opened her eyes and blinked at the blinding sunshine streaming through the lodge's open door. She shielded her eyes with one hand and looked at her husband.

He smiled and offered her a fresh bouquet of wildflowers. In his free hand, he held a bowl filled with something that smelled delicious.

"I give ye sunshine, flowers, and the gift of my smile," Gordon said. "This mornin' I've added a bowl of oatmeal porridge sprinkled with cinnamon."

Rob sat up and leaned back against the headboard. She yawned and pushed several wisps of her ebony mane off her face, unaware of how delightfully disheveled she appeared as if caught in a lover's tryst.

Taking the bowl and the spoon out of his hand, Rob tasted the porridge. "Why, 'tis delicious with the cinnamon," she said. "Ye are na eatin'?"

"When a man rises with the dawn," Gordon told her "he canna wait until the sun is high to break his fast."

"What were ye doin'?"

"Feedin' the horses and fishin' in the stream," he answered. "I've got a bucket of fish outside. Later, I'll clean a couple for our dinner and send the rest down to the valley when the others arrive this afternoon."

Rob nodded. "Where's Smooches?"

"Sleepin' in the corner. I guess the fishin' tired him out. Would ye like to bathe?"

"Aye, but—" Rob scanned the chamber but saw no tub.

"Angel, nobody bathes in a tub durin' the summer shielin'." Gordon lifted the empty bowl out of her hands and set it on the table, then grabbed two towels and said. "I'll wait for ye outside."

Rob dressed hurriedly and emerged from the lodge a few minutes later without her dog. "I couldna rouse Smooches," she said as they started down one of the paths.

The day was simply perfection, an exact replica of the previous one. Blue skies blanketed the tops of the trees, and warm sun shone down on them.

A feeling of security permeated Rob's senses. Was the rare perfection of this Highland weather a good omen? she wondered. Was there hope for Gordon and her after all? She flicked a sidelong glance at his incredibly handsome profile and could hardly believe that he belonged to her.

And how many others? the voice of insecurity intruded upon her buoyant feeling.

"So, where do we bathe?" Rob asked, trying to banish the disturbing thought into the netherworld of her mind.

"The pool in the valley is only a ten-minute walk," Gordon replied. " 'Tis beautiful at this time of day."

Rob stopped short. When he turned around, she shook her head and said, "I canna do that."

"Do what, angel?"

"Bathe in the pool."

Gordon snapped his brows together. "But why?"

"I dinna care for the water," she answered. "I'd rather be dirty."

"And stink too?" he teased her.

Rob didn't smile. Her heart was beating rapidly, and her hands at her sides already trembled with her fear. He wouldn't force her to do this, would he?

"There's nothin' to fear," Gordon assured her. "I'll teach ye to swim."

"I know how to swim but dinna like deep water," she cried.

Gordon waited in silence for her to continue.

"I had a verra bad experience once," Rob explained, praying he'd be understanding. "A crofter's daughter nearly drowned." She touched his forearm and pleaded, "Please, Gordy. Dinna force me to do this."

Gordon put his arm around her and drew her close against his body. "Angel, have I ever forced ye to do anythin' ye didna want to do?"

"Ye did so," Rob answered, nodding her head like a young girl. "Ye forced me to leave England, ye forced me to sleep outside on our journey to Inverary, and—"

"Enough," Gordon said with a smile. "I willna force ye to do this." He thought a long moment and then suggested, "We could take a pigeon bath in the stream. The water is only as high as yer waist, but if we sit, we'll get wet."

"I'd like that much better," she agreed.

Hand in hand, Gordon and Rob retraced their steps and followed another path that led away from Glen Aray. Dew still dropped lightly from the woodland trees, and the scent of heather wafted through the air. Sparkling sunbeams danced across the top of the water.

At the stream's edge, they sat down on the rocks and removed their boots and their stockings. Gordon stood first, pulled his shirt over his head, and then dropped his plaid.

Great Bruce's ghost, the man's naked, Rob thought as she stared with wide eyes at his back. Without thinking, she began to admire his broad shoulders, his tapered waist, and his wonderfully tight buttocks. What would it feel like to have his strength pressing her down in their bed?

When he moved to turn around, Rob snapped her eyes shut.

"Are ye goin' to sit there blushin'?" Gordon asked. "Or were ye plannin' on bathin'?"

Rob heard the laughter in his voice but couldn't quite summon the courage to look at him. "Gordy, yer naked," she whispered in a choked voice.

" 'Tis how I usually wash," he replied. "Do ye bathe with yer clothin' on?"

Rob shook her head but kept her eyes closed. "Ye promised ye wouldna force me," she reminded him.

"Angel, I'll never force ye to do anythin'," Gordon replied. "Besides, this water's so cold 'tis certain to shrivel me."

"I dinna ken. What do ye mean?"

Gordon chuckled. "Never mind, my innocent angel. What if I sit down so my privates are na exposed?"

" 'Twould help." Rob opened her eyes when she heard the splash of water as he sat. He looked so silly sitting in the stream and smiling at her, Rob was unable to suppress the giggle that bubbled up in her throat. The picture he presented reminded her of that night in the tavern when he'd bathed in a tub built for a dwarf.

"Yer turn, my love."

My love. Were those special words merely a sophisticated courtier's figure of speech? Or did he actually mean what he said?

"I'm waitin'."

Rob stood slowly. She dropped her skirt and then pulled her blouse over her head. She felt horribly awkward wearing only her chemise while he sat there and stared at her.

"Could ye close yer eyes until I'm sittin' in the water too?" she asked. "I'd feel ever so much more comfortable if ye werena watchin' me take my chemise off."

Gordon smiled and closed his eyes. He'd been about to tell her to leave her chemise on, but if she was willing to strip, he wasn't about to stop her. A long, silent moment passed. He heard her wading into the stream and then sensed her beside him.

"Great Bruce's ghost, the water doesna cover my—"

Gordon opened his eyes and looked at her. Her perfectly rounded breasts with their pink-tipped nipples rose above the water. When she moved her arms to cover her bared breasts, he reached out and stayed her hands.

"Angel, dinna hide yer beauty from me," Gordon said, his voice husky with long-denied need.

Rob dropped her arms and stared at him through emerald eyes large with wonder.

"Och, lass. Yer lovely." Gordon lowered his head and covered her mouth in a gentle, probing kiss. "I didna purposefully lie this time," he whispered against her lips. "I merely misjudged the water level."

That made Rob smile. And she relaxed against him.

Gordon put his right arm around her shoulder and kissed her again. He slid the top of his tongue across the crease between her lips, which parted for him. Gently and lingeringly, he kissed her, his tongue exploring the sweetness of her mouth. Caressing her breasts, he ran his thumb across her sensitive nipples and teased them into aroused hardness.

Rob sucked in her breath at the incredible sensation. And she knew desire.

"Yer ripe for me, but I willna take ye here," Gordon said, staring at her dazed expression. "Ye deserve a sweet memory of our first lovemakin', and sittin' in this stream lacks the proper atmosphere." He kissed her again and whispered, "Tonight, angel. I'll love ye tonight."

Noting the high color staining her cheeks, Gordon said, "God's balls, lass. Ye blush more than any ten women I've ever known. I'm goin' to stand now and help ye up. Close yer eyes if ye dinna want to be startled."

Gordon smiled when she instantly snapped her eyes shut. He drew her to her feet, lifted her into his arms, and carried her to shore. Ever so slowly, he slid her down the long length of his muscular frame as he set her on her feet.

" 'Tis a sinful sensation," Rob said, gazing up at him.

" 'Tis no sin for old married couples like us," Gordon told her. "Turn around and dress yerself, and I'll turn the other way."

"Verra well." Rob showed him her back and quickly toweled herself dry. Reaching for her chemise, she sensed no movement behind her and said, "No peekin'."

"Peekin' is part of the fun," Gordon replied, admiring the appealing shape of her derriere.

"Ye said we'd—" Rob turned and saw him standing there smiling at her. Instinctively, she dropped her gaze to his groin. "Great Bruce's ghost," she cried, whirling around.

Gordon chuckled and reached for his plaid. His bride was an innocent angel and an irresistible temptress. He could hardly wait to initiate her into the ways of carnal love.

"Was that Sorrow or Care we were sittin' in?" Rob asked to cover her embarrassment.

Gordon grinned and yanked her against the side of his body as they started down the path again. "Lovey, I'm aboot to newly christen it Joy," he said.

Dewey was waiting for them when they returned to the lodge. With Smooches in his arms, the giant sat in the chair in front of the hearth but stood when they walked in.

"Has everyone arrived in the valley?" Gordon asked by way of a greeting.

"Aye," the big man answered.

"Good day to ye, Dewey," Rob said. "Is Gabby aboot?"

"She's down in the valley. Did ye want her for somethin'?"

Rob shook her head.

Dewey kissed Smooches on the nose and let the pup lick his cheek. "He's verra friendly, considerin' he's English and all." The giant winked at them and added, "I see ye've been playin' Adam and Eve."

Gordon flicked a glance at his wife. Her complexion was a vibrant scarlet like a child caught in the act of doing something forbidden. What a blusher she was.

"What can I do for ye?" he asked his man.

"Nothin', I've come to do for ye."

Gordon cocked a brow at the giant.

"Ye forgot yer supply of whiskey and yer golf bag," Dewey told him. "The whiskey's on the table and the bag's in the corner."

"Thank ye," Gordon said with a smile. "Would ye care to stay a while and share a cup?"

"Gabby would kill me if I did," Dewey answered,

shaking his head. "I promised to help settle the cattle and prepare for tonight's celebration. Are ye comin'?"

Gordon turned to Rob and explained, " 'Tis Beltane Eve. Everyone gathers around the campfire at sundown. Would ye like to go?"

"If ye wish," she agreed.

"Good, I'll share the whiskey with ye tonight," Dewey said, heading for the door. As he passed Rob, he dropped the pup into her arms and disappeared out the door.

"Tomorrow mornin' the men will build Beltane's twin fires," Gordon said, standing beside her. "Before the women walk the cattle between them, lovers can leap together over the fires." His voice dropped to a husky whisper, " 'Tis an ancient fertility ritual and brings good fortune to the lovers. Will ye leap with me over the Beltane fire, angel?"

"My lord, I can think of nothin' I'd rather do," Rob answered, casting him an unconsciously flirtatious smile.

"Yer verra temptin'," Gordon said, planting a chaste kiss on her lips, "but I must clean that fish or we willna eat."

A golden glow spread across the western horizon as the sun set behind the mountains and lavender twilight descended upon the Highlands. With Smooches in her arms, Rob walked beside Gordon down the path that led to Glen Aray less than a mile away.

Advancing on the pool formed from the mingling of Sorrow and Care, Rob saw the area around the campfire crowded with women, children, and a small group of men. Every two weeks, the Campbell men returned to their duties at Inverary Castle and another contingent arrived in the glen. By the summer's end, each man at Inverary Castle had passed some time at the shieling.

"Da! Da!" two voices shouted.

Rob spied Duncan and Gavin running toward them

and glanced at her husband. With a warm smile of greeting on his face, Gordon crouched down and gathered his sons into his arms.

Standing beside them, Rob was uncertain of what to do. She feared the boys would reject her in front of their father and hoped they would refrain from crossing themselves and calling her a witch. Had attending this Campbell gathering been a mistake?

Feeling like an outsider, Rob looked toward the women and saw Kendra and her babe sitting in the midst of the female crowd. Gordon was talking with his sons, and she had no friend with whom she could speak. Rob knew she should be accustomed to being alone, but somehow that knowledge failed to lessen the ache in her heart.

Rob glanced at her beggar bead necklace as the last of the day's light faded away. Her star ruby remained placid. Apparently, the only danger to her was the awkward position of being conspicuously out of place with old friends who didn't trust her, the stranger among them. She was Inverary Castle's lady but hadn't earned their respect, and no one thought her worthy of their acknowledgment.

"Lady Rob!"

Rob turned in the voice's direction, and relief surged through her. Here were two friendly faces happy to see her.

"I hope ye are na angry with me," Gabby said, rushing to her side, leaving Dewey to follow behind. "Gordy swore me to secrecy aboot where he was takin' ye."

"I could never be angry with ye," Rob told her.

Gabby lifted Smooches out of her arms and handed the pup to Dewey, ordering, "Make yerself useful." She grabbed Rob's hand and led her to the circle around the campfire, announcing, "Inverary's lady is here. Make space for her."

Rob blushed as the faces around the campfire turned in her direction. She sat down with Gabby on her right. Only a moment passed when Gordon sat down on her left. Gavin ensconced himself on his father's lap and gave her a sidelong glance.

"Good evenin', Gavin," Rob said softly.

The boy cast her a little smile, so devastatingly similar to his father's that the sight of it tugged at her heart-strings. She shifted her gaze to his older brother who stood just behind Gordon.

"Good evenin', Duncan," Rob said.

The boy looked at her but made no reply.

"Say hello to Lady Rob," Gordon told the boy. "Then sit here beside me."

Duncan looked from her to his father, and then announced, "I'm sittin' with my mother. Are ye comin', brother?"

Secure on his father's lap, Gavin shook his head. Duncan gave him an irritated look and then walked around the campfire to sit with his mother.

Noting her husband's grim expression, Rob touched his forearm and whispered, "Dinna fault the lad for bein' loyal to his mother."

Gordon nodded and visibly relaxed.

Rob began to feel more comfortable as mundane conversations swirled around her. True darkness had descended upon the gathering, the only light being the dancing, crackling flames. Rob loved this time of the day because mysterious night shrouded her imperfection.

"Hey, Gordy," one of the men called. "Tell us the fairy banner story."

"In ancient times there lived a Campbell laird," Gordon began, his voice loud enough to be heard by all 'et hushed as though he were divulging a secret. "One day in the forest, this Campbell laird met a beautiful woman and fell instantly in love with her. He brought her o Inverary Castle and married her, but there was one hing aboot his lady he didna know. His bride was actu-ally a fairy."

All the children gasped. The men and women smiled.

"What happened, Da?" Gavin asked, turning his head o gaze at his father. "Did she cast a spell upon him?"

"No, son. The Campbell laird and his fairy bride lived happily for almost twenty years," Gordon told them. "Unfortunately, fairies canna live forever in the world of men. On the eve of their twentieth wedding anniversary —Beltane Eve, as I recall—the woman told her husband who she really was and that she had to return to her own kind that verra night. She promised to love him forever and a day. Though it saddened him to do so, the Camp-bell laird understood and rode with her to Glen Aray. His fairy wife kissed him, gave him a banner she'd made for him, and then disappeared into the mist. No one ever saw her again. That banner was a magical legacy from the fairies, and 'tis the reason the Campbells are always on the winnin' side in battle."

Everyone including Rob clapped for her husband.

"Gawd, yer givin' me the shivery creeps," Gabby said.

"I'll protect ye, hinny," Dewey told her.

"Lady Rob, do ye know any stories?" Gabby asked.

Rob blushed at the attention and was thankful for the darkness that hid her discomfort. In a soft voice, she answered, "Aye, 'tis aboot my husband's bravery."

"Tell us," several people called at the same time.

"When Gordy came to England to fetch me from my uncle's," Rob began, "we decided to tour the queen's menagerie. 'Tis where the queen keeps wild beasts. We were peerin' into the lion pit when hands pushed me

from behind. I slipped, and one of my legs dangled int
the pit. The beast was just aboot to grab me when Gord
yanked me to safety."

Everyone around the campfire clapped for their laird'
son.

" 'Twas well done of ye, Da," Gavin said.

Gordon smiled. "Well, thank ye for the high praise.'

"Who pushed ye?" Gabby asked.

Rob shrugged. "We never discovered his identity."

"Or hers."

"What d'ye mean?"

Gabby cast a meaningful look in Kendra's direction
and answered, "The culprit could be a woman. Som
women are particularly vicious."

"Are ye talkin' aboot me, Gabby?" Kendra demanded

"Ah, go suck wind," Gabby called.

"Ladies, let's not ruin our gatherin'," Gordon said, hi
lips twitching with the urge to laugh.

"She started it," Kendra said.

"And I'm finishin' it," Gordon replied, his voice stern

"I know another story aboot my husband," Rob pipec
up, breaking the strained silence that followed their ex
change. When expectant faces turned toward her, she
said, "When I was a young girl of eight, Gordon travelec
to Dunridge Castle to marry me. I told him aboot the
frightenin' monster who lived beneath my bed. Gordor
took himself upstairs and slew the nasty monster, and
always enjoyed a peaceful sleep after that."

"What happened in the room?" one of the childrer
asked.

"What did the monster look like?" another wanted tc
know.

" 'Tis late," Gordon hedged, glancing sidelong at her.
"I believe I'll save that tale for another night."

"Lady Rob, what did the monster look like?" Gavin

asked, speaking to her for the first time since that day in the garden when he'd called her a witch.

"The creature was verra hideous," she answered. "He had one gleaming, red eye in the center of his forehead and two long, yellow fangs stickin' out from between his lips. Isna that right, Gordy?"

"Aye, lass." Gordon winked at her and then stood, saying, " 'Tis time for sleepin'. Gavin, go on over to yer mother now, and I'll see ye in the mornin'."

The six-year-old hugged his father and then turned to her before heading around the campfire to his mother. "Good night, Lady Rob."

Rob smiled. "Good night, Gavin."

Gordon lifted Smooches out of Dewey's arms and handed the pup to her. Before they left, Duncan hurried over to them and hugged his father.

"I had a wonderful time," Rob said.

"The evenin' is still young, angel."

Peering at his wife, Gordon smiled inwardly when they walked into the lodge. Her gaze fixed on the bed as if it had suddenly turned into the monster she had so aptly described. The fierce lass who'd drawn her last resort on England's secretary of state feared going to bed with him. Gordon realized he needed to go slowly, woo her into ecstasy. Only then would he truly attain his own satisfaction.

After setting the jug of whiskey on the table, Gordon started a fire in the hearth to chase the evening chill out of the lodge and then lifted the pup into his arms. "Smooches and I will check the horses while ye get ready," he said, but paused at the door. "Do me a favor, angel. Dinna wear that nightgown of yers."

His request surprised Rob. "Why not?" she asked.

" 'Tis more innocent than springtime," he told her. "I feel like I'm bedded down with a twelve-year-old."

"Well, what am I to wear?" Rob asked, beginning to panic. "Nothin'?"

"Wear this," Gordon said, tossing her one of his clean shirts. Then he walked outside.

She couldn't go through with this, Rob thought in near desperation. She'd never be able to return to England if she bedded him.

You wanted this plenty at the stream today, an inner voice reminded her. *Besides, you'll never return to England whether you do it or not.*

Paralyzed with indecision, Rob lifted her husband's shirt to her face. The scent of mountain heather clung to it, and she inhaled deeply, wanting him. Again she felt his lips pressed to hers, his tongue sliding between her lips, the palm of his hand caressing her breasts, his thumb teasing her nipples.

That did it. Rob quickly undressed and pulled his shirt over her head. Its bottom edge fell to the middle of her thighs. Rolling the sleeves up, she stood near the chair and stared at the flames in the hearth.

After what seemed like an eternity, the door swung open. Rob whirled around and asked in a quavering voice, "Are ye goin' to futter me now?"

Chapter 12

Gordon stopped short, surprised by her words, and read the anxiety etched across her face. Rob was as pale as a person could get and still be breathing. She reminded him of a fledgling warrior in the midst of his first battle. Or a woman about to go to the gallows. Granted, some said that ecstasy was a little like dying, but he was no executioner. His innocent wife feared the unknown.

Stalling for time, Gordon closed the door behind him. He patted the pup and then set him on the floor. When Smooches curled up under the table, Gordon gave a silent prayer of thanks to Whomever. Getting his wife into bed was going to be a struggle, and he had no wish to fight to get the pup off the bed in order to get her there.

"Well?" Rob asked in a nervous, high-pitched voice.

Gordon looked from her pale face to her white-knuckled hand clutching the back of the chair. He dropped his gaze to her body, barely hidden beneath his shirt that only covered her to mid thigh. She looked so damned sexy. He suffered the urge to ravish her there on the floor but managed to control himself.

"Relax, angel," Gordon said, giving her his most charming smile.

Turning his back, Gordon pulled his shirt over his head and hung it on the peg beside the door. Next, he yanked his boots and his stockings off. Getting Rob into bed would be easier if he needn't stop what he was doing in order to remove any article of clothing. He'd enjoyed several women while he was wearing his boots, but his own wife deserved better than that.

Gordon paused a long moment before turning around to face her. Clad only in his plaid, he knew he looked the part of the wild, marauding Highlander. Yes, she'd seen him naked at the stream, but this night was entirely different. It was special. They both knew what was going to happen between them in a few minutes.

"Well, lass," Gordon said, casting her a boyish smile as he turned to face her. "I believe I'd like a mug of whiskey and a chance to talk with ye."

"Ye want to talk?" Rob echoed, her emerald gaze fixed on the mat of brown hair covering his chest. Her expression cleared, and color began to return to her cheeks.

Gordon nodded. She needn't sound so damned relieved. She was behaving as though he were the monster who lived beneath her bed instead of the hero who'd slain it.

Sauntering to the table, Gordon flicked a sidelong glance at her and then filled a mug with whiskey. He turned around slowly, lifted the mug in a toast to her, and downed a healthy swig. Bolstered by the liquid burning a path to his stomach, he started to cross the chamber toward her. The frantic expression on her face made him feel like laughing; he knew she would have backed away if the chair hadn't blocked her escape.

"Come, angel," Gordon said, holding his hand out in invitation. "Sit with me. We've somethin' important to discuss."

Rob shifted her gaze from his face to the chair and then back again. "There's room for only one," she told him.

"There's room for two if ye sit on my lap," he replied. "Please?" That one word *please* worked a miracle because it meant he was asking, not ordering.

Rob flicked the tip of her tongue out and wet her lips, gone dry from nervous apprehension, and Gordon almost groaned aloud at the incredibly sensual gesture performed in innocence. When she reached toward him with a badly shaking hand, Gordon firmly grasped it in his and sat in the chair, gently drawing her down on his lap.

Staring into the hearth's flames, Rob sat statue-still and rigidly erect. Was she afraid even to look at him?

"Relax, angel," Gordon soothed her, his left hand stroking the slender column of her back. "I amna goin' to bite ye."

Rob gave him a wary, sidelong glance. Her look told him that she knew exactly what he intended to do to her.

"Take a sip," he said, offering her the mug.

Rob shook her head.

"Please, do it for me," he coaxed with a smile, looking very much like his younger son.

Rob took the mug out of his hand. She pinched her nostrils together with her left hand and swallowed a healthy swig of the whiskey. She shuddered as it burned a path to her stomach and then handed him the mug.

Gordon smiled at her reaction. "Angel, ye are na supposed to hold yer nose while ye drink."

"It tastes better that way," she told him.

Gordon sipped the whiskey and then set the mug on the floor beside the chair. Gently, he drew her down to recline against his naked chest, and her head rested against his shoulder.

From beneath the thick fringe of her ebony lashes, Rob gazed up at him and waited for him to speak.

"Are ye comfortable, angel?"

"Yes."

"Now, what ye said about futterin' a few minutes ago wasna correct," Gordon told her, dropping his gaze to her emerald eyes staring so intently at him. "Animals futter because they dinna have feelin's, only urges. Men and women make love together. 'Tis a sharin' of their bodies and their emotions. Ye ken?"

"I think so," she replied, her doubtful expression telling him otherwise.

"There's nothin' to fear. And have I ever lied to ye?" Gordon grinned ruefully at his own question and said, "Forget I asked ye that. Let me put it to ye this way. Do ye believe that I'd ever hurt ye?"

Rob shook her head. "Ye saved my life at the lions' pit and helped me escape from the queen's men," she answered. "Besides that, ye slew the monster livin' beneath my bed."

" 'Tis settled then," Gordon said, pleased with his powers of persuasion. "Do ye have any questions aboot it?"

Worrying her bottom lip with her teeth, Rob dropped her gaze, and a becoming blush of embarrassment spread across her cheeks. "What does it feel like?" she asked.

"Ah, lass. What happens between a man and a woman in bed feels like warm sunshine, sweet flowers, and lovin' smiles," he told her.

That seemed to perk her interest, but a moment later her expression became skeptical. "How can I be sure ye are na sayin' that just to get me into yer bed?" she asked.

"Would the world be so peopled if makin' love wasna

pleasurable?" Gordon countered. "What I'd like more than anythin' else is one of yer kisses. Will ye kiss me, lass?"

"Yes." Rob closed her eyes and puckered her lips.

Gordon realized she was waiting for him to kiss her. "No, angel. I want ye to kiss me."

"Verra well," Rob said, opening her eyes. She leaned close and planted a chaste kiss on his lips.

"Ye didna put any feelin' into it," he complained. "I want one with emotion."

Summoning her courage, Rob covered his mouth with hers. Her lips felt soft and warm on his, her kiss uncertain yet eager.

A jolt of sensation shot through Gordon when he felt the tip of her tongue flicking across the crease between his lips. He realized she was imitating his kiss at the stream that morning.

Unable to stop himself, Gordon wrapped his arms around her and returned her kiss in kind. Taking control, he gave her a long, slow, earth-shattering kiss and put all of the tender emotion he felt for her into it.

" 'Twas verra well done of ye," he whispered against her lips. "Now, what I'd like ye to do is touch me."

"Touch ye?" she exclaimed, becoming alarmed.

"Just glide yer hand across my chest," he coaxed, his voice a soft caress. "Or wherever else ye wish."

Rob stared into his intense, gray gaze. She wanted to touch him, feel his muscles rippling beneath her hand.

Reaching out, Rob traced her fingertips across his naked chest to his shoulder and then down to the powerful muscles in his upper arm. Becoming bolder, she glided the palm of her hand up his arm to his neck and then slid it down his chest, reveling in the feel of the mat of brown hair covering it. As he'd done to her that morning, she gently flicked her thumb across his nipple and smiled when it hardened beneath her touch.

Gordon nearly groaned at the exquisite sweetness of her touch. Her fingers were silken threads sliding seductively across his skin. He held the back of her neck and, leaning close, covered her mouth with his lips.

And Rob responded, returning his kiss in kind.

"Now, I want to touch ye the way yer touchin' me," he said in a husky whisper. "May I touch ye, angel?"

"Yes," she answered.

Slowly, in an effort not to startle her, Gordon pushed the shirt off her shoulders and down her arms. It dropped to her waist, leaving her breasts bared to his heated gaze. With their pink-tipped nipples, her breasts were perfectly formed.

Gordon suffered the urge to suckle upon those irresistible pink peaks but managed to control himself. He kissed her again, and when she sighed against his lips, glided his hand across her breasts and teased her sensitive nipples to aroused hardness.

Rob felt a throbbing heat ignite between her thighs. Her breath caught ragged in her throat, and she leaned into his caressing hand, yearning for more and more of the exquisite sensations he was creating.

"Kiss me, angel," Gordon whispered, his voice seductively thick with desire.

Rob needed no second invitation. She looped her arms around his neck and pressed her mouth on his, kissing him for an eternity.

"What I'd like to do is remove our clothin' and lay across the bed while we touch each other," Gordon said. "Will ye do that with me?"

Rob nodded, but a telltale blush colored her cheeks. The becoming pink traveled down the delicate column of her throat to her breasts.

Gordon kissed her into a daze of breathless desire and then scooped her into his arms. Rising from the chair, he carried her across the room and gently laid her down on top of the fur coverlet. He kissed her hungrily as he pulled the shirt off her body, leaving her naked to his gaze.

Staring down at her, Gordon became mesmerized by her ripe breasts and tiny waist. God had blessed his wife with thighs meant to wrap tightly around him and hips suited for nurturing his seed. Yes, he'd caught glimpses of her beauty before, but the incredible sight of her naked and waiting for him made his knees weak.

Gordon leaned over her and kissed her again while he unfastened his plaid and let it drop to the floor. In an instant he lay down beside her and gathered her into his arms.

"Angel, yer so verra beautiful," he murmured against her lips as one of his hands stroked the curve of her hips.

"Yer beautiful too," she said on a sigh.

Gordon kissed her slowly and lingeringly as if time had stopped and they had an eternity to do whatever they wished. He intended to take his sweet time with the angel in his arms and coax her into doing his bidding willingly. He knew that this was the most important night of their married life; whatever happened between them in this bed would color their relationship for as long as they lived.

Gordon pulled her against the hard, muscular planes of his body. His kiss became demanding, stealing her breath away.

Responding instinctively to his passionate kiss, Rob entwined her arms around his neck and pressed her nakedness against him. For the first time in her young life, she experienced the exquisite sensation of masculine hardness touching her feminine softness. And she liked it.

"I'm goin' to love ye, angel," Gordon whispered. "Ye ken?"

"Yes, Gordy," she murmured breathlessly. "Love me."

Gordon smiled with tenderness and claimed her lips in an earth-shattering kiss that lasted forever. Rob returned his kiss with equal passion, and then some. He flicked his tongue across the crease between her lips, which parted for him, and explored the sweetness beyond them. She surprised him by following his lead. Their tongues touched tentatively at first and then grew bold, swirling together in a mating dance as old as time itself.

"Can ye feel the sun's warmth?" Gordon whispered against her lips.

"Yes."

"Me, too."

Rob moaned at his admission. His words tugged at her heartstrings and inflamed her blossoming desire.

Gordon sprinkled dozens of kisses across her temples, eyelids, nose, and throat. His mouth returned to cover hers, and he caressed her silken body from the delicate column of her throat to her thrusting breasts to the juncture of her thighs. He moved his lips down her throat and then beyond. Capturing one of her pink-tipped nipples between his lips, he suckled upon it, and the throbbing heat between her thighs blazed into an inferno of pleasure.

"So sweet," Gordon murmured when she moaned against his lips. "Spread yer legs for me."

Without hesitation, Rob did as she was told. Gordon covered her mouth with his own while he inserted one long finger inside her.

That startled Rob into alertness. Panicking, she opened her eyes and tried to skitter away from his probing finger.

"Be easy, angel," Gordon soothed her, keeping her

imprisoned within his embrace. "I want to make ye ready to receive me."

He dipped his head to her breasts and suckled upon her sensitive nipples, then inserted a second finger inside her. Judging her accustomed to the feel of it, he began to move his fingers rhythmically, seducing her to his will.

Catching his rhythm, Rob moved her hips with him, enticing his fingers deeper inside her writhing body. And then his fingers were gone.

"Gordy," she whimpered.

Gordon knelt between her thighs. His engorged manhood teased the dewy pearl of her womanhood, and she moaned at this new torture.

"Look at me, angel."

Rob opened her eyes and stared at him in a daze of desire.

"One fleetin' moment of pain," he promised.

With one powerful thrust, Gordon pushed himself inside her, breaking her virgin's barrier, and buried himself deep within her trembling body. Rob cried out in surprised pain and clutched him.

Gordon lay perfectly still, letting her become accustomed to the feel of him inside her. Then he began moving seductively, enticing her to move with him.

Instinctively, Rob wrapped her legs around his waist and met each of his powerful thrusts with her own. Suddenly, unexpectedly, she exploded as wave after wave of throbbing sensation carried her to paradise.

Only then did Gordon release his long-denied need. He groaned and shuddered and poured his hot seed deep within her womb.

They lay still for several long moments, their labored breathing the only sound within the chamber. Gordon finally rolled to one side, pulling her with him, and planted a kiss on her forehead.

With her heart shining in her eyes, Rob gazed at him and said, "Ye promised we were only goin' to touch."

"And so we did, angel." Gordon gave her a wolfish grin. "Outside *and inside*."

Rob cast him a wry smile. "If only I had known the truth aboot this lovemakin', I would have ridden to Inverary Castle and demanded my due as yer wife instead of visitin' my uncle in England."

"Thank ye for the high praise, angel." Gordon pushed the fur coverlet down from beneath their bodies and then pulled it over them, saying, " 'Tis time for sleepin'."

"I amna tired," Rob said.

"Verra well, angel. We'll talk a while." Gordon gathered her into his arms and apologized, "I'm sorry I dinna have a weddin' night gift for ye."

"Ye've already given me this ring." Without worry about him seeing her devil's flower, Rob held her left hand up and admired the band of gold with its enormous emerald.

"Still, I'd like to give ye somethin' more," Gordon replied. "What would ye like?"

Rob rolled over on top of him. Nose to nose with him, she said, "Sunshine, flowers, and the gift of yer smile."

"They're yers, angel. For ye and no other."

"For ye and no other," she whispered.

Gordon lifted her birthmarked hand to his lips and planted a kiss on her devil's flower. "Come September, I'll take ye to court where ye'll meet the king. We'll gift each other with luckenbooth broaches, and when our first child is born, we'll pin the luckenbooth to his blanket. 'Twill bring him good luck and safety in this uncertain world. Edinburgh abounds with hundreds of shops that sell everythin' from fine jewelry to—"

Glancing down at his wife, Gordon saw that she'd dropped into sleep. He held her protectively close and kissed the ebony crown of her head. Closing his eyes, Gordon joined her in a deep, dreamless sleep.

Gordon awakened early the next morning and inched toward the center of the bed, searching blindly for his wife's hot little body. It wasn't there. He opened one gray eye first, and then the other. The bed was empty. Now, where had she disappeared?

And then Gordon heard a noise on the opposite side of the chamber. He rolled over and saw her. Clad only in his white linen shirt, Rob was standing in front of the hearth and cooking his breakfast.

Leisurely, Gordon admired the enchanting picture of his wife at work. Like a dark veil, her ebony mane cascaded to her waist. Through the white linen shirt, he could see the alluring curves of her derriere and her hips.

"I never knew that gentility could boil a pot," Gordon said in a sleep-husky voice.

Rob whirled around, startled by the unexpected sound of his voice. Her lips formed a perfect O of surprise, and then she smiled. The warmth gleaming at him from the depths of her emerald eyes spoke volumes about the tenderness she harbored within her heart.

"I see yer tryin' yer hand at cookin'," Gordon said, returning her smile. Then teased, "Will it be edible, angel?"

Rob cocked one ebony eyebrow in a perfect imitation of his now-endearing habit. "I've many fine talents of which yer unaware," she told him.

"I do love surprises," Gordon replied. "Especially the kind I enjoyed last night. I'd take another helpin' of that whatever the time of day."

"Last night was hardly a surprise," Rob said, but was unable to suppress a smile. "Ye planned it out in that devious Campbell mind of yers."

"How can ye doubt me?" Gordon asked, feigning offended innocence. He winked at her and added, "I see yer wearin' my shirt, angel. The style becomes ye."

"I like its smell."

"My shirt smells?"

" 'Tis yer scent," she explained. "Mountain heather."

That made him smile. "Come over here where we can speak without shoutin'," he coaxed, patting the bed beside him.

Rob looked from him to the bannocks on the girdle over the fire and then held one finger up in a gesture to give her a minute. Grabbing the bannock spade, a long handled implement with a heart-shaped spade at the end, she lifted the bannocks out of the girdle and set them on the cooling rack. Then she wrapped them in small linen squares to keep them warm and moist.

Turning around to face him, Rob smiled as she crossed the chamber. "I found a spot of blood here on the coverlet," she said, sitting beside him on the edge of the bed, "but I rinsed it off while ye slept."

" 'Twas yer virgin's blood," Gordon told her.

"Oh." Rob blushed a vivid shade of scarlet, a brilliant red that would have shamed a rose.

"So, angel, why are ye up and aboot this early?" he asked, ignoring her embarrassment.

"As yer wife, I am duty bound to cook ye breakfast," she said primly.

Gordon cocked a brow at her, and his eyes lit with tender amusement. She was the only noblewoman he'd ever bedded who'd considered passing the night in his bed as an invitation to cook for him. All of the others had been determined upon a shopping spree down High Street.

"One night of passion and yer already a famous housewife?" he teased her.

Before she could open her mouth to reply, Gordon

yanked her down on top of him. Her smile told him she liked the feeling of his long, muscular body beneath hers.

Gently but firmly, Gordon held the back of her head steady and kissed her lingeringly. With his free hand, he began stroking the delicate column of her back; and when she sighed against his lips, he pulled the shirt up to her waist and cupped the cheeks of her naked buttocks.

"Ye've the most delightful arse," Gordon murmured against her lips.

"And ye've the most wonderful hands," Rob whispered.

"Gordy, lad, I could kill ye where ye lay," a familiar voice announced loudly. "Yer reflexes are slippin'."

Rob screamed.

In a flash of movement, Gordon grabbed the dagger from beneath his pillow, flipped his wife onto her back, and covered her body protectively. Both of them looked toward the doorway.

"Playin' Adam and Eve again?" Dewey asked, sauntering into the lodge.

"God's balls, ye gave me a shock," Gordon said. He glanced at his blushing wife and teased, "Dinna be embarrassed, angel. Yer wearin' my shirt."

Gordon sat up and relaxed against the headboard. He chuckled when his wife scurried beneath the coverlet with him to hide her naked legs from the other man's gaze.

"I knew I was right," Dewey said, leaning against the table and grinning at them. "I canna wait to tell Gabby how wrong she was."

"Aboot what?" Gordon asked.

"Gabby insisted ye hadna been layin' yer lady," the giant said baldly. "I told her ye were too much of a man to keep yer hands off such a bonny lass as yer wife."

"Well, I guess ye win," Gordon said, glancing sidelong

at his wife's embarrassed blush. "Is that the reason ye barged in here?"

Dewey shook his head and held a pail up. "I've brought ye fresh milk Gabby said Lady Rob loves to drink Old Man's milk in the mornin'."

"Thank ye, Dewey," Rob said with a smile. "I do love it."

Setting the pail on the table, Dewey nodded at her and then wandered across the chamber to the cooling rack near the hearth. "What's hidin' beneath this?" he asked, lifting the linen.

Dewey helped himself to a bannock and said, "Why, 'tis simply perfection, even more delicious than Granny Biddy's."

"How ever did a laird's daughter learn to make perfect bannocks?" Gordon asked, turning a surprised look on his wife.

"I wasna braggin' when I said I possessed many talents," Rob answered, her pride evident in her voice.

Dewey scoffed another bannock and started toward the door. "Are ye comin' to the Beltane celebration?" he asked with his mouth full of food.

"My lady's agreed to leap over the fire with me," Gordon answered, putting an arm around her.

"Then I'll see ye there later." Dewey closed the door behind himself.

" 'Tis warm in here," Gordon said, pulling the shirt over Rob's head and tossing it onto the floor. He pushed her down on her back and asked, "Now, where were we?"

"We were aboot to eat the bannocks," she answered.

"The bannocks will wait." Gordon dipped his head to her breasts and flicked his tongue seductively across her nipples. "Ah, yes. This is what I want more than anythin' else."

Two hours later, Gordon had already consumed the most delicious bannocks he'd ever eaten. Immediately after breakfast, he scooped Smooches into his arms and went outside to feed and to water their horses.

Alone in the lodge, Rob brushed her hair hurriedly. In keeping with the spring season and the warmth of the day, she'd dressed in a lightweight skirt and a scooped-neck linen blouse but left her feet bare.

"Hurry, will ye?" Gordon said, bursting into the lodge. He set Smooches down on the bed. "The Beltane ceremony will soon be beginnin'."

"I'm ready as I'll ever be," Rob said, "but I would have preferred bathin' now instead of later."

"Ye smell delightful," Gordon told her. "Ye've the scent of our lovemakin' lingerin' aboot ye." He crossed the chamber to stand in front of her, lifted a wreath of wildflowers up, and smiled. "I give ye sunshine, flowers, and the gift of my smile." With that, he crowned her with the wreath of flowers.

Rob giggled. "Thank ye, my lord. I believe I'll keep ye around for a while."

"Forever and a day," Gordon whispered, planting a kiss on her lips.

"Shall we take Smooches with us?" she asked.

Gordon shook his head. "The pup will only trouble the cattle, and I wouldna want him trampled beneath their hooves."

The great mother goddess nodded her approval upon those who celebrated Beltane. In her infinite wisdom, she granted the celebrants an idyllic day of blue skies, warm sunshine, and pure mountain air filled with the scent of the forest in springtime.

Rob appeared like one of the flower fairies as they walked down the path to Glen Aray. She hummed a spritely tune off key, and holding her husband's hand, fairly skipped along beside him. Not only had she become his wife in fact as well as name, but she was about to attend her first Beltane celebration.

"I'm so verra excited," Rob said.

"I would never have guessed," Gordon said dryly. He cast her a puzzled, sidelong look and asked, "Have ye never attended the MacArthur's shielin'?"

"No," Rob answered honestly. Before he could question her about that, she said, "Tell me what happens."

"Twin fires are lit from the nine kinds of wood collected and dried last March," Gordon told her. "There are branches of birch for the ancient goddess, oak for the ancient god, fir for birth, willow for death, rowan for magic, apple for love"—he pulled her close and kissed her—"vine for joy, hazel for wisdom, and hawthorn for purity. Beltane honors the sexual union of man and woman. Lovers drink from a May bowl that contains wine, strawberry, and sweet woodruff. Afterwards, they leap over the fire together. Lastly, the cattle are led between the twin fires, which purifies them."

By the time they reached Glen Aray, a crowd of men, women, and children had already gathered near the pool. Farther away, the cattle grazed in one large herd. Still dark, the kindling for the twin fires awaited the moment when the Beltane celebration would begin.

As the laird's only son and heir, Gordon received the honor of lighting the Beltane fires. Rob watched him proudly as he torched one and then the other. A resounding cheer arose from the spectators.

"Gordy and Lady Rob must drink from the Beltane bowl and leap over the fires first," Gabby announced in a loud voice. "Inverary will prosper if our future lord and his lady be fruitful."

"Come, angel," Gordon said to Rob. He took the bowl out of Gabby's hands and lifted it to his wife's lips so that she could take the ritual sip. Following his lead, Rob did the same for him.

After passing the May bowl to Gabby, Gordon scooped Rob into his arms. He took a running leap over the first fire, and then the second. Releasing her, he slid her slowly down the long length of his body.

Wild cheering and whistles of encouragement erupted from the watching Campbell men.

Rob blushed, recalling the intimacies they'd shared the previous night. In spite of her embarrassment, she looped her arms around his neck, pressed her body against his, and kissed him. She wanted no Campbell clansmen doubting the fact that she was truly Gordon's wife in every sense of the word.

"Did I mention that leapin' over the fire together will insure that ye get with my child?" Gordon asked, placing the palm of his hand against her burning cheek.

"Lyin' is a terrible sin," Rob teased him. "Ye'd better ask the priest for absolution the next time ye attend church."

"Are ye worried for my soul, angel?" Gordon grinned. "I promise we'll be together for all of eternity."

"Aye, but where?" she asked. "I dinna doubt ye'd force me through the gates of hell if it suited yer purpose."

"Och, angel. I was hopin' ye'd put a good word in with the Lord for me," he said, then brushed his lips against hers.

Next, Dewey and Gabby leaped together over the twin fires. Another couple followed them. Soon the time arrived for purifying the Campbell cattle by marching them between the fires.

Gabby took charge of the ceremony as the older children ran to the far end of the valley to herd the cattle toward them. "Inverary's new lady will lead the first cow through in order to bring our clan good luck," Gabby announced.

"What am I to do?" Rob whispered to her husband, trying to hide her left hand within the folds of her skirt.

"Dewey will rope the first one," Gordon answered. "Use the rope to coax the cow between the fires."

Embarrassed at being the center of attention, Rob stepped forward and took the rope from Dewey. She recalled how worried the MacArthurs had been that she would kill the cattle with her touch and so hid her devil's flower within the folds of her skirt. Using only her right hand, Rob tried to pull the cow toward the fires. Unfortunately, the cow refused to budge.

"Use both hands," Gordon called from where he stood.

Reluctantly, Rob grabbed the rope with two hands and started to lead the cow between the fires. She prayed that no one would notice the evil deformity that marked the back of her left hand.

Everyone cheered when she finally managed to drag the cow to the other side of the twin fires. Glistening perspiration beaded her forehead and upper lip. Rob knew her fear of being labeled a witch, not her exertions, had made her clammy with sweat.

While Gordon ran to the back of the herd to help the older children usher the cattle toward the fires, Rob stood beside Gabby on the sidelines and watched. Sensing a presence beside her, she glanced to the left.

"Good mornin'," Rob greeted the little boy who stood there.

"I'm verra sorry I made ye cry," Gavin apologized, placing his hand in hers. He cast her his charming smile, so much like his father's, and asked, "Can I still be yer hero?"

Rob grinned, and her heart filled with boundless joy.

"Ye'll always be my hero," she said, giving his hand a gentle squeeze.

"Angel, are ye ready for yer bath?" Gordon called, drawing their attention as he advanced on them.

Rob blushed as anticipation for her husband's body heated her. For once, Gordon had spoken truthfully. Making love was all that he had promised, and more.

"Can I come too?" Gavin asked.

Rob bit her bottom lip to keep from giggling at her husband's surprised expression. She wondered how he would handle this without hurting the boy's feelings.

Gordon knelt on one bended knee in front of the boy in order to be eye level with him. "Lady Rob and I are goin' bathin' without any clothin'," he told his son.

"Ye mean doup-dippin'?" Gavin asked.

"Aye, and ladies dinna like bein' naked in front of more than one man at a time," Gordon explained. "So ye'll stay behind this time."

"Oh." The boy's expression drooped.

Gordon leaned close to his son and whispered into his ear, "Rob and I are goin' to see aboot gettin' ye that sister ye want."

Gavin perked up at that.

Gordon stood then, and taking his wife's hand in his, led her away from the gathering. As they walked toward the path, Rob glanced over her shoulder at the six-year-old. Gavin stood alone and watched them retreating. He appeared so utterly forlorn. Rob felt the insistent tugging at her heartstrings. She knew better than most how miserable being alone was.

"Gordy, look at Gavin," Rob said. "We canna leave him behind."

"Duncan will play with him," Gordon told her.

"Duncan is playin' with the older boys and willna want him taggin' along," Rob replied.

"We're goin' bathin'," Gordon said. "I dinna want him taggin' along either."

"I'll wear my chemise."

"Gavin will get over it," Gordon assured her, taking her hand firmly in his. "The lad must learn to stand up for himself."

"He's a six-year-old bairn," Rob said, yanking her hand out of his grasp. "I canna leave him standin' there."

"The boy has a mother."

"And a heartless father, to boot."

At that, Rob retraced her steps across the clearing until she reached the boy, who gave her a puzzled smile. She held her hand out to him and asked, "Will ye come along with us?"

Obviously torn between going and staying, Gavin stared at her offered hand in apparent indecision. Finally, with his mind made up, he shook his head and said, "Go on and make my baby sister."

Rob bit her bottom lip to keep from laughing. "Yer father and I decided to wait until tonight to make her," she explained.

Gavin's expression cleared. He reached for her hand and said, "In that case—"

"Gavin!"

Rob and Gavin turned toward the voice.

"Come here at once," Kendra called from where she stood with a group of women.

Gavin looked at Rob and shrugged. "Perhaps we'll bathe together another day."

"I'd like that verra much," Rob said. "Will I see ye tomorrow?"

"Damsel, I'll be right here," he told her.

Rob curtsied. "Thank ye, my lord-hero."

Gavin grinned and bowed from the waist. Turning on his heels, he dashed toward his mother.

Rob watched him a moment and then lifted her gaze to the voluptuous, dark-haired beauty. Kendra stared hard at her, and there was no mistaking the cold hatred leaping at her from the dark eyes.

Rob lifted her chin a notch and turned to leave. By chance, she glanced down at her beggar bead necklace, and a ripple of fear danced down her spine.

Her star ruby had darkened redder than pigeon's blood.

Chapter 13

Rob saw no one but Gordon during the next two weeks.

Under cover of darkness, a heavy blanket of gray clouds shrouded the mountains and the glens of Argyll. Before dawn, those sadly drooping clouds yawned. Sheets of rain slashed the land, and blasts of howling wind swirled around the mountains and slapped the woodland trees.

The women and the children remained hidden within their stone and turf beehive shelters during those long, lonely days. Mothers used this quiet time to knit warm stockings for winter. Only the older children ventured outside to tend the cattle that huddled together among the rocks.

Gordon and Rob, alone in their lodge, passed the better part of those two weeks in bed. When they weren't making love, she cooked and cleaned for him while he escorted her pup outside and tended their horses.

"Wake up, angel. The sun is shinin'."

Rob opened her eyes and saw Gordon sitting beside

her on the edge of the bed. Brilliant sunshine streamed into the chamber through the open door and bathed the lodge in a yellow glow. Her husband offered her a freshly picked bouquet of wildflowers and the gift of his smile.

"Have I already slept for forty days?" Rob asked, sitting up and leaning against the headboard.

"Only fourteen," Gordon answered her. "I've made ye breakfast this mornin'." He set a bowl of oatmeal porridge on her lap.

Rob looked at the porridge and felt her stomach lurch sickeningly. She covered her mouth with her hand and gulped the nausea back.

"I'll eat later," she said in a muffled voice.

"Are ye ill?" Gordon asked, worry creasing his brow.

Rob managed a faint smile and shook her head. "I'll be fine once I feel the warmth of the sunshine and breathe the fresh air," she assured him.

"Dewey's waitin' outside for me," Gordon told her. "Would ye care to go fishin' with us?"

"No, Smooches and I will walk to Glen Aray and visit with Gabby," Rob said, refusing.

"I'll meet ye there later," Gordon said, and then leaned close to plant a chaste kiss on her lips. After setting the bowl of porridge on the table, he winked at her and left the lodge.

Two hours later, Rob completed her housekeeping chores and her morning toilet. Leaving the lodge, she scooped Smooches into her arms and started down the path to Glen Aray.

Everywhere she looked, Rob saw voluptuous nature in bloom. The trees seemed greener; a colorful variety of wildflowers adorned the woodland; lush blossoms promised a bountiful harvest. The morning air resounded with bird song as grackle, robin, finch, and wren went about the business of nesting and feeding their young.

Birds signify new beginnings, Rob remembered her aunt telling her. Was she about to experience a new beginning in her own life? Did Gordon cherish her? Her husband certainly behaved as if he did. Could the Campbell clansmen accept her as their lady? They'd seemed to have accepted her at the Beltane celebration, but why had her beggar bead necklace darkened? Was it only because Kendra harbored such negative feelings for her?

That must be the reason, Rob concluded. She wasn't in any real physical danger from the other woman. Her star ruby had sensed the negative feelings emanating from the dark-haired woman.

Keep a guarded eye on the ruby today, Rob told herself. She reached to touch the beggar bead necklace and stopped short. She'd forgotten to wear it. Should she return to the lodge to get it? Where was the sense in that? She was closer to the glen than the lodge, and in no real danger.

Rob continued walking along the path and hummed a merry tune to herself. Gavin's apology renewed her dream of acceptance, and she hoped she'd see him on her way to look for Gabby. Perhaps the three of them could play games together.

Leaving the path behind, Rob started across the valley of Glen Aray. The sunshine on her shoulders warmed her, the grass beneath her bare feet tickled, and the mingling fragrances of myriad wildflowers wafted through the air and made her nose twitch pleasurably with their scents.

Rob felt wonderfully alive. The day and the valley were simply perfection. She was home in the Highlands; and for the first time in her life, she felt that she truly belonged there. In spite of Old Clootie's mark, her husband's people accepted her. And their acceptance was all she'd ever wanted.

Sublime happiness made Rob giddy, and she twirled in

a circle like a young girl. Her gaze fell on one of those deadly glenside sundew blossoms. A butterfly struggled for freedom on the flower's sticky tendrils, and a feeling of foreboding washed over her.

Rob paused and watched the butterfly. Leaning close, she lifted it to freedom. *Now the sundew flower would starve.*

Rob banished the disturbing thought from her mind. Letting the death of a flower trouble her was ridiculous. She'd done the butterfly a good turn that day. Perhaps the favor would be returned to her on another day.

Rob strolled across the valley in the direction of the natural pool formed from the mingling of Sorrow and Care. Even from this distance, she spied the older children swimming in the pool. A group of women, including Gabby and Kendra, sat together and talked animatedly. Apparently, they were as happy with the idyllic day as she was.

And then she saw Gavin. The six-year-old sat alone on a rock and watched the other children, including his brother, romping in the water. Her heart ached at his dejected expression. The boy seemed so alone, a feeling she well understood.

"Gavin!" Rob called.

With a smile of greeting lighting his face, the six-year-old turned in her direction. When Smooches dashed forward to greet him, Gavin reached out and patted the pup.

"Is aught wrong?" Rob asked, sitting beside him.

"The others willna play with me," Gavin answered, looking longingly at the boys frolicking in the pool. "Duncan said I'm too little."

Rob felt the insistent tugging at her heartstrings. She knew from experience what rejection was. "The others canna keep ye from swimmin'," she told him. "They dinna own the water."

"I dinna know how to swim," Gavin admitted. "Some day I'll swim out away over my head. Perhaps I'll float across the seas to the New World."

Rob smiled. "Yer father will be here by and by. He'll give ye yer first swimmin' lesson then."

"I'd like that." The boy's expression brightened with hope. Then he asked, "When will my baby sister be arrivin'?"

Rob stifled a giggle, but wondered about her morning queasiness. Could that be a sign that she was carrying her husband's child? No, that couldn't be. They'd only been intimate for a few weeks, and surely getting with child took longer than that.

"Gettin' a sister isna as easy as ye may think," Rob told the six-year-old, "but yer father and I are tryin' really hard to accommodate ye . . . There's a shallow stream in the woods near yer father's lodge. If the weather holds tomorrow, would ye care to go ticklin' a trout with me?"

"What's that?"

His ignorance surprised Rob. "My brothers taught me how to tickle a trout when I was younger than ye. Has yer father never showed ye?"

Gavin shook his head.

"Well, ye wade into a stream and stand perfectly still," she explained. "Ever so slowly, ye submerge yer hand into the water. Fish, as ye may know, are curious creatures. When one swims close to investigate, ye stroke its belly with one finger. Once its paralyzed with pleasure, ye flip him onto the shore."

Gavin grinned. "And then what?"

"Why, ye cook him up and eat him," Rob said. " 'Tis a grand way to pass a summer's afternoon."

The six-year-old lost his smile and remarked, " 'Tisna grand if yer the fish."

"I do believe yer a lover, not a fighter," Rob said, lifting his little hand in hers and planting a kiss on it.

"Good day to ye, Lady Rob," Gabby greeted her, and plopped down on the ground beside them. "I'm verra excited and canna wait 'til this summer's gone."

"Why?" Rob asked, surprised. Winter lasted a long time in the Highlands. Most people relished the coming of summer and savored each day of its warmth.

"Gordy told my Dewey that he planned on takin' ye to Edinburgh to meet the king," Gabby answered. "Since I'm yer tirin' woman, I'm goin' too. Dewey will come along and play the part of Gordy's valet."

Rob giggled. "I canna imagine Dewey bein' a verra good valet."

Gabby burst out laughing, and Gavin smiled, though it was obvious from his expression that he had no idea what a valet was. Suddenly, shouts of alarm sliced the air and drew their attention.

"*Help!* The cattle are dyin'!" one of the older boys shouted, racing across the glen toward them. The others on duty with him ran close behind him, but the group stopped when they reached the women.

Rob scooped Smooches into her arms and stood to watch what was happening. Gabby and Gavin stood when she did. Even the children playing in the pool swam to the water's edge and listened.

"Tell us what happened," one of the women ordered. "And for God's sake, speak slowly."

"I dinna know for sure," the boy answered. "Everythin' seemed peaceful; but then the cow keeled over, shuddered for a minute, and died."

"Just the one?" Kendra asked, her alarm apparent in her voice.

"Aye, the cow Lady Rob led between the Beltane fires," he said.

In unison, the women turned around and stared at her. The suspicion in their gazes told Rob that her worst nightmare was coming true.

"The witch killed the cow with her evil touch," Kendra spoke up.

"Aye, look at her left hand," a second woman agreed. "Old Clootie marked her as his own."

"Shut yer foolish mouths," Gabby snapped, taking a step toward them. "The laird will have yer tongues for voicin' such lies."

Rob squared her shoulders proudly. She held her left hand out toward the women who leaped back quickly in fear.

" 'Tis a birth stain, not the devil's mark," Rob told them. "I am yer new lady and have yer best interests at heart. Never would I do anythin' to jeopardize yer welfare."

Silence reigned for several long moments while the women mulled that over in their minds. In the end, Kendra ruined whatever chance Rob had for winning the women's trust.

"I heard her mother is a Sassenach witch," Kendra said. "She passed that infernal ability along to her daughter. Look at her Sassenach dog. Why, 'tisna a dog at all. 'Tis a cat and her witch's familiar."

"Suffer a witch to die," one of the women agreed.

"The laird will kill the lot of ye if ye dare to lay a finger on her," Gabby warned.

"She cast her witch's spell on Gordy and the laird," Kendra insisted. " 'Twill be broken once she's dead."

"Aye, let's drown her and her cat," a woman said.

"Let's have done with it," another agreed.

Gabby stepped protectively in front of Rob as the group of women started forward. That gave Rob the chance she needed.

"Take Smooches and run into the woods," Rob ordered Gavin, thrusting the pup into his arms. "Follow the woodland path and find yer father."

Without hesitation, Gavin clutched the pup close against his chest and dashed toward the forest. "Da!" he shouted. "Help! Murder!"

"Fetch yer brother back here," Kendra ordered Duncan.

The boy looked from Rob to Gavin and then his mother. Finally, he shook his head and refused to budge.

"Ye must go through me to get to Lady Rob," Gabby informed them.

"Get her!" one of the women shouted.

Five of the women rushed Gabby who, in spite of her healthy size, was unable to fend them off. The women tackled her to the ground and then sat down on top of her. Gabby struggled in vain.

Kendra and two other women grabbed Rob, who fought frantically for freedom. They dragged her to the water's edge and shoved her to her knees. Kendra pushed her head toward the water.

"Gordy!" Rob screamed, and then sucked in her breath as her head plunged beneath the water's surface . . .

Strolling leisurely down the path that led to Glen Aray, Gordon and Dewey heard the screams for help. Both men dropped the fish they'd caught, raced toward the valley, and burst upon a shocking scene.

Clutching Smooches to his chest, Gavin was running toward them and shouting for help. Beyond the boy, five women sat on top of Gabby, who was cursing them loudly and struggling to buck them off. At the water's edge, Kendra and two women were drowning his wife.

Gordon reached them in mere seconds. He yanked the

two women away from his wife, tossed them aside, and then grabbed Kendra.

Gordon lifted the dark-haired beauty and slapped her hard, then dropped her to the ground beside her accomplices. He pulled his gasping wife to safety and held her protectively close within his embrace.

"Gordy, I didna do it," Rob rasped, weeping and clutching at him. "I—I swear I am no witch. 'Tis a birthin' stain, not Old Clootie's touch. I never killed the cow."

"She's a lyin' witch," Kendra screamed. "She killed the cow with her touch and cast a love spell on ye."

"Aye, the spell will be broken when she's dead," one of the women agreed.

Several others nodded, but dared not speak to the laird's son.

" 'Tisna so, Gordy," Rob sobbed. " 'Tisna so."

Gordon looked from the women to his sobbing wife. In a flash of awareness, he realized what her life had been at Dunridge Castle. Everything fell into place. Now he understood why she'd never attended a MacArthur shieling. *And why she wished to remain in England.*

The Highlands abounded with ignorant people who believed in Old Clootie. His wife had passed her entire life as an outlander in her own home. While he'd been futterin' Inverary's maids and flirting with the jades at court, the angel in his arms had waited for him to rescue her as he'd done the day he'd slain the monster beneath her bed.

"My wife is an angel and the lady of Inverary," Gordon said, his voice clipped with fury, his gaze on the women cold with accusation. "Yer continued good health depends upon rememberin' that. I'll suffer no qualms aboot dispatchin' anyone who dares to touch her."

"And if Gordy doesna get you, *I* will," Dewey spoke up. "The lot of ye disgust me." He glanced at Kendra and added, "Fergus willna be pleased aboot this."

Gordon lifted Rob into his arms and started walking across the glen toward the path that led to their lodge. "Dewey, bring the dog," he called over his shoulder.

Gabby gently lifted Smooches out of Gavin's arms and said, "Thank ye for yer help."

"Thank ye, lad," Dewey added, placing a hand on the six-year-old's shoulder. "We'll take Lady Rob's pet to her."

"Will she be well?" Gavin asked.

Dewey nodded, saying, "Gordy will take good care of her."

Together, Dewey and Gabby followed Gordon toward the woodland. With hot tears rolling down his face, Gavin stood alone and watched them leave.

Rob had stopped weeping by the time they reached the lodge. Dewey hurried ahead and opened the door for them. With his wife still in his arms, Gordon followed his man inside, and Gabby walked behind.

"Ye can put me down now," Rob said softly.

Reluctantly, Gordon set Rob on her feet. She stood beside the chair and stared like an unseeing statue into the darkened hearth.

"Can I get ye or ye lady anythin'?" Dewey asked.

"Privacy," Gordon said, flicking a worried glance at his wife.

"I'll send ye supper later," Gabby offered, setting Smooches down on the floor.

"I'll make us supper," Gordon said in refusal.

"*I'll* make it," Rob told him in a voice barely louder than a whisper.

At Gordon's nod, Dewey and Gabby left the lodge. As soon as the door clicked shut behind them, Gordon approached his wife. He felt uncertain about how to ease her pain. God's balls, he felt a bit shaky himself. He'd nearly lost her to the women's superstition. What if he'd delayed going to the glen? His wife would be dead instead of standing here in the lodge with him. That thought nearly felled him, but he knew he had to present a strong facade. His angel was in pain and needed his strength to get through this.

"I want ye to rest on the bed a while," Gordon said, standing behind her. "I think both of us need to sit down."

Rob nodded once and started to turn toward the bed. In the next instant, she crumpled to the floor in a dead faint.

"God's balls," Gordon swore. Lifting her into his arms, he carried her across the chamber to the bed and sat down beside her.

What should he do now? Gordon wondered. He had no experience with swooning women, but then recalled that first night at Devereux House and waited for her to regain consciousness.

Relief surged through Gordon a few minutes later when her eyelids fluttered, and she began to revive naturally.

"Dinna move yet," he said, placing the palm of his hand against her pale cheek.

Gordon drew her blouse over her head. After removing her skirt, he covered her with the blanket. Then he walked to the table and poured a dram of whiskey.

"Sit up slowly and sip this," Gordon ordered, perching on the edge of the bed.

Rob did as she was told, but kept her eyes downcast as if she feared meeting his gaze. Leaning back against the headboard, she sipped the amber liquid.

Gordon smiled as she grimaced against its taste. "Ye've been ill lately," he remarked.

" 'Tisna every day I'm almost drowned," she replied without looking at him.

With one hand, Gordon gently raised her chin a notch and waited until she lifted her gaze to his. " 'Twill never happen again," he promised.

"I—I'm no witch," Rob said, her emerald eyes glistening brightly with fresh tears.

Gordon leaned close and planted a chaste kiss on her lips. Then he pulled his boots off. Leaning back beside her against the headboard, he gathered her into his arms.

"Yer an angel," he whispered, dropping a kiss on the ebony crown of her head. *"My angel."*

"The Campbells will never accept me as their lady," Rob said with a heavy sigh. Wearily, she rested her head against his shoulder. "Ye must annul our marriage for the sake of the clan. I can return to Uncle Richard's."

"Annulment is impossible once the vows have been consummated." Gordon sounded calmer than he actually felt. No matter the consequences, he would never let her go.

"A divorce, then."

"Absolutely not."

Rob gazed at him through eyes that mirrored the raw pain in her heart and her soul. "Ye must divorce," she said in an aching whisper. "Livin' like an outsider will destroy me."

"They'll accept ye in time and love ye as one of their own," Gordon insisted.

Rob shook her head. "Ye canna force them to accept me any more than my own father could force the MacArthurs. He once told me that the clan is stronger than the laird. Consortin' with me can only taint their loyalty for ye."

Gordon suffered the overpowering urge to murder every ignorant MacArthur who'd ever shunned his precious wife. How they had hurt her. Probably beyond healing. Her pain became his pain, and Gordon knew he could never bear to let her go. Together, they would get through this ordeal, and somehow he would find a way to force his clan to accept her.

"For better or for worse, yer my wife and willna be returnin' to England," Gordon told her, though not unkindly. "The Campbells will accept ye as their lady."

Rob held her left hand up for his perusal and said, "Old Clootie's mark will always come between them and me."

"What a silly chit ye are," Gordon teased her. He lifted her hand to his lips and pressed a kiss on her birthmark. "Ye carry the flower of Aphrodite, not Old Clootie's mark."

Rob stared at him blankly.

"Dinna ye ken what I'm tellin' ye?"

She shook her head.

"Aphrodite was the legendary Greek goddess of love," he told her. "This flower is her symbol."

That seemed to surprise Rob. "Then why do people believe 'tis the mark of the devil?" she asked.

"Holy church convinced its people that lovemakin' was sinful except to procreate," he explained. "Over the course of a dozen centuries, people forgot that the flower originated with a love goddess. Naturally, the church had a hand in suppressin' the flower's real meanin'."

"But why?"

Gordon grinned. "Bald fat men, who canna wiggle their waggles, govern the church and dinna want anyone else havin' fun."

Rob giggled.

"Yer laughter sounds as divine as an angel at play," Gordon said, brushing his lips across her temple.

"But how did ye learn this?" Rob asked.

"Among other thin's, I enjoy readin'."

With one long finger, Gordon lifted her chin and dipped his head to meet hers. His mouth covered hers in a long, slow, healing kiss. When she entwined her arms around his neck, Gordon drew her down on the bed. Within mere seconds, his lips persuaded her to forget the afternoon's painful events.

"Come, Smooches," Rob called, opening the lodge's door. " 'Tis time to do yer duty."

She stepped outside and savored the warmth of the midday sun on her face and shoulders. Without warning, a dizzying wave of nausea swept through her and forced her to sit down on the ground to await its passing.

Rob felt thankful that Gordon had gone fishing with Dewey that morning. At least her husband wasn't around to witness this latest seizure. His constant hovering was beginning to grate on her nerves.

Since that nearly fatal day at Glen Aray three weeks earlier, Gordon had been as attentive as a man in love. But how could that be? What her husband wanted was a legitimate heir for Inverary. He would have that some day, but not from her.

Rob knew she hadn't long to live. Some unknown but horribly debilitating malady had caught her within its grip. Now she need not consider divorce; she'd be dead before one could be obtained.

When the queasiness passed, Rob got to her feet slowly. Clad in her oldest skirt and blouse, she appeared like a barefoot peasant girl. However, no peasant would wear an emerald-adorned wedding band or a necklace that sported a star ruby.

Glancing down at her beggar bead necklace, Rob saw that the star ruby was darker than pigeon's blood. A chill of apprehension rippled down her spine, and she jerked into rigid alertness.

Like a doe sensing danger, Rob lifted her head and, turning slowly in a circle, scanned the surrounding woodland. Had Kendra and the other Campbell women come to finish what they'd begun three weeks earlier?

Serenity pervaded the air, and Rob detected no lurking danger. She reached up and touched the star ruby. As she did, the image of Gavin flitted across her mind's eye.

Some day I'll swim away out over my head . . .

Rob recalled the boy's words to her. Gavin was in danger! Reason fled and instinct surfaced.

Rob scooped Smooches up, shut him inside the lodge, and ran down the path that led to Glen Aray. Fear for the boy blinded her to nature's glory. She never saw the green lushness of the trees or the wanton wildflowers adorning the path. Even the chorus of sweet bird song fell upon deaf ears.

Gavin is in danger. That thought echoed within the corridors of her mind, making her pulse beat faster, urging her on and quickening her pace.

The closer Rob got to the glen, the faster her feet moved; but she never felt the stones and the twigs beneath her bared feet. Only that urgent sense of foreboding sent her careening down the path. Lighter than an angel's touch, invisible hands on her back seemed to push her along.

"Gavin!" Rob screamed, bursting into the glen.

And then she heard the shouts for help. In the middle of the mountain pool, Gavin struggled to stay afloat while Kendra stood at the shoreline and screamed for help. All the women and the children appeared frozen in shock, unable to move to save the six-year-old.

Without breaking stride, Rob reached the shoreline and ran straight into the water. Hands on her arm jerked her back.

"Dinna touch my son," Kendra cried. "Stay away from him."

Rob whirled toward the woman. In one swift motion, she clenched her fist and swung, striking Kendra full on the face. She shoved the hysterical woman to the ground and dived into the water.

The shock of the cold mountain water nearly stole Rob's breath away. Though hampered by her skirt, she swam toward the middle of the pool just as Gavin sank beneath the water.

Tucking her legs up, Rob dived beneath the surface. The sparklingly clear water made it easy for her to see him. She reached out, grabbed his shirt, and pulled him up with her. Breaking the surface, Rob clutched him against her breast. His small head lolled against her shoulder like a drowned kitten's.

With a strength born of desperation, Rob finally got Gavin back to shore. The boy was deathly pale, his lips tinged with blue.

"Stay back," Rob ordered, feeling the others crowding around her. Everyone, including Kendra, obeyed the authority in her voice.

Please God, let him live, Rob prayed as she rolled Gavin onto his stomach and began to pound rhythmically on his back. She hit him again and again until he retched water tinged with blood. Then she flipped him onto his back, pressed her mouth to his, and breathed life into him. An eternity seemed to pass before his eyelids fluttered open, and familiar gray eyes stared dazedly into hers.

"He's alive," one woman gasped.

"Lady Rob brought him back from the dead," another added.

" 'Tis a miracle," said a third woman.

"Someone fetch a blanket for him," Rob ordered.

Feeling a hand on her shoulder, Rob looked up and saw her husband kneeling beside her. She peered at the crowd in time to see several Campbells making the sign of the cross.

"Lady Rob *is* an angel," Dewey said, passing Gordon a blanket.

Rob shook her head. "I'm a flesh and blood woman, nothin' more."

" 'Tis the Lord's mark stainin' yer hand, not Old Clootie's," Gabby insisted. "Ye were touched by an angel."

Chapter 14

 Touched by an angel?

That absurd notion flabbergasted Rob. Only three weeks earlier these superstitious Highlanders had tried to drown her for being a witch, and now they were hailing her as an angel. Of course, she much preferred their acceptance to their murderous intent; but if their attitudes could change so quickly, what prevented them from turning on her again? How could she feel secure living among them?

"I'm a woman," Rob said simply, glancing at their awed expressions. "But perhaps the Lord did help me save Gavin." She wrapped the blanket tightly around the boy and smiled at him, saying, "Dinna move. Yer father will carry ye home."

Rob stood when her husband scooped his son into his arms. She flicked a grateful smile at Gabby who'd placed a woolen shawl around her shoulders.

"I'm takin' Gavin to my lodge," Gordon told Kendra.

"No, he needs me," she protested.

Gordon opened his mouth to argue, but Duncan piped

up, "Sleepin' in the same lodge as a witch will frighten Gavin."

Rob flinched visibly. Without thinking, she moved her right hand to cover her birthmark. How could she ever hope to win the Campbell's acceptance if her husband's own sons rejected her?

"Lady Rob is no witch," Gordon told the boy.

Duncan looked confused. "But Mama said she was."

"Dinna argue aboot it now," Rob said, touching her husband's arm as he rounded in anger on Kendra. " 'Tis done and past. Gavin will want to recover with his mother by his side." She noted the angry twitching of a muscle in his cheek and pleaded, "Please, Gordy."

He glanced at his trembling son in his arms and nodded once. "I'll meet ye at the lodge after I take Gavin to his mother's."

Kendra lifted her youngest son by Fergus out of one of the women's arms, flicked a sour glance at Rob, and walked away. Following in her wake, Gordon started across the glen in the direction of a cluster of beehive-shaped hovels.

"The bitch never even thanked ye," Gabby muttered, drawing her lady's attention. "Dewey and I will walk ye back to yer lodge."

"I can find my own way," Rob said. "Besides, I'd prefer being alone for now."

Clutching the shawl tightly around her shoulders, Rob stepped forward, and the milling crowd of Campbells parted for her. She'd only gone ten yards when a familiar voice called out, stopping her in her tracks.

"Lady Rob!" Duncan raced toward her, quickly closing the distance separating them.

"Yes, Duncan?"

"Thank ye for rescuin' my brother."

Rob smiled. "Yer verra welcome."

"And . . ." The boy dropped his gaze to his bare feet and added, "I'm sorry I made ye cry."

Rob felt renewed hope swell within her breast. She reached out, lifted his chin, and waited until he raised his gaze to hers.

"What's done is past and forgotten," she assured him.

The boy smiled with relief.

"Ye'd better hurry home and help yer mother care for Gavin," she said.

Duncan nodded. Turning on his heels, he ran across the glen in the direction his parents had taken.

When Rob reached the lodge, Smooches attacked her with love. She dropped the damp shawl onto the floor, scooped the pup into her arms, and hugged him. After setting him down on top of the bed, she removed her wet garments and donned one of her husband's shirts. His scent of mountain heather clung to it and soothed her badly frayed nerves.

Feeling depleted of energy, Rob lay down on the bed. The enormity of almost losing Gavin hit her with the impact of an avalanche. What if her ruby hadn't darkened? What if she hadn't reached the glen in time? What if she'd been unable to make him retch the water he'd swallowed?

The door swung open suddenly. Gordon grinned at her and held the fish he'd earlier caught high into the air. "Are ye up for cleanin' fish?" he asked.

Rob looked from his smiling face to the dead fish. Covering her mouth with one hand, she leaped off the bed and made a mad dash for the door. Outside, she dropped to her knees and heaved dryly while her husband gently held her head. When her spasms passed, she leaned heavily against his legs.

"Should I take that as a *no*?" Gordon asked, caressing the top of her head.

Rob managed a faint smile. "Yer verra funny, my lord."

Gordon lifted her into his arms, carried her inside the lodge, and set her gently down on the bed. After pulling the coverlet over her, he discreetly tossed the dead fish out the door.

Sitting on the edge of the bed, Gordon yanked his boots off and then lay down beside her. "Feelin' better?" he asked, gathering her into the protective circle of his embrace.

"Aye, but too much excitement and the smell of dead fish is a sickenin' combination," Rob answered. "How's Gavin?"

"Badly frightened." Gordon cast her a thoughtful look and said, "Tell me, angel. How did ye know what to do?"

"Well, I saw that my star ruby had darkened," she replied. "Then Gavin leaped into my thoughts and—"

"I meant, how could ye know what to do to revive him?" Gordon interrupted. "I didna think ye could swim."

"I told ye I could swim," she said, "but I hate the deep water."

"Tell me how ye knew to revive him."

"Verra well, but ye must promise not to feel sorry for me."

He gave her a puzzled smile and nodded.

"Once when I was a young girl, I sneaked out of the postern gate and wandered to the shore of Loch Awe," Rob began, careful to keep her gaze fixed on his chest lest she see pity in his eyes. "I heard the children playin' and wanted to join in their fun. As I neared them, they"—her voice cracked with remembered pain—"they called me a monster and ran away."

Gordon felt his heart lurch. How could the MacArthurs have been so cruel to his beautiful wife, his angel?

Revenge against them for hurting her leaped into his mind. When he became the Duke of Argyll, he'd—

"Dinna pity me," Rob whispered, reaching up to touch his cheek as she gazed into his eyes.

"I wasna pityin' ye," Gordon lied.

Rob recognized the pity shadowed in his gaze and knew he was lying, but loved him for not telling her the truth. She cast him a knowing smile and then continued. "One of the crofter's daughters became hysterical with fear when I chased after her. In her desperate flight away from me, she fell into the loch. Fortunately, my father had come searching for me. He dived into the water and pulled the girl to shore. His pounding on her back and breathin' into her mouth revived her finally."

"Did the children never play with ye?" he asked, one hand stroking her back soothingly.

"I never ventured to the loch again," Rob said. A rueful smile touched her lips when she added, "I remember demandin' that my father order the children to play with me."

"And did he?"

Rob shook her head. "My father said that he couldna force the children to play with me because the clan is stronger than the laird."

An aching tenderness for the angel in his arms swelled within Gordon's chest. He brushed his lips across her temple and said, "So ye befriended the cook who taught ye to make perfect bannocks."

Rob pinkened. "And Old Man's milk too."

"Forgive me, my love," Gordon whispered.

"For what?"

"For failin' to send ye the doll I promised."

"I forgave ye for that long ago," she told him.

Gordon dipped his head, and his mouth covered hers in a lingering kiss meant to heal. She was his exquisitely beautiful wife, and he wanted to erase a lifetime of painful memories. Easing her troubled spirit for the next two hours was easy, and they dropped into a sated sleep.

Early the following morning, Gordon awakened and rose from their bed to stoke the embers in the hearth. He dressed noiselessly and then perched on the edge of the bed to study his wife in sleep.

A smile touched his lips as he traced one long finger down the side of her silken cheek. His wife was brave and bonny and vulnerable.

And he loved her.

God's balls, when had he fallen in love with her? Gordon wondered. Love was for women and fools. Well, he wasn't a woman so that made him a fool.

Gordon knew without a doubt that admitting his love for her would be a grave mistake. He'd seen too many men at court ruled by the women whom they loved. When they were old and gray and drooling in their dotage, he would tell her he'd loved her for all the years of their marriage.

Leaning closer, Gordon pressed a kiss on her parted lips. When her eyelids fluttered open and she wrapped her arms around his neck, he chuckled huskily against her mouth.

"Good mornin', angel," Gordon greeted her. " 'Tis early yet, but I've important business needin' my attention. Are ye up for makin' me a stack of bannocks while I'm gone?"

Rob smiled drowsily and nodded, saying, "Yer wish is my command, my lord."

"Och, fibbin' is a terrible sin," he teased her. "Be certain ye dress decently because I just might return with company."

"Who?" Rob asked, perking up.

" 'Tis a surprise." At that, Gordon gave her a quick, teasing kiss and left the lodge.

Humming a bawdy tune, Gordon marched down the path to Glen Aray. This summer's shieling had been eventful. He'd made Rob his wife in fact as well as name and nearly lost her to his clansmen's superstitions. Then there was the matter of his youngest son who would be lying in an early grave if not for his wife's swift intervention.

And he'd fallen in love.

That startling fact brought a smile to his lips. Realizing that he was grinning like an idiot, Gordon schooled his features into an expressionless mask. If he chanced to meet anyone along the path, they'd think he'd lost his wits.

A few of the shieling's events had gotten out of control. As the future Duke of Argyll and Campbell laird, Gordon decided he needed to exert his authority. His wife had been ill lately and needed his protection. Kendra had poisoned Duncan and Gavin against Rob. Setting that straight was his duty.

Unannounced, Gordon barged inside one of the bee-hive-shaped hovels and grinned at the provocative sight that greeted him. Leaning against the doorway, he said in an overly loud voice, "Age is slowin' yer reflexes, Dewey. I could kill ye where yer layin' yer wife."

Startled by the intrusion, the bucking couple on the pallet snapped their heads around. Gabby shrieked with outraged embarrassment, but Dewey threw back his head and hooted with laughter.

"Get off me, ye bumblin' oaf," Gabby ordered. "He can see everythin' God gave me."

"Playin' Adam and Eve, are ye?" Gordon teased. "I'll wait outside, and ye might as well take yer time aboot it. Ye willna be returnin' to yer nestin' until tomorrow."

When Dewey appeared a few minutes later, Gordon started walking in the direction of a certain hovel. "Escort Kendra and her bairn back to Inverary," he ordered his man. "Pass the night there, and when ye return in the mornin', bring Granny Biddy with ye."

"Granny Biddy?" Dewey echoed. "She willna want to come up into the mountains."

"Tell Biddy that Rob's been ill recently," Gordon said, "but I dinna want to alarm the lass by forcin' her back to Inverary."

Dewey nodded in understanding.

When they reached Kendra's hovel, Gordon entered without announcing himself. He nudged Kendra awake and said, "Pack yer belongin's. I'm sendin' ye back to Inverary. The boys are stayin' here with me."

"I dinna want that witch near my sons," Kendra told him.

Gordon clenched and unclenched his hands, fighting the urge to strike her. "I didna ask what ye preferred," he said in a voice that brooked no argument. "If ye ever again accuse my wife of bein' a witch, I'll have Fergus beat ye within an inch of yer life, and then I'll cast ye out of Argyll."

Kendra clamped her lips shut and packed her few belongings. With that completed, she walked over to the pallet where Duncan and Gavin slept. Gently shaking them awake, she smiled at their sleepy expressions and gave each a kiss on the cheek.

"Fergus needs me at Inverary," she told them. "Yer father is here to take ye up to his lodge so ye needna miss any of the shielin'."

Turning away, Kendra lifted the baby from her pallet. Duncan and Gavin kissed their half-brother. After casting Gordon a sullen look, Kendra walked out the door.

Gordon stared at his sons who returned his stare. "I

want to talk to ye aboot Lady Rob," Gordon said, joining them on their pallet. "But ye must swear never to tell her we had this conversation. Can I trust ye?"

"Ye can trust me," Duncan said, "but Gavin canna keep secrets."

"I'll keep this one," the six-year-old promised. "I'd do anythin' for Lady Rob."

"Because the MacArthur children feared the mark on Rob's hand, they refused to play with her and hurt her feelin's," Gordon told them. "Lady Rob had a verra lonely childhood. Not only that, but she's been feelin' puirly lately."

"She willna die, will she?" Duncan asked.

"No, Dewey's bringin' Granny Biddy back from Inverary to help her get well again," Gordon answered. "I want to be certain that ye boys treat Lady Rob kindly. She loves the both of ye verra much, and 'twould be a shame if ye added to her worries by makin' her feel worse than she already does. Can I trust ye to guard her feelin's?"

"Ye can count on me," Duncan said.

"Me too," Gavin agreed.

"Come along then." Gordon rose from the pallet, adding, "Rob's makin' us a mountain of bannocks, and Dewey said they're even better than Granny Biddy's. If we dinna hurry back to the lodge, Smooches will gobble them up and save none for us."

Rob grabbed the bannock spade and lifted the last of the bannocks from the girdle over the hearth. Being careful not to drop them, she set the bannocks down on the cooling rack and then wrapped them in linen to keep them moist and warm until her husband returned.

Where had Gordon gone? Probably to see Gavin, she

answered herself and wondered how the boy was feeling this morning.

Touched by an angel.

Rob stared at the devil's flower staining the back of her left hand. How unpredictable these people were. One day the Campbells reviled her for being Old Clootie's hand-maiden, and the next day they regarded her as a saint.

Rob heard the door opening behind her. Wearing a smile of greeting, she whirled around but then stared in surprise as her husband's sons followed him into the lodge. Smooches reacted to their presence first. The pup dashed across the chamber and lovingly attacked the boys.

"Look who's with me," Gordon said needlessly, set-ting a pail of milk down on the table.

Recovering herself, Rob gave him a puzzled smile and said to the boys, "Are ye hungry? Yer just in time to help me eat that stack of bannocks."

"I could eat the whole thin' myself," Duncan said, dropping his satchel on the floor.

"Me too," Gavin agreed, and set his own satchel down beside his brother's.

"Are ye ready, sons?" Gordon asked. When they nod-ded, he turned to Rob and gestured toward the open door, saying, "We give ye sunshine . . ."

"And flowers," Duncan said, handing her a freshly picked bouquet of heather, buttercups, and dandelions.

Gavin winked at her. "And the gift of our smiles."

Rob giggled. "Thank ye, my lords. I canna think of any three thin's I'd prefer." She filled a mug with water and placed the flowers in it, then set it on the table. "Drag those stools over here," she ordered. "Who wants Old Man's milk?"

"I do," Gavin answered.

"So do I," Duncan said.

"Me too," Gordon added.

Rob served them the bannocks and then mixed four mugs of zested Old Man's milk. Gordon sat down in one chair while she sat in the other. The boys sat on the stools. Rob couldn't help thinking that being here like this made her feel part of their family. A warm feeling of acceptance and security enveloped her.

"These bannocks are as good as Granny Biddy's," Duncan said.

"Even better than hers," Gavin corrected him.

"Yer an incorrigible flatterer," Rob told the six-year-old.

"What's that?" he asked.

" 'Tis a handsome rogue who always tells the ladies what they *wish* to hear," she explained.

"That sounds like lyin' to me," Duncan said.

"Well, sometimes tellin' the truth isna the kindest thin' to do," Rob replied.

The boy looked at his father for verification.

Gordon shrugged and nodded.

"We're stayin' with ye for the rest of the shielin'," Gavin spoke up.

Rob flicked her husband a questioning look and asked, "What aboot Kendra?"

"Fergus needed her at Inverary," Gordon lied for the benefit of his sons. "I suppose he missed her company."

"Dinna ye want us with ye?" Gavin asked, drawing her attention.

"Great Bruce's ghost, of course I want ye here," Rob answered. "What larks the four of us will share."

Gavin pointed at Smooches and said, "Ye mean, the *five* of us."

"I stand corrected," Rob said with a smile.

Gordon and Duncan went fishing after breakfast, but Gavin chose to stay behind. Rob and the boy wandered outside and sat beneath a birch tree while Smooches scurried about and inspected the immediate area.

"Tell me aboot when I'm supposed to lie," Gavin said, gazing up at her with piercing gray eyes so much like his father's.

"Yer never supposed to lie," Rob told him, hiding a smile. "However, there are two kinds of lies. A bad lie almost always hurts someone, but a good lie keeps a loved one from becomin' hurt or angry. So a bad lie causes pain, but a good lie prevents it."

"I ken what ye mean," Gavin said. "If Grandfather asks me if I'm payin' attention to my lessons, I should say yes even if I'm not. Grandfather is an old man, and we dinna want to upset him."

"Exactly." Rob reached out and picked a dandelion. "Close yer eyes. I want to see if ye love butter."

"How can ye do that?" the boy asked.

"If I put this dandelion beneath yer chin and it reflects yellow, that means ye love butter," Rob told him.

At that, Gavin closed his eyes and lifted his chin.

"Oh, I see that ye simply adore fresh butter," she said.

Gavin giggled and said, "Let me try."

Rob handed him the dandelion, closed her eyes, and lifted her chin. His voice sounded very close when he said, "Ye love butter too." She opened her eyes and found him practically nose to nose with her.

Gavin gifted her with his father's devastating smile. Unexpectedly, he lifted her left hand and pressed a kiss on her birthmark, saying, "I love ye, Lady Rob."

Tears welled up in her eyes, but she brushed them away with her fingertips. "I love ye, too."

"Why do I see tears in yer eyes?"

" 'Tis joy, sweetie," Rob told him. "Ladies always cry when they're happy."

Gavin threw himself into her arms, and Rob hugged

him close. How she wished his father would say those same words to her. Great Bruce's ghost, she'd done what she vowed never to do, what she'd struggled against these many long months. She'd fallen in love with Gordon Campbell.

That night Rob learned what being married with children really meant. Gordon placed the fur throw down on the floor in front of the darkened hearth, and she covered the boys with a blanket. Smooches insinuated himself between them beneath the blanket.

Rob undressed in the darkness and, for modesty's sake, donned one of her husband's shirts. She climbed into bed and snuggled close to him. Lying there within the circle of his arms made her feel secure. When Gordon leaned close and covered her mouth in a sweet kiss, she entwined her arms around his neck and pressed herself against him.

"Lady Rob?"

"Yes, Gavin?"

"Can we eat bannocks for breakfast tomorrow?"

"If ye want."

"I do."

"Me too," Duncan called.

"Verra well," she said. "If ye dinna sleep now, I'll be too tired to cook for ye."

Silence reigned for several long moments.

Once again, Gordon leaned close and kissed her. Rob flicked her tongue across the crease of his lips, and their kiss deepened into smoldering passion. She felt his long fingers gliding up her legs, and her breath caught in her throat when he stroked the dewey pearl of her womanhood.

Noiselessly, Gordon moved to cover her body with his own, and Rob guided him inside her. The bed creaked in protest as they began to move as one.

"What are ye doin'?" Gavin asked loudly.

Gordon and Rob froze and then heard Duncan say, "They're makin' ye a baby sister."

"Thank ye," Gavin called.

Gordon and Rob struggled against their laughter and lost. Surrendering to the inevitable, Gordon rolled off his wife and pulled her close against the side of his body.

"Good night, angel."

"Good night, husband."

"Granny Biddy," Gavin cried, dashing across the lodge yard.

Hurrying out of the stable where he'd been grooming the horses, Gordon felt a surge of relief at the sight of the old woman with Dewey and Gabby. With Biddy's expertise, he would learn what ailed his wife. Even now, Rob lay on the bed inside the lodge because she'd become dizzy and nauseous at breakfast.

"Thank God yer here," Gordon said, helping the older woman dismount. "Rob's ill and needs yer tendin'."

"What a journey I've had," Biddy complained. "My bones ache, and my puir backside is sore. I'll never make it back to Inverary alive. I'm the one who needs tendin'."

Duncan and Gavin giggled out loud, earning themselves a frown from the older woman. Gordon hid his smile, and Dewey rolled his eyes. Only Gabby was solicitous of her.

"Come rest over here a minute," Gabby said, taking her grandmother's arm.

"I'll rest when I'm dead," Biddy snapped, slapping the helping hand away. "Get the haggis from Dewey and bring it inside." She rounded on Gordon and ordered, "Ye wait out here."

Gordon inclined his head and whispered to Dewey, "Does she think to cure my wife with haggis?"

Dewey shrugged but said nothing. Five minutes

passed, and then another five. Ten minutes grew into thirty, and then an hour.

Gordon stared at the lodge's closed door. Each passing moment etched deepening anxiety across his features. God's balls, what was taking so long? Rob must be terribly ill. What would he do if he lost her? That disturbing thought made his heart sink to his stomach. Accustomed to having her near, he couldn't imagine life without her now.

"Is Lady Rob goin' to die?" Duncan asked, apparently sensing his father's tension.

Gordon glanced at the seven-year-old and wished he knew the answer. "No, son," he said. "Lady Rob will be better now that Granny Biddy is here."

"Is that a good lie or a bad lie?" Gavin asked.

Puzzled, Gordon turned to his youngest son and said, "I dinna ken what ye mean."

"Lady Rob told me that—"

The lodge's door opened. Wearing the fiercest scowl Gordon had ever seen on her face, Granny Biddy marched outside. Gabby followed behind her grandmother.

Braced for the worst, Gordon stepped forward and asked, "Well?"

"I ought to slap ye silly for draggin' my brittle bones all the way up here," Biddy snapped, surprising him. "The laird *is* correct; ye do possess the sense of a donkey."

"What's wrong with my wife?" Gordon demanded.

"Nothin' is wrong with her, ye blinkin' idiot," Granny Biddy shot back. "Yer seed hit its mark."

"Ye mean she's pregnant?" Gordon asked.

Duncan and Gavin shouted with glee and jumped up and down. Dewey hooted with laughter, and Gabby grinned at the amazed expression on Gordon's face.

"I love ye," Gordon vowed, hugging the old woman. He planted a smacking kiss on her lips and then headed for the lodge.

Rob was sitting on the edge of the bed when he walked in. She cast him a shy smile and asked, "Did Biddy tell ye?"

Gordon nodded and sat beside her on the bed. "Why didna ye tell me?" he asked. "I've been sick with worry for ye."

"Ye have?"

Gordon smiled and put his arm around her shoulder, gently drawing her against the side of his body. "Of course I was worried," he whispered, brushing his lips across her temple.

"I didna know myself," Rob admitted, her eyes downcast. "I thought I was dyin'."

Gently, Gordon turned her head toward him and waited until she lifted her gaze to his. He planted a kiss on her lips and whispered, "Thank ye, angel."

Rob pasted a sunny smile onto her face, but her thoughts were troubled and blinded her to the tenderness in his expression. A simple *thank you* for bearing his child wasn't enough; she desperately needed to hear those three magic words, *I love you*.

But what else could she expect? Disappointment had dogged her entire life. Why should this be any different? Perhaps she should consider herself fortunate that her husband respected her enough not to lie to her. That would be even more unbearable than knowing the truth.

June brought warm, dry breezes to the upper pastures and mountains. The summer mornings filled with the melodic sounds of bird song, afternoons heated beneath brilliant sunshine, and calm evenings brought displays of fireflies down in the glen. In the woodland garden, lady's slipper orchids bloomed as did the mistletoe in the oaks. Midsummer Eve and the full mead moon came and went.

Sudden, severe thunderstorms arrived with the month of July. By mid August, goldenrod appeared in the glen and hinted at autumn's blaze of color. The screech of blue jays replaced the sweet songs of robins and wrens, which vanished suddenly. When the full barley moon shone in the night sky, the Campbells counted the dwindling days of summer and their shieling.

One sunny August morning, Rob and Gavin sat together outside the lodge. With them were Gabby and Smooches. Though the six-year-old had been invited to go swimming with his father and his brother, Gavin preferred staying with Rob and stubbornly refused to go anywhere near the water.

"Let's play court," he suggested.

"How do ye do that?" Gabby asked.

Gavin leaped to his feet and bowed to Rob. After giving her his devastating smile, he asked, "My lady, will ye dance with me?"

"I'd be honored," Rob replied, rising from the ground. She curtsied to the boy, and they began the pavane as she'd taught him.

"I've nobody to partner me," Gabby complained. "What aboot me?"

Gavin stopped dancing and looked at her. "Lord Smooches is free for this dance," he said, pointing to the pup.

Gabby lifted Smooches into her arms and then pranced around the lodge yard. "Why, Lord Smooches, what a divine dancer ye are," she exclaimed in a loud voice, making Rob and Gavin laugh. "Yer so verra light on yer feet."

"What are ye celebratin'?" a familiar voice asked.

Rob smiled at her husband and said, "We're dancin' at the king's birthday gala."

"Lord Smooches is partnerin' me," Gabby called.

"Should I be jealous?" Dewey asked.

"I want to dance too," Duncan said.

"We must pack our belongin's and ride to Inverary this afternoon," Gordon said as Mungo MacKinnon followed him into the lodge yard.

"All of Scotland knows aboot the queen's death," Mungo said, flicking a hate-filled glance at Rob.

"James wants us in Edinburgh by the second week of September for her memorial service," Gordon said. "Dewey and Gabby will accompany us."

"By the way, yer brother snatched Isabelle Debrett on the eve of her weddin'," Mungo told Rob with obvious relish. "The king is furious aboot it too. He just might name yer brother an outlaw."

Rob paled by several shades, and then began rubbing the stain on the back of her left hand. Turning a worried gaze on her husband, she echoed, "Dubh is an outlaw?"

"Dinna fret aboot that," Gordon said. "I can handle Jamie. Besides, the Debrett lass probably wished to disappear with Dubh. Perhaps he rescued her instead of snatched her." Looking at Mungo and Dewey, he added, "Come along, lads. We'll share a mug of whiskey."

Rob watched their retreating backs as they walked to the lodge. How could they behave so casually about Dubh being named an outlaw? Had he really abducted Isabelle on the eve of her wedding? Her marriage to whom? Apparently, while she'd been summering in the mountains, the world had continued without her. How did she dare—?

"Lady Rob, can I go to court with ye?" Gavin asked, interrupting her thoughts.

"I dinna think so, sweetie." Noting the droop in his expression, she added, "I need ye at Inverary to care for Smooches. Will ye do that for me?"

Happy again, Gavin grinned and nodded. "Damsel, I'll guard Lord Smooches with my life."

"Shall we go inside and pack our belongin's?" Rob asked.

Gavin nodded. Taking their cue from her, Gabby and Duncan started toward the lodge.

Rob reached for Gavin's hand and turned to follow them, but glanced at her beggar bead necklace. The star ruby had darkened redder than pigeon's blood.

How provoking, Rob thought. The moment Mungo MacKinnon appeared, her star ruby warned her of danger. Well, she carried her husband's child within her body and would take no chances with the babe's safety.

The time for strapping her last resort to her leg had arrived.

Chapter 15

Great Bruce's ghost, how would she survive the Stuart court?

Rob furiously rubbed a finger back and forth across her devil's flower as she gazed out the window from her husband's chamber at Holyroodhouse Palace. Having arrived in Edinburgh late the previous evening, she hadn't actually met any courtiers but felt the nervous hives rising upon her body.

That Gordon was the king's confidant and an insider at court worried her immensely. How could she measure up when critical gazes searched her for flaws? She could never fit in here; Old Clootie's mark prevented her acceptance. Rob knew that as surely as she knew her own name.

Anxiety and insecurity mingled in a deadly combination and stole her peace of mind. Rob wished she were back at the shieling, or anywhere else that wasn't here. Had it only been last autumn that she'd been an innocent maiden flirting with Henry Talbot at Devereux House? Last autumn seemed like a lifetime ago.

So many things had happened since then. The most important, of course, was that she would become a mother early in February. *If she survived the Stuart court.*

"Those gloves ye wanted are here," Gabby called from the other side of the chamber. "Gawd, there must be a dozen pair of them."

Relieved, Rob closed her eyes and said a silent prayer of thanks. Her aunt had remembered to pack the fingerless gloves Gordon had given her, and her uncle had shipped her belongings to Campbell Mansion.

Exposing her deformity at court required more courage than Rob possessed. What if the king's courtiers saw her devil's flower and started making the sign of the cross whenever she passed by? She'd heard the rumors of how superstitious King James was. Why, he even believed in witches.

Rob forced herself to take several deep, calming breaths. Becoming too frightened could mar her babe. In an attempt to free all those troubling thoughts from her mind, she concentrated on the picturesque scene outside her window.

The chamber had a perfect view of Holyrood Park and the esplanade that led to Edinburgh Castle. Early autumn wore its most serene expression that day. Brilliant sunshine touched the land, and clear blue skies kissed the distant horizon.

The seasons changed early in these northern climes. Though only mid September, the oaks and the birches and the elms had already gone to gold while the pines and the spruce and the fir remained evergreen. Several trees had even changed their golden garb to orange and red. Meanwhile, the green lawns of summer were rapidly browning.

In London, summer would just be passed its ripening peak and waning; but here, in Edinburgh, autumn had arrived with all of its colorful beauty. Strangely, Rob felt an aching melancholy as she surveyed the glory of nature outside her window.

"Which gown will ye be wearin'?" Gabby called.

"The black and gold brocade with my black shawl," Rob answered, glancing over her shoulder. "Dinna forget the black gloves."

Rob gazed out the window again while she tried to summon the courage to accompany her husband into the mob of noble strangers attending the memorial service for Scotland's late queen. The service was set for precisely twelve noon. She had no doubt that Gordon would be annoyed if he returned to their chamber and found her clad in her bed robe.

And then Rob saw him.

A magnificent rider on horseback caught her attention as she turned away from the window. Even from this distance, she recognized her husband. A smile touched her lips as she admired the incredibly virile picture he presented.

From the opposite direction, a woman on horseback rode straight for Gordon. Rob noted the heavy mass of gloriously red hair cascading down the woman's back and her impeccable dress.

Gordon jerked his mount to an abrupt halt and gifted the lady with one of his devastating smiles. The woman halted her horse beside his.

Great Bruce's ghost, Rob thought. How could two horses stand *that* close without biting or kicking each other?

Gordon reached for the woman's hand and raised it to his lips. The woman laughed in response, retrieved her hand, and then gracefully dismounted. Gordon wasted no time in dismounting too.

When they faced each other, the woman threw herself

into Gordon's arms. She looped one arm around his neck, pulled his head down, and kissed him passionately.

Rob clutched her belly as if trying to protect her unborn child from his father's betrayal. Unable to move away from the window, she felt her world crumbling down around her.

Once a womanizer, always a womanizer, echoed within her mind.

"What's so interestin' outside?" Gabby asked, standing beside her. "Holy horseshit, 'tis Gordy kissin'— Come away from the window and dress, or ye'll be late for the service. Never mind aboot that. She's probably an old friend or—or . . ."

"Or somethin'," Rob finished.

"Exactly."

MacArthur pride forced Rob to lift her chin a notch. She would remain calm for her baby's sake and ask him for an explanation. Brushing a tear from her cheek, Rob told herself to keep a tight control over her emotions and prayed that Great Bruce's ghost would give her strength.

After removing her bed robe, Rob crossed the chamber and searched through one of her satchels. She fastened the garter with the black leather sheath to her leg and placed the last resort inside.

"Will ye be needin' that blade?" Gabby asked.

"Aunt Keely told me that at court friends come and go, but enemies tend to accumulate," Rob said. "Certainly, wearin' my last resort canna hurt."

"Whatever blows yer gown up, dearie," Gabby replied. "Dewey and I will be sittin' with the other retainers in the rear of the chapel. Holler if ye need me."

Gabby drew the black and gold brocaded gown over her mistress's head. After slipping her arms inside its sleeves, Rob turned around so the tiny buttons in the back could be fastened.

"Suck in yer gut." Gabby chuckled. "The gown barely fits, so I'd better start lettin' the seams out on the others."

Rob set the beggar bead necklace over her head and frowned at the star ruby. The magical stone had darkened redder than pigeon's blood on the day that Mungo MacKinnon arrived at the shieling and hadn't faded yet. The sight of its constant danger warning was beginning to give her the creeps. Rob could almost feel the evil lurking in the shadows at Holyrood Palace and itching to grab her as she passed by.

Rob pulled on her black, fingerless gloves and felt much better. Hiding Old Clootie's mark gave her confidence. She wrapped the black cashmere shawl around her shoulders just as the door swung open.

"I hope yer ready," Gordon said, smiling at her as he walked into the chamber. "I've already been to the High Street."

Rob whirled around at the sound of his voice and stared at him. In spite of her worries, she couldn't help admiring her husband. Dressed in his Campbell plaid with a white shirt and black doublet, Gordon appeared a magnificent figure of a man, and she could well understand why the ladies were attracted to him. However, he had insisted on their marriage and dragged her out of England. She expected—no, demanded—faithfulness from her husband.

"We ladies take longer," Rob said, managing a faint smile.

" 'Tis well worth the wait," Gordon told her, planting a kiss on her lips. "Ye look divine."

Rob captured his piercing gray gaze with her own and asked without preamble, "Who was that woman?"

Gordon slid his gaze to Gabby and said, "Dewey is waitin' outside for ye." Once the tiring woman had gone, he turned his attention on his wife and gifted her with his devastating smile.

No man should be this handsome, Rob thought, steeling herself against his charm. "Who was that woman?" she repeated, sounding shrewish even to herself.

"What woman?" Gordon asked, cocking a brow at her tone of voice.

Rob cocked her eyebrow in a perfect imitation of his gesture. "The woman ye were kissin'."

"I wasna kissin' her," Gordon replied. "She was kissin' me."

"What the bloody hell is the difference?" Rob cried, irritated and hurt by his evasiveness.

"If ye had watched a moment longer," Gordon said, his gray eyes lit with amusement at her obvious jealousy, "ye would have seen me push her away."

Rob flushed with embarrassment and dropped her gaze to the floor. If he spoke the truth, she'd just made an arse of herself.

"Who is she?" Rob asked in a quieter voice.

"Lady Kerr, Mungo's cousin, who's recently been widowed," Gordon answered. "She's a good friend of mine."

"And Lady Kerr thought to renew her friendship with ye?" Hearing the jealous sarcasm in her own voice, Rob turned away from him and wandered across the chamber to the window. "Is it needful that I attend this memorial service?" she asked without looking at him.

"What's the problem, angel?" His voice was close behind her.

Rob turned around slowly and told his chest, "I've never attended court and dinna know how to go aboot. Besides, I dinna like meetin' new people. What if I do somethin' wrong?"

Gordon tilted her chin up and waited until she lifted

her gaze to his. "Be yerself," he said. "Everyone will adore ye."

"But what if they dinna?" she asked, her worry apparent in her voice. "What if I canna fit in with them?"

What if they recognize Old Clootie's mark on my hand? was left unspoken.

"God's balls, lass." Gordon chuckled. "Raise no more devils than I'm able to lay . . . I've brought ye a gift."

"Why?"

"Because yer my adorable wife and soon-to-be the mother of Inverary's heir."

But not because he loves me, Rob thought.

Gordon produced a solid gold luckenbooth broach and pinned it to her shawl. The heart-shaped broach was customarily exchanged between a betrothed couple and later pinned to their child's blanket for good luck and safety.

"I considered the traditional silver," Gordon said, brushing his lips across hers, "but then I decided that particular metal much too cold for a hot-blooded woman like ye."

When he produced a second golden brooch, Rob asked in confusion, "Why did ye purchase two?"

"Ye must pin this one on me," he told her.

Taking the broach out of his hand, Rob smiled shyly and fastened it on his white shirt for all to see. Then she stood on her tiptoes and planted a kiss on his lips.

"I'd love to pursue the invitation yer lips are offerin'," Gordon said. "Unfortunately, we're late for the memorial service. Are ye ready?"

Rob shook her head and reached inside her black shawl to free her beggar bead necklace. She laid it on the outside and said, "I dinna want to be caught unaware. Now I'm ready for anythin'."

Leaving their chamber, Gordon led Rob through a

confusing maze of corridors to a narrow, stone staircase. Three stories down, they reached ground level and walked outside into the bright sunlight. Glancing back at the palace, Rob wondered how she would find her way back to her chamber.

"There's an interestin' legend that goes along with the abbey," Gordon said, leading her around to the right.

"What is it?" Rob asked, managing a faint smile. At that moment, she could not have cared less about legends. Her main concern was surviving the next several hours.

"On the day of the Holy Rood," Gordon began, "King David I was hunting in this area and became lost from his companions. His horse threw him, and a great stag appeared ready to gore him. Suddenly, a magical mist rolled in aboot him, and a hand carrying a cross reached out of the mist. When the king grasped the cross, the stag took flight. And so King David vowed to build an abbey on the verra spot where the miracle happened."

"Aye, 'tis a verra interestin' tale," Rob said distractedly.

Gordon flashed her a sidelong smile and said, "Look over yer shoulder, angel. Do ye see Edinburgh Castle in the distance?" When she nodded, he told her, "Legend says there's an underground passage that leads from Holyrood Palace to the castle. There's an interestin' tale that goes along with that theory . . . Now, are ye ready to go inside?"

Rob gazed up at her husband and noted the softness in his gray eyes as he stared at her. He was being kind and trying to keep her mind off her worries.

Reaching up, Rob placed the palm of her right hand against his cheek. "Thank ye, Gordy."

"Damsel, the pleasure is mine," Gordon replied, sounding very much like his youngest son.

"Ye do remind me of Gavin."

"I'll take that as a compliment."

Located beside the palace, Holyrood Abbey possessed ironwork as intricate as Scottish politics. Beyond its gates, sprawling gardens surrounded the abbey. The burial place of Scottish kings, the abbey echoed with past majesty and power.

Rob grabbed her husband's hand as they walked through the abbey's entrance and felt him give her an encouraging squeeze. Gordon started down the center aisle, forcing her to step with him or struggle for freedom.

Crowded to overflowing with Scotland's nobility, the chapel was dimly lit by filtered sunlight that streamed inside through the stained glass windows. At the end of the aisle, a thousand candles brightened the sanctuary with its intricately carved font, ornate screen, and enormous pulpit.

Uncomfortably, Rob felt scrutinizing gazes directed at her as she walked down the aisle with her husband. She sent up a silent prayer of thanks that her gloves hid Old Clootie's mark.

Midway down the aisle, Rob spied Mungo MacKinnon who sat beside a red-haired woman. Much to her relief, Gordon kept walking. Rob had no wish to sit with Mungo and certainly not when he escorted the woman who'd kissed her husband that very morning.

Three quarters of the way down the aisle, Gordon stopped and gestured her into the wooden pew. Then he sat down next to the aisle.

Seeing her husband nod to the nobleman on her right, Rob peered around at him and gave him an ambiguous smile.

"So, this is the bride?" the older gentleman asked.

Confused, Rob glanced at her husband, but he was smiling at the man.

"Uncle George, may I make known to ye my wife, Rob MacArthur," Gordon introduced them. "Angel, this old rogue is the Earl of Huntly, my late mother's oldest brother."

"I'm verra pleased to meet ye," Rob said.

The Earl of Huntly smiled at her and then lifted his gaze to his nephew. "Yer bride is bonny," the earl said. "I hope ye willna waste any time makin' yer father a grandsire."

"My wife and I have already taken care of that business," Gordon told him. "Inverary's heir is risin' in the oven."

Rob gasped and flushed with angry embarrassment. She cast her husband a withering look and then lifted her upturned nose into the air. She intended to set her crass husband straight as soon as they returned to their chamber.

The two men chuckled at her expense.

" 'Twould appear the lass is modest too," the earl said. "Count yer blessin's, Gordy. Ye could have ended up with one of these Edinburgh jades."

Gordon lifted his wife's hand to his lips, pressed a kiss on it, and said, "I count my blessin's each night when I crawl into bed beside my angel."

Rob flicked him a sidelong smile and would have spoken, but the trumpets blared the noon hour and the king's arrival. She stood when everyone else did as the king made his stately way down the aisle toward the sanctuary.

Dressed in the royal Stuart colors, King James with his reddish hair and doleful-eyed gaze marched slowly past his courtiers. Rob bowed her head as he passed their pew. However, her curiosity got the better of her, and she kept her gaze on him. Surprisingly, the king walked with a decidedly unregal, shambling gait and, if she wasn't mistaken, his mouth dribbled at the corners.

"I didna see our fathers as we entered," Rob whispered, sitting down after the king was seated.

Gordon shrugged. "I'm certain they're somewhere in this crowd."

The memorial service for Scotland's deceased queen began with several long prayers. Unexpectedly, a metallic clinking sound reached Rob's ears and then grew increasingly louder as the moments passed. Rob wondered if the noise was part of the service and looked at her husband. His perplexed expression told her that he was also wondering about the strange noise.

Clanking metal and voices raised in angry protest drew everyone's attention. Bursting into the chapel, three men dressed in full armor stood at the head of the aisle. Rob glanced in alarm at Gordon and then at the king, who'd risen from his seat of honor and stood there staring in shock at what he saw.

Half rising from the pew, Rob spied the three men. Their armor had to be at least a hundred years old.

The three knights of yore stepped forward. Slowly but with grim determination etched across their faces, the three men clanked their way toward the altar. Every step they took was a cacophony of rusting, squeaking armor.

"Great Bruce's ghost," Rob cried softly. "What are they doin'?"

"I do believe *our fathers* are makin' a point," Gordon said dryly, the hint of an amused smile flirting with the corners of his lips.

"They've even dragged Uncle Percy along with them," Rob said. "Gordy, do somethin'."

"Relax," Gordon whispered. "I canna do anythin' to prevent them from makin' fools of themselves."

"By all that's holy," King James bellowed, the dribble at the corners of his mouth flowing freely. "Campbell and MacArthur, what is the meanin' of this intrusion upon our solemnity? Our court is in deepest mourning for my late mother, the queen."

The Duke of Argyll clanked his way five steps forward. Duke Magnus tried his best to bow, but the heavy armor prevented his kneeling. Instead, he cavalierly inclined his head at the young monarch.

"Full armor *is* proper mournin' attire for our murdered queen," Duke Magnus called in a voice loud enough for all ears to hear.

Murmurings erupted from the crowd. Rob saw several of Scotland's ageing magnates nod their heads in agreement with her father-in-law.

"God's balls, but I'll need to do some fancy talkin' later," Gordon muttered, a muscle in his right cheek twitching.

Rob watched in growing horror as her own father, Iain MacArthur, clanked forward to stand beside his Campbell kinsman and called, "The proper memorial service for our murdered queen is a declaration of war."

"I agree," added Percy MacArthur after clanking his way forward to stand beside his brother.

"God's wounds!" King James bellowed, his face mottling with rage, his dribbling flowing faster. "If ye dinna back yerselves out of this chapel, I shall pull down my breeches and show ye my arse."

Duke Magnus held his hand up and said, "Anythin' but that, sire."

Iain and Percy MacArthur chuckled. More than a few spectators, especially those who remembered Queen Mary's grace, joined in their mirth.

"Arrest these rebels," the king shouted.

"Dinna move from this pew," Gordon ordered Rob, yanking his hand out of hers as he bolted to his feet.

Gordon marched down the aisle toward the king. Behind him hurried his uncle, the Earl of Huntly.

Reaching the king, Gordon dropped to one bended knee and asked, "Yer Majesty, may I be heard?"

King James nodded at his favorite golfing and hunting companion.

" 'Tis a monumental misunderstandin'," Gordon said, flicking a look of disgust at the three middle-aged men in armor. "These old warriors are merely relivin' their youth and fightin' old battles."

"I can still disown ye," Duke Magnus growled at his son.

"Mayhap I'll take my lassie back and annul yer marriage," Iain MacArthur added.

"These old warriors knew our late queen personally and worshipped the verra ground upon which she walked," Gordon went on, ignoring his relatives' outbursts. "Their intense emotion over her sudden death has made them unstable. However, as ye always say, rashness of action is ill-advised. Could we adjourn to a more private chamber to discuss this gently?"

King James stared at Gordon for an excruciatingly long moment, but nodded finally.

"All will return to this chapel at the noon hour tomorrow," the king announced.

Escorted by Gordon, King James marched back down the aisle. The three clanking Highlanders followed behind them with the Earl of Huntly.

Titillated by what they'd just witnessed, the Scots nobility started talking all at once. Slowly, in groups of two's and three's, they left their pews and walked outside.

With her hands folded in her lap, Rob sat perfectly still.

No one spoke to her, but she did catch several people casting curious looks in her direction.

What was happening in the king's privy chamber? she wondered. Would her father and father-in-law be arrested? Would her unborn child have the chance to meet his grandfathers? And now what should she do? Wait here for her husband or leave with everyone else?

Rob rose from the pew and followed the last of the courtiers out. She would remain within sight of the abbey. Once he finished calming the king, Gordon would surely come looking for her.

Stepping outside, Rob felt the sunshine on her face and breathed a sigh of relief. After being enclosed in that crowded chapel, the day's combination of warm sun and crisp air refreshed her.

Rob felt conspicuously out of place as she wandered across the browning lawns of the esplanade toward a spot where several oak trees stood together. Everyone milling about knew Gordon and had seen her walk down the abbey's aisle with him, but no one bothered to approach her. Was she doomed always to play the unhappy outsider? Perhaps she should introduce herself to them?

No, that wouldn't do. Without her husband by her side, Rob knew she hadn't the courage to approach anyone. If only she knew the way back to her chamber, she could make a graceful exit.

Leaning against one of the massive oaks, Rob stared at the abbey and willed her husband's quick return. From the corner of her eyes, she spied two young noblewomen advancing on her. Rob stood proudly erect but kept her gaze fixed on the abbey.

"Lady Campbell?" the brunette said, smiling.

"Yes?"

"I am Lady Elliott." She gestured to her blond companion. "This is Lady Armstrong."

The blonde smiled and nodded at her.

"I'm pleased to make yer acquaintance," Rob said, but something in their polite smiles troubled her. She had the uncanny feeling that these women were not as sincere as they wished her to believe.

"We're verra pleased to meet Gordy's bride," Lady Armstrong said.

"Ye know my husband personally then?" Rob asked.

"Verra well," Lady Elliott answered.

"Intimately," Lady Armstrong said, flicking a sidelong glance at her companion.

Rob noted the byplay between them and realized that one or both had bedded Gordon. Determined to put a brave face on the matter, she lifted her chin a notch and gifted them with an insincere smile.

"Any friend of my husband's is a friend of mine," Rob said. "Ye must call me by my given name, Rob." Seeing their surprised reactions to her boy's name, she added, "My father named me in honor of Robert the Bruce, and Gordy thinks 'tis adorable."

"Call me Catherine," said Lady Elliott.

"I'm Jean," the blonde added.

"We couldna help noticin' the unusual gloves yer wearin'," Lady Elliott remarked.

"Why, Catherine, 'tis all the latest rage at the Tudor court," Rob informed them as if the two sophisticated beauties before her were country milkmaids. She hoped the Lord would forgive her lies. "All the English ladies at court are wearin' them. I've recently passed a year visitin' Uncle Richard, the English Earl of Basildon."

That bit of unsolicited information surprised the two beauties.

"Yer uncle is the English queen's Midas?" Lady Elliott asked.

"Why, his fame has even reached us here in Scotland," Lady Armstrong added.

"Dearest Uncle Richard is as wonderful and kind as he is rich and influential," Rob replied, pasting an insincere smile on her face. Behaving obnoxiously was incredibly easy.

"Oh, dear. Here comes trouble," Lady Elliott said, gesturing to the right.

Rob glanced in that direction. Mungo MacKinnon and the red-haired woman were advancing on them.

"Good day to ye," Mungo greeted them, and then turned to Rob. "May I make known to ye my cousin, Lady Kerr."

Rob looked at the voluptuous, fiery-haired beauty and managed a faint smile. "I'm pleased to make yer acquaintance," she said.

"And I'm pleased to meet Gordy's bride," the redhead returned. She wasted no time in perusing her rival's charms.

Rob knew the other woman was searching for flaws. When the redhead's gaze dropped to her thickened middle, Rob placed one hand over her belly and announced, "I'm afraid yer discernin' eye has discovered my little secret. I carry Inverary's heir."

Lady Kerr lost her smile. "Congratulations are in order then."

Rob nodded, satisfied that she'd managed to drop the other woman's composure several notches.

"I'm certain we'll be seein' a great deal of each other," Lady Kerr drawled, recovering herself. "Call me Livy."

Rob froze, but willed her expression to remain passive. "Did ye say *Livy*?" she asked.

"Yes. Is there somethin' wrong?"

Before Rob could reply, another voice spoke, "Lady Campbell, is it really ye?"

Rob turned toward the voice and saw the Earl of Both-well standing there. A tall, well-built man, Francis Hep-burn-Stuart possessed auburn hair and heavenly blue eyes and an unlimited supply of charm.

"I'm pleased to see ye've fully recovered from yer long journey from England," the earl said, bowing over her gloved hand. "Have ye brought that Sassenach dog of yers to court?"

Rob grinned and shook her head, saying, "We left Smooches at Inverary."

"Come and walk aboot with me," the earl said, offer-ing his hand. "We must renew our acquaintance."

"I'd be delighted, my lord," Rob said, placing her hand in his.

Escorting her away from the others, Bothwell whis-pered, "I thought ye needed an escape route from that group."

"My Lord Bothwell, how perceptive ye are," Rob re-plied, making him smile. "I suppose yer intervention puts me in yer debt."

"I'll remember that," he said. "And how goes the married life?"

"I'm expecting Inverary's heir," she told him.

"The verra best to ye, then." The earl smiled at her. "Ye know, lass. When I met ye at Hermitage, I had my doubts aboot yer survivin' here at court."

"But why would ye think that?"

"Ye appeared such a pathetic creature when ye sat at my table."

Rob gave him a sidelong glance and warned, "My lord, I'm wearin' my last resort. If ye ever again refer to me as *pathetic,* I'll be forced to end yer life."

Bothwell threw back his head and shouted with laugh-ter. He stopped walking and turned to face her. "I'm verra glad to hear that because ye'll need spunk to survive the pretty vultures at court," he said. "Now, suppose ye tell me why ye drew yer blade on the English queen's minister."

"Suppose ye tell me where my brother is," Rob countered.

"Dubh took to the heather after he snatched the Debrett chit," the earl told her. "I believe they're hidin' somewhere in the Highlands."

"So he did abduct her," Rob said.

"Well, Dubh thought he was abductin' her," the earl replied, "but the lady insists he rescued her from an unwanted marriage."

" 'Tis a relief," Rob said with a smile. "And, for yer information, I drew my dagger on Walsingham because I'd overheard him speaking aboot Queen Mary's execution. We needed to keep the secret for fear he'd toss my uncle into the Tower."

"Gordon Campbell has chosen his bride well," Bothwell complimented her. "Yer a braw lassie."

"My lord, do ye think my father and my father-in-law are endangered by what they did today?" Rob asked abruptly.

Bothwell shook his head. "Jamie favors Gordon and will listen to reason. Ye, however, look a little peaked. Why dinna ye retire to yer chamber and rest until yer husband returns."

"I dinna know the way," Rob admitted, and then felt the heated blush rising upon her cheeks.

Bothwell smiled. "All ye need do is ask a page to escort ye there."

Feeling foolish, Rob returned his smile and said, "Thank ye, my lord. I believe I'll do that."

Once inside her chamber, Rob lay down on the bed. Her stomach churned with worry for her father's well-being, and her head pounded with another, equally troubling thought.

Lady Lavinia Kerr had recently been Gordon's mistress and wished to resume her affair with him. Rob knew that as surely as she knew her own name.

But, for what did Gordon wish? That was the most disturbing thought of all.

Chapter 16

God's balls, but the king's dribbling boded ill for his success.

Alone with the angry king in the privy chamber, Gordon knew he needed a strategy that would put James in a kinder, more merciful frame of mind.

Gordon lifted two crystal goblets off the desk and then cast the pacing king a lopsided smile. After laying them down on their sides on the floor, he reached into the royal golf bag to withdraw two putters and a handful of golf balls.

"We may as well practice while we confer," Gordon said, offering the king one of the putters.

James relaxed visibly, and a slow smile stole across his face, banishing his irritated expression. Nothing in the whole wide world soothed him more than golfing and hunting.

Taking the putter out of his friend's hand, James waited for Gordon to set the golf ball down on the floor.

Then he sidled up to the ball and aimed for the goblet. His face split into a broad grin when the ball hit its mark.

"Yer kin are intent on incitin' war with England," James said as his friend set his own golf ball down on the floor.

Gordon flicked a glance at the young monarch, aimed for the goblet, and hit his mark. "My father and his kinsmen are nothin' but old warriors livin' in the past," he disagreed. "Their agein' minds canna see beyond vengeance to the ultimate prize, bein' named Elizabeth's successor. The old girl canna live forever, ye know."

" 'Twas a particularly good shot ye just made," the king complimented him.

"Thank ye, sire." Gordon set another golf ball down in front of the king.

"I'm a lovin' son," James said, and then aimed for the goblet. "Horrified outrage was my initial reaction to my mother's death, and my own inclination was toward declarin' war. After all, Elizabeth could have sent her home instead of executin' her."

Jamie betrayed her, Gordon recalled his wife's words. *The English offered to return her to Scotland, but her own son refused her sanctuary because he feared sharing his crown with her.*

James putted the golf ball into the goblet and added, "War wouldna honor her cherished memory, but would only serve to eliminate any chance I have of bein' Elizabeth's successor. After all, what's more fittin' to my mother's memory than havin' her only son wear the crown that she coveted."

"I agree with ye on that point," Gordon said, hitting his ball into the goblet.

"To that end, yer rebellious relatives should be punished for disturbin' the peace."

"With all due respect, I disagree with ye on that

point," Gordon said. "My father and his kinsmen are na beyond reasonin'. Besides, the Earl of Basildon is MacArthur's brother-in-law and one of the most influential men in England, not to mention the richest . . . Care to place a small wager on our game here?"

James nodded. "A gold piece?"

Gordon smiled and tossed a gold piece onto the desk. Then he set a golf ball down on the floor in front of the king.

James took careful aim and hit the ball into the goblet. Gordon also hit his mark.

"Another good shot," the king complimented him. "Yer game is improvin'."

"If my game is improvin', 'tis because I'm learnin' from the verra best, namely yerself," Gordon said smoothly.

James smiled, obviously pleased by the flattery, and hit his next ball into the goblet. Gordon followed suit.

"As I was sayin', Basildon favors ye to be Elizabeth's successor," Gordon continued. "He also possesses the uncanny talent to fatten yer coffers. God's balls, but everything the man touches turns to gold."

Always in need of coin, King James brightened at that. Gordon tossed another gold piece onto the desk and then set a golf ball down in front of the king. Flicking a sidelong glance at him, Gordon felt relieved to see that the king's dribbling had slowed considerably.

"Tell me more," James ordered after sinking the ball into the goblet.

"My wife is Basildon's niece," Gordon went on, setting his own golf ball down on the floor. "I was a guest at his home while in England. Many times during my stay there, Basildon spoke of when ye would succeed Elizabeth. However, if ye harm his Scottish kin, I dinna know if he'll back ye when the moment comes to name a successor. He does enjoy considerable influence with Elizabeth. Perhaps, ye should exhibit those noble qualities for which ye've become renowned."

Giving the king time to digest his words, Gordon took careful aim and hit the ball. He hid a satisfied smile when the golf ball veered to the right at the last possible moment and missed its mark.

"Aha! I've beat ye," James said. He confiscated the gold pieces and then leaned against his desk. "To which of my noble qualities do ye refer?"

"Patience and mercy, Yer Majesty." Gordon looked at the king and felt immensely relieved that the royal dribbling had almost stopped.

"Verra well, my friend," James said. "But Campbell and MacArthur must apologize now and again in public at the memorial service. Elizabeth's emissary is scheduled to arrive tomorrow. Because of yer relatives, I must keep him waitin' an extra day."

"So?" Gordon cocked a brow at the king. "*Ye* control this unfortunate situation with England. Ye dinna need to give Elizabeth yer attention at the verra moment she demands it. She's the one who's squirmin' on her throne." Gordon held a golf ball up and asked, "Are ye goin' to give me the chance to win my gold back?"

King James grinned. "We'll go golfin' after the service tomorrow, and in the evenin' ye can present yer bride to me at supper."

"Sire, we'd be honored to attend," Gordon replied, inclining his head. "I'll fetch those stubborn old war horses to ye."

Gordon stepped into the corridor outside the privy chamber. His father and his in-laws had removed their rusty armor and stood with his uncle, the Earl of Huntly.

Before speaking, Gordon removed his handkerchief from his pocket and made an exaggerated show of wiping the nervous sweat from his brow and his upper lip. Finally, he cast them a wholly disgusted look and said, "I had to do some fancy talkin'. Now, get in there and grovel."

"I grovel to no man," Duke Magnus announced.

"Neither do I," Iain MacArthur said.

"Nor I," Percy MacArthur added.

The Earl of Huntly chuckled. Gordon ran his hand across his face in exasperation.

"Inverary's heir is risin' in my wife's belly," Gordon told them, giving each of them a cold stare. "Would ye spoil his future with yer prideful pigheadedness?"

All three instantly appeared shamefaced.

"Gettin' the Campbells and the MacArthurs attainted willna bring Queen Mary back from the dead," Gordon added for good measure.

That did it. One by one, the three men nodded their compliance. Gordon led the way into the privy chamber, and the Earl of Huntly followed behind.

"Huntly, what d'ye do here?" King James asked.

"With yer permission, Sire, I'd like to stay," the earl replied, bowing to the king. " 'Tisna every day I get the chance to see my illustrious Campbell brother-in-law grovelin'."

The king smiled. "Be my guest, then."

In unison, the three old war horses went down on bended knee. "I'm verra sorry for disturbin' the realm's peaceful solemnity," Duke Magnus spoke first.

"So am I," Iain said.

"Me too," Percy added.

"Are ye prepared to apologize publicly?" the king asked.

All three nodded. Only Gordon saw the reluctance in their gazes.

King James smiled with satisfaction. "Rise, then. Yer forgiven."

Duke Magnus and Percy MacArthur stood, but Iain MacArthur remained kneeling. When the king arched a questioning brow at him, Iain said, "I want to discuss the matter of my oldest son bein' named an outlaw."

"He abducted that English chit," the king reminded him.

" 'Tis untrue, Yer Majesty. Dubh *rescued* her from a forced marriage," Iain argued. "Besides, I recently received information that my son has taken the honorable action of marryin' the lady."

"Well, that could put a different spin on the situation," James replied without committing himself.

"What better method of preparin' to rule two countries than to have the nobility intermarry," Gordon piped up, and nodded almost imperceptibly when his father-in-law sent him a grateful look.

"Why, 'tis an excellent idea," King James agreed. "I'll discuss yer son's marriage with Elizabeth's emissary, and perhaps she'll withdraw her official protest. Ye may leave me now."

The four older men bowed to the king and backed their ways out of the chamber. Gordon started after them, but the king called, "Gordy, dinna forget aboot our golf game tomorrow."

"Sire, I'm countin' the hours," Gordon said, flashing the young monarch a grin. "I hope I've enough luck to win my gold back."

" 'Tis expertise that makes a man a winner," James told him.

Gordon inclined his head and escaped out the door. Outside in the corridor, he gave his father and in-laws a disgusted look and, without a word to them, marched down the corridor.

Intending to fetch his wife from the abbey, Gordon retraced his steps outside and started to cross the lawns that separated the palace from the abbey. He stopped when he heard someone call his name and turned around. The Earl of Bothwell, Mungo MacKinnon, and Lavinia Kerr were advancing on him.

"Gordy, we've met yer bride," Lavinia said by way of a greeting. "When I saw ye this mornin', ye never mentioned that she's with child."

God's balls, Gordon thought, turning a frigid gaze upon her. This was all he needed to make his day complete. First the king had called for his kin's imprisonment, and now Lavinia Kerr had introduced herself to his wife. God only knew what words had passed between them.

Gordon flicked an accusing glance at Mungo, who smiled unrepentantly and shrugged.

"How did yer audience with Jamie go?" Bothwell asked.

"It ended reasonably well," Gordon answered. "If ye'll excuse me, my wife is waitin' inside the abbey."

"She isna there," Bothwell told him.

Gordon arched a brow at him.

"Lady Rob wished to retire to her chamber," Bothwell said. "I escorted her back to the palace."

"Thank ye, my lord." Without another word, Gordon retraced his steps to the palace. Reaching his chamber, he paused outside the door for a long moment and wondered in what mood he'd find his wife. Meeting Lavinia Kerr could not have been pleasant. For the first time in his life, Gordon regretted the liaisons he'd had with court jades like Lavinia. Well, he couldn't change the past so he would be forced to deal with the present as it was.

Gordon stepped inside the chamber. With her back turned toward the door, Rob sat in a chair pulled close to the window and appeared to be doing her needlework.

That she knew he'd returned was apparent in the almost imperceptible stiffening of her delicate shoulders.

Gordon smiled to himself. Ready for battle, was she? His wife was never more adorable than when angered.

Noiselessly, Gordon walked across the chamber. He lifted the curtain of her hair, lightly kissed the nape of her neck, and said in a husky voice, "I'm partial to this ebony mane of yers."

"To what were ye partial before?" Rob asked, her voice colder than a Highland blizzard. "Blondes, brunettes, and redheads?"

"I dinna ken, angel." Gordon leaned against the wall beside the window and folded his arms across his chest. "Explain yerself."

Rob raised her glittering emerald gaze and stared at him straight in the eye. "I met Ladies Elliott, Armstrong, and Kerr."

It was worse than he'd expected. Experienced in court intrigue and strategy, Gordon knew that the best defense was a superior offense. He returned her stare unwaveringly and said, "And?"

"And I'd bet the family fortune that Campbell Mansion's housekeeper isna called Livy."

Gordon flashed her a wicked grin and winked at her. "Ye'd make yerself a fortune, angel. I'm guilty as charged."

"Ye lied to me," she cried.

"Give over, angel. I've passed the last hour kissin' the king's arse so that our fathers wouldna be tossed into the Tolbooth."

Rob dropped her gaze to the knitting in her lap. Her thoughts were incredibly easy to read. Gordon knew by the way she worried her bottom lip with her teeth and the rosy stain upon her cheeks that, though angry, his wife felt guilty for failing to think of their fathers first. In that case, he could afford to be generous.

"Be at peace, angel," Gordon said. "Our fathers are na in any danger. I've managed to set thin's aright with Jamie." He knelt down on one bended knee to be eye level with her and vowed, "All those jades ye met today are from my past. Yer my present and my future. Just like our weddin' band says, 'Ye and No Other.'"

"I saw ye kissin' Lavinia Kerr this mornin'."

"I wasna kissin' Livy. She was kissin' me," Gordon insisted. He glanced over his shoulder at the window and said, " 'Tis barely two of the clock and early enough for a visit to the High Street. I know a good tavern where we could sup."

"Are ye tryin' to purchase my forgiveness?" Rob asked, arching a perfectly shaped ebony brow at him. "I canna be bribed."

Gordon shook his head and cast her his devastating smile. "I'm tryin' to court an angel."

That brought the hint of a smile to her lips, and Gordon knew the bluster had gone out of her. "Are ye knittin' Smooches a new sweater?"

Rob shook her head and held her handiwork up for him to see. " 'Tis a blanket for our son."

"Well, Gavin will be disappointed if the bairn isna a girl," he said. "Now, how aboot that ride up the High Street, lovey?"

A short time later, Gordon and Rob sat astride their horses and left the palace stable yard. Glancing sidelong at her husband, Rob was unable to hold onto even a smidgen of her anger. Gordon was a handsome and virile man and several years older than she. They'd married so young; she couldn't have expected him to remain faithful while she grew into womanhood.

Gordon led Rob south on the Cannongate and

pointed to its sites of interest. On the right was White Horse Close where Campbell Mansion with its enclosed courtyard and gardens was located. A little farther ahead stood the Cannongate Tolbooth where prisoners wasted away and beyond that John Knox's house, Mercat Cross, and St. Giles Cathedral.

Edinburgh Castle, situated on Castle Rock, rose in the distance only a scant mile away. Nor' Loch and the Esplanade lay in the foreground.

An enormous wooden structure built on the Esplanade caught Rob's attention, and she wondered what it could possibly be. Halting her horse abruptly, Rob pointed toward the structure and asked, "What's that?"

No answer.

Rob turned in her saddle to look at her husband. Gordon's expression had become grim.

"Well?" she asked.

" 'Tis the gallows where the executioner strangles and burns those convicted of witchcraft," he answered.

Rob paled by several shades. She glanced down at her left hand, covered by her riding gloves, but never bothered to check her beggar bead necklace, since the star ruby had permanently darkened. Rob realized that danger, more sinister than being shunned as an outcast, surrounded her in Edinburgh.

Stopping in the Upper Bow, Gordon purchased several court gowns for Rob and instructed the dressmaker to deliver them to Holyrood Palace. At the goldsmith's shop, Gordon gifted Rob with emerald earrings mounted in a traditional gold setting; and at the Lawnmarket, Rob easily persuaded Gordon to buy her yards and yards of various fabrics which could be fashioned into gowns for their baby.

"Are ye hungry?" Gordon asked as they left the Lawnmarket's shops behind.

"Famished."

Gordon escorted Rob to Princes Street. Seated inside MacDonald's Tavern, they stuffed themselves with boiled mussels and clams seasoned with herbs, scones dipped in honey, and fruit tarts dressed with nuts and spices.

"Tell me what happened durin' yer interview with the king," Rob said.

"Because of my expert arse-kissin', our fathers got off lightly," Gordon told her. "They apologized to Jamie and have agreed to apologize publicly at tomorrow's service."

"I canna believe my father agreed to do that," Rob replied. "For years he's been complainin' aboot Jamie's lack of interest in his mother's plight."

Gordon shrugged. "I didna say they *liked* the idea, but it was either a public apology or the Tolbooth."

"I dinna know if I like attendin' the court," Rob told him. "Danger swirls like a thick fog around every step a person takes."

"Dinna worry that pretty head of yers," Gordon said, covering her hand with his own. "We'll soon be returnin' to Inverary. After all, Jamie canna fault me for wantin' my heir born in Argyll."

That lightened Rob's mood considerably. "Did the king mention my brother?"

"Yer father says that Dubh married Isabelle Debrett," Gordon told her.

"Bothwell told me that Dubh and Isabelle are hidin' in the Highlands," Rob replied. "Isabelle's my verra best friend and now she's my sister-by-marriage. I only hope that the king doesna outlaw Dubh."

"Give me a few days, and I'll take care of that too," Gordon assured her. "By the way, we're suppin' with the king tomorrow evenin'."

"Great Bruce's ghost, I've nothin' to wear," Rob cried in a horrified whisper.

Gordon chuckled. "Ye women are all alike. Whenever somethin' special happens, ye'll die if ye canna have a new gown and geegaws to match. We men dinna care aboot such thin's. Why canna ye be more practical like us men?"

Rob batted her ebony eyelashes at him and cast him a flirtatious smile. "Would ye really want me to be more like ye?" she asked.

"Angel, yer perfect the way ye are," he answered, leaning close to kiss her cheek.

At meal's end, Gordon tossed several coins on the table. Then he stood and helped Rob rise from her chair.

"Are we bankrupt?" she asked.

"Well, I can tell ye that keepin' a wife happy is more expensive than I ever realized," he teased her.

"But worth every gold piece?"

"And then some."

Gordon steered Rob through the crowded tavern. Just as they reached the entrance, the door swung open unexpectedly. Mungo MacKinnon and Lavinia Kerr stood there, blocking their path.

"Gordy, what a coincidence meetin' ye here," Mungo said by way of a greeting.

"Good evenin', Gordy," Lavinia said with a smile. "Lady Rob, we meet again."

Gordon nodded to acknowledge them, but a smile split his face when Rob spoke up.

" 'Twas a good evenin', *Livy*." The other woman's name on her lips sounded like a foul oath.

"What lovely emeralds yer wearin' on yer ears," Lavinia said, ignoring the insult.

"I do love my husband's newest gift," Rob replied, reaching up to touch one of her emerald and gold earrings. "The emeralds match my weddin' band. Gordy has superb taste in jewels."

"Yes, I know." Lavinia fingered the sapphire necklace that exactly matched her blue eyes.

Rob stiffened in surprised anger and stared coldly at the voluptuous redhead. She should have known she'd never win in a verbal fight with the gloating she cat standing in front of her. Why, the bitch probably had years of experience in behaving obnoxiously.

"Mungo, I'm golfin' with Himself after tomorrow's service," Gordon said, breaking the strained silence. "Yer welcome to join us."

"Aye, I will."

"We've just been shoppin' in the Lawnmarket where I've purchased lace in every color available," Lavinia said, casting Rob a feline smile. "Since those unusual gloves of yers are such a rage at the English court, I intend to have a pair that matches every gown I own."

Rob realized in that instant that Lavinia knew she'd lied to Ladies Elliott and Armstrong. Damn Mungo MacKinnon's blabbing mouth to hell. Now, the red-haired vixen would try to discover what lay hidden beneath the gloves. If Mungo MacKinnon hadn't already blabbed about that too.

"If ye'll excuse us," Gordon said. With a farewell nod to Mungo and Lavinia, he ushered his wife outside and then asked, "What was that aboot?"

When Rob looked at him, misery had etched itself across her delicate features. "I've just been neatly trapped in a lie," she admitted.

"Angels dinna lie," Gordon said with a smile.

"Well, I did."

"Aboot what?"

Embarrassed, Rob dropped her gaze and confessed to his chest, "I told Ladies Elliott and Armstrong that my fingerless gloves were the height of fashion at the Tudor court."

Gordon threw back his head and shouted with laughter. Then he yanked her against his body in a sidewise hug.

" 'Tisna funny," Rob said. "I could see in Lavinia Kerr's eyes that she knew the truth of the matter. What will I do when she blabs to the king that I carry Old Clootie's mark on my hand?"

Gordon leaned close and planted a kiss on her lips, saying, "Dinna fret aboot such nonsense."

Rob glanced over her shoulder in the direction of Edinburgh Castle's esplanade. "That scaffold doesna seem like nonsense to me," she said in a small voice as a ripple of dread danced down her spine.

"Listen to me, angel." Gordon turned her to face him. "Any man or woman who calls ye a witch is as good as dead. I'll guard ye with my life."

"Why?" Rob asked, searching his eyes for the truth.

"What kind of a question is that?" Gordon asked. "Yer my wife and carry my bairn. What better reason could there be?"

Because ye love me, Rob thought. She managed a faint smile, looped her arm through his, and said, "I'd trust ye with my life any day of the week and twice on Sunday."

"That's my girl," Gordon said, patting her hand. He nodded at the tavern's boy to fetch their horses.

If only he loved me, Rob thought, unable to banish the ominous image of that scaffold from her mind. *If only he loved me and we were back in the mountains at the summer shieling.*

While Gordon and Rob rode north on the Cannongate toward Holyrood Palace, Mungo MacKinnon and Lavinia Kerr sat inside MacDonald's Tavern. They spoke together in hushed tones about the Marquess and Marchioness of Inverary.

"I canna believe that little, mousy nobody from the mountains will be the Duchess of Argyll one day," Lavinia complained with a pout, surprised and irritated at having lost her masculine quarry to another woman.

"That mountain mouse isna a nobody," Mungo replied. "She's Dunridge's only daughter and the Earl of Basildon's niece."

"I canna understand why she'd lie aboot those gloves bein' the latest rage at the Tudor court," Lavinia went on heatedly, missing her cousin's look of amused speculation. "She's tryin' to make fools of us."

Mungo shook his head. "Gordy's wife has good reason to cover her hand."

"Is she deformed?" Lavinia asked, brightening at that prospect.

Mungo chuckled at the hopeful note in his cousin's voice and answered, "In a manner of speakin'."

"Tell me what ye know."

"Rob MacArthur is the green-eyed daughter of a Sassenach witch and carries the proof of it on the back of her left hand," Mungo told her, his hatred apparent in the hard edge to his voice.

His words and his emotion startled Lavinia. "I dinna ken yer meanin', cousin."

"Brigette MacArthur caused the deaths of my father and my aunt," Mungo explained, "and I've been waitin' all my life to exact my revenge."

"What do ye mean?" Lavinia asked. " 'Twas twenty years ago that yer father disappeared and yer aunt took an arrow meant for Menzies."

"Because of Brigette MacArthur, I grew to manhood without a father," Mungo said, his voice bitter. "I found letters from my late Aunt Antonia provin' Lady MacArthur's guilt in his death."

"How could Brigette MacArthur have killed yer father?" Lavinia scoffed. "Where would she even have met Uncle Finlay?"

"Aunt Antonia hated her MacArthur sister-in-law and wanted her dead," Mungo told her. "As a favor to his beloved sister, my father disguised himself in a Menzies plaid and abducted Brigette MacArthur. He planned to leave her on the infamous Lady's Rock in the Sound of Mull. However, while my father was attemptin' to drown her, the bitch managed to drown *him* . . . I almost dispatched Dubh and Rob MacArthur when we were in England. Too bad for me, the devil's spawns have the devil's own luck."

"The Earl of Dunridge is in Edinburgh for the memorial service," Lavinia remarked. "Why dinna ye challenge him and be done with it?"

"I'm bent on revenge, not suicide," Mungo replied dryly.

"Then why dinna ye kill Brigette MacArthur?" Lavinia asked.

"I'll get to her as soon as she leaves the protection of Dunridge's walls," Mungo answered, an unholy smile lighting his expression. "As a matter of fact, I'm plannin' on executin' the whole damned MacArthur clan into extinction. I'm startin' with the daughter. She's easy prey bein' so near at hand."

"Ye canna hold the daughter accountable for the mother's crimes against ye," Lavinia tried to reason with him.

"Who's side are ye on?" Mungo snapped.

Lavinia flicked him a cool gaze. "*My side*. And what's this proof she carries?"

Mungo made a protective sign of the cross and said,

"The witch bears the devil's flower on the back of her left hand. I saw it while we were travelin' north."

Lavinia burst out laughing. "Cousin, ye surely dinna hold with such foolish notions?"

"King James believes in witches."

"So?"

"So I need yer help," Mungo told her. "When we sup with the king tomorrow evenin', I want ye to draw the witch into an argument. 'Tis then we'll force her to unmask her hand for all to view. The verra next mornin' ye'll feign an illness, and I'll complain to the king that she cursed ye. 'Tis certain Jamie will sentence her to death for practicin' witchcraft. I'll have the beginnin' of my revenge on the MacArthurs, and ye'll marry Gordy and become the future Duchess of Argyll."

"Are ye daft?" Lavinia exclaimed, determined not to be connected with such a risky business. "She carries Inverary's heir. Do ye actually believe Gordy will let ye get away with this?"

"Gordy has the anvil with which to forge another brat."

Lavinia chuckled throatily but then shook her head. "Cousin, I willna be a party to killin' the chit."

"I thought ye wanted Campbell," Mungo shot back.

"I did," she hedged, "but realized that others at court are even more appealin'."

"Like who?"

She smiled at him. "Like none of yer business."

"Livy, let me put it to ye this way," Mungo said with a smile that did not quite reach his eyes. "Do what I ask, or I'll whisper in yer father's ear that he'd best make a second marriage for ye. I heard Old Man Ramsey's lookin' for a wife."

"That stinkin' swine?" Lavinia cried. The revolting thought of bedding a fat, toothless old man with body odor made her relent. "Verra well, I'll draw her into an argument, but I willna feign illness."

"Ye instigate an argument," he agreed, "and I'll take care of the rest."

Mungo tossed a few coins on the table, and together they rose from their chairs and started toward the tavern's entrance. "By the way, save me a place beside ye at tomorrow's memorial service," he said. "I'll be a tad late."

Lavinia stopped walking and whirled around to face him. "Why?" she asked, suspicious.

"I've somethin' to do," he answered.

"Like what?"

Mungo raised his brows at her and cast her an unholy smile that sent shivers rippling down her spine. "Like none of yer business, dear cousin."

Chapter 17

"Well, I could be happy if only—"

"That arrogant pup better make ye happy or I'll—"

Rob reached up and placed a finger across her father's lips, the same gentle gesture for silence that he'd used with her when she was a child. Smiling into his dark eyes, she looped her arm through his.

"Let's walk aboot," Rob said. "I'll explain what I mean."

When he nodded, Rob led her father across the browning lawns outside Holyrood Abbey toward a cluster of oak trees that stood together like old friends. She breathed deeply of the mildly crisp air and admired the oaks' autumn garb of gold, orange, and red leaves.

With her father by her side, Rob felt relaxed and secure. Though he'd always enjoyed a reputation for fierceness, Iain MacArthur had been her first and best champion. Her father had always saved time for her in spite of his myriad duties as chief of the MacArthur clan. She smiled inwardly, remembering how he'd joined her and her imaginary friends several afternoons each week for a mug of cider and an animated chat. And then there were the many times when he'd held her protectively close while she wept because none of the other children would play with her.

Casting him a sidelong glance, Rob wondered how best to explain herself. Implying that her marriage to Gordon Campbell was less than perfect would definitely be a mistake, especially since he'd just been forced to apologize publicly to a king for whom he harbored no respect.

Sometimes lyin' is kinder than tellin' the truth . . . Rob recalled the day she'd given that piece of advice to her cousin, Blythe. If only she'd heeded her own words, she wouldn't be facing the difficult task of convincing her father that all was relatively well.

"I only meant that I wished my husband loved me," Rob said. "Like ye love Mother."

"I'm positive Gordy loves ye," Iain assured her. "Why, yer the most lovable woman in the world."

"Da, I believe yer a tad biased," she said with a smile.

"I may be biased, but I'm tellin' ye the truth," her father replied.

"Gordy has never professed his love."

Iain put his arm around her. "Sometimes a man finds sharin' his deepest emotions difficult. That doesna' mean he lacks those deep emotions. Remember, love is as love does."

"But why would men want to hide their feelin's?"

"There are as many reasons as there are men," Iain answered. "Usually, a man fears lettin' his woman see how vulnerable he is."

"I canna believe that aboot Gordy," Rob replied. "Why, he's the bravest man I know. Besides ye, that is."

Her diplomacy brought a smile to her father's lips, and

he planted a paternal kiss on her forehead. "Other than that complaint, how are ye feelin'?"

"I'm fine now that the mornin' sickness has passed." Rob blushed and dropped her gaze to her shoes. "At first I thought I was dyin' of some terrible disease."

Pleased by her admission, Iain MacArthur chuckled. He'd raised his only daughter to be innocent and modest, if not exactly biddable.

"And I do love Gordy's sons as much as if they were my own," she added, peeking up at him from beneath the thick fringe of her sooty lashes.

"Ye always did have a generous heart," Iain remarked, his dark gaze warm with tenderness. "I'm glad that yer husband's past indiscretions dinna bother ye overmuch."

"So why didna Mother journey to Edinburgh with ye?" Rob asked, steering their conversation away from her husband's indiscretions.

"I insisted she remain in Argyll," Iain answered. "Yer mother is no shrinkin' wallflower and says whatever pops into her mind. At the moment, Jamie Stuart isna verra high in her regard. She thinks he's an unnatural, betrayin' brat."

"I harbor the same belief." Rob dropped her voice to barely a whisper and told him, "I met Queen Mary when I was in England."

"Ye did?" Her father appeared interested.

Rob nodded. "I persuaded Uncle Richard to take me to Chartley when we were in Shropshire that summer before her—" She broke off, unwilling to say those horrible words. "Oh, Da! She seemed so pathetically lonely. My heart ached for her. Jamie refused her refuge when the English offered to send her home." As soon as the words slipped from her lips, Rob regretted them.

"I didna know aboot that," her father said, his expression grim. "I doubt Cousin Magnus knew either."

Rob touched his arm. "Nothin' will bring her back from the dead now."

Iain MacArthur smiled at his daughter's remark. She sounded almost exactly like her husband. Perhaps, the match between them had been a good one.

"Will Dubh be safe from prosecution?" Rob asked, her worry apparent. "Isabelle is the only real friend I ever had. If Dubh and she are happy together, I wouldna want to see them torn apart."

"Listen to ye," Iain chided her, giving her a sideways hug. "Why must ye carry the whole world's problems on yer delicate shoulders? I forbid ye to fret aboot anythin' more than deliverin' a healthy babe. Yer brother and his bride are well and will remain that way as long as I have life in my body. Besides, yer mother would surely kill me if I let any harm befall her firstborn."

Rob tilted her head and gazed up at him. A smile flirted with the corners of her lips, and she said, "Da, I love ye."

"What a perfectly heartwarmin' picture," Duke Magnus remarked, approaching them. "I suppose there's somethin' to be said in favor of sirin' daughters."

"The lasses always love their fathers," Percy MacArthur agreed.

"Hello, Uncle Percy," Rob greeted him, planting a kiss on his cheek. "I do hope Aunt Sheena fares well."

"Everyone is fine," he said.

Rob kissed her father-in-law's cheek, saying, "Good day, Yer Grace."

"I am now yer father too and want ye to call me Da," Magnus told her. "How's that first granddaughter of mine?"

"She's growin' bigger every day," Rob said, blushing, sliding her hand to her belly. "Gabby says I'm double the size I should be."

"Gavin will be verra pleased by the news," Duke Magnus said.

Rob smiled and would have spoken, but a voice behind them drew their attention.

"Hello, darling."

"Great Bruce's ghost, 'tis Henry," Rob cried, whirling around. She threw herself into his arms. "What are ye doin' here?"

"I'm acting as one of Elizabeth's emissaries," Henry answered. "Roger Debrett is here too, but he's gone off to explore a few possible business ventures in town."

"Roger Debrett, ye say?" Rob echoed. "Would Lord Roger put a good word for Dubh in with the king? Ye knew my brother eloped with Isabelle?"

"I'd hardly call what Dubh did an elopement," Henry said dryly. "However, I'd do just about anything for you, darling, and will discuss this matter with Roger as soon as he returns." He grinned at her and observed, "I see that marriage to Inverary has put a happy glow on those pretty cheeks of yours."

When the three older men cleared their throats, Rob finally remembered she wasn't alone. She flicked an embarrassed, apologetic smile at them and made the introductions. "This is Henry Talbot, the Marquess of Ludlow, Uncle Richard's brother-in-law. We became close friends in England. Henry, these are my father-in-law, the Duke of Argyll, my own father, the Earl of Dunridge, and my uncle, the Earl of Weem."

The three Highland lairds shook hands with the Marquess of Ludlow. All three knew exactly how close the marquess had been with Rob, but no one mentioned it.

"Ye know, Henry, returnin' to the Highlands wasna as disastrous as I had believed," Rob told him. She blushed, adding, "Come February, I'm goin' to be a mother."

Henry smiled, genuinely happy for her. "Since you're

not pining away for love of me as I had hoped, I'll share *my* news with you. I wed your Irish cousin, Shana, who arrived at your uncle's last spring for an extended visit."

"Ye married my cousin?" Rob cried in surprise, her pride injured. "Why, my trail to Scotland hadna even cooled, and the dust hadna covered my tracks."

Henry flicked a helpless glance at the three older men who were smiling at his predicament. "I didn't marry for love," he added hastily. "The lady needed a husband's protection for political reasons." He winked at her, asking, "How about that Samhuinn kiss I never got?"

Rob cast him a flirtatious smile. Married her cousin, had he? Well, she was about to give him a teasing taste of what could never be his. Regardless of her relatives' presence, Rob entwined her arms around his neck, pulled his handsome face down to meet her, and claimed his lips in a sweetly tantalizing kiss.

"Get yer paws off my wife." The voice belonged to Gordon.

Rob leaped away from Henry and turned to her husband. *Her angry husband.* With his golf bag slung over his right shoulder, Gordon stood two feet away and glared with murderous intent at them.

Wearing a sardonic smile, Henry faced his former rival and asked, "What's wrong with a little welcoming kiss between such *intimate* friends?"

"Fuck ye and the horse ye rode in on," Gordon snapped, echoing the words the other man had once spoken to him.

"I arrived in one of my brother-in-law's ships," Henry replied, his smile broadening. " 'Tis faster than a horse."

Recognizing the dangerous glint in her husband's eyes, Rob placed herself between the two men. She flicked a silent plea at her watching relatives. No help there. The

three Highland lairds were grinning at the scene un-
folding in front of them.

"Gordy, yer makin' a public spectacle of us," Rob said.
"Everyone is watchin'."

"Perhaps the startlin' sight of my pregnant wife lettin'
this Sassenach paw her shocks them," Gordon replied.

"Easy, lad," Iain MacArthur warned. "I ken that yer
jealous, but I willna allow ye to speak disparagin'ly of my
daughter."

Rob snapped her head around to stare at her father.
Could it possibly be true? Did her husband care enough
about her to be jealous? No, that couldn't be. He would
have professed his love for her long before this.

"Henry is yer cousin-by-marriage," Rob informed her
husband.

"I dinna ken."

"He married my Irish cousin, Shana."

At that, Henry nodded at his former rival and offered
his hand in friendship. Finally, Gordon relaxed and accepted it.

"We'll be takin' our leave now," Iain MacArthur spoke
up.

"Are ye leavin' Edinburgh today?" Rob asked, giving
her father a hug.

"No, we'll pass the night at Campbell Mansion,"
Duke Magnus answered. "We'll be leavin' in the
mornin'."

"I wish we were goin' with ye," Rob said, casting her
husband a pleading look. She wanted to be away from
court and the dangers waitin' to grab her.

"Jamie willna delay us long," Gordon assured her.
"He knows I want my heir born at Inverary."

Rob kissed her father good-bye. Standing between her
husband and her former suitor, she forlornly watched the

three Highland lairds walk toward the palace's stable yard to get their horses.

"So, did ye bring yer wife to Edinburgh with ye?" Gordon asked.

"Ah, my bride's having a difficult time adjusting to the married life," Henry replied. "I left her temper cooling in the Tower."

"Ye locked her in the Tower of London?" Rob cried in horrified surprise.

"Well, I tried lockin' her in her chamber," Henry defended himself, "but she escaped out the window. I wasted a whole day and a night searching for her."

Gordon slapped the other man's back in easy camaraderie, saying, "Ye know, *cousin*, the lasses can be a royal pain in the arse."

Rob opened her mouth to scold both men but heard someone calling her husband. She turned to see Mungo MacKinnon advancing on them, and a shiver of dislike for the man rippled down her spine.

"Gordy, are ye ready?" Mungo called.

"We're golfin' with the king," Gordon told Henry. "Join us, and I'll share my clubs with ye."

Henry nodded in agreement. " 'Tis better than waitin' the extra day to see him."

"How well do ye golf?" Gordon asked.

"I've never golfed in my life," Henry answered.

Gordon grinned. "Good, the king will love ye." When he turned to Rob, his expression softened. "And what will ye do while I'm gone, angel?"

"I'm plannin' on sewin' baby clothes with that fabric we bought," she answered.

"Be certain ye take a long nap," Gordon answered, leaning close to plant a chaste kiss on her lips. "I dinna want ye yawnin' in the king's face tonight."

"I'll try to control myself," Rob said with a smile. She

watched the three of them walk away and then headed for her chamber lest one of her husband's former mistresses corner her and ruin her good mood.

"Bring me the gown," Rob called, strapping her last resort onto her left leg.

Gabby hurried across the chamber and helped her mistress don the forest-green and gold brocaded gown. After fastening the tiny back buttons, she said, "Turn around, Lady Rob . . . Och, yer beauty will shame all the other ladies."

"I doubt that," Rob replied with a rueful smile. She glanced at her bare hands and added, "Please fetch me the green gloves."

"I canna find them," Gabby answered. "Where did ye put them?"

"In the chest."

"There are na any gloves in yer chest."

That's odd, Rob thought. She crossed the chamber to her wooden chest, dropped to her knees, and opened its lid. Several pairs of gloves should have been lying on top of the pile of clothing.

Sticking her hand down deep, Rob searched for the lacy gloves but only managed to produce a chemise. She tossed it over her shoulder, and the search began in earnest.

Rob grabbed the top layer of stockings and garters and tossed them into a pile on the floor behind her. Next came her chemises and nightshifts. Those went flying over her shoulder too.

Each passing moment brought a rising swell of panic within her breast. She was positive she'd carefully placed her fingerless gloves on top of the heap in her chest. Where could they be? She couldn't sup with the king unless she wore those gloves to cover her deformity. Perhaps she'd accidentally placed them in her husband's chest.

Rob attacked Gordon's wooden chest with a vengeance. Every article of clothing it contained ended in the heap on the floor behind her.

"My lady, what are ye doin'?" Gabby asked.

"I need those gloves," Rob cried. "I canna wear the black ones because they dinna match this gown and will only bring attention to my hand."

Rob leaped to her feet and went for her gowns. She shook each one out vigorously and then tossed it onto the floor.

Gordon's pranking me, Rob decided. When he returned to their chamber that morning to fetch his golf clubs, he'd hidden her gloves. But where?

Breathing heavily from her exertions, Rob raced across the chamber to the bed. She dropped to her knees, yanked the bottom edge of the coverlet up, and peered beneath the bed.

"Fetch me a candle," she ordered. " 'Tis dark under here."

"Are ye ready?" Rob heard her husband call as the door swung open. She lifted her head in time to catch his surprised expression as he surveyed the shambles in the chamber.

"God's balls, what happened?" Gordon demanded.

"I canna find my gloves," she answered. "Do ye know where they are?"

Rob watched him flick his hand at Gabby, who immediately left the chamber, and then asked, "Do ye think someone stole them while we were out today?"

"Get off yer knees," Gordon ordered, crossing the chamber to tower above her.

"Aboot what are ye angry? I'm the one whose property's been stolen."

"This chamber looks like the north wind swept through it." Gordon gently but forcibly lifted her to her feet, saying, "Ye dinna need those gloves."

"The king will see Old Clootie's mark if I dinna wear them," Rob replied, nervously rubbing a finger back and forth across her birth stain, her desperation apparent in her voice and her expression.

"Ye dinna carry Old Clootie's mark," Gordon insisted, reaching for the black gloves she'd worn that day. He held them up in front of her face, saying, "Like a crippled man, ye've made these gloves a crutch, and I regret givin' them to ye." He marched across the chamber and tossed the gloves into the hearth's fire.

"Great Bruce's ghost," Rob exclaimed, feeling weak legged as if he'd struck her with the blunt end of a claymore. She plopped down on the edge of the bed and covered her face with her hands.

Oh, God, she thought in a panic. Her husband would force her to attend the king. Once he'd seen her deformity, Jamie would send her to that scaffold outside Edinburgh Castle, and the babe she carried would die with her.

"Angel, listen to me." Gordon knelt in front of her and took her hands in his. When she gazed at him, he said, "I only purchased those gloves because I was tryin' to win yer favor. No one will think less of ye because ye carry a pretty birthmark on yer hand."

"But King James believes in—"

"Jamie is superstitious only in theory," Gordon interrupted her. "Yer the Marchioness of Inveraray and soon-to-be the mother of my heir. He willna say a word against ye. With me by yer side, ye need fear no man—not even a king. Accept yerself for who ye are, and everyone else will accept ye."

When I accepted myself, everyone else accepted me, Rob

recalled the advice Aunt Keely had given her that long ago day in Devereux House's great hall.

"I do love ye with all of my heart," Rob vowed, throwing herself into his arms.

With his arms encircling her protectively, Gordon planted a kiss on the ebony crown of her head and said, "I know ye do, angel."

He didn't return her love, Rob decided in the next instant, her heart breaking with that painful knowledge. Though she was carrying his child, her husband refused to profess any love for her. Did he harbor any tender feelings for her? Did he feel the emotions but fear the words as her father had suggested? If only she knew what he felt, perhaps she could live without the words.

Gordon tilted her chin up and smiled, asking, "Now, are ye ready to meet the king?"

Setting her heartache aside for the moment, Rob managed a faint smile and answered, "I'm ready as I'll ever be."

"That's my angel," Gordon said, and planted a chaste kiss on her lips.

When they left their chamber, Gordon guided Rob down a long corridor that led to the northern section of the palace where the royal apartments were located. They passed the apartments of the late Lord Darnley, the king's father, and walked until they reached an audience room. From there, a stairway led to the king's private audience chamber, and at the head of the spiral staircase was the king's supper room.

"This is the verra chamber where assassins dragged Rizzio from Queen Mary's presence and murdered him," Gordon whispered as they reached the top of the staircase.

Rob said nothing. Treachery abounded here; it was as tangible as the stones beneath her feet. She made a protective sign of the cross and hid her left hand within the folds of her gown before stepping inside the supper room. She only hoped that treachery wouldn't reach out to grab her that night, but the knowledge that she'd strapped her last resort to her leg gave her the courage to place one foot in front of the other until she stood inside the chamber.

Rob spared a quick glance around. The room's starkness surprised her, especially since her aunt had told her of the luxury of the English court.

Disappointment surged through her as she spied Mungo MacKinnon, Lavinia Kerr, and several of her husband's former mistresses accompanied by their husbands. Apparently, she'd be forced to face Gordon's past indiscretions all evening. Seeing Henry Talbot and Roger Debrett, as well as the Earl of Bothwell, calmed her rioting nerves. At least, she'd have three allies in attendance. Four, if she counted her husband.

"This way, angel," Gordon said, drawing her toward the king.

Being certain to keep her deformed hand hidden, Rob dropped King James a deep curtsey and bowed her head.

"Stand," James bade her.

With her husband's assistance, Rob rose and lifted her gaze to the king's. The sight of his dribbling mouth sickened her stomach, but her placid expression never altered.

"So yer Gordy's bride," the king said with a wet smile.

"Yes, Sire," Rob replied, fighting her nausea.

"Gordy tells me yer with child," James remarked. "He wants his heir born at Inverary too."

Uncertain of what to say or to do, Rob nodded and flicked a sidelong glance at her husband.

"Apparently, Lady Rob is a woman of few words,"

James remarked. "I admire that trait in a female. 'Tis proper for a woman to be seen and not heard."

"My opinion mirrors yers," Gordon smoothly replied.

The king reached out and slapped Gordon's shoulder in easy camaraderie, whispering loudly, "I hope ye didna tell yer wife how much gold ye lost to me today."

Gordon grinned. "Well, Sire, I daresay she knows now."

The king chuckled. "Come and sit beside me at supper, my friend. Lady Rob can sit on yer left."

Gordon nodded. "Thank ye for the honor, Yer Majesty."

King James headed for the supper table already set for fifteen. When he moved, everyone else in the chamber moved too.

Rob was relieved when Henry Talbot sat beside her and Roger Debrett sat directly opposite her. At the far end of the table were Mungo MacKinnon and Lavinia Kerr. At least, she'd be spared the ordeal of dealing with them as she supped.

The servants arrived with their supper. A salad of damsons, artichokes, cabbage lettuce, and cucumber in a vinaigrette arrived first. Next came fresh sturgeon and chicken baked in caudle and fritters. The last course consisted of scraped cheese with sugar, quince pie, marchpane, and wafers with hippocras.

Keeping her left hand hidden on her lap, Rob sat quietly throughout supper and let the conversations swirl around her. Sitting between Gordon and Henry Talbot made her feel secure. As long as she called no attention to herself, she would survive the evening.

" 'Tis an excellent feelin' in this time of our mournin' to have my friends offer me comfort," King James was saying.

What a lying hypocrite, Rob thought, losing her appetite. She'd always assumed that the king would be nobler than any other person in the realm. Apparently, she'd been mistaken. Noble or not, a king was subject to the same human frailties as the basest commoner in his realm.

"Yer brother-in-law is the renowned Earl of Basildon," King James said, looking down the table at Henry as supper came to an end. "Tell me aboot Elizabeth's 'Midas.'"

"Lady Rob is his blood niece and passed more than a year in his household," Henry replied. "She can probably tell you more than I ever could, although I will gladly share anything of interest that I can."

When the royal gaze shifted to her, Rob squirmed uncomfortably in her seat. She cleared her throat and said, "Sire, I would be honored to answer any questions ye have concernin' my uncle."

"I want to know aboot his business ventures," the king said baldly.

Business ventures? She knew nothing about her uncle's businesses. Apparently, James wanted inside information in order to fatten his own coffers. At a loss for words, Rob sent her husband a silent plea for help.

"Yer Majesty, my wife knows less than nothin' aboot business," Gordon said with a smile, giving the king an arch look. "Why, I canna recall even seein' her read a book, which is as it should be. Women were meant for breedin' and child rearin'." At the king's look of disappointment, he added, "However, while I was a guest at Basildon's, we closeted ourselves in his study each night and discussed business. I've made several successful investments for clan Campbell." He dropped his voice, "I would be honored to share that information with ye, Yer Majesty, but hesitate to do so in such a crowd as this."

King James nodded with satisfaction. "Well, Gordy, I'm glad yer father had the foresight to marry ye off to the Earl of Basildon's niece. How aboot a game of chess while we discuss the advice Basildon gave ye?"

"With pleasure, Sire."

King James and Gordon rose from the table and sat in the chairs near the hearth. Between them on a table rested a chess set, and the two began to play. Henry Talbot and Roger Debrett stood near them to watch as well as to discourage any would-be eavesdroppers looking to fatten their own purses.

Feeling conspicuously out of place among these strangers who knew each other, Rob carefully hid her left hand within the folds of her gown and wandered across the chamber to stare out a window. Night shrouded Edinburgh Castle in the distance, yet she felt the presence of its horrifying scaffold with every fiber of her being.

How long would Gordon's chess game take? Rob wondered, desperate to escape the chamber and the king's presence. She knew without looking at her star ruby that insidious danger lurked within the palace's darkened corners and awaited the predestined moment when he would step forward to claim his due.

"Good evenin', Lady Rob."

Turning toward the voice, Rob pasted an insincere smile onto her face and greeted the woman, "Good evenin', Lady Kerr."

"And where are yer gloves this evenin'?" Lavinia asked with a sarcastic smirk. "I thought we'd never see ye without them since they're the latest rage at the Tudor court."

"My pregnancy makes me unwell this evenin'," Rob said, fearing the redhead would notice her devil's flower. "Please go away and leave me alone."

"I'll leave after we've cleared the air between us."

"Can it wait until the mornin'?"

Lavinia stood her ground. "No."

"What is it ye wish to say to me?" Rob asked, irritated not only with the woman but her own husband whose past had brought her to this uncomfortable moment.

"How does it feel to know ye've separated two people who truly love each other?" Lavinia asked, her voice low so that no one else could hear.

"Dinna talk in riddles," Rob snapped. "Speak straight if ye've somethin' to say."

"Ye realize Gordy and I were lovers?"

Rob stiffened and gave her a curt nod. "I had an inklin' that somethin' illicit had passed between ye, but yer the interloper since he'd already married me."

"Gordy only married ye to suit his father," Lavinia informed her, giving her a feline smile. "As a matter of fact, Gordy and I were abed when the message to fetch ye arrived from Argyll."

Rob flushed with appalled anger, and rage simmered in her blood. How many other women in this room were waiting to have this same conversation with her? Damn Gordon Campbell and his unbridled lust!

"Go away, Lady Kerr," Rob managed to choke out, her stomach churning with her angry humiliation and her pain.

Encouraged by the obviously anguished expression on Rob's face, Lavinia went in for the kill. "Gordy planned on ridin' to Dunridge Castle and then droppin' ye off at Inverary. He was in a hurry to get back to my arms. Yer waywardness ruined our plans."

Pushed beyond endurance, Rob reached down and, in one swift motion, flicked the bottom edge of her gown up to draw her last resort. She pointed the deadly little dagger in the general vicinity of the other woman's flawlessly beautiful face and threatened, "Go away, ye adulterous jade, or I'll give ye so many scars no man will want to look at ye much less bed ye."

"She's goin' to kill me," Lavinia screamed, leaping back several paces.

In the next instant, everyone rushed across the room and surrounded them. Pushing his way through the small crowd of shocked spectators, Gordon demanded, "God's balls, what are ye doin'? Ye brought a dagger into the king's presence? Are ye daft?"

Speechless at being blamed for this confrontation, Rob could only stare at her husband. Why was he shouting at her? She glanced toward Lavinia, whom Mungo MacKinnon had protectively encircled within his arms. King James, dribbling a river of saliva, stood beside them.

"Yer blamin' me?" Rob asked her husband.

Gordon held out his hand and ordered, "Give me the blade."

"The plague and the devil take ye," Rob cursed Lavinia as she passed her dagger to her husband.

"Get these bickerin' bitches out of my sight," King James ordered.

Needing no second invitation to leave, Gordon grabbed Rob's wrist in a bruising grip and yanked her out of the chamber. Silence reigned as he pulled her through the maze of dimly lit corridors.

When they finally reached their own chamber, Gordon exclaimed, "I canna believe ye drew a dagger in the king's presence."

"Are ye worried for yer whore's life?" Rob shouted, exploding with outraged humiliation. "I ken ye had affairs, but I dinna relish havin' yer lightskirts accost me."

She plopped down on the edge of the bed and placed a hand against her belly as if that could calm its churning. Watching her husband pace the chamber, Rob felt defeated and hot tears brimmed in her eyes. "I willna contest a divorce, Gordy. Ye can even use Old Clootie's mark as the reason. I just want to be away from here. Attendin' this court is makin' me sick."

"Aboot what are ye talkin'?" Gordon asked, stopping his pacing to fix his piercing gaze on her.

"I dinna want a husband on yer terms," she answered, lifting her chin a notch.

"Ye really must be daft," Gordon countered. "Do ye think I'd ever let ye rule our marriage?"

"I'll have a husband who's faithful or none at all," Rob said, squaring her shoulders proudly and looking him straight in the eye. "Besides, ye'll be happier if ye wed the woman ye love."

Some unrecognizable emotion flickered in his piercing gray gaze, and his expression softened on her. Gordon sat beside her on the edge of the bed and put his arm around her, drawing her close.

"I never loved Lavinia Kerr," he told her. "I took what she offered and nothin' more."

His admission left her depleted of energy. "I dinna like attendin' the court," Rob said, her misery obvious. "I want to leave."

Gently, Gordon brushed his lips against her temple. "Tomorrow mornin', angel," he promised. "After ye apologize to the king, I'll ask his permission to leave. If he wants me to stay in Edinburgh, we'll move into Campbell Mansion. Will that suit ye?"

Rob nodded, and secure in his embrace, rested her head against his chest. Though outwardly calmed, Rob's thoughts were troubled. Her husband insisted he never loved Lavinia Kerr, and she believed him. Yet, he refused to profess any love for her.

Rob sighed raggedly. Perhaps some day he would develop a fondness for her. Until then, she needed to concentrate on the babe she carried. Danger surrounded her, and any danger to herself placed her unborn child at risk.

Great Bruce's ghost, she'd kill the man or the woman who jeopardized her baby.

Chapter 18

"Brava, Livy. Ye performed most excellently this evenin'." Mungo MacKinnon smiled with satisfaction as he watched his cousin pacing angrily back and forth in front of the hearth in her chamber.

"Humph," Lavinia snorted delicately, throwing him an irritated glare. "I canna believe that Highland mouse had the audacity to draw her dagger on me."

"I'd say Gordy was more than a little surprised too," Mungo replied, pleased that the opening act of his scheme for revenge against the MacArthurs had gone so well. " 'Twas even better than I'd planned. Not only did the stupid twit draw her dagger in front of the king but she also cursed ye in the presence of witnesses."

"So what will ye do now?" Lavinia asked, flicking him a sidelong glance as she passed him in her pacing.

"In the mornin' I'll whisper in the king's ear aboot her devil's flower and then accuse her of practicin' witchcraft." Mungo reached out and grasped her forearm, saying, "Cousin, yer pacin' is makin' me dizzy." He gently forced her to sit in the chair and ordered, "Stay put, and I'll fetch ye a glass of wine."

When she nodded in agreement, Mungo crossed the chamber to the table. Ah, yes, he thought with an inward smile of supreme satisfaction. Events were progressing rather nicely. Perhaps his luck was about to take a turn for the better.

Mungo glanced over his shoulder to be certain his cousin wasn't watching and then pulled a glass vial from inside his doublet. He stared at its contents for one brief moment. The apothecary had insisted that this amount of calcinated, fresh tree bark would reduce a person to a retching state within a few minutes. Though the illness wouldn't be fatal, the nausea and the stomachache would last two or three days.

Without remorse, Mungo emptied the powdery tree bark into a goblet and poured the wine. After filling a second goblet, he carried them back across the chamber and then passed Lavinia the goblet of tainted wine.

"I salute yer fine actin' ability," Mungo said, raising his goblet and drinking.

"I wasna play actin'," Lavinia told him, and sipped her wine. "Despisin' that mouse comes easily."

"I ken what ye mean," Mungo replied, sitting down in the other chair and stretching his legs out.

For the next half hour, the two cousins drank their wine and spoke of inconsequential matters. Mungo kept a sharp eye on his cousin and her slowly paling complexion while he awaited the illness' onslaught.

Suddenly, Lavinia placed a hand against her belly as if she felt uncomfortable. "Cousin, I dinna feel verra well," she said. "Would ye call my tirin' woman for me?"

Struggling against a smile, Mungo shot to his feet. "Of course, I will. I'll also fetch the king's physician."

As he passed her, Lavinia grabbed his hand and looked

up at him with an anxious expression. "Ye dinna think she really is a witch?" she asked.

"I dinna know," Mungo answered with a shrug. "But I'm positive the king's physician can make ye feel better."

On the opposite side of the palace, down the winding maze of corridors from Lavinia's chamber, Gordon sat in the chair in front of the hearth in his own chamber. Rob, dressed in her night shift and robe, cuddled in his lap and rested her head against his shoulder. She'd dropped into an exhausted sleep as they'd been speaking about their baby's impending arrival only a few months from then, and Gordon was reluctant to awaken her just to put her to bed.

Gordon glanced down at her sweet expression. His wife was indeed an angel, no matter that she possessed the foolish habit of drawing her dagger at precisely the wrong moment. *A Highland angel with an imp's temperament.* That's exactly what she was. Despite the long years of personal sorrow, Rob had an enormous heart and more love to give than any ten women put together.

Without a doubt, Gordon knew that no other woman in God's universe would have accepted Duncan and Gavin unconditionally as she had. He knew she'd been profoundly disappointed when he failed to profess his love for her. And he knew that he must tell her he loved her, even if she tried to manipulate him because of his tender regard for her.

His wife accepted his bastards, professed her love for him, and nurtured his heir inside her body. He owed her those three words she longed to hear . . . *I love you.*

Bang! Bang! Bang! came a pounding on the door.

Rob awakened in an instant and, though drowsy, peered up at him through emerald eyes that mirrored her alarm. Gordon shrugged and shook his head.

Again sounded the insistent pounding on their chamber door.

"Open up, Inveraray," a voice ordered. "By order of His Majesty, King James, I charge ye to open this door."

"Give me a minute," Gordon called as Rob rose from his lap.

"Am I to be arrested for drawin' my dagger in the king's presence?" she asked, worriedly rubbing a finger back and forth across her devil's flower.

Gordon planted a kiss on her forehead and asked, "Would I let Jamie do that to ye?"

Rob gave him a wobbly smile and shook her head.

Gordon crossed the chamber, unbolted the door, and opened it a crack. Five men of the king's personal guard stood there.

"What do ye want?" Gordon demanded.

"Ye and yer wife will accompany us to the audience chamber," the man in charge answered.

Gordon glanced in his wife's direction and then shifted his gaze back to the man. "My wife is already dressed for sleepin'," he told him. "Will ye wait while she changes into a gown?"

"No." The man stood his ground. "She's to accompany us now."

"I'll fetch her," Gordon said with a curt nod. When he turned around, he regretted ever leaving Argyll.

"Dinna fret," Gordon said, noting her pale face and wrapping a shawl around her shoulders. "At times James is given to dramatics. 'Tis a trait he inherited from his mother. Do ye trust me to protect ye and handle him?"

Rob nodded once, but was unable to speak.

Putting his arm around her protectively, Gordon guided his wife toward the door. He felt the tremors of fear that shook her body and cursed himself for insisting she accompany him to Edinburgh. If he'd only known then what dangers awaited them at Holyrood. Ah, well, there was nothing to be done now. Even a blind man saw keenly through hindsight.

Gordon felt the first inkling of true apprehension when they walked into the audience chamber. With the exception of Lavinia Kerr, everyone who'd attended supper that evening was there, and Mungo MacKinnon stood near the king.

Gordon flicked a questioning glance at the Earl of Bothwell who almost imperceptibly shook his head in obvious disgust. Next his gaze slid to the English emissaries, Talbot and Debrett, who also appeared none too happy.

Though he felt the stirrings of unease in the pit of his stomach, Gordon forced himself to give his wife an encouraging squeeze. Together, they stepped forward toward the dais, but the king's voice stopped them.

"Stay where ye are," King James ordered, gesturing with his hand.

Gordon halted instantly. Noting the river of dribble emanating from the king's mouth, he asked with a smile, "Yer Majesty, may I be heard?"

"No," came the king's bitterly cold reply. "MacKinnon, step forward and repeat yer accusation."

Mungo MacKinnon walked forward until he stood only inches from Gordon and Rob, who shrank back from him. For the first time, Gordon recognized the unmasked hatred in his friend's gaze when he looked at Rob.

"Gordy, I'm verra sorry aboot this," Mungo said, flicking him an apologetic look. "Yer wife's curse has sickened Livy. Even now, the king's own physician is tendin' her."

"Dinna be ridiculous," Gordon snapped, unable to

credit what he was hearing. He shifted his gaze to the king to make an argument in his wife's defense.

In that instant, Mungo snaked his hand out and grabbed Rob's left wrist. She screamed and struggled to free herself.

"Rob MacArthur is a witch who wears Old Clootie's mark," Mungo shouted, holding her hand up for all to see.

Everyone in the chamber except Bothwell and the two English emissaries shrank back from the unholy sight. As if fear were contagious, each man and woman made a protective sign of the cross to ward the evil eye off.

"God's balls, I'll kill ye," Gordon growled, lunging for Mungo. He tackled the blond man to the floor, and enraged beyond reason, he grabbed his throat and began squeezing the life's breath from his body.

"Cease!" King James shouted, spitting saliva. "Stop, I say!" His royal command fell on deaf ears.

In the end, saving Mungo MacKinnon required the strength of three men. Lords Bothwell, Talbot, and Debrett pulled a struggling Gordon off the other man.

"Ye canna help yer lassie if he tosses ye in the Tolbooth for murder," Bothwell whispered into his ear.

Gordon stilled instantly at the earl's warning. He'd settle with MacKinnon at a later date. After all, revenge tasted best when served cold.

"MacKinnon, do ye actually believe Gordy's wife is a witch?" King James asked.

"Aye, I do." His answer came out in a breathless rasp.

"I dinna believe that the English queen's Midas would harbor a witch in his household for more than a year," the Earl of Bothwell spoke up, drawing his royal cousin's attention.

Henry Talbot took his cue from the Border lord and

remarked, "Aye, Rob is the Earl of Basildon's favorite niece."

"Why, Rob is as much his daughter as the six he sired," Roger Debrett added.

"Basildon sired *six* daughters?" James echoed in apparent surprise.

The Earl of Bothwell forced himself to laugh loudly. " 'Twould seem that Basildon knows much aboot fattenin' England's royal coffers but little aboot fuckin' a woman." Everyone in the chamber chuckled, relieving the tension, and he added, "The man should have done it with his boots on."

Relaxing a bit because of the unexpected levity, King James shifted his gaze to Rob, who stood there trembling visibly. The cold speculation vanished from his eyes as he looked at her.

"Rob MacArthur is the daughter of a green-eyed witch," Mungo MacKinnon cried, indignant. "The proof lies on the back of her left hand. Her Sassenach mother caused the deaths of my father and my aunt."

" 'Tis a lie!" Rob cried, speaking for the first time.

"I have proof enough and demand retribution," Mungo called, ignoring her outburst.

"I'll give ye retribution." Gordon clenched his fist and struck the other man full on the face, sending him sprawling on the floor and a river of blood gushing from his nose.

"Enough!" the king shouted, his saliva spraying those closest to him, who dared not dry themselves in his presence.

King James slid his gaze from Mungo to Gordon to Rob while he debated the best action to take. Finally, he shifted his gaze to Mungo and said, "Verra well, MacKinnon, but yer retribution must be monetary. Name yer price, and Gordy will pay ye." *Or else* was left unspoken.

"Fifty thousand gold pieces," Mungo called, holding his handkerchief against his bleeding nose. "And if he canna raise it, will ye put the witch to death?"

"I'll consider it." King James looked at Gordon and said, "Ye've six weeks from tonight to deliver the gold. Until then, both Mungo and ye are banned from my court. Yer wife, however, will remain here as surety."

"No," Rob exclaimed, and then swooned.

Gordon caught her before she hit the floor and cradled her in his arms. Before turning away, he said in a low voice, "MacKinnon, yer a walkin' dead man."

"He's goin' to kill me," Mungo whined in protest.

"Gordy, if MacKinnon meets with an untimely accident," the king threatened, clearly irritated, "I'll charge yer wife with witchcraft and hang her from yonder scaffold. Do ye understand?"

"I can guarantee Mungo's safety," Gordon replied, inclining his head. "For the next six weeks, at least."

Without waiting for royal permission to leave, Gordon whirled away and carried Rob out of the audience chamber. The Earl of Bothwell cast his royal cousin a wholly disgusted look and followed him out, as did Henry Talbot and Roger Debrett.

There was a hole in her world where Gordon had once stood.

Those autumn days dawned depressingly overcast and rainy as if the angels on high sympathized with her plight. Utterly disheartened, Rob passed the first week of her lonely confinement in a blur of tears and a deep, dreamless sleep. Though Henry Talbot tried several times to gain admittance to her chamber, she saw no one but Gabby and refused to eat except for a bowl of broth each evening.

At the beginning of her second week of miserable isolation, Rob arose from her bed and passed the long hours each day sitting in front of the hearth and staring despondently into its mesmerizing flames. She refused to sew more baby clothes. Why go to all that trouble for a child that would never be born? Raising fifty thousand gold pieces would be impossible for Gordon. Who would pauper themselves for a woman they'd never accepted?

By the third week, Rob toyed with the idea of escaping but was uncertain of how that could be accomplished. Security at Holyrood was excellent. Besides, Gordon and she would forever be branded outlaws. No one thwarted the will of the king.

On the twenty-first evening of her confinement, Rob sat in the chair in front of the hearth. She stared at her devil's flower and traced a finger across it. The skin on her left hand felt no different than on her right hand. How could such a tiny flaw bring her a lifetime of misery? The dark, delicate flower jeopardized her and her unborn child, but evil lurked within the heart, not the back of a hand. Unless . . .

Rob flicked a sidelong glance at Gabby who sat in the other chair and knitted a blanket for the baby that would never be born. "Do ye think I really could be a changelin'-witch?" she asked the other woman.

Gabby snapped her head round and stared at her incredulously.

"There might be such bein's," Rob went on. "Perhaps, the fairies stole the true MacArthur daughter and left me in her place. What d'ye think?"

Gabby grinned. "I think ye sound even stupider than my Dewey."

"Well, 'tis possible," Rob insisted, disgruntled by her insult.

"Fairies and changelin'-witches dinna exist," Gabby replied, shaking her head.

"How do ye know?"

"Granny Biddy told me." Gabby lowered her voice and added, "There exist such bein's as ghosts, though. If my granny saw how thin ye've become, she'd murder me and make me one of them."

"I amna hungry," Rob said, and then sighed. Apparently, their nightly argument about eating supper was about to begin.

"If ye sicken while I'm on the watch and Granny Biddy kills me," Gabby threatened, "I swear I'll come back to haunt ye."

That remark made Rob smile. "Verra well, bring me a bowl of soup."

"With a slice of bread and butter?"

Rob nodded reluctantly.

Gabby leaped out of her chair and dropped the knitting onto her lap, ordering, "Work on this until I return."

Rob stared at the knitting and dropped a hand to her belly. Her beautiful baby would never wear the gowns and the blankets she'd made for him. And what would Gordon do when she and their baby were dead? Would he find another, more suitable wife? Or would he howl a protest and seek revenge for their deaths?

The chamber door opened and closed with a quiet click. Then Rob heard the bolt being thrown.

"Set the tray on the table," she said without looking up. "I'll eat in a few minutes."

"Ye'll eat now, angel, or ye'll do without."

Rob bolted out of her chair at the unmistakable sound of her husband's husky voice. She whirled toward the door and dropped her mouth open in surprised confusion.

The voice belonged to her husband, but the figure in the shadows was a woman of gigantic proportions.

Dressed in a skirt and a cloak, the long-haired woman set the supper tray on a nearby table.

"Who are ye?" Rob demanded. "Identify yerself."

The woman flicked the hood of her cloak back. Then she reached up, yanked her flowing mane of dark hair right off her head, and tossed it onto the floor.

Casting her a devastatingly familiar smile, the woman said, "Dinna ye recognize yer own husband, angel?"

With a soft cry of joy, Rob sprung to life. She ran across the chamber and threw herself into his arms.

With a groan of sublime relief, Gordon crushed her against his hard masculine frame. He dipped his head, and his lips captured hers in an earth-shattering kiss that melted into another. And then another.

When he finally lifted his lips from hers, Rob wrapped her arms around him and rested her head against the comforting solidity of his chest. " 'Thwartin' the king's will is risky business," she said. "Ye shouldna be here."

"I couldna stay away another moment." Gordon tilted her face up and gazed into her eyes. "I love ye with all of my heart and my soul."

Rob burst into tears at that. She lowered her head and hid her face against his chest.

"I thought admittin' my love would make ye happy," Gordon said, holding her protectively close within the circle of his embrace.

"I—I am h-happy."

"Then why are ye weepin'?"

Rob looked up at him. "Because ye love me."

That made Gordon smile. "Ye'd really be weepin' and wailin' if ye knew what I went through to get to ye."

"Tell me."

"As ye've seen, I dressed like a woman," Gordon said, his disgust apparent in his voice. "Then Talbot insisted I play the role of his Edinburgh paramour."

"Henry helped ye?"

"God's balls, but I dinna like the feelin' of a man's arms around me," he added ruefully.

Rob giggled at that.

"That's my girl," Gordon said, brushing the tears from her face. Then, "Talbot will be returnin' to escort me back to Campbell Mansion in less than two hours. Gabby told me ye hadna been eatin'. Will ye sup first?"

Rob shook her head. Without modesty or shame, she said, "I want ye to love me."

Gordon flashed her his devastating grin. "With pleasure, my lady."

They divested themselves of their garments where they stood. Naked, Gordon pulled her softness against the hard planes of his body and kissed her as if he would never let her go, pouring all of his love and his need into that single, stirring kiss. For a long moment they stood entwined and cast one long shadow on the wall.

Finally, Gordon scooped her into his arms and gently placed her across the bed. Pausing before joining her, he worshipped her with his eyes.

Gordon dropped his heated gaze from her hauntingly lovely face to her swollen breasts with their enlarged dusky nipples, the proof that his seed grew within her womb. Lower his gaze drifted to her curvaceous hips and rounded belly.

With a groan of mingling emotion and need, Gordon dropped to his knees on the floor in front of her. He glided the palms of his hands up the sides of her hips and kissed the mound of her swollen belly.

"The babe has grown," he whispered hoarsely.

"Yes," she answered on a sigh.

Gordon slashed his tongue up the moist valley between her thighs and heard her sharp intake of breath at the exquisite sensation. Cupping her buttocks, he held her steady while his exploring tongue made her writhe with hot desire.

Up and down, Gordon flicked his tongue in a gentle assault on her womanhood. He licked and then kissed her dewy jewel as his talented fingers teased and taunted her sensitive nipples.

Surrendering completely, Rob cried out and melted against his tongue. She clung to him desperately as wave after wave of throbbing pleasure carried her to paradise and beyond.

When she stilled, Gordon stood and gently drew her toward the edge of the bed. He positioned himself between her thighs, plunged his manhood deep inside her, sheathing himself to the hilt, and groaned at the wet, hot spasms caressing him. Ever so slowly, he withdrew and then eased forward again, piercing her softness, teasing her again and again until she trembled with rekindled need. Holding her hips steady, Gordon thrust deep and ground himself into her throbbing softness.

With mingling cries, Gordon and Rob exploded together, and then lay still as they floated back to earth from their shared paradise. When he regained strength enough to move, Gordon stood and gently turned her lengthwise on the bed. He lay down beside her and cradled her in his arms.

Rob sighed with contentment and said without preamble, "Tell me again, Gordy."

"I love ye," he whispered, brushing his lips across her temple. "I love ye more than life itself."

"And I love ye." Rob rolled over on top of him and asked, "How long have ye loved me?"

Gordon encircled her with his arms and smiled as if remembering. " 'Twas that verra first day, I think."

"At Uncle Richard's party?"

"No, angel. 'Twas when ye insisted I kill the monster

beneath yer bed or ye wouldna agree to become my wife."

Rob gave him a rueful smile. "Yer lyin', Gordy."

"God's balls, 'tis the truth," he insisted. Then, "When did ye begin to love me?"

" 'Twas that day in my father's hall when ye knelt before me and kissed my birthmarked hand."

"Ye werena sayin' that when I rode to England to fetch ye home," Gordon teased, cocking a brow at her.

"My mother taught me that a lady always plays hard-to-get," Rob countered, casting him a flirtatious smile and batting her ebony lashes at him.

Gordon chuckled. He caressed the slender column of her back and cupped her buttocks. "I never knew angels had such seductive arses."

Rob leaned close and captured his lips with her own. Her kiss was gently probing and would have lasted for an eternity, but a light rapping sounded on the chamber door.

Rob lifted her head and listened, then said, " 'Tis Henry lookin' for ye."

" 'Tisna time," Gordon whispered. "Ask who it is."

"Who's there?" Rob called.

"Lavinia Kerr," came the answer. " 'Tis urgent that I speak with ye."

Rob looked at her husband in alarm. When he nodded, she called, "Just a minute."

"Throw my clothes and boots on the bed," Gordon whispered. "We'll draw the bed curtains, and she'll never realize ye are na alone."

Exhibiting more energy than she had in three weeks, Rob leaped off the bed, gathered her husband's clothing and wig, and tossed them onto the bed. While he pulled the bed curtains shut, she donned her night shift and bed robe, and then hurried across the chamber.

Opening the door a crack, Rob peered at the redhead and asked in a coolly polite voice, "What can I do for ye, Lady Kerr?"

"I need to speak with ye."

Rob cocked a brow at her. "Aboot what?"

"Please, I need yer help," Lavinia whined, her anxiety etched across her expression. "May I come inside?"

Rob hesitated for a fraction of a moment, but then nodded and opened the door, allowing the other woman entrance. Lavinia walked past her into the chamber.

The two women sat in the chairs in front of the hearth. Rob waited for her guest to speak and prayed that Henry Talbot wouldn't arrive while Lavinia was there.

"I'm verra sorry for yer troubles," Lavinia began. " 'Tis all Mungo's fault, of course. He forced me to pick a fight with ye that evenin'."

Rob stared at her in surprise.

"Mungo wanted to accuse ye of practicin' witchcraft," Lavinia explained. "I refused to feign an illness, but then really did become sick. Ye didna curse me into an illness, did ye?"

That did it. "I've heard enough," Rob said curtly. "Please leave, Lady Kerr."

"Forgive me," Lavinia apologized, holding her hand up in supplication. "Yer expression tells me yer innocent. Mungo must have slipped somethin' into my wine that night. He hates the whole MacArthur clan, ye know, and has waited a lifetime for his revenge."

"Why does he blame my mother for his father's death?" Rob asked.

"A long time ago, his father abducted yer mother but drowned when she made good her escape," Lavinia answered. "The MacArthurs never knew 'twas Finlay Mac-Kinnon because he was wearin' the Menzies plaid. Yer father and the Menzies chieftain were embroiled in a feud at the time so everyone assumed 'twas a Menzies who snatched yer mother."

Rob closed her eyes. Now she knew who'd tried to push her into the lions' pit at the queen's menagerie and who was behind the attempt on her brother's life at Hampton Court.

"If yer truly sorry," Rob said, looking at the other woman, "ye'll go to the king with this information."

"I canna do that," Lavinia cried. "Mungo threatened me too. Besides, Jamie willna listen now that he's seen yer—" she hesitated—"yer mark."

"Then why are ye tellin' me this?" Rob asked.

"I need yer help," Lavinia admitted. "In order to protect myself permanently from Mungo, I've set my sights on becomin' the king's mistress but canna seem to catch his eye. I want ye to give me a love potion."

Rob burst out laughing. "I amna a witch, Livy, and canna mix ye a love potion."

Lavinia's expression drooped. "I ken why ye dinna want to help me."

In spite of the harm done to her, Rob was unable to ignore the other woman's disappointed expression. Her husband's professed love had opened her heart again, so she could sympathize with another's plight.

"I canna give ye a love potion," Rob said, "but I can tell ye what worked for me with Gordy."

Lavinia perked up. "What?"

"Ye must feed the king cockle bread," Rob answered, and could almost hear her husband's silent laughter from where he hid behind the bed curtains.

"I dinna ken."

"Cockle bread is an aphrodisiac cake," Rob explained. "Ye knead a small piece of dough, mold it against yer privates, and then bake it. Feed it to Jamie, and he'll be fairly droolin' to get his hands on ye."

"Shall I . . ." Lavinia blushed and dropped her gaze. "Shall I touch myself first so my love juices soak the dough?"

Rob struggled against the laughter bubbling up in her throat. "Well, I suppose it couldna hurt and may even help yer cause."

"Thank ye so much," Lavinia said, rising from her chair, giving her a pleased smile. "So that's how ye managed to snatch Gordy from me. I just knew ye needed some help. I'm indebted to ye, Lady Rob, and I'll certainly send Gordon whatever gold coins I can spare for yer ransom."

"Every coin helps," Rob said dryly. She closed the door and bolted it behind her guest.

Hurrying across the chamber, Rob yanked the bed curtain aside and asked, "Ye heard?"

Gordon burst out laughing but sobered quickly. "I'll kill that MacKinnon bastard."

"Dinna do anythin' rash," Rob said, snuggling into his embrace. Then, "Will ye be able to raise the gold?"

"Dinna fret aboot that, angel." Gordon planted a kiss on her lips. "Ye'll be sleepin' beside me at Campbell Mansion three weeks from tonight, and the mornin' after that ye'll be ridin' beside me on the road to Argyll."

Rob reached up with her birthmarked hand and caressed his cheek, saying, "Gordy?"

Hearing the question in her voice, Gordon turned his face to kiss the palm of her hand and vowed, "I do love ye, angel. Like our weddin' band says, 'Ye and No Other.' "

Their lips met in a sweetly devastating kiss. And then a knocking sounded on the chamber door.

" 'Tis Henry," the muffled voice said. "Open the door."

"One moment," Rob called.

Gordon gave her a quick kiss and then rose from the bed. "Go on and let him in while I dress."

Rob padded on bare feet across the chamber and admitted Henry. She bolted the door behind him.

Henry winked at her and bowed over her hand, saying, "I see that your husband's conjugal visit has brought the rose's bloom to your cheeks, darling."

"Thank ye for yer help," Rob said, her blush darkening with her embarrassment.

" 'Twas my pleasure," he replied. "Well, *almost* my pleasure. Are ye ready, Inverary?"

Rob looked at her husband and dissolved into giggles. Over his breeches and shirt, Gordon had donned his skirt, long-haired wig, and cap. Then he covered the whole outfit with a woman's hooded cloak.

"Good Christ, Inverary. You're the ugliest woman I've ever seen," Henry remarked. "My reputation as a connoisseur of beautiful women will never recover from this."

Rob walked straight into her husband's open arms. "I think yer the most handsome woman I've ever seen."

"Thank ye, my love." Gordon dipped his head and kissed her.

"Ahem." Henry Talbot cleared his throat.

Gordon glanced up at the other man. "Verra well, Ludlow. I'm comin'. And keep yer hands off me as we leave."

"I assure you, Inverary. Walking with my arm around your shoulders is a supreme sacrifice on my part," Henry shot back.

Gordon gave Rob another quick kiss. "Have a care for the babe, angel. I'll see ye in three weeks."

And then he disappeared out the door.

After bolting it behind them, Rob closed her eyes against the tears that threatened to spill. A lump of raw emotion formed in her throat, and she tried to gulp it down.

Gordon loved her. Surely she could muster the courage to survive whatever the next three weeks brought her.

Chapter 19

I love ye more than life itself. Ye and No Other . . .

Those magical words of love heartened Rob and gave her the inner strength needed to endure another three weeks of lonely, frightened isolation. And then the final moment arrived when gold would decide her fate.

On the evening of her forty-second day in captivity, Rob stood between two of the king's guard beside the dais at the front of the royal audience chamber. All of the Stuart courtiers milled about and spoke in hushed tones, and Rob wondered if they'd attended the proceedings to see her hanged as a witch or walk free.

On one side of the milling throng stood Lavinia Kerr. The Earl of Bothwell, Henry Talbot, and Roger Debrett stood together on the other side of the chamber. Mungo MacKinnon waited on the opposite side of the dais for his gold. King James, his mouth dribbling a river, stood between Mungo and Rob.

Though pride forced Rob to maintain a serene expression, every nerve in her body tingled in a riot of barely suppressed panic. She stood on trembling legs and prayed she wouldn't embarrass herself by swooning like a coward.

Where was Gordon? she wondered. Would this be the night she slept beside him at Campbell Mansion as he'd promised? Or would this crowd of courtiers attack her like a pack of wolves and drag her to yonder scaffold on Edinburgh Castle's Esplanade?

And then Gordon appeared in the hall's entrance. Looking none too happy, he paused there until the courtiers quieted and all their gazes fixed upon him, and then he started forward.

Clutching her swollen belly, Rob swayed on her feet. She just knew from the expression on her husband's face that he'd been unable to raise the fifty thousand gold pieces necessary to free her.

Committing an insultingly outrageous breach of protocol, Gordon ignored the king and halted in front of Rob. Perhaps for the final time, he gifted her with his devastating smile and lifted her hands to his lips.

"Damsel, yer hero is here," he whispered in a husky voice. "How do ye and the babe fare, my love?"

Unable to find her voice through her constricting fear, Rob managed a wobbly smile and nodded that she was well.

Turning away from her, Gordon stepped in front of the king and bowed. "Sire, I've come to collect my wife," he announced.

"Even a deaf man hears the clinkin' of gold," King James replied. "Have ye the means to free her?"

Like a true Prince of Argyll, Gordon flicked a contemptuous glance at Mungo MacKinnon and then, with every ounce of arrogance he possessed, nodded at the king. "Shall I have it brought here, Sire?"

"Please do," King James said.

Gordon looked over his shoulder and nodded at Dewey, who opened the audience chamber's door and beckoned to someone in the corridor. A line of seven Campbell warriors, dressed in their battle plaids and carrying enormous burlap sacks over their shoulders, marched into the hall and through the crowd toward the dais. The first Campbell warrior emptied his sack of gold pieces in front of the king, making the crowd of courtiers gasp.

"Ten thousand gold pieces from my father, the Duke of Argyll, and myself," Gordon announced.

The second Campbell warrior stepped to the dais and emptied his sack at the king's feet.

"Ten thousand gold pieces from Iain MacArthur, the Earl of Dunridge," Gordon said.

Great Bruce's ghost, she'd never seen so much gold in her life! Rob glanced at the king whose gaze seemed glazed as it fixed on the small heap of gold at his feet. She peered at Mungo MacKinnon whose eyes held the same greedy gleam as the king's.

And then Rob knew her husband's ploy. Gordon was bent on enticing King James with the gold promised to Mungo. MacKinnon would lose the gold and a rich, influential ally in himself. It would be his revenge against a trusted friend's betrayal.

As each of the five remaining Campbell warriors stepped forward and emptied his sack of gold at the king's feet, Gordon announced its contributor: "Five thousand gold pieces from Percy MacArthur, the Earl of Weem . . . Five thousand gold pieces from George Gordon, the Earl of Huntly . . . Five thousand gold pieces from Francis Hepburn-Stuart, the Earl of Bothwell . . . Five thousand gold pieces from Henry Talbot, the

Marquess of Ludlow . . . Five thousand gold pieces from Lord Roger Debrett, the heir to the Earl of Eden."

" 'Tis five thousand gold pieces short of the price," Mungo insisted, though his gaze rested longingly on the incredible pile of gold. "By yer own word, Sire, the wench stands trial for witchcraft."

Rob swayed precariously on her feet. Would she be dragged to yonder scaffold for lack of five thousand gold pieces? A merciful God could not be so cruel to her.

Fixing her gaze on the king, Rob saw the uncertainty playing across his face, and the royal dribbling had worsened with Mungo's outburst. The price had been set at fifty thousand gold pieces, and even the king was at a loss about what to do unless MacKinnon agreed to take the slightly smaller sum.

"Sire, I am honored to present my wife's final benefactor," Gordon announced, gaining everyone's attention. He nodded at Dewey, who opened the corridor door again and beckoned to someone outside.

Dressed completely in black like Old Clootie himself, a tall well-built man with a shock of burnished copper hair stepped into the audience chamber. He paused for maximum effect and then strode forward with an arrogant, predator's grace.

"Uncle Richard!" Rob exclaimed in surprise, drawing the king's attention.

The crowd of spectators erupted in excited murmurings as the undeniably impressive English earl advanced on the dais.

" 'Tis the Earl of Basildon."

"Elizabeth's 'Midas.' "

"England's favorite son."

"The earl with the golden touch."

Reaching the dais, the Earl of Basildon glanced at Rob

and cast her an unmistakably fond smile. He looked at King James and bowed from the waist.

"Yer Majesty, I present Richard Devereux, the Earl of Basildon," Gordon made the introduction.

"Welcome to Scotland, my lord," King James greeted him with a broad smile. "How fares my dear cousin, Elizabeth?"

"The queen is well and sends her fondest regards to her closest living relative," Richard replied. "And, I am most honored to meet finally with Scotland's monarch."

King James grinned. He'd heard the lure of a promise in the words *closest living relative.* "And I have long waited to meet Elizabeth's financial wizard."

Richard Devereux inclined his head at the compliment and said, "Your Majesty, may I approach you and be heard?"

King James nodded.

Rob watched as her uncle flicked an insultingly disdainful look at Mungo MacKinnon, who appeared none too happy, and then walked around the pile of gold pieces. Reaching the king, he gave the young monarch an ingratiating smile.

"Your Majesty, when news of my beloved niece's detainment reached me in London, I entertained but three thoughts," Richard said in a voice that carried to the far corners of the chamber. "First, I thought a terrible miscarriage of justice was victimizing Rob. Regardless of the stain on her hand, my wonderful niece is no witch. Then I decided I must immediately journey to Scotland and help settle this horrible misunderstanding. What upset me the most was the fact that fifty thousand gold pieces would secure her freedom."

"I warrant 'tis a great amount of money," King James agreed.

" 'Tisna fair," Mungo cried. "Ye set the price at fifty thousand, and there it stands."

"Your Majesty, allow me to make myself perfectly clear," Richard said. "The incredibly *low* price for her release angered me more than anything else. My beloved niece is certainly worth at least one hundred thousand gold pieces. Anything less is exceedingly insulting."

Rob gasped, as did everyone else in the chamber. Great Bruce's ghost, was Uncle Richard here to help her or to see her hanged? She looked at her husband, who was smiling as if enjoying himself immensely.

"I insist upon paying the true worth of my beloved niece," Richard added.

Rob stared at her uncle, and then she knew his game. It was a bribe, of course. Uncle Richard was bribing King James to win her freedom and to keep her free for all the days of her life. She watched her uncle raise his hand and gesture at the seven Campbell warriors who again stood in the rear of the hall. They marched forward and, one by one, emptied sacks of gold pieces at the king's feet.

"Fifty-five thousand gold pieces from the Earl of Basildon," Gordon announced, and then winked at her.

Rob longed to fly into his arms, but stood rooted to the floor. Was she free to leave or not? She looked at the king for an answer.

"Ye would pauper yerself for a favored niece?" King James was asking her uncle, his disbelief apparent in his voice.

"Pauper?" Richard Devereux cocked a copper brow at the king and then smiled. "Your Majesty, 'tis merely pocket change."

Mungo MacKinnon was unable to control his greed a moment longer. Without royal permission, he started forward to claim his ransom in gold.

Rob watched her uncle lean close to the king and

whisper in the royal ear. Whatever he said brought a smile of satisfaction to Jamie's face.

"Hold, MacKinnon," the king ordered. "Ye set the price for the lives of yer father and yer aunt at fifty thousand gold pieces."

Mungo nodded, but shifted his gaze to the Earl of Basildon. He seemed to mentally steel himself for the unexpected.

"Tell me, Mungo lad," King James said pleasantly. "I wondered if ye'd set the price for yer own life at—let's say, one hundred thousand gold pieces? Is yer life worth that much?"

Mungo nodded. "Yes, Sire."

King James turned to Gordon and ordered, "Step forward, Inverary." Then, "Draw yer dirk and kneel."

As if he knew what was coming, Gordon smiled and drew his dagger. Then he knelt in front of the king.

"I demand ye swear on yer dirk, that most solemn of all yer Highland oaths, that ye'll never seek revenge on Mungo MacKinnon for past deeds," King James ordered.

Holding his dirk high, Gordon said without hesitation, "I swear by this dirk and all that is holy to refrain from revengin' myself on Mungo MacKinnon for past crimes."

"MacKinnon, ye may leave with yer life," King James said with a smile. "However, I do claim these gold pieces for savin' ye from Campbell's wrath."

Mungo opened his mouth to protest, changed his mind, and clamped his lips together. He'd been beaten and knew it. With a deferential nod at the king, Mungo turned on his heels and left the chamber.

Rob could scarcely control herself. She longed to fly into her husband's arms. Apparently, Gordon felt the same because the look he fixed upon her was filled with yearning and promise. Neither moved for fear of angering the king.

"My lord, I hope ye'll enjoy my hospitality for a few days," King James was saying to her uncle. "I've several questions of a financial nature to ask ye."

Richard Devereux smiled. "Your Majesty, I'd be honored to extend whatever advice I can." The earl shifted his attention to Gordon, and the king's gaze followed him.

"Well, Inverary, I dinna relish the prospect of yer wife givin' birth in my audience chamber," King James said. "Are ye takin' her home or no?"

At that, Rob gave a soft cry of joy, flew the short distance to her husband, and threw herself into his embrace. Their lips met in a hungry, earth-shattering kiss; the world faded into nothing but the two of them. Only the loud applause of approval that erupted from the courtiers in the hall yanked them back to the reality of the audience chamber.

Lifting his lips from hers, Gordon opened his mouth to speak but then frowned, saying, "Look at yer necklace."

Rob glanced down at her beggar bead necklace. The star ruby, darker than pigeon's blood for so many weeks, faded back to its original color.

Rob looked up at her husband and smiled, saying, "Aunt Keely spoke honestly. I believe the danger disappeared out that door a few minutes ago."

"I love ye, angel," Gordon said, unable to resist planting another kiss on her oh-so-inviting lips.

"And I love ye," Rob vowed. Ignoring the milling courtiers who still watched them, she grasped his hand and guided it to her belly which shifted with their baby's movement. With her heart shining in her eyes, Rob said, "Take us home, Gordy. Take us home to the Highlands where we belong."

Gordon nodded and lifted her hands to his lips. He kissed her right hand first and then gazed at the delicate devil's flower staining the back of her left hand before dropping a kiss on that too.

"Damsel, yer wish is my command." At that, Gordon scooped her into his arms and carried her out of the audience chamber.

He arrived on the eighth day of February, the first anniversary of the death of Mary Stuart, during the worst Highland blizzard in recent memory. Gordon named his son Hunter in honor of that remarkable summer shieling when he'd managed to make an angel his wife.

She arrived unexpectedly five minutes after her brother. Rob named her daughter Mairi in honor of Scotland's deceased queen.

Late the following morning when the excitement over Inverary's newest arrivals had eased somewhat, father and mother rested in their chamber. Leaning against the bed's headboard, Rob cradled her daughter in her arms while Gordon sat beside her and nestled his son against his chest.

When a knock sounded on the door, Gordon looked at his wife and asked, "Are ye ready for company, angel?"

Rob nodded, saying, "I do hope Gavin likes his new sister."

"Enter," Gordon called.

The door swung open slowly. Then a boy's voice ordered, "No, Smooches!"

Duncan and Gavin dashed into the bedchamber behind the wayward pup. The duke followed the boys, scooped the pup into his arms, and grinned at the proudly smiling parents.

Duke Magnus supervised the boys' inspection of their new brother and sister, and then remarked, "I suppose this makes amends for yer callin' me 'an old warhorse relivin' past battles.' "

"Why should Hunter and Mairi absolve him of sin?" Rob teased, glancing sidelong at her husband. "*I* did all the laborin'."

"He's so small," Duncan said, standing beside his father.

"And she's wrinkled," Gavin gasped in a horrified whisper, standing beside his brother.

"All babies are small and wrinkled," their grandfather told them. "The skin smoothes out as they grow."

"I dinna remember bein' that small," Duncan announced.

"Me neither," Gavin agreed.

"Are ye ready boys?" Duke Magnus asked.

Both boys nodded and knelt on bended knee beside their father and baby brother. The duke drew his jewel-hilted dagger and passed it to his oldest grandson.

Duncan accepted the dagger and held it high. "By all that is holy and this sacred Campbell dagger, I pledge my unwaverin' loyalty to Hunter Campbell, the future laird of Inverary and Argyll."

Gavin took the dagger out of his brother's hands, held it high, and promptly forgot his speech. He flicked an embarrassed grin at Rob and vowed, "Me too."

"Thank ye, sons," Gordon said. "I'm verra proud of ye."

" 'Twas lovely," Rob agreed.

"I'm teachin' Hunter how to raid the other clans," Duncan announced.

"And I'll teach Mairi how to dance," Gavin said with a smile.

" 'Tis time for our lessons," Duke Magnus said. "Ye can visit yer brother and sister this afternoon."

Gordon glanced at Rob, who nodded in answer to his silent question. "Duncan, Lady Rob and I would like ye to stand as Hunter's godfather if yer willin'," he told his son.

"Aye, I'll do it," Duncan accepted, puffing his chest out with pride.

"Gavin, come over here," Rob said. When the boy walked around the bed and stood beside her, she asked, "Do ye like yer baby sister?"

Gavin nodded. With one finger, he touched the tiny palm of the baby's hand and smiled when she closed her fingers around it.

"Would ye be willin' to stand as Mairi's godfather?" Rob asked.

"I'll protect her with my life," Gavin vowed. His gray eyes, so much like his father's, gleamed with excitement.

"And will ye slay the monsters beneath her bed?" Gordon asked.

Gavin nodded solemnly and then leaned close to his sister, whispering, "Damsel, yer hero is here."

Duke Magnus ushered the boys toward the door; but at the last moment, Gavin ran back to the bed. "I love ye, Lady Rob," the boy said, planting a kiss on her cheek. "Thank ye for my sister."

"Yer verra welcome," Rob replied with tears welling up in her eyes. "I love ye too."

Gavin kissed her cheek again and said in a loud whisper, "Do ye suppose Mairi will want a sister too?"

Gordon chuckled, earning an unamused look from his wife.

Rob turned to the boy and answered, "Perhaps Mairi will want a sister. We'll ask her when she gets older."

When his father and his sons had gone, Gordon rose from the bed and gently set Hunter in his cradle. Then he lifted Mairi out of her mother's arms and placed her in her own cradle beside her brother's.

Returning to the bed, Gordon gathered his wife into

his arms. He kissed the crown of her head when she sighed with contentment.

"I want to thank ye for my son and my daughter."

"Yer verra welcome, my lord." Rob smiled into his piercing gray gaze, but sudden tears welled up in her eyes when she said, "And thank ye for giftin' me with a home where I truly belong."

"Shall I say the words?" he asked softly.

"Well, ye did promise to say them for all the days of our lives."

"I do love ye more than life, my sweet angel," Gordon vowed in a voice hoarse with emotion. "Ye and no other."

"And I love ye, Gordy," Rob whispered as his lips claimed hers. "Ye and no other."